# In the time of
# Dragon Moon

BY Janet Lee Carey

Kathy Dawson Books

AN IMPRINT OF PENGUIN GROUP (USA) LLC

# KATHY DAWSON BOOKS

Published by the Penguin Group
Penguin Group (USA) LLC
375 Hudson Street
New York, New York 10014

USA/Canada/UK/Ireland/Australia/New Zealand/India/South Africa/China
penguin.com
A Penguin Random House Company

Text copyright © 2015 by Janet Lee Carey

Library of Congress Cataloging-in-Publication Data
Carey, Janet Lee.
In the time of dragon moon / Janet Lee Carey.     pages cm
Summary: "In AD 1210, Uma, a healer raised by a tribe of people native to Wilde Island, must complete an impossible task for the English queen or be burned alive, and her only ally is the part dragon, part fairy Pendragon prince who is struggling with a secret of his own" — Provided by publisher.
ISBN 978-0-8037-3810-2 (hardback)
[1. Kings, queens, rulers, etc.—Fiction. 2. Healers—Fiction. 3. Kidnapping—Fiction.
4. Racially mixed people—Fiction. 5. Dragons—Fiction. 6. Fairies—Fiction.
7. British Isles—History—13th century—Fiction. 8. Fantasy.] I. Title.
PZ7.C2125In 2015
[Fic]—dc23     2014032216

Printed in the United States of America
1  3  5  7  9  10  8  6  4  2

Designed by Jennifer Kelly
Map illustration by Jennifer Kelly. Copyright © 2015 Penguin Group (USA) LLC
Text set in Stempel Garamond LT Pro

To Justina Chen and her
daughter, Sofia Headley.
Pathfinders.

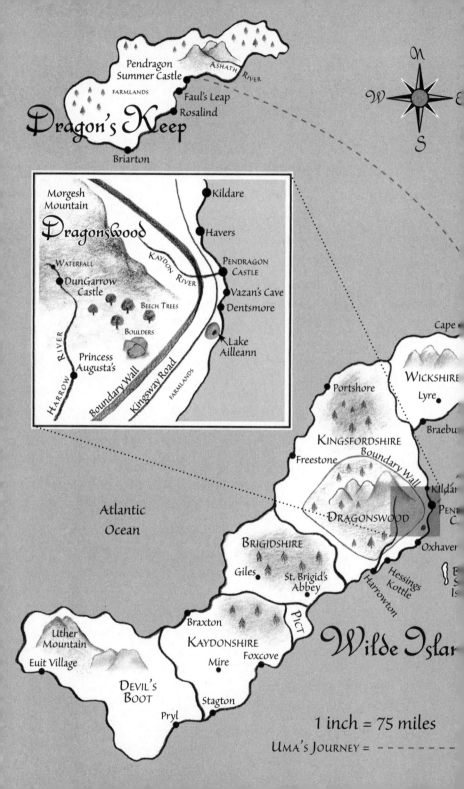

# Contents

# PART ONE

# Captive

# CHAPTER ONE

# Euit Village, Devil's Boot on Wilde Island

## FALCON MOON
### *April 1210*

KNIFE IN HAND, I crouched under the willow. Father's dragon skimmed over the river, her crimson scales blazed blood red across the surface. Her searing cry rang through the valley. Dragons live more than a thousand years; their turning eye sockets allow them to look forward and back, seeing past and future, patterns in time we humans can never see. My eyes were fixed on smaller things.

*Today he will tell me. Today I will know.*

I took my knife to the ends of my hair. Crow-black strands in my hand, red-toned where the morning sun struck them. The auburn from my English mother was nearly swallowed by the black, but I could not hide what I was: a girl, a half English. Under the willow, I covered the strands with soil. I'd buried much in this secret place.

Tying back what remained, I went to wash Father's medicine pots in the river.

"Uma!" Ashune raced down the muddy riverbank, her baby screaming in her arms. "Help him please!"

I scrambled ashore, dripping. "What's happened?"

"A bee stung him. And he . . . look!" She pulled back Melo's blanket. His waving arm was red and swollen as a rotting plum. I gripped his tiny wrist. He wailed as I pulled the stinger out.

"Was he stung in other places?"

"No, just here." Her eyes were wide. "Why is it so swollen?"

I heard a wheezing sound between cries. His throat was swelling shut. "It's a bad reaction."

Ashune hugged him to her chest. "He needs medicine, Uma."

My father, the Adan, was the only healer in our village. He'd gone to Council Rock to speak to the elders on my behalf. I didn't expect him back for hours.

Melo coughed, shuddered.

"Help him, Uma. Please!"

"I can't. Only the Adan can—"

"You're the Adan's apprentice," she cried. "Look at him. He can hardly breathe!"

"Wait here." I raced uphill to the healer's hut and ran my hand along the shelves. This could cost me my apprenticeship. But how could I let Melo suffocate? All Father's hard work bringing Melo into the world would be in vain if he died, and Father was away just now because of me.

I grabbed the elixir I'd seen Father use and a jar of sooth-salve.

Little Melo was turning blue by the time I reached him again.

"Hold his mouth open, Ashune." *Holy Ones, help me help him.* Our law was clear. No one but the Adan could heal the sick, but still I spilled three green drops on Melo's tongue. *So the law is broken in drops,* I thought.

"Swallow it, little one, swallow." *Breathe.* The world grew silent as I listened to his ragged sounds between each cry. I could not hear the wind in the branches, the rushing river; only Melo struggling for air.

"It's not working," Ashune cried.

"Pray," I said. I dosed him again, gently ran my fingers along his throat to help him swallow.

Melo was conceived thanks to Father's magnificent fertility cure. *Breathe.* Our small Euit tribe needed every child. *Live.*

Melo squirmed, sucked in air, and shuddered all over. He kicked in his blanket. Was the soft brown color coming back to his face? I gripped the elixir jar tight, watching him. He took a few more breaths that didn't sound thick or strained. And with his breathing, other sounds returned—the breeze in the willows, the singing river.

"Holy Ones, you did it." Ashune wept with joy, rocking her boy between us. She was a year older than me, eighteen when she bore Melo. It wasn't an easy labor.

I wanted to hold him too: weep and rest my cheek against his downy head, but I had never seen my father do such a thing when he cured the sick. A healer kept his dignity. And his distance.

I rubbed the sooth-salve on Melo's swollen arm, scooped out more of the ointment, and wrapped it in a leaf. "Rub this twice more on him today. Hide it in between."

Ashune took the leaf.

"Tell no one you came to me," I said.

"I won't tell."

She looked at me, silent a moment. The word *Euit* means "family." Our chieftain said we were one family. We all belonged. It wasn't that simple for me. Ashune's mother caught us playing by the river together when I was six, she seven, and told her to keep away from the half English. I looked more like Father than Mother, with his skin, high cheekbones, and dark eyes, but that did not count for much back then. I knew I didn't belong. Not long after that, I buried my girl's clothes under the willow, left my mother's side, and went to serve my father the Adan to become a person of value in the tribe.

Ashune rocked Melo. "Thank you, Uma." Since the day her mother dragged her off, things had been awkward between us.

"I have washing to do," I said, glancing down at the pots. She hesitated, but I waved her on. "Go. Melo should sleep."

Ashune's colorful woven skirts brushed past clumps of wild iris as she climbed back up the riverbank. Melo made a contented cooing sound. He was one of just five infants born to us after nine years of emptiness and waiting. No one knew why our women had stopped having children. Had some plague infected us? Had something entered our food or water? We still didn't know, but after years of seeking, my father found the plants he needed to make his fertility potion.

I'd held Melo the night he was born. Today I'd cured him—maybe even saved his life. My heart swelled, tightening the binding cloth around my breasts as I watched Ashune heading back to the village.

IN OUR FAMILY hut just before dinner, Mother gave me a new belt with twelve red dragons woven in it. Her green eyes shone with delight above her freckled cheeks. The belt was her wordless way of telling me she expected good news when Father came home. I clung to the belt, admiring her fine craftsmanship. Hoping. More than that, believing she was right.

Mother said, "I wove some of my hair into each dragon." She'd done the same with Father's sixteen-dragon belt. Her auburn strands gleamed in the red wool, adding vibrant orange tones. I hugged her before cinching it around my waist like a power charm, then stepped outside to wait for the Adan. *Today he will tell me. Today I will know.*

In the hut, Mother sang to herself as she grilled the tuki peppers, *Poppies and roses in her hair. She is queen of the May.*

*Oh sing to her gladly and never sing sadly, she is the light of our day.* She loved the English ballads from her childhood, but I was no queen of the May.

I looked beyond the cone-shaped rush roofs to the thick forest climbing steeply beyond the village and felt a small flutter of excitement as Father came down the trail with his herbing basket.

I knelt and touched the Adan's feet with reverence before he entered our hut. At dinner I could hardly eat around all my unasked questions. Father, for his part, seemed to be chewing his thoughts. I'd served as his apprentice for ten years, but no girl has ever become an Adan. If the chieftain agreed today, I'd be the first.

Father hadn't accepted my help that first year; still I persisted. He did not like girlish chatter, so I was silent. He did not like weakness, so I stayed strong. He was never ill, so I was never ill—or if I was, I never let him know it.

I rubbed the old scar bisecting my palm. *Tell me, Father.* He bit. He chewed.

"I spoke with the chieftain about you," Father said at last, dusting the crumbs from his mat. "Your path is chosen, Uma."

I hooked my thumb through my new belt, tugging the flying dragons tighter against my waist, circling Uma Quarteney. Healer. Adan.

Father said, "You are to marry the hunter Ayo Hadyee in the time of Fox Moon."

My stomach seized. "M . . . marry? But my healer's path . . . Didn't you ask the chieftain, Adan?"

"You have been a great help to me, Uma, but I've put things off too long. I should have started training a male apprentice sooner."

"What male could learn as much as I already know?"

"Mi tupelli," he said softly.

*Mi tupelli*—my lad. The nickname raked my heart. "Don't call me that. Not now!" His brows flew up. I'd never raised my voice to him before.

"It's been decided," Father said. "As a female, you can be an Adan's helpmate. Never a healer."

"Then why this?" I tugged my tunic down to the fox mark below my collarbone. "Why did you burn the pattern of my Path Animal on my skin if I was never meant to be a healer?"

Such burns were reserved for warriors, elders, healers. I gloried under the excruciating pain the night he pressed the tip of the hot wire to my skin again and again until the tiny fox was complete. I took it as a sign I would become an Adan. A healer would not be shunned for being half English. A healer is needed. A healer belongs. And more than anything, I'd wanted to belong.

Father took Mother's hand. "Paths can change directions, Uma. I know you dreamed of more, and for a time I also thought . . . but our laws guide us. It's good for you to marry. You know how much we need children."

"I'm needed as a healer. People have learned to accept me as your apprentice." An acceptance that was hard-won. "I know how to help you treat our women with Kuyawan so they can have the children we need. Who else can do that?"

Father's mouth was a stern line.

I said, "Does Ayo even want to marry a half English, a girl who does not cook or garden or weave, a girl who has dressed as a boy most of her life?" The look on Father's face told me what I needed to know.

Mother said, "I understand how you feel, Uma."

"No, you don't."

"Believe me, I do. I know how hard you've worked. I've seen it. It hurt for me to give up my midwife practice and come here to live a different life, learning Euit ways so I could marry your father, but I did it."

"You did it because you love him! I don't love Ayo Hadyee."

"You can learn to love him, Uma. It's what your father wants for you."

"No! It's what *you* want!"

I shot out the door. I didn't know why I raced to the healer's hut until my hands were on the jars I'd washed that morning, until I was hurling them across the room, breaking them against the wall.

"Uma, stop." Mother came in, took my hands, and pulled me back outside. People had poured out of their huts, curious to see where the crashing sounds had come from. "Go back to your meals," I shouted. "Leave us!"

A hot wind scoured us from above. Father's red dragon, Vazan, must have heard the sound of breaking jars from the healer's hut. She dove from the clouds and roared a warning fire over our heads. I pushed Mother away, wanting to scream fire right back at Father's guardian. But no human breathes fire.

Or so I thought then.

THE NEXT DAY, after convincing Father to let me work beside him until Fox Moon came, I helped him attend my uncle Sudat, who'd accidentally cut his leg while skinning a goat. I was soothing my uncle with a smoking sage bundle as Father stitched the wound, when I heard horses' hooves and shouting in the distance.

Father kept chanting as he stitched. The far-off shouting turned to screams. The Adan did not allow himself to be distracted, but I peered out the door.

"Adan," I screamed. "King Arden's army!" I'd not seen the king's soldiers since I was small, when they'd burned our huts and forced us farther south. "They're armed!"

A soldier raced up and slashed an old man's neck right in front of our hut. Blood spurted onto the murderer's boots and breeches.

Now people were running, scattering like goats frightened by a mountain lion. Two armed men burst into the healer's hut.

"Are you Adan?" the taller one barked. Father looked at him. He did not say yes. He did not say no. But the soldier saw what Father was doing to mend my uncle's leg. The shorter man grabbed me, shook the smoke bundle from my hand, and stomped it out with his boot.

"Are you the famous healer who cured infertile women?" the tall one asked. "Answer me!"

"Yes," Father said.

Sudat groaned, "My leg." His gash still gaped open. The soldier shoved Father aside and drove a dagger through my uncle's heart, silencing him. I stopped the scream that came up my throat. It was like damming a river.

He turned his bloody blade on Father. "Pack all your medicines, old man. The queen of Wilde Island commands your presence."

Father loaded his trunk. I watched the dagger's point as if my eyes alone could keep Father alive.

The second soldier let me go. "Help him pack, boy. Stinks in here." I did as I was told, wrapping the tincture jars, the fertility herbs we'd gone so far across the mountain to find. Father packed his herbal book and locked the trunk. He was whispering, praying to the Holy Ones. I was too sick with fear to pray.

The army encircled our village. Our warriors and the red dragons were away hunting. We were defenseless. Ashune hid in the trees with Melo. People ducked behind boulders, bushes, huts. The soldiers chained Father's wrists and prodded him up the steps into the jail cart.

I raced up and jumped in the cart with him. Father pushed my shoulders. "No, Uma. Stay here with your mother."

I gripped the iron bars so he couldn't throw me outside.

A soldier jabbed me with his sword, slitting my pant leg

where I crouched, clinging to the bars. "What are you doing, boy?"

"I am the Adan's apprentice. He needs me."

They looped a cold chain tight around my wrists, chained Father's ankles and mine, and shut the metal door with a clank. Then the army set out, their lead chargers stirring up choking dust.

Through a brown cloud I saw Mother run out from our hut, her red hair streaming behind her as she raced after us calling my father's name, calling mine. "Uma, no!"

I gripped the bars, afraid, as two soldiers grabbed her arms, stopping her. But they did not put the sword to her throat.

For once I was glad she was not like the other women in our village.

For once I was glad she was English.

## CHAPTER TWO

# Journey to Pendragon Castle

FALCON MOON TO FOX MOON

*April to May 1210*

IT WAS A grueling three-week journey. Half the army followed the king's son, Prince Desmond Pendragon, north out of Devil's Boot. The other half had stayed behind, surrounding our village. The queen wanted Father alive, but what would happen to Mother and everyone we left behind? What would the army do to them? My anxious thoughts churned in rhythm with the cart's relentless wheels.

On the third day, I felt a rush of warm wind. "Father, look." Large red wings cut through the thin clouds above. His dragon, Vazan, had found us! Her muscled body spanned the length of seven horses; twice that again if you measured her snout to tail. She skimmed down on wings as large as mainsails. Men shouted, straining to control their frightened horses. I gripped the bars, hoping she'd roar fire, kill our captors, even as I knew she wouldn't do such a thing. Reds abided by the dragon treaty. They no longer killed humans. Or ate them. But at least she frightened the king's men. Father winked at me as the cavalcade fell apart, horses galloping this way and that ahead of us.

Mother had told me stories about the royal Pendragons whose blood was mixed with dragons. But on our journey north, I never once saw Prince Desmond Pendragon behave like a man with noble dragons' blood. One night he staggered drunk to our cage. "You're looking at your next Pendragon king," he said. "Call me Your Royal Highness."

"Your Royal Highness," we said, dry-tongued with thirst. We'd learned to obey. We were whipped when we did not.

"I'd order you to bow, but you're chained up, so." He shrugged and laughed. "By God, you Euit dogs stink! As soon as Mother sees you and your boy here, she'll realize you're a fraud. Healing infertile women. Ha. That's a joke. I bet you used your own prick, old man."

He staggered off. Devil! His words dug a pit of shame so deep in me I could not show my face to my father.

We were rarely fed, but one soldier with a crooked nose secretly shared his rations with us. "Here, eat," he said pushing bread through the bars one night, dried meat another. We learned his name was Sir Geoffrey.

FOX MOON WAS a silver bracelet in the sky the week we reached the northeast coast and saw Pendragon Castle rising tall and dark on the edge of a cliff.

The closer our rattling jail cart got to the castle, the more my chest tightened. I could hardly breathe by the time we crossed the drawbridge. Father saw my face and wrapped his large hands around mine. He had never done that before. I looked down at our hands in astonished wonder.

"You did not have to come with me, Uma," he whispered.

"I did. I couldn't let you go alone."

Soldiers hauled us through the wide castle door, down a chilly torchlit hall, our ankle chains clanking, and forced us up spiraling tower stairs to a room on the second floor. The minstrel's music dulled to a wary halt as they dragged us inside. Girls and women put down their stitchery and stared.

Queen Adela sat on an ornately carved high-backed chair, wearing a velvet gown as purple as fresh bruises. The color set against her pale skin brought out the sheen of her hair, dark brown with a few silver strands thin as spider's silk. She was beautiful and severe.

Mother told me witches had attacked her when she was younger, putting out her eye with a poker. The fey folk fashioned her a glass eye to replace it. When she'd regained her strength, she'd sought revenge as a witch hunter. That was before she'd become the queen, but I saw ferocity in her still, or was that just my fear looking back at me?

"Leave us!" she commanded. A dozen ladies-in-waiting dropped their sewing on the benches and scurried out behind the musicians. Only one woman remained at the queen's side.

She was even paler than the queen, if that was possible.

A single blond strand poked out from under her shoulder-length veil. I was used to warm, brown skin. These two made me think of snow and shiver.

Four blue eyes appraised us as if we were strange animals the guards had just deposited on the floor. I knew we stank. I wanted to say, *We do not bite,* but knew better.

Father cleared his throat.

"Remain silent until Her Majesty addresses you," said the woman. "You are filthy," she added, flicking out a colorful lacquered fan and fanning the queen.

Queen Adela asked, "Is it true you helped infertile women, Adan?" Her blue glass eye glinted in the afternoon light. "Is it true that they bore children after taking your cure?"

"It is true," Father said.

"Call me Your Majesty!" she growled. "Who had you whipped?" she added, eyeing the long ragged tears in Father's shirt.

"Your son, Prince Desmond, Your Majesty."

The queen stared down at her lap. "My son, my son, my one and only son," she whispered in a singsong voice, pinching her velvet skirts and pulling them apart as if she'd lost her son somewhere in the folds.

"What's that?" she said, glancing toward the empty alcove to her right where the musicians played when we'd first come in. "Take it away," she said to the empty space. "The pudding causes upheaval to my stomach." Then she went back to pinching her skirts.

I heard Father's slow intake of breath. No one had warned

us that this queen, who'd abducted us, whose army held our people captive, this fey-eyed, former witch hunter, was mad.

THE WOMAN WHO entered our tower room the next morning was the same elegant English one who'd stood by Queen Adela. "I am the queen's companion, Lady Olivia," she said. "I have come to welcome you on your first official day here at Pendragon Castle. You bathed?" she asked, sniffing the air, her delicate nostrils flaring. We had scrubbed as best we could and changed into the new, strange English clothing. (They'd stolen our clothes and burned them.) A stale odor still haunted the armpits of my used scribe's outfit, but I liked the ink-stained sleeves. Father looked his part in his dark physician's robes. At least we both still wore our dragon belts.

"Yes, we bathed, thank you," Father replied, looking up from his worktable. They'd housed us in a tower chamber called the Crow's Nest where the queen's physicians had lived. The windows faced all four directions. I'd unlatched the iron grid work and opened them first thing to air out the room.

"That's 'thank you, *my lady*,'" Lady Olivia said, still hovering near the open door as if she might make a quick escape. "You must learn castle etiquette if you want to keep your life. You are called upon to help Her Majesty. She is desperate for another child. She gave a son to the king sixteen years ago now. It's a queen's duty to mother the king's children. *Many* children," she added, her sharp blue eyes on Father.

"Her Majesty feels she's failed her husband. Do you understand the importance of your mission?"

Father gave a single, stern nod.

"Her last physician displeased Her Majesty. He's in the dungeon awaiting judgment. She's executed physicians for their foul treatments that promised everything and did nothing." Lady Olivia paused a moment. "I tell you this as a warning. She is not getting any younger."

"I am the Adan," Father said, head high. "I have the medicine she needs."

"News of your miracle cure has spread far and wide. That's why Her Majesty sent for you."

*You mean stole him.*

"I hope for your sake there's more to it than market gossip."

I flinched. "My father is the best—"

"Hush, Uma." He brushed his sleeve, removing her comment with a slow downward swipe of his hand. Father could do that. I couldn't. Her insult entered my blood like venom.

Father turned. "Am I to treat the other condition?"

"The . . . other?" Lady Olivia looked behind her suddenly, checking to see we were still alone.

"We saw her refuse the pudding, my lady. How often does she speak to people who are not there?"

Lady Olivia crossed the room, her heels clicking with purposeful steps. "Listen, Adan. That is your name, isn't it?"

"It is my title."

"No one speaks of the queen's . . . episodes. She is unwell, and gossip-mongering—"

"I am no gossipmonger, my lady. I plan to treat both maladies."

She moved to the worktable, whispering, "If you have something to balance her mind, give it to her. But I warn you." She looked around again. "Never talk about her moods with anyone but me. You understand, Adan?"

She left us, shutting the door behind her. Father took out his scale and weighed the huzana leaves he used for his fertility cure, his hands flying swift and sure as birds. Mine were shaking as I struck the flints and lit the brazier to seethe the queen's potion. "What do you think Queen Adela will do with the physician in the dungeon, Adan? Will she execute him like she did the others?" I was thinking about us, about our future here.

"Be present with what you are doing, Uma."

"How will you treat her . . ." *What did she call them?* ". . . her episodes, Adan?"

This made him stop and look up. "The English do not understand about balancing the four sacred elements of earth, wind, water, and fire in the body. What imbalance did you see in this queen, mi tupelli?"

"She is not balanced by earth, she has some fire." I was guessing.

"The queen is ruled by wind," he said. "Her scattered thoughts and phantom visions are caused by wind mind."

I felt the barb of failure in my gut. "You will use earth element plants to ground her?" I said, still wanting to appear knowledgeable. He ignored my attempt.

"I need the water seething, Uma."

I watched him work as I heated the water, steam ghosting between us.

"You are too anxious for what you want, Uma. Begin by wanting what you have."

Father chanted the Euit plant names as he dropped kea stems and huzana leaves in the simmering pot. I decided to be present with what I was doing, and chanted with him.

Every plant has a name, and the name holds the secrets of its origin—the dreams the earth fed its roots, down in the dark underneath. The name awakens the plant's healing powers. I knew the powers these plants held, the power to bring new life.

IN THE QUEEN'S aviary, the Adan gave Queen Adela the curative. After questioning my father about its name and its efficacy, she drank it down, watching Father over the chalice rim.

When she finished, Her Majesty dabbed her lips with her kerchief, then tossed birdseed to her songbirds, causing a small winged riot in the cage as they fluttered down. I felt sorry for the birds. Mother loved birds, especially small, bright finches. She would never hold them hostage the way this queen did.

"I am a generous queen. I plan to free your village if your cure works, Adan. Give me a child and my husband's soldiers will break camp and march north again."

She held out her hand. Lady Olivia mouthed to Father, *Kneel and kiss her ring.*

I took a breath. My revered father knelt to the Holy Ones in prayer and he bowed to his red dragon, never to another person. I felt a small landslide somewhere behind my ribs as he stepped closer, bent his neck, and put his lips to the queen's ruby ring. The stone was as red as a wound. It flashed when she withdrew her hand and held it out again, this time to me.

I fell to my knees. The landslide had already occurred, though it did not make falling to the floor any easier. The ruby was frigid, a smooth dead thing, only slightly colder than Queen Adela's hand.

"My son told me the soldiers had to kill some Euit men to bring you here," she said to Father when I stood and backed away again. "If your healing tonic works, I will be content and so will the king. The men will have died in a good cause."

Sickness washed up my throat. *A good cause?*

We turned to go.

"Face Her Majesty as you leave her presence," instructed Lady Olivia. "Head lowered, back out." Yesterday the guards had hauled us out in chains; today we walked out backward.

Later in the Crow's Nest, I attacked the rushes with a broom to sweep the fury out of myself over the butchery back in Devil's Boot, over my uncle and the rest of the men these English were content to kill in their *good cause.*

# CHAPTER THREE

# Pendragon Castle, Wilde Island

SNAKE MOON TO WHALE MOON
*June to July 1210*

O N THE LAST night of Snake Moon, someone
pounded on our door. "Let us in. Now!" I slid the
bolt aside and was brutally flung back as six armed palace
guards with leashed hounds flooded in. Two dogs rammed
into the worktable and set the measuring scale swinging.

"What is this?" Father asked, steadying the scale with one
hand.

The pock-faced guard yelled, "Search!" He bounded to
the wardrobe and threw our cloaks on the floor. The dog
at the end of his leash jammed his head inside and sniffed
around. I stood back alarmed as the king's men unleashed
the other dogs. Three raced over and sniffed Father's bed
on one side of the room, others pressed their noses under
my mattress behind the screen. The palace guards slit both
mattresses, and felt around in the straw. The dogs sniffed

both before they lost interest and bounded over to Father.

"Arms out!" said Pock Face.

How dare he shout at the Adan. "What is this about?" I demanded.

"You too, boy!" he barked.

The palace guards patted down Father and me. The bald, stout man patted under my arms, ran his hands down my ribs, then across my chest, where he paused a moment. I recoiled inside, terrified he'd detected my true shape under my bound breasts. But he passed his hands over my hips and slid them down my breeches. I looked away when he was done. Four dogs were sniffing Father's trunk, barking and growling.

"Open it!" Pock Face shouted.

Father pulled out his trunk key and paused, curling his weathered fingers around it.

I pushed through the men, wedging myself between growling hounds and trunk. The dogs snarled, their sharp teeth inches from my thighs, but I fixed my eyes on them, standing guard beside my father. "Why should he open it?" I said over the menacing growls. "The Adan's medicines are in there. The dogs should not spoil the queen's—"

"Stand back, boy!" Pock Face shoved me aside, throwing me hard against the wall, the thud as I hit it shaking my bones.

He drew his knife on Father. "Open it, Euit savage, or feel my point!"

Father knelt and slid the key in the lock. I clenched my

teeth as the hounds jammed their wet noses in, sniffing the Adan's valuable herbs. If any of them drooled on our precious curatives! Pock Face squatted and swiped his hand around inside, feeling herb bundles and tincture bottles, then stood, his eyes narrowed on the small leather sack he held out. "What's this?"

"No!" I made a grab for it. Too late. He slit the sack down the middle. Precious earth from Devil's Boot spilled on the floor. I dove for it, and the dogs beared their fangs. One leaped closer and snapped my sleeve. I reared back in terror, pressing myself against the wall as men and dogs trampled the small pile of sacred earth, all we had from home.

"What is this?" Sir Geoffrey Crooked Nose hurried into the tower room. He grabbed the two threatening dogs who had me up against the wall and pulled them back by their collars.

Pock Face looked up at Sir Geoffrey with a grin. "Following orders, sir."

Sir Geoffrey leashed the hounds, tossed the leads to the men, and glared at the slit leather sack. "And you destroyed this man's property because?"

"Thought it might be the missing coin purse, sir."

So that's what this was about? The English thought us thieves?

Sir Geoffrey surveyed the room. "Any coin purse found?"

"None we could turn up, sir. But these being foreign devils, thought we'd look here first, if you know what I mean."

Sir Geoffrey waved his hand. "Go. You've got lots of

other rooms to search." The men tromped out with the dogs. On the floor against the wall, I heaved a sigh. Handing me what was left of the leather sack, Sir Geoffrey bowed stiffly to Father. "I'm sorry to have disturbed you, Adan," he said under his breath before raising his head again. "You are free now to go about your work."

I stood up, shaking with anger.

"Why did they come in here?" Father asked.

"A cutthroat slit the lute player's throat last night and stole his coin purse."

Father and I looked at each other. Some elders called the moon the *Murderous Moon* at the end of its cycle. But even though we'd honored the end of Snake Moon with a ritual before we'd bedded down for the night, a man had still died here.

Sir Geoffrey hung our cloaks back in the wardrobe. "Men and hounds are searching the entire castle for the murderer." He stuffed some straw in my slit mattress, placed it on my pallet, and turned to me. "Bolt your door when I'm gone and keep yourselves safe until we catch the cutthroat." His brown eyes held me a moment longer. "I'm sorry for the roughness of my men."

His penetrating eyes felt too invasive. I folded my arms across my chest, suddenly afraid he saw me for what I was—a woman in scribe's clothing—then turned my back and knelt by the trunk to scoop up the spilled earth. By the time I'd gathered it all into a pile, Sir Geoffrey was gone.

———

A KITCHEN SPIT boy was seized later that day and punished so severely they had to call my father down to the dungeon.

"King wants him kept alive till his public hanging tomorrow," said the stout guard who'd patted me down earlier.

"I didna do it," the boy sobbed. In the rank dungeon cell, I pulled more bandages from the medicine basket while Father leaned over the cot. The king's soldiers had cut off his hand and tried to stop the excessive blood flow with tight leather straps before calling the Adan down.

The guard leaned against the doorframe watching. "Oh, he's guilty, right enough. Cried out his crimes when we stretched him on the rack, didn't you, spit boy?"

"But I didna. I s . . . said I did it to stop the pain. They—" He was crying too hard to say more. I breathed through my mouth against the stink of sweat, blood, fear, and urine, and tried not to look too deep into the boy's pale eyes set close together in his thin grimy face.

"I wouldn't kill no one never," sobbed the boy.

"He's a lying thief," said the guard. "We found the money sack under his straw mattress. Did it for the money, didn't ya? Kitchen work don't pay enough, is it?" he said, looking over Father's shoulder. "And we found the knife he killed the musician with besides."

"Someone put it there!" the spit boy cried.

"Shut him up or I will," the guard growled at Father.

"Hold still," Father said softly to the boy. "I'm nearly done, and I have something for the pain."

"What's that?" The guard stepped up to Father's back. "Don't give him nothing. Pain's a part of the punishment. Just keep him alive for his hanging, that's all."

"That's not right," I argued.

"What do you Euits know of right and wrong?" he spat. "You're done now, the both of you. Get out." He shoved us down the dim dungeon hall.

"Father, I'm sure he's telling the truth. What can we do?"

The Adan approached another guard near the base of the dungeon steps. "Tell me," he said, "if the king wants the boy hanged tomorrow, why cut off his hand?"

"Oh, hands go off for thieving. Hanging's for the murder, see?" He squinted at Father in the dim torchlight.

"He says he is innocent," Father said.

"Oh, they all say that. But he confessed on the rack."

"Anyone would under such torture," I snapped, stepping closer, my hands curling to fists.

"What's that, boy?" the man growled, reaching for his knife. Father yanked me away from the armed man. He dragged me firmly up the dungeon stairs, led me down the hall, and pressed me into a dark alcove.

"What were you thinking down there, Uma?" he whispered fiercely. "If you attacked one of the guards, they'd throw you in a cell. Do you want that?"

"I couldn't help myself," I said in a choking whisper. "It's horrible, Father. They'll hang an innocent boy. Can't we go to the queen and say something to stop it?"

"What can we say that they she will hear?" Father said. "We are captives ourselves here, Uma."

"We're not in a cell. Not about to be hanged."

Hearing footsteps, Father pressed himself closer to the wall in the dark alcove and whispered the chant *"havuela"*— become. I did the same, hoping my Euit skills were strong enough to blend into the walls as swiftly and easily as my father had done.

Prince Desmond came down the hall, arm in arm with Lady Olivia's daughter, Bianca. I heard the swish of her silken gown just before they passed us. Bianca glanced aside; I tensed under her luminous blue eyes, but she did not seem to see us. I let out a silent sigh as they trailed down the hall in their colorful riding clothes, heading for one of their afternoon rides together.

Father waited silently until the halls were empty again before he faced me and put his warm hand on my shoulder. "I would say something if I thought it would change things for that boy," he whispered, "but it won't. You know it won't."

"It's not right. Nothing is right here."

"Nothing will ever be right here, Uma. I will do what is needed to satisfy the queen so we can go home to a free people. We cannot upset the balance of this. If we both die here, who will free our tribe?"

I looked into his sad eyes and nodded.

"Until we can go home, guard your power, mi tupelli."

He touched the dragon belt encircling my waist. "Never trust the English. You are the fox. They are the hounds. You must learn to survive. Promise me."

FATHER WORKED. We survived. Still, the queen's frustrations with the Adan's cure sharpened. One afternoon late in Whale Moon she clicked the chalice rim against her teeth, glanced up at Lady Olivia, and said, "How long has Adan been serving us?"

"He came in May on Saint Florian's Feast Day, Your Majesty. Nearly three months ago."

"Three months," she repeated. "And still I am not with child!"

"It can take time to conceive, Your Highness," Father said.

"I beheaded Master Fenns, that cloying little man who leeched me dry. We've already had a hanging last month," she mused before turning to Lady Olivia again. "I much prefer a burning. A double one," she added, looking at Father and me. "If you fail me, you and your faithful apprentice can burn together, Adan. What do you think of that?"

*Burn?* I grabbed Father's arm, the floor pitching underfoot.

"Tying two to a stake would be unusual. What do you think, Lady Olivia?"

Lady Olivia clutched her throat as if she were choking on a mouse. "Un . . . usual, yes, Your Majesty."

The queen put out her hand for my father to kiss her ring.

As Father knelt, I noticed his narrow shoulders. He'd grown so thin working day and night for the queen; I could count the bony knobs along his neck. The sight startled me. The English did not know how to spice their food. You might as well chew ash. Still, I promised myself I would make him eat more; sleep more so he'd regain his strength.

That night I brought him ox-tail soup and thick buttered barley bread. Father got up from his prayers and waved it aside. "The Holy Ones have given me a vision," he said, eyes sparkling. "I've seen where I must go to harvest the special remedy for the queen."

Adans were gifted with visions. I'd never argued with him when he'd had one. Now I couldn't stop myself. "You are overworked, Father. You need to eat, to rest."

"I am the Adan," he said.

"You treat our enemy."

He flipped to the first page of his Herbal and pointed to a line in the *Adan-duxma*—the healer's creed: *Adans heal the wicked and the righteous alike.*

I knew the line, I'd memorized the *Adan-duxma* as a part of my training. "But she will not let you go."

Ignoring me, he flung the window open and called his dragon to the tower, a silent call, a summoning. He called Vazan this way when he truly needed her. Always I pricked my ears, hoping to hear some small sound from him. But the only sounds were those of pumping wings against the night sky as Vazan came to us like a great dark shadow. The room filled with her sharp peppery odor, the tang of rusted metal, her familiar spicy scent. Father crawled out onto the window ledge and carefully mounted her, swinging his leg over the base of her long neck.

"I will return by morning," Father said. "Keep the door bolted, mi tupelli."

Of course I would keep it bolted with a murderer still about. I leaned against the sill, wanted to call, *Don't go!* Instead I jammed my hand outside, crying, "Take this!" He took a slice of the barley bread. A moment later he was gone.

He'd vanished just as quickly other times back in Devil's Boot; days when he'd gone to gather herbs too far away for me to journey with him. Always I felt his leaving with the hot wind stirred by Vazan's wings. Back then I'd gone home to our hut, watched Mother's freckled hands fly, weaving bright patterns on her loom. I'd ask her for a song or story to ease my sadness. I'd give anything to see her, hold her, hear her smooth, low voice now.

I'd never felt this alone.

I ate some buttered barley bread, hoping Father would eat his. The English bread was good, but it sat in my stomach like a lump. I couldn't face the ox-tail soup. I crawled into my narrow bed behind the screen. In my dreams Father and I were tied back to back to a stake. And burned. I bit my nails down to the quick that night and had to lick the blood from my fingers before I dressed.

"What did you do to yourself?" Father asked, looking at the swollen fingertips when he returned later the next morning.

"I . . . dreamed she burned us."

"She won't, Uma." His brown eyes were soft above his sunken cheeks. "My medicine will work. I am the healer who will cure her. Trust me. You do trust me?"

"Yes, Father." He looked so tired. "Why don't you rest, Adan."

"I have to work," he said. "A child cannot grow in the queen when her mind is so troubled." He pulled the bapeeta plants he'd gathered from his herbing basket. I recognized the five-point leaves that looked like an infant's hands. "This herb will calm Her Majesty's wind mind," he said.

We turned the leaves over. The undersides had more tiny pollen dots than ferns do. I helped him scrape the pollen dust into packets. It was the dust he wanted.


I WAS AFRAID Her Majesty would detect the bapeeta in her curative brew. But Father was a master, adding just enough honey to hide any telltale bitterness. She took her morning and evening doses without comment that day. Father was pleased, but I saw his exhaustion the moment we left Her Majesty's room that evening. Halfway up the stairs to the Crow's Nest, he hunched over and clutched his arm, his brown face gray as if he'd bathed it in dust.

"You're ill, Father."

He waved my words away, went up and unlocked his Herbal. I took out his ink and quill and watched him draw the bapeeta. This plant differed from the ones that grew down south; the leaves here a smaller, brighter green. The

Adan was careful to note such differences. He traced the shape of the leaves top and bottom, the pollen dotting the undersides, and wrote the Euit words beside it, noting the variations of color. He stopped a few times to grip his upper arm and draw in breath.

"Please take some medicine, Adan."

"Uma. Let me work!"

I backed away, hurt. I could see he was in pain. Why would he never admit it even to me? Why would he never take any of his own medicine when he needed it?

Father worked another hour, finished the page, got slowly to his feet, and went to his bed. He usually prayed before he lay down, but I saw how little strength he had tonight.

"Eat a little first, Adan."

"Not now, Uma." Father turned and faced the wall. I covered him with the moth-eaten wool blanket. *He needs his rest,* I thought. *He'll feel better tomorrow.* I was wrong.


HE NEVER WOKE the next morning. When I went to check on him, he was cold. He'd been dead for hours. My legs went out from under me. I fell with my head on his chest. I had not let him see me weep since I was a small child. Now the flood came rising up, roaring, breaking the banks inside me.

## CHAPTER FOUR

# Pendragon Castle, Wilde Island

## WHALE MOON
### *July 1210*

PALACE GUARDS POUNDED on the door. Sobbing, I swayed on my feet. Pock Face barged in with a second guard, saw my father's body, then grabbed me and muscled me through the castle.

In Queen Adela's bedchamber, I dove to the floor, prostrating myself.

"Your Majesty," Pock Face said, "we could not bring your physician with your morning tonic. The man is dead."

"Dead?" she asked, her voice cracking with the word.

"Yes, Your Majesty."

"Was he murdered in his bed?"

"Doesn't look like murder, Your Majesty." Pock Face sounded disappointed. "What shall we do with the leftovers?" he added, stepping closer to where I lay on the floor to jab my ribs with his boot.

"Wait outside in the landing, both of you, until I call for you again."

They shuffled out, leaving me alone with Queen Adela and Lady Olivia.

"Look at me," said the queen. I raised my head off the floor. Her Majesty selected a sweetmeat from a tray on the small table at her side. The glint coming off her golden fingerbowl stung my eyes that were still raw from crying.

"Tell me how he died. Did he take his own life?"

"No, Your Majesty," I said, shocked. "The Adan would never do that."

"Disease, then." She leaned out from her chair narrowing her eyes. "A physician who cannot cure himself."

I swallowed. "He would not take his own medicine, Your Majesty," I said hoarsely. "He believed in using it only on his patients." *On you!*

She huffed. "What a ridiculous way to die."

She'd burn me now. I'd welcome it. It hurt too much to breathe with Father gone. I felt part dead already. But I heard my father's voice: *Never trust the English. You are the fox. They are the hounds. You must learn to survive. Promise me.*

I was still on the floor. "Your Majesty, let me try and help you."

Her lip twitched. "How can you help me?"

"I worked beside the Adan for years, Your Majesty."

She flung the fingerbowl. It struck my temple before it hit the floor and rolled under her vanity. "He lied to me. Stop groveling," she added. "And stand up. I said leave the room!" She spoke these last words to the vacant place by the door. By now I'd grown used to her addressing the air.

On my feet, I brushed away the rushes clinging to my breeches. Queen Adela studied me and smiled. "I see you." She touched her cheek with her forefinger, pointing to her fey eye.

*See me? What does she mean?*

"You think you have fooled *me* in those scribe's clothes, young woman?"

My knees began to wobble.

Lady Olivia blanched, blinking rapidly as if seeing me for the first time.

I gripped my dragon belt. "Your Majesty, I can explain. In our Euit tradition . . ." *No, don't tell her that.* "I chose to dress this way in service to the Adan because—"

"I don't want to hear anything about your quaint tribal customs. I am the queen of Wilde Island, and I have waited sixteen years to have a healthy second child. Your father promised me a marvelous cure. If this was not a lie, tell me why I am not already pregnant."

*Because you are going mad and the king fears visiting your bed. Because you are too old.*

"The remedy does not always work right away, Your Majesty. One woman took Kuyawan for six months before she conceived. In time she birthed a healthy boy." Ashune and little Melo.

The queen's mouth curved down. I wasn't convincing her.

"I have studied beside the Adan all my life. I know his

remedies. Please give me the chance to help you have the child you want, Your Majesty. I promise I can do it."

"Come here, Pippin." The queen picked up her lapdog and stroked his head, her face now strangely serene. I'd seen her quick mood changes before. They did not mean anything.

"You beg me for a chance," she said. "What do you have to offer that your father did not?"

Sweat dripped down my back. *Nothing. He was a great healer.* "Time, Your Majesty."

"Time?" The queen squeezed Pippin's neck. He yelped before he struggled free and jumped down to hide under the table. "I have given your father too much time already.

"Guards!"

Pock Face rushed in with a second man, they grabbed my arms and started dragging me from the solar.

"Wait, please. You haven't taken the cure a full six months, Your Majesty. What if just a few more doses—"

"Stop a moment," Queen Adela said, raising her hand. The men held me firmly, pinning my arms against my sides as if I might fly away.

"Three months more," she mused. "That would be October's end," she said, tapping her armrest with her long nails, a sound like hungry woodpeckers searching for food.

October's end. By the death of Dragon Moon. I wasn't sure it gave me enough time, but it was too late to retract my words.

She fixed her eyes on me. "If I give you this chance, Uma, the first thing you will do is to destroy those foolish clothes." She turned to her companion. "Lady Olivia, your daughter is about Uma's height, if a little rounder, is she not? Have Bianca give my new physician two of her prettiest gowns. I'm remembering a blue velvet one with pearls along the neckline."

Lady Olivia's face went hard as ironwood. "Yes, Your Majesty."

Pock Face lost his grip a moment and stared at me bewildered.

The queen stretched out her hand. "You may show your gratitude now, Uma."

I crept forward and kissed her ruby ring, keeping my head low. "Thank you, Your Majesty." I would live a little longer. But her offer meant nothing if she didn't mean to release my tribe once she got the child she wanted.

Queen Adela withdrew her hand. "Take her out. I am finished with her until she's properly dressed."

I saw my reflection in the queen's vanity mirror as the guards led me to the door: a girl-boy in dirty tunic and breeches, with a dark, tear-stained face.

"Oh, and Uma?" The men paused, holding my upper arms tight. "You have hidden yourself from us in many ways while you worked in the shadow of your father. Now I will bring you into the light. We will see if you bloom *or burn*."

I HIKED UPHILL to my father's grave.

How could I live without him?

I was his daughter—and the son he never had.

He was my teacher and my solid earth.

The queen had refused him the dignity of a gravestone. I sang to the Holy Ones as I set out the symbols of the four sacred elements at his gravesite, where I'd carved his name onto a driftwood plank: rich soil from Devil's Boot, an osprey feather, a bowl of seawater, and my flint box to burn an oak branch. He deserved a large gathering, not the songs of a single soul, but I was the only one here to perform the rite.

The Adan had already started his long walk home to heavenly Nushtuen. His Path Animal, owl, would guide him. I hoped my prayers would help.

I was about to light the cleansing fire when a shadow overcame the hill. Vazan stormed in, her hot gust blowing me off my feet. I flung my hands back to catch my fall and landed with a thump as she settled noisily on the summer grass.

One eye on the grave, the other on me, she lowered her great head. I brushed myself off and stood again, facing her. Her nostrils flared as she sniffed the earthen mound. She gave a smoky huff when she caught my father's scent.

"Uma!" She blazed fire over Father's grave. I leaped back. She'd nearly singed my feet. The raw flames lit the oak branch at the foot of Father's grave. I didn't need the tinder box now. She completed the fire rite.

Her large silver eyes were iced with anger. "How did the queen kill your father?"

"She didn't . . . Father worked and wouldn't stop to eat or rest. He hid his pain from me."

"But you saw it," she said.

"I saw it. He . . . wouldn't let me treat him," I said past the lump in my throat.

Vazan dug a talon into the soft grave soil. She was all wind and fire, not bound to earth as humans are, though she loved her rich hunting grounds around our volcano. Her bond to my father showed in the great sacrifice she'd made leaving her cave in Devil's Boot to follow us north. Smoke billowed from her nose. Her breaths were long sighs. Dragons do not cry.

I breathed in her smoke, gray grief between us. At last she spoke.

"There is no one to heal this infertile queen now. She will leave the king's soldiers in Devil's Boot. We'll lose all our freedom to these English vermin!"

"I have the herbs to cure infertility, and I have the Adan's book." The keys to Father's trunk and his Herbal clinked as I pulled the necklace out to show her.

Vazan flattened her ears against her head. "What good are the herbs and this book? Men have the power to heal. Women do not have that power."

"You are female, Vazan. You are powerful."

"Yesssss," she hissed, "but I am dragon. You are girl."

I crossed my arms. My chest ached. Bound in cloth, wrapped in sorrow, I had no heart to argue here at Father's grave, but battle is dragon's bread. "We both want the same thing. I have to treat the queen so she'll keep her promise. What other choices do we have?" She blinked at me. I went on. "Back home, the elders say a woman cannot heal, but the English don't live by our laws. The English have women healers. They have midwives. Mother was one."

Vazan flicked a clump of dirt off her talon. "There is no trusting these Pendragon royals. I have watched them. They don't even display their dragon scales, as if they are ashamed of them."

It was true. Prince Desmond supposedly had a scale patch on his arm. I'd never seen it. Most men rolled up their sleeves to spar in the weapons yard. He never did.

"So you plan to stay," Vazan said.

"I must stay. I promised the queen I'd keep treating her."

"With your father's herbs."

"Yes."

"You are the Adan's daughter," she conceded.

She curled her long tail around Father's grave. The spikes along the end were like a row of black upright daggers near my feet. "Will you take the voyage to Dragon's Keep?"

"What voyage?"

"Do you have eyessss and earssss?"

I sighed. "Tell me."

"The king plans to visit his brother Duke Bion on Dragon's Keep. Your father knew this. You'll see more Pendragons there if you go. It's where the Son of the Prophecy lives; the firstborn with dragon, human, and fairy blood combined." I knew the fairy's song about Duke Bion's son, the Son of the Prophecy. I'd learned it at my mother's knee.

"When is King Arden leaving?"

"A few weeks. The queen plans to go along. Your father was concerned about it."

My eyes fell to the mounded soil. "He had every reason to be. I need to talk the queen out of taking the journey. Egret Moon would be a dangerous time for her to travel by sea. She'd be at the mercy of the wind, even more than she already is."

"Any breeze can change her wind mind, Uma, but you won't change it."

"I hope you are wrong."

Vazan flicked her tail, the spikes rising to my waist before the scaled flesh slapped the ground again.

Was she going to leave me now that Father was dead? I felt a sharp jolt of fear. I pinched the red dragons on my belt, as if by squeezing hard enough, I could make her stay. *Ask her.* I glanced up at her noble head. The thin smoke coiling between us softened the shades of her red-orange scales. *I need you, Vazan. Don't go. Please don't leave me alone.*

I couldn't say the words out loud.

"You are crying, Adan's daughter."

She lowered her head and breathed a warm wind on my face, drying my tears.

# CHAPTER FIVE

## Voyage to Dragon's Keep

### EGRET MOON
*August 1210*

VAZAN WAS RIGHT. Queen Adela didn't listen when
I warned her that the journey would be perilous for
her. I was told to bring my medicine trunk along and leave
my opinions behind.

Her Majesty was seasick on the voyage. She blamed me
for her foul mood and putrid stomach, so I was relieved
on the fourth day when the sailors spotted land at last, and
thankful to be mixing her potion in the ship's galley for the
last time.

I rolled up the ridiculous, bell-shaped sleeves of Bianca's cast-off gown, then stirred the brew, chanting the plant
names. *My medicine will work*, Father said. *I am the healer
who will cure her. Trust me.* I did trust him and his medicine,
but I wondered. Was I skilled enough?

The bapeeta powder darkened the simmering potion. I'd

added an extra dose to calm Her Majesty before we reached Dragon's Keep.

When fists pounded on the door, I slid the bolt aside to find Prince Desmond. His clothes reeked of sweat and spilled ale.

I held the door firm. "The queen's remedy is nearly ready, Your Royal Highness."

He forced his way in and kicked the door shut with his boot heel. The jolt rattled the pots hanging from their hooks. He wrinkled his nose. "Stinks in here."

"It must be the whale oil lamp, Your Royal Highness."

I turned away. He stepped closer, wrapped his arms around me, and pressed himself up against my back, his wide hands gripping my waist. I tensed. I'd seen these same hands slit an old man's throat back in Devil's Boot. "What are you doing, Your Royal Highness?"

"You know what I am doing."

*Holy Ones help me.* Offend the prince and I'd end up with my neck in a noose. I touched his arm to free myself and felt a scaly rough patch of skin under his sleeve. *Dragon scales,* I thought, withdrawing my hand.

"You must let me go. I have to bring this remedy to Her Majesty now."

"Remedy? Mother thinks she has to have more children to please my father, but I don't need any royal snot-nosed siblings crawling underfoot." Desmond's ale-breath was hot against my neck. In public he looked at me as if I oozed maggots. He had never touched me like this before, but his favorite, Bianca, had stayed behind on Wilde Island. I was here.

His hands slid down my waist and lingered at my hips. My insides crawled. "I like this gown, Uma. So much better than the filthy boy's clothes we found you in." The night he learned I was female, he had had me whipped in front of him for my deceit. I gritted my teeth as my skin tore under the jailer's whip while Desmond watched. *I'm surprised you did not scream,* the prince said later, sounding disappointed. That was a little over three weeks ago. The scars had healed. The painful memory hadn't.

"And you've done things to your hair." He tugged the braid I'd carefully tied with a blue ribbon, jerking my neck back so hard my head hit his shoulder.

*Keep calm. Think what a castle maiden would say.* "Such flattery, Your Royal Highness, but I have to take the infusion from the fire now."

"Are you saving your virtue? Who would stoop to marry you?" He nibbled my neck, then sucked my skin the way he ate swan meat off the bone. I felt his breath on my cheek as he began to slide his fingers up the front of my laced bodice.

The door swung open with a bang. We flew apart, but not soon enough. Sir Geoffrey Crooked Nose had seen us in a backward embrace.

"Her Majesty wants to know what has been keeping you so long." His face was hard in the shadows.

Desmond grunted, brushing past him. Sir Geoffrey turned and glowered at the door after he left before he faced me again. "You had better watch your step with him if you don't want your head on the chopping block."

"I did not . . ." How could I say this? "I did not ask for His Highness to come inside, Sir Geoffrey. Please don't think—"

He looked at me a moment longer. Said nothing and left.

I wiped Prince Desmond's slimy kiss off my neck with three vicious swipes. Would he come to me again when we made landfall? Please, Holy Ones, I would have a door that locked.

WHEN I REACHED the deck, just barely managing not to spill the entire potion on the way up the rocking stairs, I heaved a breath. A few stars hung in the twilight sky. Prince Desmond stood at the prow with his mother, father, and Lady Olivia, taking in Dragon's Keep, our first sight of land. Sir Geoffrey hovered near the royal family with the rest of King Arden's private guards. I held back in the shadowy doorway, hoping the prince would leave his mother's side.

I couldn't bear to go near him.

The prince cracked a joke. His father laughed and pounded him on the back. He turned to his mother, and said something I couldn't hear from my hiding place. Queen Adela looked past him as if he weren't there. I caught his brief, hurt look before he faced forward again.

The island's black mountains lay like a sleeping bear atop the sea. Tiny specks of light winked near shore. We would arrive soon. Queen Adela needed to take her potion before we landed. Still I held back, sick at the thought of crossing Prince Desmond's path.

Sir Geoffrey pointed at the sky above the dark water. "Look, Your Majesties!"

Two dragons sped toward us, the green and copper-scaled kind that can grow as large as warships. But as they flew closer, I saw they were no bigger than Vazan. *Young dragons then*, I thought. And then I saw the riders. A rare sight for me. In my village only a few chosen elders flew on reds. Vazan had never let me ride her.

I watched them wing closer to our ship. Prince Desmond sometimes rode an old dragon who'd spent the last few months of his life dining on table scraps near the king's stables—not what I considered to be much of a dragon. Not like the noble Vazan. Not like these.

I watched transfixed. The dark-haired figure sitting proud on his dragon called down to us.

"Welcome to Dragon's Keep!" He caught sight of me by the door as his dragon skimmed down. The beast's wing knocked against the mainsail. I gripped the doorframe to steady myself as the ship tilted to the right. The queen let out a wild scream.

"Get away, dragon!" Desmond shouted, waving his arms overhead.

The coppery green beast backwinged out of reach. "I'm your cousin Jackrun Pendragon," called the rider over the queen's piercing screams. "Here with my sister, Tabitha. Don't you recognize us?" I looked from Jackrun to Tabitha, saw her neck scales shining in the ship's torchlight.

Desmond threw his head back. "Get away from my mother, clodpole!"

I hurried toward Her Majesty, tripping over the coiled ropes on my way to the prow, spilling more precious remedy on the deck before finally passing the chalice to the king. "Your Majesty, please give her this," I pleaded. "It will calm her."

He held it out to his frightened wife. "My dear," he shouted over her wails, "it is my brother's children flying out to greet us. They mean us no harm. Drink this. It will soothe you." She reared back like a wild horse, her eyes darting from chalice to husband, her face contorted with confusion, but she seemed to understand at last. I heaved a sigh as she drank the warm brew and pressed the empty silver cup against her flushed cheek.

"That's better," King Arden said, wrapping his arms around her. "You're all right now." He shot me a grateful look as he handed back the chalice. I lowered my eyes. The calming effect in the potion did not work that quickly. For now, the king's arms supported Her Majesty while Lady Olivia patted her back, murmuring soft words like a mother soothing a frightened child.

Jackrun Pendragon glared at his cousin before he cupped his hand to his mouth, calling down to his aunt and uncle. "Please forgive us for startling you, Your Majesties. We came to escort you across the bay."

He signaled his sister and flew ahead of the royal vessel. The dragons dove over and under each other as they moved toward the distant harbor, coiling a golden chain of fire for the ship to follow.

Sir Geoffrey hummed the fairies' song "Fey Maiden"

under his breath as the shining fiery chain lit the dusky sky ahead of us, spilling gold reflections on the dark water below. Mother had taught me all the verses.

> *In the enchanted woodland wild,*
> *The Prince shall wed a Fairy child.*
> *Dragon, Human, and Fairy,*
> *Their union will be bound by three.*
>
> *And when these lovers intertwine,*
> *Three races in one child combine.*
> *Dragon, Fey, and Humankind,*
> *Bound in one bloodline.*
>
> *O Bring this day unto us soon,*
> *And forfeit weapons forged in strife.*
> *Sheath sword, and talon, angry spell,*
> *And brethren be for life.*

Three races in one child combined. The "child" in the song was Jackrun, a young man now, leading us toward his island with chains of dragon fire.

In that moment, on that ship, four months after leaving the only home I had ever known, I was watching my own fate. But at the time, I merely prayed he was not at all like his cousin.

# CHAPTER SIX

# Pendragon Summer Castle, Dragon's Keep

## EGRET MOON
### *August 1210*

THE CASTLE ON Dragon's Keep was built like the castle back on Wilde Island, but smaller. It perched like an ornamental hat on the distant bluff with high towers and a crenellated guard wall. King Arden called it the summer castle, a place he'd visited with his family when he was a boy. His younger brother and his family lived here year-round now.

"Carry the physician's trunk," Sir Geoffrey called to a cabin boy. I turned as the lad rushed toward me.

"No, thank you. I have it." No cabin boy would take my father's precious medicines. I'd carried it onto the ship, I could carry it off.

"It looks heavy," Sir Geoffrey said. "You are sure?"

"Yes." He'd looked out for me from the start. I didn't know why. Sir Kenneth passed us, his arms and neck muscles bulging as he hefted one of the queen's trunks more than twice the size of mine. I glanced up at Sir Geoffrey. "I never thanked you for what you did for Father and me," I said in a hushed tone so no one on the busy deck would overhear. "If there is anything I can do to repay—"

"Think nothing of it. I chose to offer the food. They were starving you. A dead physician cannot heal anyone."

He saw me start and realized his words made me think of my father, but it was too late to take them back. I knew he hadn't meant to hurt me.

"I'm sorry for your loss," he said, lowering his head a little to make his speech more private. "I am sure you miss your father." He paused, adjusting his belt. "I have to go, but if you should need anything . . ."

I looked down, feeling his kindness, unable to speak.

He stood a moment longer before walking across the gently rolling deck.

The ship creaked like old bones as I struggled down the gangplank with the trunk and took my place at the end of the procession walking two-by-two down the long curved quay for shore.

An enormous dragon twice the size of the ones who'd escorted us in swooped down and landed by the welcoming party, folding his wings and shaking himself a little as a seabird will do when it alights on the beach.

"Welcome to Dragon's Keep, Your Majesties," he hissed, his voice like rough rocks tumbling down a ravine. King Arden gave him a hurried nod and whisked his wife up the beach toward the waiting horses.

I rested the Adan's trunk at my feet. The dragon's spicy breath loosened the hair at my temples, warmed my body. Closing my eyes, I was home, bathing in the steaming pools in the hills far below Mount Uther's volcanic rim. I could almost smell the slight sulfurous scent, mixed with the delicious odors of the lush green forest.

When I opened them again, I saw I had stayed too long. The king's men had stepped past the great dragon and we were left alone.

"I am Lord Kahlil. Welcome to Dragon's Keep." His low, rumbling voice greeted me in Euit. I was surprised. Dragons are masters of many languages, but our tribe is small now. I thought only the reds still bothered to learn our tongue.

I'd learned to guard my speech among the English, but just this once I let my words sing. "Thank you, Lord Kahlil. I am the queen's physician, Uma Quarteney. I am full in being here," I said in formal Euit before reverencing him with a bow and a hand on his scaly foot. The scales were leathery and warm.

Lord Kahlil gave a low, smoky sigh. Mother had told me stories about this dragonlord. He'd been a friend to the Pendragons for generations. Jagged scars ran down his long neck. A few teeth were missing, but the rest of his fangs looked sharp enough to eat his prey, bones and all. I hitched up my skirts and lifted Father's trunk.

"You carry a great weight," he said.

"I guard the queen's medicines."

"I do not mean the trunk."

A shiver raced up my spine. Great dragons like Lord Kahlil, who lived a thousand years or more, had a long view. They saw patterns far beyond what we could see. Did he see "a great weight" in my past, the losses I carried since the English came, since Father died, or was he speaking about the future? My future.

I was working up the nerve to ask Lord Kahlil, when he turned and began to walk up the long beach toward the castle.

Suddenly the dark shore felt vast, like the waters I'd just crossed.

I stood in the darkness with nothing but the summer's night wind surrounding me, until a ring of torchlight encircled me, and a man's strong hand reached for Father's trunk. He'd sneaked up from behind.

I started, turned, and came face-to-face with Jackrun Pendragon. "Let me help you with that," he said.

I held the trunk firm. "I can manage."

His hand was still out. I caught the scent of sweat, the peppery aroma of dragons coming off his skin. "The beach is tricky in the dark. Driftwood lies everywhere like a giant's bones. You'll need a hand and my torchlight if you don't want to fall."

Our eyes locked. He seemed to read my hesitation, note my tight grip on the trunk.

"You've nothing to fear," he said. "Let me introduce myself."

"I know who you are," I said. His face was much leaner than his cousin's, but he had the same well-shaped nose over full lips. Traces of his Persian heritage showed in his gold-brown skin, and dark curls. Fiery rings surrounded the dark pupils in his green eyes.

A swirling gust, swift and hot, stirred us both. Lord Kahlil wheeled overhead, coming closer with each spiral, his great wings outstretched like sails, the night clouds deep red above him. Jackrun's black cloak and my gray one slapped against each other like battle flags.

My hair ribbon flew off, and Jackrun chased after it, returning just as the beast winged out to sea.

"What was that?" I asked, still watching the retreating dragon. "Was he angry with me or—"

"Not angry, I'm guessing. I think he sees you have the help you need." He reached again for the trunk.

I paused. It *was* heavy. "Just carry your end."

He cocked a smile. "As you wish."

I tucked the ribbon into my mother's woven belt, watching Jackrun out of the corner of my eye as we walked up the dark beach toward his father's castle, the trunk swinging to and fro between us.

Jackrun slowed his pace as we skirted a large driftwood log. "My dragon, Babak, startled the queen. I saw you bring her a potion. You calmed her. Are you her lady's maid? Tell me your name so I can thank you properly."

*Jackrun Pendragon had waited on the beach to thank me?* "I am no lady's maid. I'm Uma Quarteney, the queen's physician."

He stopped. "You must be a very gifted healer to have risen so high in your profession at such a young age."

I gaped at him. A fluttering sensation passed along my chest as if my secret fox mark moved below my collarbone. No one had ever called me a gifted healer.

"Did I say something wrong?"

I tightened my grip on the trunk. He knew nothing about me.

He kicked up the sand as we walked on. "What ails the queen that she needs to bring her personal physician with her?"

*Infertility. Madness.* "Weak stomach," I said, landing on a half-truth. She *had* lost her appetite at sea. I wasn't about to discuss her real maladies with her nephew.

"Well, thank you for what you did back there, Uma Quarteney."

We climbed the wooden stairs up from the beach to the grassy bluff, then stopped three stones' throw from the castle to rest and catch our breath.

Jackrun jammed the torch handle in the grass and got on his knees. Running his fingers along the dragon carvings encircling the Adan's trunk, he said, "Very fine workmanship. Matches the pattern in your belt. Who made it?"

"A woodcrafter carved it for my father down in Devil's Boot."

"Where is your father now?"

I couldn't speak past the ache in my chest.

"I'm sorry," said Jackrun. "I did not mean to—"

I fingered the silky places on my belt where Mother had woven her red hair into one of the dragons. She didn't know what had happened to Father, unless Vazan had flown home to Devil's Boot and told her. My hands went clammy.

Jackrun stood again. "I'd like to see Devil's Boot someday."

"It's a lush and dangerous place," I said with pride.

"Yes, with a living volcano, so I've heard."

That living volcano had saved us when I was small. I had terrible memories of the English army burning our village, marching us south, closer to the mountain. When we reached the foothills, Mount Uther had rumbled, and spewed smoke and molten lava. The English army fled. We celebrated that year and every year after that with our explosive volcano dance. The only dance the red dragons admired, aside from the one we did on Dragon Moon.

Jackrun said, "I plan to explore all of Wilde Island."

"You've never seen it?"

"We've kept clear of it."

"Why?"

"It is a long story, Uma Quarteney."

"Because you are the Son of the Prophecy?" I asked.

He looked surprised. "Some call me that. The firstborn with dragon, human, and fairy blood was supposed to be king, able to rule everyone, every race fairly. My mother married the wrong brother for that."

I rubbed the long scar on my palm. "Rule every race fairly? Even the Euit people? My people?"

"Of course. Your people deserve respect like anyone else," he said.

*Not if you ask Prince Desmond,* I thought. "That would be very different than it has ever been before."

"It was all a dream anyway. My mother made her own choice. She infuriated the fairies, especially my grandfather. My parents fled Wilde Island to escape his vengeful magic, and took sanctuary here before I was born."

"And you've been safe here on Dragon's Keep?"

"It depends what you mean by safe. We haven't gone unpunished." He hefted my father's trunk.

I blocked him. "I will take one end."

He shook his head. "You guide us up to the road with the torch while I carry it for you, Uma Quarteney." I surprised myself, letting him. He carried it along the bluff toward the castle with ease.

"It's a long way from Devil's Boot to Pendragon Castle. I envy your journey. You must have seen the whole east coast of Wilde Island along the way."

He looked wistful, imagining a pleasant journey on horseback, not at all like the one I'd taken locked in Prince Desmond's jail cart. *As soon as Mother sees you and your boy here, she'll realize you're a fraud. Healing infertile women. Ha. That's a joke. I bet you used your prick, old man.*

Jackrun must have heard me moan. I hadn't meant to make a sound. "You're tired after the long voyage," he said. "I'll take you to your room. Then I'll have to leave you and dress for dinner. My mother has planned an elaborate feast. The Great Hall will be crammed with islanders to welcome the king."

"But no dragons?"

He laughed. "I would love to squeeze them in, but our Great Hall is not *that* great."

"The queen will be relieved."

"And you? Will you be relieved?" He looked at me out of the corner of his eye.

"I won't be there."

"Why? You must be hungry after the voyage."

"I have work to do."

The wind followed us through the open double doors, troubling my torch and the ones in the wall sconces. Servants hurrying down the hall with food trays stopped to bow to Jackrun before going on.

We mounted the spiral stairs in one of the four castle towers. "Tell me about the red dragons who live down south near your volcano," Jackrun said. "I've never seen one."

"They are fiercely independent."

"Like you?" he asked.

"What do you mean?"

"I had to fight to carry this heavy trunk for you," he said, setting it on the third-floor landing. "Reds are too independent to take refuge in Dragonswood, I've heard." He opened the door. "Your room, my lady."

Inside, he lit the torches on the wall, the candles on the table. I sneezed from the thick dust, and looked around. Splintered chairs were stacked in one corner by a coverless bed. The worktable I would need to prepare my medicines was slanted. The rickety wardrobe door hung askew. A storage room for castle cast-offs.

"I'm sorry about this, Uma." Jackrun grabbed some rushes from the floor and waved them around at the thick cobwebs. "I'll send a servant upstairs to clean your chamber right away."

I grabbed some rushes and did what he was doing, both of us waving our arms as if we were greeting an exuberant crowd. We worked until our rushes were thickly matted. Evicted spiders scuttled along the walls heading for refuge in the piled chairs and behind the wardrobe. The room reeked of rat piss. I missed my small, friendly hut back home with its bed of fresh reeds, with the scent of the mountainside that could not be kept out. No amount of cleaning would change the intense confinement of these thick stone walls.

But I didn't feel completely lost in the tower room until Jackrun bowed and took his leave.

## CHAPTER SEVEN

# Pendragon Summer Castle, Dragon's Keep

EGRET MOON
*August 1210*

I PULLED FATHER'S belt from the trunk. The red dragon's wings seemed to move as it slowly uncoiled. His belt
was longer and thicker than mine. Made for a man. I rubbed
my thumb across the horned owl engraving on the buckle,
Father's Path Animal.

Jackrun complimented me on the beach. *You must be a
very gifted healer to have risen so high in your profession.*
He didn't know my story. I was doing a forbidden thing. I
was an untried female. I'd never been allowed to mix cures
or treat the sick while Father was alive.

I looped the Adan's belt above my own, cinched it in to
feel the pressure of it against my waist. Mother wove the red
dragons with love; Father had worn them when he followed

the visions the Holy Ones gave him to the places where the healing plants grew. He'd worn this belt when we harvested the herbs for his greatest remedy, Kuyawan—beloved child.

But what powers did I have? The Holy Ones hadn't blessed me with visions. My Path Animal had never guided me to healing herbs.

I locked the trunk. A servant came in and dropped the bedding on my straw mattress. She eyed me warily, and stayed just long enough to flit the dust cloth around here and there before she bolted for the door.

"Wait," I said, putting out my hand. "Give me the room key, please. I need it."

The girl screwed up her face. "I weren't told to do that, miss," she said, and flew down the stairs, probably frightened by the sight of the first Euit woman she had ever seen.

Sir Geoffrey had offered help: *If you should need anything* . . . But he would have no authority to get me a room key. I would have to work it out somehow if I did not want to sit up with my back pressed against the door, knife in hand all night long, waiting for Prince Desmond.

They'd left me no firewood to seethe the queen's morning tonic. I would fetch my own wood; breathe fresh air before I was forced to stay inside for the night.

Downstairs, I used my Euit training to move unseen through the torchlit halls, whispering the chant, *havuela*— become—to help me blend in with my surroundings. I found it much harder to blend indoors than out, but I'd been forced to learn how among the English who lived their lives in stone boxes. That and silent feet took me beyond the courtyard gate, out into the clean-scented summer night.

I circled the corner of the castle and crossed the dirt road to walk in the long grass, the sea to my right, the harbor to my back, the woods two hundred yards or so ahead. I was in no hurry. I felt myself expanding under the scattered stars. It was good to be outside. I was reveling in my stolen freedom, when the sound of distant pounding feet made me turn.

A man in courtier's clothing raced from the castle, flying across the road and down the steps to the beach. Not wanting to be caught out alone, I stood very still as he ran along the sand. He stopped suddenly, thirty strides or so downhill from me, leaned toward the brambles, and roared fire.

We should all balance the four sacred elements of earth, wind, water, and fire in our being. But no man breathes fire. Yet my eyes did not lie. His flames lit the brambles, the ignited wood burst into a brilliant golden blaze. I watched transfixed, saw his face in the glowing light.

*Jackrun.* My fingers curled to fists as he shouted flames in sharp, bright javelins. I heard the rage in his roar. Terror blazed through me. And something else. Exhilaration at his unleashed power.

A few birds flew upward, crying out, to escape. One slower than the rest caught fire and beat its flaming wings before it fell.

Sparks popped and flew up like tossed jewels over Jackrun's dark head. He hurled hunks of sand to put the fire out and kicked up more with his boots, moving like a fighting man who'd thrown off his weapons in favor of his hands and feet. It was then he looked up toward the bluff and saw me.

I could have become a part of the blowing grass tickling my arms, night's darkness, but I didn't. I clung to a slender stalk of pampas grass as he made his way up the bluff with long forceful strides.

"What are you doing here, Uma?" he demanded. Smoke puffed from his nose and mouth.

"You breathe fire," I said, still only half believing what I'd seen.

He wiped his brow. His eyes were the colors of green earth and flame.

"Listen." He grabbed my shoulders, shook me once, then dropped his hands again. "You cannot tell anyone what you saw." His face was all passion and anger. Heat wafted off his skin. He'd been kind when he helped me carry Father's trunk. Now I wondered who he was.

"Surely others know?"

Silence.

"Your family?"

He stood very still, his arms crossed, but the silent yes I saw in him made him grip his upper arms tighter.

"Your uncle, the king, and his wife, the queen?"

"No," he said, firmly, "not them."

His eyes fell on my double-belted waist. I'd put on Father's belt—missing Mother, missing Father, feeling alone on this strange new island full of English—and forgotten to take it off. "If you have been given this power," I said, "why hide it?"

Jackrun began pacing the bluff, keeping his path small, as if the grass caged him. "Just give me your promise."

*Never trust the English,* Father said. I could not make promises so easily anymore. I needed to gather information as sure coin to use if I needed it. "I know some warriors in my tribe who would love to have such power."

He barked a short, bitter laugh. "You don't know what you're saying, Uma." His feet moved, his arms, his hands. "I have to get back," he added, glancing toward the castle.

"And I have firewood to gather," I said. *You are the fox. They are the hounds. You must learn to survive.*

"I'll give you a hand," he said. We headed down the hill. Summer stars winked above, a treasury of diamonds. On the beach I slipped off my shoes and felt the sand between my toes as Jackrun rolled up his sleeves, fell to his knees, and dug a hole with his bare hands to bury the dead bird he'd burned. When he was done, he patted the small mound with care as if he were tucking in a child.

He stood tall again, brushing off his hands. Green dragon scales covered his right forearm, each diamond-shaped scale the size of a coin.

"I nearly burned Desmond tonight over that," he said, looking down at his scaly arm. "Not my scales, but my sister's. He insulted Tabitha. He called her neck scales repulsive in the middle of the feast, loud enough for everyone to hear. She ran from the table in tears." He swiped a hand through his hair, a swift, hard pass as a man skins an animal with a sharp blade. "He's the same callous bastard he's always been."

I tasted the words *callous bastard,* liking the sound. The callous bastard had shed the blood of my people, the callous bastard whipped me and my father, the callous bastard slobbered on my neck, reached up the front of my dress.

Jackrun was on the move again, this time walking to the shore. Water hissed up to our feet, touched his boots and my bare toes. I pointed across the sea at the dragon flying under the stars, black as a torn piece of night. It might be Jackrun's dragon, Babak, or Lord Kahlil. Too far away to tell. Dragons combine earth, wind, and fire in their bodies. They have a power like the sun. Jackrun had this same life force in him.

"You are the only one who can do what they do with fire."

Jackrun's mouth tightened. He hooked his thumb around the jeweled dagger at his belt.

"You don't understand. It's dangerous. I'm dangerous."

"You didn't harm Prince Desmond tonight," I said. "You ran outside before you burned him."

"He deserved to burn." His body was rigid. He glared down at me. I kept his gaze.

"Yes. He does." *Had I spoken the words out loud?* For a moment his fire had released me.

"Uma Quarteney." Jackrun's gaze softened. Then he crouched to fill his hands with seawater and rinse his face. Water ran down his cheeks and chin, his wrists and arm scales. He looked calmer when he stood again. "You remind me of someone," he said. "Someone I lost years ago."

I waited for him to explain, taking in his thoughtful mouth, the weight of sorrow around it. But he never told me who he was thinking of. We circled the beach, gathering firewood. Jackrun broke a longer branch across his knee with a loud crack.

"You still haven't given me an answer, Uma."

I paused, cradling my driftwood. Time in the water had made the wood's surface smooth as skin. What would Jackrun's scales feel like? Thick and leathery? Rough as bark? "I'll keep what I saw to myself if you will do something for me."

He gave a wary sigh as he faced me. "Of course there is a price. What is it?"

"I need the key to my tower room. The servant would not let me have it."

Jackrun's shoulders eased. He stepped closer, stretching his hand over mine a moment like a hovering bird, then took my branches and added them to his stack to carry for me.

"Key it is," he said.

# CHAPTER EIGHT

# Pendragon Summer Castle, Dragon's Keep

## EGRET MOON
*August 1210*

J ACKRUN'S MOTHER, THE duchess Tess Pendragon, waylaid us in the castle hall, parting us as soon as we came in as a tiny island parts a river. She asked Jackrun to step into the family presence chamber with her and called a servant to carry my firewood upstairs. As soon as the gangly boy stacked the wood and left the tower, I shoved the wardrobe in front of the door—one way to keep Prince Desmond out until I had the key—then opened the windows and cleaned the room by torchlight, chasing dust and shadows until I sat alone exhausted on the bed.

The ropes below the straw mattress creaked under my weight. I knew I should rise, set out the four sacred elements, offer myself to Creator, and pray to the Holy Ones. Father would have done that, grateful to arrive safely on a new island without accident or injury. But I was too tired. I felt a strange rocking motion in my body as if I were still aboard the ship. I decided to rest a little and wait for Jackrun and the key.

Jackrun came to me in my dreams. Not breathing fire or riding his dragon. He had filled a bowl with seawater. I looked inside and saw a bright orange starfish. In the dream I asked how he'd found the power to pull a star down from the sky and he laughed.

Thunderous pounding outside the tower door woke me hours later with a start. I raced across the room thinking it was Jackrun. Lady Olivia's muffled voiced called, "Uma! For God's sake, open up!"

The heavy wardrobe scraped against the floor as I pushed it aside. Lady Olivia shivered in her long robe at the top of the stairs. "The queen!" she said. "She is in a bad way. Crying in her bed. Shouting at people who are not there."

"I'll mix the calming cure."

"No time. Bring what you need and make it in her bedchamber. Come on!"

I unlocked the trunk. Jackrun hadn't come with the room key. I might miss him if I left, but I couldn't think of that now. I gathered the medicines, locked the trunk, and followed Lady Olivia to the queen's bedchamber.

The red curtains had been drawn back on Her Majesty's bed. She was writhing as we entered; twisting the sheets and covers into thick cloth snakes. "Let me go, you filthy witches," she was crying. "Untie me!"

Lady Olivia approached the bed. "She relives the night the witches tormented her and put out her eye when she was a girl. I tried to wake her, but it is not a dream. It is more like some fit. Your Majesty," she said, sitting by her, "your physician is here."

"My eye!" she screamed, pushing Lady Olivia away. "Get away from me! Please don't put out my eye!" Her scream sent ice up my spine. Lady Olivia forced a hand over Queen Adela's mouth. However late it was, someone was bound to hear us if we couldn't quiet her. I shook as I mixed the sleeping remedy and the bapeeta in honey. Mother had told me the story of how the queen lost her eye on All Hallows' Eve, but it was one thing to know a tale, another thing to be drawn into the agony as if it were happening here and now, to hear the pitiful, frightened cries of the victim as she relived it.

On the bed, Lady Olivia was doing her best to muffle the screams. "Ouch," she cried, cradling her hand. "She bit me!"

Someone pounded on the door. "Your Majesty? Are you all right?" Lady Olivia flew to answer the knock as I spooned the honeyed cure into the queen's mouth.

"No," the queen said, tears wetting the side of her face below her living eye. Still she swallowed the mixture.

"A nightmare," Lady Olivia was saying to the person on the far side of the door. "Her physician is attending her. We will call you if we need any assistance."

Queen Adela breathed fast as a frightened bird, but she took a second spoonful. I'd made sure to add extra honey to entice her. "Now we wait," I said.

Lady Olivia sat again and began a lullaby my mother used to sing to me. For a brief moment I thought I smelled the scent of my mother's hair.

I stepped back, overcome, as I watched this woman's way of healing, a way to calm fears, ease pain with song. This was not Father's way, and so not mine. Shaken by the childhood feelings the song unleashed, I told myself to do what the Adan would do and went about recapping the honey, cleaning the medicinal spoon as I waited for the cure to take effect.

The queen rested her head on her companion's shoulder, her face ashen under her wildly tangled hair. The room began to quiet. *Ona loneaih,* I thought in Euit, *be you well.* I heard Her Majesty whimper as a young child would do after a bout of crying. Then she let out a sudden, violent snort and pushed Lady Olivia off the bed onto the floor.

I jumped back as Queen Adela leaped onto her feet with tremendous energy that seemed almost inspired.

"You can't have her," she shouted to the ceiling. "She's mine!"

"What has happened?" asked Lady Olivia, stepping back, afraid now to come near her.

"Another memory," I guessed. "The medicine hasn't taken hold yet."

The queen screamed, "Get away from my witch pyre, dragon!" She raised her leg as if mounting a horse, and rode off in her mind, her body jiggling up and down in an imagined gallop. "Bring back that witch. Witches have to burn!

Tanya has to burn! Riders, go after that thief of a dragon and bring the witch back to me!"

The queen's body tottered and I was afraid she would fall. "Help me with her," I said.

Lady Olivia moaned and crumpled to the queen's bed, gathering the blankets to herself and hiding her face in them. I'd never seen her so affected by the queen's distress.

"Your Majesty," I said, speaking softly. "This is only a dream." My eyes were drawn to a painting on the bedside wall of a dragon breathing fire as he flew over the trees. If this painting brought on Her Majesty's current nightmare . . . I took it down and turned it to face the wall.

"Bring Tanya back, you thief!" the queen cried.

I inched up to her right side, put my arms about her, and held her. Until at last her body quieted to a series of trembles so strong I felt the quaking in my own.

She cried a little. "Where is—?" She shuddered, turning her head to me. "I am so tired, Uma," she whispered.

She gripped my double-belted waist as I led her back toward her bed.

Lady Olivia still hugged the blankets, shaking. It took some coaxing on my part to get her to release them. "I am sorry, Uma," she said, her breath catching as we tucked Her Majesty in. "I . . ." She looked like a stunned woman pulled out of the wreckage.

"It's all right. You were overcome." I felt the same, but I did not say so. The Adan was never shaken. He was reserved, proud. The queen relied on me to treat her as competently as my father would. It unnerved me to be so undone.

"I'm thirsty," the queen said, sitting up. "What are you doing here, Uma?" she asked as Lady Olivia fetched her cup.

"You were having trouble sleeping, Your Majesty."

"I see," she said, yawning. "Well, I can sleep now." She drank to the dregs and lay down again, her dark hair spreading out like wet seaweed around her head.

We watched her eyes close, her face serene now in the candlelight.

Lady Olivia sighed and glanced up. "It is over, I think. Thank you, Uma."

"We both worked together."

She shook her head. "It was you and your potent medicine put her back to sleep," she whispered.

"My father's medicine."

"You must learn to take a compliment, Uma. He is not here. You are the one who serves Her Majesty now."

*And I'm the one she will burn if I fail,* I thought, looking down at the queen. The queen's eyelids fluttered, pale as moths. I remembered Father's warning: *If we both die here, who will free our tribe?* Already the Adan was in the grave. Did I have the skills to give Her Highness the child she wanted? What if the elders back home were right? What if a woman did not have the ability to become a true healer? I didn't move, sat poised as rock hoping Lady Olivia could not read my fear as I broke into a cold sweat.

# CHAPTER NINE

# Pendragon Summer Castle, Dragon's Keep

EGRET MOON
*August 1210*

THE QUEEN WAS in the walled garden the next morning, playing ball with a little curly dark-haired boy of two or three, and her lapdog, Pippin. I came up to Lady Olivia as the boy raced after the red ball, squealing, "Mine!" Pippin reached it first and caught it in his mouth, his tail wagging furiously.

"She slept through the night," Lady Olivia said, with her usual untouchable tone. The woman who had buried her face in the blankets like a terrified vole was gone. Her silks shone, her face was powdered, her skin scented with hyacinth perfume. I decided I liked the woman I'd met last night who was less proper, more human. The woman who had sung a lullaby, cried.

"There is something I must speak with you about," she said sternly. We both ducked as the tossed ball flew over us and splashed in the fountain at our backs.

"Retrieve it, Lady O.," said the queen, lifting the hem of her elegant gown as she crossed the lawn. Lady Olivia threw me a look that asked, *Why should a person of my station have to fetch it?* before she curtsied in resignation, rolled up a lacy sleeve, and turned for the fountain.

I offered Queen Adela her tonic while we waited on the gravel path. It was less than an hour after breakfast, a good time to drink it. The little boy on the lawn didn't seem to need the ball. He ran in circles now, romping on the grass with Pippin.

"He is a delight," the queen said. "So like Desmond at that age. I'd almost forgotten." She swallowed the brew and licked her lips. I thanked the Holy Ones for my ample supply of honey that made the potion tasty. "I will reward you if you help me have another child," she said with sudden brightness. "This," she added, lifting the emerald necklace from her throat. "This will be yours if you succeed."

I blinked at the expensive jewels. "Thank you, Your Majesty, but . . ." I paused. "What I truly want—"

Her eyes flared. "What you *want*? Don't tell me you do not appreciate my gift!"

I curtsied, afraid. "I like it very much, Your Majesty." The smile I tried on did not quite fit. My cheeks felt hard. "It is beautiful. Much too good a gift for me. You are exceedingly generous. But if you wish to give me anything, more than any jewel, any gift, all I really want is to go home to a free people."

"Why?"

"Wh . . . why?" *By the Holy Ones, how could she ask that?* "When the soldiers leave my village, we can all live without fear." There. I'd said it. The naked confession made me shiver.

"Your skills are wasted there, Uma. You could have so much more. You could practice medicine anywhere you like. This necklace would buy you a pretty house and good land with a few servants to tend it."

"My home is in Devil's Boot, Your Majesty," I said, though saying it didn't make it true. *Would I be any more welcome there now than I was when I left?*

Lady Olivia returned with the dripping ball. The queen raised a brow at it until Lady Olivia sighed and used her skirts to dry it off. Satisfied, Her Majesty took it out to the boy and dog again.

Lady Olivia peered at me. "Are you all right, Uma?"

"Fine, my lady."

She shook water droplets from her hand and rolled her sleeve back down. "What did she say to you?"

"I talked of home," I admitted.

"You miss your tribe," she said.

"I'm worried about what the king's troops might do to them while I'm away."

We watched the boy and frisky dog run into the bushes after the ball. Jackrun's sister, Tabitha, came into the walled garden, the sun catching gold-brown gleams in her hair. Her fey blood from her mother's side showed in her graceful steps as she passed the fountain. "Is Kip out here?"

Lady Olivia nodded toward the hedge. "Your little brother has been playing catch with the queen." The hiding boy giggled in the bushes. More laughter and squealing erupted as Tabitha moved toward the hedgerow. Queen Adela joined her. "Where is Kip?" she called, the game of catch turning into hide-and-seek.

"Your talk of home brings up the matter we need to discuss," Lady Olivia said under her breath. "It is a matter of discretion between the sexes."

I felt my spine go taut as a tugged rope.

"I spoke with Sir Geoffrey at breakfast this morning. He told me about the incident between you and Prince Desmond in the ship's galley."

My jaw dropped before I said, "Incident?"

"He was right to come to me with his concern. It is Sir Geoffrey's job to keep an eye on Prince Desmond, and mine to watch out for you."

Her explanation did no good. I felt betrayed. I'd thought of Sir Geoffrey as a friend, or at the very least as someone who wished me well. I'd made it clear I hadn't wanted Prince Desmond's attention.

"Kip? Where's Kip?" Tabitha called in a singsong voice, peering through the bushes.

"I do not know what your customs are regarding unwed men and women back home in Devil's Boot," she continued

in a half whisper. "We've talked before about courtly manners. I thought you understood our strict rules of decorum.
I was shocked when Sir Geoffrey told me—"

"I did not approach the prince, my lady."

"You must have done something to attract him." Her
shrill voice had risen above a whisper.

I shook my head. "I don't know what Sir Geoffrey told
you, but—"

"He told me very little. He is a man of discretion." She
had a bitter look, as if she'd eaten hax root. I knew she expected her daughter, Bianca, to marry the prince someday.
I'd seen Bianca and Prince Desmond together often my
first months at court, and I'd heard the rumors flying. His
Highness made it clear he was interested in the prettiest girl
among the eligible maids. He'd given her one of the finest
horses in the king's stable. I hoped Lady Olivia didn't think
I was trying to lure him away from her daughter. If anything, I felt sorry for Bianca.

"Please believe me, my lady. I did not seek his attention."
I scraped my shoes in the gravel like an impatient mare
wanting to run.

"Listen closely, Uma. You will keep your distance from
now on. He is royalty. He is the Pendragon heir. You are a
queen's servant." Her face was growing redder. "You should
do nothing more than curtsy when he passes you in the hall.
I've taught you how to behave in court. I expect you to com-
ply with my instructions. Your life depends on your actions
both medical and moral in these next few months."

"Of course I know that! My lady," I added in a brutal whisper.

"Good," she snapped.

A child's high-pitched scream came from the hedgerow. Kip ran out of the greenery, crying, "Bee! Bee stinged me!" Pippin followed, barking at his heels.

Kip's screams turned to tears as we ran to him. I joined Tabitha, who was on her knees.

"Where did it sting you, honey?" she asked.

"My . . . my neck."

The tiny stinger protruded just below his ear. "Let me," I said to Tabitha over Kip's sobs. Pinching the stinger between my nails, I carefully pulled it out.

"Oweee!" Kip cried. Tears rolled down his pink cheeks. I looked at the red spot. It didn't surprise me that the bee had stung his neck. Egrets are slender-necked, and necks are vulnerable in Egret Moon. But I was glad to see the swelling had already stopped. This wasn't the kind of dangerous re-action little Melo had back in Devil's Boot, just an ordinary sting.

"Poor little Kip," the queen crooned. "It must hurt terribly."

"He will be all right soon, Your Majesty," Tabitha said. "You're a brave boy, aren't you, Kip?" Her little brother was still sobbing.

Queen Adela flicked my shoulder. "Run and fetch an ointment for him, Uma."

She considered my medicines hers, and rarely shared

them. A little surprised, I left the garden. In my chamber I unlocked Father's trunk, thankful I had a key to protect the medicines inside. I still had no door key. Had Jackrun tried to bring it up last night while I was with the queen? I found the corked ointment jar and pulled it out. Kip wouldn't need the breathing cure I'd used on Melo.

I locked the trunk, remembering Melo's soft cheek, still wet with tears as he sucked in breath after breath. Four males and one female had been born to the women who'd used my father's medicine. Both sexes were needed to ensure our small tribe's survival. The Adan had planned to treat more women with Kuyawan, hoping they would have girls. Now I used all our precious Kuyawan to help *one* woman—the one woman who'd ordered the army down to hold my people captive.

It was deeply wrong.

Kip was in the queen's lap when I returned. He sniffed a little as he ate sweetmeats from her hand. "He looks much better already, Your Majesty."

Queen Adela smiled up at me, her face radiant with joy. I had never seen such a look from her before. *This is what she has been missing*, I thought. *Her son is grown. It's been years since she had her own child on her lap.* I pulled the stopper from the jar.

"Careful with him now, Uma," she warned.

"Yes, Your Majesty." She watched like a doting mother as I salved the pinkish swollen spot on Kip's neck.

"Bee!" he said, whimpering.

Queen Adela wrapped her arm around him. "It is all right, Kip. My physician will help that nasty sting go away. And when you are better, we will play catch again."

I joined Tabitha in the shade of a cherry tree. "Thank you for helping Kip," she said.

"It was my pleasure." *The queen is very taken with him,* I thought to say before deciding not to. "Your chain of fire was beautiful last night."

She smiled. I was sad to see thick lace wrapped around her neck hiding her dragon scales.

"You don't need to wear that," I said softly. Tabitha fingered it a moment, blushed, and dropped her hand. I wondered how long it would take for Desmond's caustic remarks to fade, how long she would continue to keep her scales covered.

"Have you seen Jackrun this morning?" I still needed that key.

"He's usually out fighting in the practice yard this time of the morning."

I nodded, liking the sound of that. "But," she went on, "he left before dawn with Babak to invite the island fairies to the masked ball we are having in honor of the king's visit tomorrow night. Do you dance?" she asked, giving a graceful swirl, her lavender skirts flaring out.

"Not your courtly dances," I admitted.

"But others? Euit dances? Maybe you can teach me some?" I thought of our men in their impressive clothes and headdresses, of how proud Father looked as Mother helped him into his colorful costume for the ceremonies, the complicated Moon Dance steps our men did in the center of our circle, and the wilder courtship dances where our warriors truly shone.

"The dances are very . . . bold."

"Good," she said. I liked her for that.

She gave me a smile I didn't know how to receive. When I was small, I'd tried to play with the other girls. Their mothers tugged them away. Later those same mothers let me in their huts when I trailed behind my father. The women were warmer. Still, I'd wondered if their smiles were genuine or if they only welcomed me to please the Adan.

AN HOUR LATER I was peering through the iron grille of my tower window, watching Jackrun and Babak soar high above the earth. I traced the fox mark below my collarbone. Fox is an earth animal, and I am mostly earth, but a person needs to balance all four sacred elements to be whole. I needed more wind, more sky. I clutched the bars, and felt a deep tug inside watching the freedom Jackrun had every day of his life and likely took for granted. One day I would ride a dragon higher than this tower. Feel wings draw me up.

I pulled off my slippers, unlatched the grillwork, swinging it open and hooking it to the wall. The narrow ledge outside the window was less than three feet wide. I studied it a moment, then threw my leg over the sill and climbed out.

Laughter drifted up from the garden far below as I stood pressing my back against the rough stone wall. Falling from this height would kill me. But my feet were sure. I inched farther to the left so I could not be viewed by those in the garden below. Back in Devil's Boot, I'd learned to scramble along the cliffs with Father to pick precious herbs caught in the cracks. These walls were stone as cliffs are stone, and the ledge was more generous than some of the dangerous places I'd explored. The river that ran along the back side of the castle into the dark forest beyond gleamed bright silver in the sun.

"Uma?" A woman's voice called from inside my tower room. I braced myself against the wall.

"We were made to climb the steps for nothing," another whined. "Where's that healer got to?"

Two female servants entering my herbarium without permission. I gritted my teeth.

"You'll have to go back downstairs and say we couldn't find her."

"Not me, I won't."

"Maybe she'll be back. Look, there's her shoes. She can't have gone far barefoot."

"She might have another pair. Look how sandy they are!"

I crept back toward the window.

"Ou! It stinks in here!" Rustling sounds.

"What do you suppose this is?"

"Witch potions. Look now. This packet is full of dirt. You think she doses the queen with dirt?" They laughed.

*Do not touch my medicines!* I pressed my back harder against the wall to keep from jumping in through the window.

"You go look for the queen's physician. I'll stay here in case she comes back."

"Lazy slug!"

"I'm not."

"Then I'll stay."

"Stay with her smelly potions, then, and you can stink like an Euit."

There were more noises from within as if the two were struggling. Then the door slammed. *Am I alone again? Have they both gone?* I dared not go in through the window if one of them was still inside. I waited, then heard scraping noises in the tower room. The woman must be moving a chair. Was she about to stand on it and meddle with the herbs I'd hung from the rafters this morning? I peered in, saw her on the chair reaching up. Her back was to me.

Leaping to the floor with a thump, I pulled her down, and covered her mouth to stopper her scream. The woman was three times my weight, short, and balding. Her mud-brown eyes were wide as she screamed into my hand.

"You do not enter my room without asking. I am the queen's physician. No one touches my medicines. Do you understand?"

The woman nodded, her fat tears wetting my thumb. I did not like frightening her, but she was toying with herbs that could not be replaced without a three-week journey south on horseback all the way to Devil's Boot once I was back on Wilde Island.

"I will remove my hand if you promise not to scream."

Another nod.

I released her and wiped my hand on a rag. "Now tell me why you are here."

The woman sniffed. She held her chin up, trying to look down at me, but she was too short. "Prince Desmond wants to see you for his headache. I'll never come back here," she added. "No one can make me." Her muddy eyes were all anger as she backed out the door. I saw her give the sign against the devil before she thudded down the steps.

I closed my door again, huffing. I couldn't ignore the royal request even if his headache was a fabrication to lure me to his room. The *Adan-duxma* said: *Adans heal the wicked and the righteous alike.* My father never lost his focus when he'd mixed the queen's cures, despite her brutality. I needed the competence to mix this cure without bile rising in my throat, but I couldn't calm myself.

I set out my mother's pinch pot bowl filled with water, my father's leather pouch of sacred earth. Breathed in the light breeze whispering from the still open window, lit a candle, and leaned into the power of the four sacred elements for balance, hoping that would be enough.

The small evicta seeds were night black in the pale onyx mortar. I'd used evicta for the queen's pain, and once or twice to treat Bianca's headaches back in Pendragon Castle. But the king's guard hadn't let Father use the painkiller on the spit boy with the severed hand. What was Prince Desmond's trivial little headache compared to that boy's wretched pain? I felt my anger boiling up again and glanced over the four elements for help. *You can do this. A true Adan heals the wicked and the righteous alike.*

Head down, I chanted evicta's name to release its potent power, crushing the small seeds with Father's heavy stone pestle. The door opened and shut again with a thunk. I knew who it was before looking up.

Too late to stop him. The prince was already in my herbarium.

# CHAPTER TEN

# Pendragon Summer Castle, Dragon's Keep

## EGRET MOON
*August 1210*

"HOW LONG DOES it take to answer a summons?" he said, coming toward me.

"I was only just told you have a headache, Your Royal Highness. I am mixing your medicine now."

He pressed up close to me at the table. "What is that stuff?"

"Seeds that will cure your head pain," I said, crushing them harder, wishing I could do to him what I was doing to the seeds.

"I like it when you lean over like that." He was eyeing my low-cut gown. I straightened up, quickly. The prince grabbed my wrist and removed the pestle from my hand. He dropped the pestle by the mortar with a thud, crushing me against the worktable. "Do you remember when I found you in Devil's Boot, Uma?"

My eyes were on his chin. I did not look up. "Yes, Your Highness."

"Your father made you dress like a boy. He worked you like a slave. I saved you from that."

*Saved me? You abducted us!*

"I thought you would want to thank me for the favor," he said, running his free hand up to my chin. He pinched my jaw, forced my head back, and pressed his thick lips against mine. I tasted the fried fish and ale he'd just downed for breakfast. I shouldn't move. You do not cross the king's son; still, I pushed him off.

"You should know better than to push me away, Uma!"

Thumping sounds came from the window behind us as something large flew past. The sound vanished as quickly as it had come.

*Think. Make some excuse.* "Your Royal Highness, I cannot allow myself to be with you in that way."

"Why not? What's the matter with you?"

I was slowly inching back. "I cannot give myself to another."

He grabbed the stone pestle. "Come here or feel this on the back of your head."

I ran. He lunged at me, swinging the heavy pestle. I ducked, but not low enough. The stone pestle cracked against the side of my head. I reeled from the pain. He pushed me to the floor, straddled me, and held my arms down against the planks.

"Well now," he said, smiling. His dark hair fell about his

plump face as he leered down. Head throbbing, I struggled under his bulk. Lights flitted around us. *Don't pass out! Breathe.* I couldn't suck in enough breath under his heavy weight. He shifted, uncoiling himself like a snake, and slid down, lying on top of me as if my body were his bed. I screamed. He clamped his hand over my mouth.

I squirmed under him, tried to kick him off. He was too strong, too heavy. *Grab the table leg, overturn it on him.* My outstretched fingers were inches from it. I strained, desperate to reach it.

The prince was breathing hard as he slid his cold hand up my leg and tugged at my small clothes. Thumping noises again. Babak's head appeared just outside the window. On dragonback, Jackrun peered down at us and recoiled, seeing Desmond stretched on top of me with his hand over my mouth. He dove through the window, rolled to a stand, and loped toward us, agile as a mountain lion.

"Get away from her!" He grabbed Desmond's arms and pulled him off of me. I curled up on my side, clutched my stomach, and tried to catch my breath as they rolled on the floor, straining and grunting. There was a sickening smack as Desmond punched Jackrun in the mouth. They tumbled past me and rammed into the worktable, knocking it over. The stone mortar flew off and struck my neck. I gasped at the shock of pain as black seeds spilled around me. Mother's water dish broke by my shoulder. The candle landed in the rushes, setting them alight.

Desmond drew out his knife, slashed Jackrun's upper

arm. Jackrun screamed into his clamped teeth, forced Desmond on his side, roared fire behind his back.

"Jackrun," I shouted. He was about to set Prince Desmond's hair and clothes on fire. Jackrun looked up.

Sir Geoffrey burst into the room. "What's this?" He pulled the two apart, stomped out the burning rushes with his boot, and picked up the broken candle. "You very nearly set the whole room on fire."

Shaking, I came to my feet, one hand on the overturned table for support, one hand on my swelling neck where the mortar had struck it, a worse pain than the lump already forming on my head.

"I was protecting Uma," Jackrun said, clutching his bleeding arm.

"Protecting her from what?" Desmond said. "We were doing fine until you interfered." Jackrun's body went rigid. He swayed on his feet as if he was about to spring on Prince Desmond and throw him to the floor again.

Desmond swung around on Sir Geoffrey. "And who sent you?" he asked, cleaning the blood from his knife on one of my linen cloths in three swift motions. "Did I call for your help?"

"Your Royal Highness—"

"I can handle my own battles, you meddlesome bastard. Breathe a word of this, and I'll tell what I know about you, and you'll be hanged for your own filthy sins!"

Sir Geoffrey's cheeks flushed dark.

I glanced at Jackrun. *Filthy sins?* What did Prince Desmond know about Sir Geoffrey—enough to make him blush? The prince sheathed the knife and left.

Jackrun kicked aside the blackened rushes. I was glad for the candle in Sir Geoffrey's hand. The rising smoke from Jackrun's fire was rank, but it told no tales.

Jackrun's lip was bleeding, but the slashed arm worried me more. "Your arm is badly cut." I went to him.

He drew back. "It's nothing. It's not deep."

Sir Geoffrey's eyes moved from me to Jackrun. "How did this start?"

Jackrun licked the red droplets from his split lip. "Desmond was . . . he was on top of her. He nearly—" His hand was on his dagger as he searched for words.

Sir Geoffrey's face hardened. He had caught me with Prince Desmond before. What was he thinking now? I felt too sick, too raw to explain, but the man glared at me. "I didn't ask him to my room," I said finally under my breath. "I was preparing a cure for Prince Desmond's headache when he came up on his own. Please don't tell Lady Olivia."

Sir Geoffrey nodded sternly toward the door. "Best for you to leave now, Jackrun."

A shadow flicked across the room. Babak had circled the tower again to look inside.

Jackrun said, "I'll send a servant to help clean up this mess, Uma."

"No, please don't, Jackrun." I didn't want anyone else up here. My heart felt like a wadded rag. I needed to be alone.

Jackrun glanced back once as he headed for the stairs. His

split lip was already beginning to swell. I saw the question in his look. *Are you all right?* I could still feel the wintery place where Prince Desmond had run his cold fingers up my leg. I answered with my eyes. *You came just in time.*

AS SOON AS they left, I shoved the wardrobe in front of the door, spat in the fireplace. Disgust still poisoned my mouth as I stripped off my gown to my small clothes and bathed every place Prince Desmond touched me, swiping my lips with the damp cloth to annihilate his kiss, and washing all the places he'd run his hand along my leg. I shuddered, remembering how close he'd come to overtaking me completely. Last, I bathed my injured head and the swollen place on my neck. The linen strip was pink with blood when I pulled it from my head. Every touch in those places made my flesh sting.

I breathed against the throbbing in my head and neck. The Adan's trunk had cures for my pain. There was still some evicta in an unopened pouch along with the seeds strewn across the floor during the fight. All I had to do was crush some, put it in my mouth with a little bit of honey.

I shook, fighting the temptation. The Adan didn't use the herbs on himself. The evicta was for my patients, not for me. I gathered the pieces of the broken bowl Mother made for me when I was thirteen, wanting her here. Needing her here. My eyes stung as I wrapped the broken bits, and tucked them in the trunk. I retrieved what evicta I could still use on the queen, every seed precious, and threw the burned rushes out the window.

I changed into my other gown. The blue velvet matched Bianca's eyes, not mine. The pearls adorning the neckline were pale as her skin. An English gown for an English maid.

If I had married Ayo, I'd be wearing the long blouses and colorfully patterned woven skirts of an Euit woman. Would I have felt more at home in them than I did in Bianca's gown after dressing as a boy so many years? I wrapped my dragon belt around my waist. The gown's wide sleeves had bothered me when I'd tried to work; now they gave me an idea.

I strapped the leather sheath of my father's herbing knife to my upper arm. The bell-shaped sleeves hid it well. Prince Desmond would never touch me again. The weight of the knife handle, the sharpness of the blade would keep me company from now on.

My stomach was queasy, sick from the fight, raw with hunger. No one had bothered to tell me where I was supposed to dine while we were here on Dragon's Keep, if I was expected to eat in the Great Hall, or in the kitchen with the servants as I often did back on Wilde Island. I headed down the stairs.

Two servants bearing trays full of dishes stopped to gawk at me in the hallway on their way to the kitchen. I paused outside the kitchen door, unsure now if I should go in. Jackrun came around the corner, heading back toward my herbarium stairs.

He'd thrown a chain mail vest over his tunic, strapped a

sword to his side. Fighting gear. Was he going to challenge the prince? He peered down at my bruised neck. "Did he do that to you?" he whispered fiercely. "I could smash him flat."

"No. The mortar struck me there when the table fell."

He tilted his head and brushed his fingers across my neck, gently tracing them under the swollen place. I held my breath until he dropped his hand again.

"I came by last night with the key," he whispered.

My heart pounded in my ears, nearly drumming his whispers away. "I thought you might have. I was called to the queen's room."

"So we missed each other." He stepped back, his hand strangling the sword hilt. "Now you've been hurt because of me."

"Not because of you." My eyes stung. *Leave now,* I told myself, *before you burst into tears in front of him.*

"If I'd known that bastard was after you, I'd have—" He snapped his mouth shut as a scullery maid came out the kitchen door. We both tensed until she passed us, water sloshing in her washbucket.

"This isn't the place to talk," he said. His eyes were piercing as he drew close to me again. Hearing footsteps, he glanced back.

"Are you ready?" a red-haired man of an age to Jackrun asked, hurrying up to us. He smiled and bowed. "I'm Griffin. You must be the lovely queen's physician." He took my hand and kissed it. His scabbard clanked against his chain mail vest as he bowed.

Flustered, I drew my hand away. Jackrun clapped his friend on the back. "Please excuse Griff, Uma, he is only part human on his mother's side and comes from a long line of fey folk."

"A proud line," interrupted Griff, "and it's in your blood too." He turned back to me. "My father taught me how to treat a lady. You don't mind, do you?"

I was at a loss for words.

"Leave her be, Griffin."

Griffin's freckles gathered in a tighter bunch as he grinned. "The weapons master waits. We're late for the practice yard already."

"I'll meet you there."

"I see," Griffin said, glancing at the two of us. "Excuse me, my lady." He bowed again and left.

"Uma," Jackrun said. Drawing something from his pocket, he put his hand over mine. Warm skin. Cold metal. The key. He searched my face, the gold flecks in his green eyes like fires lit in small encampments in the trees. "I'll make it up to you. Tell me what you want me to do and I'll do it."

The words *You already fought for me* caught halfway up my throat. Jackrun closed my fingers around the key, turned heel, and headed down the hall. Just before he disappeared, he looked back. "Come to the masked ball tomorrow night."

"I have no costume."

"Don't worry about that," he said, and was gone.

In the kitchen, Cook passed me a hunk of barley bread and cheese and promised future meals that I could take to my room if I came to the kitchen after the serving was done in the Great Hall.

OUTSIDE, AROUND THE corner past the stables, I followed the sound of cheering and found Tabitha in a small crowd, watching the men in the weapons yard.

Jackrun fought his knight in one ring, Griff in the other. Swords bashed and clanked in the fierce competition. In Devil's Boot, our warriors were proficient hunters, using bows and arrows or poisoned darts. We were not a people of the sword.

I followed Jackrun's quick, skilled movements. He'd rolled his sleeves up, and the sunlight played fire on his dragon scales. A few onlookers grunted as the opponent hit Jackrun broadside; applauded when Jackrun recovered, and made a similar strike a moment later.

Young Tabitha fixed her eyes on Griff—a man her brother's age and she just fourteen—but a lady can look.

I bit the sharp cheese, watching Jackrun. A lady can look.

# CHAPTER ELEVEN

# Pendragon Summer Castle, Dragon's Keep

## EGRET MOON
*August 1210*

I WAS OUT gathering fresh rushes mid-morning the next day when I heard the jingling sound of bridles. A fairy cavalcade had crossed the wide stone bridge and was coming up the road. I stepped aside with my bundle and watched transfixed as the riders paraded toward me in their shimmering clothes.

I'd never seen fey folk growing up in Devil's Boot. None of my mother's tales prepared me for the pageantry I saw now. The very air sparkled around them. They were wind and water, air and light.

The fairies were long and lean and easy in their saddles. Some were as pale as the English; others as dark as or darker than my people. The tallest rider wore a king's crown and a robe of dazzling white. He gazed down at me from his black charger. I shivered under his stark look until he passed.

A dozen or so children rode ponies decorated with flowers in the long procession. Tiny will-o'-the-wisps no larger than dragonflies flitted playfully around the children, their winged bodies flashing in the sunlight. Last came the wagoners driving painted carts stacked high with goods battened down with heavy, colorful tarpaulins. The stacks swayed to and fro as I turned and followed the carts down the road toward the castle.

AT DUSK, I learned what the fey folk had brought us in their painted carts; costumes for the masked ball. The king and queen had the first pick. Both were trying on masks, their colorful cloaks brighter than Lady Tess's paintings of dragons and fairies on the chamber walls. They were parading back and forth in the queen's chamber when I came in and stood by Lady Olivia with Her Majesty's tonic.

"You look like a peacock," Queen Adela said to her husband, clapping her hands.

"A proud cock I am too," he laughed, turning and strutting in the feathered headdress.

I'd watched Father painting the thin yellow beak of his Egret Moon mask when I was eight. Everyone had to make new masks the year after the English soldiers came and burned the Moon Month masks and regalia in our huts before moving us south. Father had let me touch the long white egret feathers on his dance robe. I sang with Mother and everyone that year, watching the men dance in all new costumes, honoring the death of the old moon, the birth of the new. I felt the song in me now, wanting to rise up my throat.

"How do I look, Lady Olivia?" the queen asked, twirling in a petaled cloak.

"Like a living garden, Your Majesty."

"Like summer itself," added the king, grabbing her and kissing her.

"She'll have him in her bed after the ball," Lady Olivia said to me under her breath. "Your remedy has a chance tonight."

BACK UPSTAIRS, A soft dusky light fought its way through the iron grating, barely reaching the floor. I lit a taper to help the light along, turned and found a costume on my bed. Who had brought it up?

The half facemask was cut in the shape of a water lily. Two eye slits hid neatly in the bright white petals. The gown's skirts were earth brown at the hem, a shimmering watery blue above. The wide silky sleeves moved like flowing water when I touched it. What would it look like on?

I opened the wardrobe and paused. The jagged crack running down the mirror cut me in two. The split image I saw startled me: Uma of Devil's Boot, Uma of the Pendragon court. I spread my feet apart, trying to span my two worlds. My heart felt wedged in the crack between them both.

I recognized my mother in my large eyes, my shapely lips, my strong, slim figure. *Mother. I saw how people shunned you when I was young. You were so strong. I watched you weaving the most beautiful patterns, slowly gaining the trust of the other women.* I wasn't that strong. After the king's soldiers burned our village and pushed us south when I was seven, after I learned how many times the English conquerors attacked our tribe, and drove us off our land, I wanted to bury myself from shame at my Englishness.

*Did you understand why I became mi tupelli to serve Father? That I felt I'd die if I did not belong completely to my tribe? There is so much I want to say to you now. I'm sorry I hurt you. So sorry. I hope;* my finger traced the curve of my jaw on the cold glass. *Holy Ones, I hope I'll see you again.*

I did not close the wardrobe door on my reflection, not yet. I'd opened it to try my costume on. What would I see then? I pulled off my gown, slid the silky costume over my head, and turned, feeling the swish of cloth against my skin. It was softer than Bianca's gowns, and lighter, I could move in it, dance in it. The gown flowed with me. *Like wearing water,* I thought, turning slowly, tilting my head this way and that, lowering myself and rising in the pattern of the Moon Dance. I stopped. We hadn't been allowed to do the Moon Dances when I was seven, the months when the soldiers were with us. We didn't begin again until after Mount Uther rumbled and smoked, scaring the English away.

Here I was, admiring my costume when for all I knew the elders back home were forbidden to wear theirs, forbidden to dance. "And what are you doing about it?" I asked my cracked reflection.

*This,* I thought, removing the costume to shrug on my well-worn gown. *This,* I thought, strapping the pouch of sacred earth taken from Devil's Boot to my belt. *This,* I thought, heading down the stairs for the king's rooms.

"What is it, Uma?" King Arden asked when I came in and curtsied. A plump tailor was circling the king, measuring and making small adjustments to his plush purple costume.

"Your Majesty, I have come to ask you for a favor."

"How much longer do I have to hold out my arm?" he barked at the tailor.

"Just a moment longer, Your Majesty." Sweat ran down the back of the poor man's neck.

"Out with it, Uma."

"Please, Your Majesty. I've come to ask if you will bring your troops home from Devil's Boot."

"Why should I do that?"

"I promise you I'll see my mission through, Your Majesty. If you set my people—"

"Enough, man!" he said to the tailor. "Help me take this thing off."

The two men struggled a moment entangled as two cats in yarn. "Now leave us," said the king. The man scurried out with the costume, minus the mask. The king studied his chessboard a moment before he looked up at me again.

"That's an ugly bruise. What happened to your neck?"

"I . . . fell, Your Majesty."

He'd left his window ajar. Wolves howled in the woods beyond the castle. Egret Moon would die in four nights' time. In September, Wolf Moon would be born, a time when wolves came into their power—already the packs were restless.

"I will do all the queen asks of me, Your Majesty," I said. "My people should not have to suffer while I'm here."

"Who said they were suffering?"

"There was bloodshed when the soldiers took us, Your Majesty. I don't know what's happened since I left, what sort of restrictions have been laid upon my tribe, but—"

"A king should be surrounded by his offspring," he said gruffly. "My wife wants assurance you will help her have more children."

"Holding my people captive does not help with that, Your Majesty."

"You have continued your father's work to make her fertile?"

"Yes, Your Majesty, that's what I was hired to do as her physician."

"That is what your father was hired to do, Uma, and he failed." He rubbed his thumb along the onyx bishop.

I could almost feel that rough thumb pressing against my own bruised neck as he moved the bishop slowly, square to square. "Tell me, Uma. Is she fertile?"

My heart thumped. "The Adan's medicines are powerful, Your Majesty. She has been taking them long enough now to be able to conceive," I said carefully.

"Good. You may leave me now."

He'd dismissed me without answering what I'd come for. "Sire, the soldiers. Can you order them home please?"

"You still have family down there?" he asked.

"My mother, Your Majesty."

The king gazed at his chessboard a moment. "My wife arranged to keep our men down there until she has a child. I agree with her. You say you're committed to seeing this through. I know the army's occupation keeps you focused, Uma."

He flung the words so casually at me. I'd seen delegations come to Pendragon Castle to argue behind closed doors as I'd passed down the halls with the queen's medicines. Some men left the king's rooms smiling, signed scrolls in hand. But I was an Euit woman. I had nothing to bargain with, no way to make offers or counteroffers, no idea how to tempt, lie, or wheedle to get what I needed.

I backed out of the room, through the door, under the sentries' crossed pikes, away from any hope of freeing my people until the queen had her child, if she ever did.

# CHAPTER TWELVE

# Castle Green, Dragon's Keep

## EGRET MOON
*August 1210*

AT THE MASKED ball, I scanned the crowded Great Hall for the queen. The room was riotous with movement, color, and sound. The tables overflowing with food and ale had been shoved against the walls to allow for dancing. Three giant candelabras swung to and fro overhead as the revelers twirled each other around. Some dancers spilled out onto the terrace above the castle green. This ball was nothing like the courtly dancing I'd seen at Pendragon Castle back on Wilde Island, where couples lined up facing one another and moved with prim, orderly steps.

I saw Lady Olivia across the room. She was dressed in black and wore a silver eye mask. I knew her by the way she held her chin like royalty, though she was only the queen's companion. She gestured to me. Her formality set against everyone else's noisy abandon made me smile. Somehow through my water lily costume, she had known me too. I wondered what had given me away.

"There." She pointed to the royal couple dancing near a garlanded column.

"It's madness in here," I said over the music. "Is Her Majesty all right?"

"She is fine and more than fine. For now," she added.

"For now," I said, knowing what she meant. The noise, the crowd, the wild costumes could stir her mind to sudden storm. I had a sealed cap of honeyed bapeeta in my waist pouch to calm the queen at any moment tonight if needed.

"Do you know how to conduct yourself at a ball?" Lady Olivia asked.

"I watched one back on Wilde Island."

"Observing is not the same as attending." I'd grown used to her etiquette lessons, but still I felt myself wilting as she laid down the rules for my evening. "You understand?" she said.

"Yes, my lady."

I looked around the crowded room. Where was Jackrun? What costume had he chosen? Would I be able to spot him as easily as I'd spotted Lady Olivia?

Elbowing my way out to the wide terrace above the castle green, I stopped with a gasp. The masked ball indoors was tame compared to the one out here: Lady Olivia's courtly manners thrown to the wolves, literally—wild wolves, hinds, and boars roved among the dancers. My nose caught the musky scent of fur. I was feeling for my knife when a half man, half horned bull danced past, his lady draped in gray webs and wearing a spider mask. The man's giant bull's head and furry torso seemed far too real.

Two giant snakes, coiled together in dance, bumped my shoulder and sent me reeling into a tall fey man who swept me in his arms and twirled me round and round before he let me go and bowed, the tips of his coiled ram horns sharp as pikes.

I'd had enough of the terrace. I raced downstairs, my feet seeking solid earth. A band of fey musicians played on the outdoor stage. The lawn glowed with hundreds of torches set on poles. Castle servants and fey children wove in and out with trays of food and drink. Will-o'-the-wisps flitted over my head as I searched the crowd; some flew toward the castle, others swirled over the fairy musicians who had paused on stage to refresh themselves. A half horse, half man sitting by stacked drums held his mug between his hooves.

Amid the whistling, growling, and high-pitched laughter, I heard Prince Desmond shouting, "How dare you!" A large wine stain soaked the front of his costume. A fey child crawled about on hands and knees trying to retrieve the chalices rolling helter-skelter on the lawn. The fey boy must have crashed into him with his tray.

"Sorry, sorry," the boy was saying.

"Sorry," Prince Desmond mimicked, kicking him hard in the rear. The crowd gasped as the boot sent the boy flying forward, landing flat on his face inches from the tray.

"It was an accident," a fey man snapped.

"The boy didn't mean to," said a woman guised as a monarch butterfly at my side.

I heard fierce whispers, a deep feral growl that made the hair on the back of my neck stand up. Costumed creatures in the crowd seemed to grow larger, wilder all around me. There was far too much magic here.

A man in a fox mask stepped from the crowd. On his knees, he picked up the rest of the silver chalices, placed them on the tray, and helped the boy up to a stand.

Prince Desmond left, angry or bored or both. Butterfly Woman hissed at his back. The tensely knotted crowd began to slowly loosen and wander off.

Sir Geoffrey still stood a few feet away, disgust etched on his face. The tall fey man to his right leaned down and spoke with him. Hearing angry tones, I strained my ears, but I couldn't make out what they were saying.

Fox Mask mussed the fey boy's hair, saying something cheerful, I guessed. The boy sniffed a little, then laughed before he left with his tray.

Dancers swirled across the wine-soaked grass between me and Fox Mask. He stepped around them in long easy strides. His gait told me who he was before he spoke.

"You like the costume?" Jackrun asked.

"Did you choose it for me?"

"I told you not to worry about what to wear," he said.

Jackrun's choice to come to the ball as my Path Animal made me feel vulnerable, exposed, even if he couldn't possibly have seen my mark. I was about to tell him how real his full head mask looked, when the boy he'd helped a moment ago scampered up, tray reloaded with fresh wine.

"Thank you, Senni," Jackrun said, lifting two goblets from the tray.

"You were kind to help him," I said, taking the goblet he handed me as the boy disappeared back into the crowd.

"Desmond's a fool to risk the fairies' wrath," he snapped.

The boy hadn't sparkled with magic the way his elders did. "Perhaps he didn't know Senni was a fey child?"

"He knew!"

I started. Not at the vehemence of his remark, but because I'd looked down at the side of my goblet and caught Jackrun's true face reflected in the silver cup.

"Caught me," he said.

"I don't understand."

"You thought this was a mask," he said, pointing to the fox head. "It's something else, a fey glamour spell. It fools the eye, but hold a mirror or any shiny surface like this up to a fairy glamour and you will see the truth. We can trick each other, but reflections do not lie."

"The wolves and wild boars?" I asked, glancing around.

"Some shape-shifting going on here tonight," Jackrun admitted. "A full animal form is achieved through shape-shifting, but most choose fairy glamours for a ball. A glamour takes much less skill and allows more energy for dancing." I thought of the half man, half bull who'd danced past me on the veranda, shivered, and downed the goblet all at once.

Jackrun watched me, amused. "Hungry?" he asked, leading me to a long table laden with food of every kind.

I swayed a little from the strong wine that was already beginning to make my head float, and steadied myself against the table. Jackrun's true reflection still shone on my shiny chalice. I noticed the lanky fey man nearby under his unicorn glamour. Just down the table a half girl, half deer was nibbling at the fruit. Jackrun's sister, Tabitha, looked up at me, startled, before she pranced away.

Jackrun covered my wrist with his hand and slowly but firmly pushed my goblet down. "No one likes to be exposed," he whispered. I left the reflective chalice on the table and backed away.

"You haven't eaten," he said.

"I don't like bland English food."

He swept a hand over the many dishes. "You must want something. Tell me what you want."

"An egret feather." I wasn't sure if the elders would be allowed to do the Moon Dance two nights from now. Someone needed to.

Jackrun pretended to look for it among the cheeses. "No feather here," he said at last. "You have particular wants."

I didn't apologize.

"What do you need it for?"

I hiccupped and shook my head. Jackrun grabbed something from the table and gestured for me to follow him to a stone bench bathed in torchlight near the wall. My skirts

rippled like water as I sat. My head still felt light enough to
float away with my skirts.

"You might like this," Jackrun said, peeling an orange.
"Take a segment," he offered.

"Drop your guise first. Please, if we are going to eat together."

"It's a masked ball," he protested, but the fox glamour faded and I was left looking at the Jackrun I knew; his
thoughtful brows, his fierce eyes, and lower lip still swollen
lopsided from the blow Desmond gave him.

I reached for the orange. *It is shaped like a smile,* I
thought, cupping the cool wedge in my hand.

"Shall we both eat at the same time?" he challenged. We
raised our hands in time with the music. I bit, squirting liquid in my eye. The juice stung and I had to squint a moment,
but I laughed all the same. It was delicious. When he offered
me another piece, I took it.

"Now will you tell me what you need the feather for?"
Jackrun said.

I swallowed the new segment. "You English study the
moon cycles."

"Our astrologers and alchemists do."

"We follow the way of animal moons."

"What animal moon is it now?"

"Egret Moon."

He leaned closer. "So the feather is for some Euit cere-
mony?" he asked, interested.

I regretted what I'd blurted out earlier. Jackrun was English; what if he didn't understand?

Jackrun asked, "What are the names of the other moons?"

I watched the fey dancers twirling on the trimmed English lawn. This ball belonged to the fairies. I wanted to talk about something that belonged to me, if only for one night. I told Jackrun about the twelve moons, only touching the surface of our beliefs, not because Jackrun would be too slow to understand, but because there was so much about moon months I could not explain in one hour or six or twelve. I revealed that each animal moon related to parts of the body. "As with any month, the moon animal empowers some people and hinders others. Egrets have slender necks. Egret Moon strengthens some people's throats, they sing with power, they can speak with clarity and insight and sway men's minds." *Egret Moon hadn't lent me her powers when I tried to sway the king,* I thought before I went on. "Others lose their voices. We see more sore throats this month, and those who die often die from broken necks."

My hand nearly wandered to my throat, but Jackrun had already reached up, gently touching my bruise. "The swelling's gone down," he said. "Does it still hurt you there?"

"It feels much better." My skin sang where he'd brushed it even after he drew his hand away. *How restoring a touch can be,* I thought, *a healing that has nothing to do with plants or potions.* The revelation surprised me. Father had never mentioned touch.

"Tell me more," he said, offering me another orange segment. I chewed and let the cool sweet liquid fill my mouth.

The Holy Ones ruled the four sacred elements of earth,

wind, fire, and water, I told him, which were also a part of the moon months, each animal representing an element. "Falcon Moon, a time of wind; Bear Moon, a time of earth . . . "

"And the animal moons are strongest when the moon is full," he guessed.

I shook my head. "There are three times of heightened power: at the new moon's birth, at its fullness, and on the night of its death."

"Why is it powerful when its light is dying?"

"At death the tips are knife-sharp. It does not want to be replaced by a new moon. The dying moon can be like a wounded animal lashing out."

He named a few animal moons, repeating them as if to keep them in his mind; last he whispered, "Dragon Moon," staring at the white flesh inside of the orange peel.

"That is the strongest of all the animal moons because it carries all three elements of earth, wind, and fire."

"Why not water?"

I laughed. "Everyone knows dragons hate water," I said, surprised he would ask. "It goes against their nature. Have you ever seen one swim?"

"It would be unusual," he said with a playful look. "When will Dragon Moon come?"

"In October."

Jackrun said, "We call that one Hunter's Moon. So do the fey folk."

It pleased me in some deep reaching way down to my bones to learn my Euit people had a more complex relationship with the moon than the magical fairy folk. I thought I would tell Jackrun about the Murderous Moon, but changed my mind. It reminded me of the death I might face at the end of Dragon Moon.

Jackrun stood, held out his hand, and helped me up. "Dance with me." His fingers were sticky, but so were mine. Before I could say no, he had me in his arms. His fox guise appeared again as he swept me into the crowd. I felt clumsy at first, not knowing the steps, but the fairy music pulsed through my body as he led me on. He laughed when I stepped on his foot and we didn't stop.

Later we spun past Prince Desmond, who seemed to have forgotten the spilled wine now his arms were around a shapely costumed maiden. Jackrun's body tensed before he yanked me away from his cousin, wheeling me deeper into the crowd. We turned and turned, the starry sky spinning overhead.

"Dragons," Jackrun said, stopping and looking up. The thin strands of clouds drifting in the night sky turned red. A hot, spice-scented wind swirled in as the dragons flew over the castle turrets. The bright blazing ring they breathed as they wheeled overhead reminded me of the red dragons' fire on the birth night of Dragon Moon, the only Moon Dance the reds ever took part in. The sight made me hunger for Devil's Boot, for other dragons, other dancers, another kind of celebration that happened only one place in the world with a small tribe that might someday die out, a language lost, a people lost. I swayed on my feet, feeling the fire circle as if it burned around my heart.

"Babak's up there," Jackrun said, shaking me from my thoughts.

I looked at him, pointing at his dragon. "You could be adding your fire to theirs," I whispered.

His fairy glamour melted away. "Uma, you don't understand what you're saying."

"What?" I asked. "Tell me."

He gripped my wrist and dragged me through the noisy revelers, past a bear juggling knives, couples kissing in the shadows. His large hand was too tight around my wrist, his skin too hot. We moved farther and farther away on the lawn, deeper into the dark. I could have pulled back and dug my feet in. But I wanted to go with him. He'd rolled up his sleeves when he'd fought in the practice yard, proudly showing his dragon scales. Why hide his greater dragon's gift from everyone as if he were ashamed of it?

But before he could say anything, Lady Olivia called, running up to us. "Uma? I have been looking everywhere for you. The queen needs you."

Jackrun had stepped away from me the moment she'd called out, sliding into his fox guise. He remained behind in the shadows as we raced back for the castle.

WE FOUND LADY Tess trying to manage Queen Adela in the corner of the Great Hall. The duchess had removed her cat mask to speak to the queen, who laughed and swayed, conversing with a pillar.

"I think she's had too much wine," Tess said.

Lady Olivia and I both knew her babbling could not be blamed on wine alone. The duchess had done her best to quiet Her Majesty; still, revelers gaped at us, some speaking behind their hands. At least King Arden was too busy dancing with a pretty fey woman to notice me dosing his wife with the bapeeta I'd brought. The queen licked the honeyed spoon. Now we only had to wait.

I wanted to run back outside and find Jackrun, but I was trapped here until Her Majesty's mind was sound.

"You are enjoying the ball?" Lady Tess asked, flicking a spot of paint from her wrist. I'd heard she had an artist's studio somewhere in the castle. Her thumbnails were misshapen. It was strange to see warped, discolored nails on such finely shaped hands.

I looked up. "Yes, my lady."

"Some of the fey glamours and shape-shifters might upset you if you aren't used to them," she said. "They used to frighten me."

"I'm not nervous, my lady."

"She is a strong young woman," Lady Olivia said proudly.

"I can see that," the duchess said, pausing to tug the tip of her cat's tail out from under her shoe. She watched the guests in her Great Hall. She was close to Queen Adela's age, yet she looked too young to have a seventeen-year-old son, but maybe her fey blood added the youthful blush to her skin.

For a moment I let myself wonder how different things

would be if Tess had followed the fairies' plan, married Prince Arden in his youth, and become our Pendragon queen.

I would be at home in Devil's Boot. My father would still be alive, my people free. I felt an ache so deep I put my hand over my stomach.

"Are you well?" Lady Tess asked.

"Yes, my lady. I . . . must have spun too fast dancing outside just now."

She smiled, and looked about again. Her eyes sparkled when she fixed them on her husband, who was joking and laughing with a fey man at one of the refreshment tables. I saw that things could never have been any different than they are. She'd choose the same man now. The love between this man and this woman had changed our island's history.

"Her Majesty will be fine now, Lady Tess," Lady Olivia said. "We can attend to her if you need to get back to your other guests."

I watched the duchess of Dragon's Keep slip her cat mask on again. It was adorned with silver whiskers, but otherwise very plain. She was half fey and could have used a glamour spell, like Tabitha or Jackrun, for tonight's ball. For some reason she had chosen not to.

Lady Olivia and I tempted Queen Adela with sweetmeats, watched her eat, waited. When at last a calmer, more controlled queen went out to dance with her husband again, we breathed a mutual sigh. If she remained balanced, happy, the king might visit her bed tonight.

"You are a fine physician, Uma," Lady Olivia said.

"Thank you, my lady." I wasn't used to compliments. It was like eating unfamiliar food. I had to chew on it a while.

"I heard about the incident between Prince Desmond and the fey boy on the lawn," Lady Olivia said, tapping her foot and craning her neck to follow the king and queen on the dance floor.

"Who told you, my lady?"

"All the fey folk are talking about it. Were you there?" she asked pointedly. "Did you see?"

I nodded.

"What did you think, Uma?"

I wasn't sure what to say to this woman who favored the prince and hoped he'd marry her daughter. "I think it was . . . dangerous," I admitted under my breath.

"Yes, the fairies can be devious and dangerous. It is not good to cross them. I don't trust them myself."

I looked about anxiously, hoping no fey had overheard her. A moment later I excused myself, headed for a refreshment table by the side doors, and slipped back outside.

Down on the green, I found Jackrun in his fox glamour, dancing with a partner under the circling dragons. The woman in his arms wore shining fish scales and fan-shaped wings like the magical sea folk Mother used to tell stories about. Her rippling laughter when he swung her around made me think of the dangerous water women who lured fishermen to the deeps, and drowned them.

She'd pulled her sea woman mask up. A human girl, her skin soft and pale, not one of the fey folk using a glamour spell. She was nearly as pretty as Desmond's favorite back home, Bianca, but not quite. Jackrun held her close. One arm tucked under her wing. My hands itched for a silver chalice so I could catch his true expression, but something made me step back into the jumbled crowd as he whisked her away past the row of torches.

## CHAPTER THIRTEEN

# Pendragon Summer Castle, Dragon's Keep

### EGRET MOON
*August 1210*

A TAPPING SOUND awakened me that night. *Not the door*, I thought groggily, *the window*. I opened the shutters and jumped back. A long black dragon's talon pressed against the glass.

"Uma?" Jackrun's muffled voice said from somewhere outside.

"What are you doing?" I asked, poking my head out. Jackrun clung to Babak, who hung nearly vertical, his tail wrapped like a vine around the tower below for extra support, his claws gripping the tower ledge, and his wings flapping slowly.

"Here." Jackrun handed me a long white egret feather. I took it, surprised.

"You left the ball," he said.

"Physicians do not have time to dance." *And you were dancing with a mermaid when I came back out.*

"I see." His eyes were piercing as if he'd read my thought. "We cannot stay," he added. A moment later Babak lost his grip and plummeted down, flipping nose to tail before he straightened out again, wings pumping. I sucked in a startled breath.

Jackrun clung to his dragon's back, laughing. Yes, laughing.

"Thank you for the feather!" I called as Babak winged toward the bay, unsure if he could still hear me.

Jackrun was both dragon and fairy, hot-tempered and human, a man who loved swordfights and oranges. Who did not mind retrieving feathers.

The sun wouldn't rise for a few hours. I took off my nightshift, belted my gown, and strapped my knife to my arm before locking the door. Drunken revelers were sprawled everywhere in the downstairs hallways, sleeping in wrinkled costumes, masks askew, snoring in chorus.

When I reached the beach, I spotted Jackrun and Babak flying out toward the water. Above me, partway up the cliffs, were caves. I shed my slippers and climbed up to one in my bare feet, settling in the cave's mouth, on the lip.

I leaned my head against the rough wall and closed my eyes. Had the king gone to the queen's bed to make a child tonight? If my Kuyawan medicine finally worked, if the queen conceived. If . . . if . . .

A roaring sound somewhere beyond the receding tide drew my eyes to the sea again. Babak breathed silken fire over the water. Below him, Jackrun swam in the illuminated ocean, moving through the shining light as if through fire. I knew how cold this sea was even in late August.

Babak flew up, folded his wings, and dove snout first into the bay with a splash. My jaw dropped. The dragons I knew never let themselves get wet. They could barely tolerate the rain, yet here was Babak diving, bathing. Letting his wings get wet.

I hugged my knees to my chest, watching two creatures of fire reveling in water. I am more earth element than water, but both played a part in my making. Father hadn't meant to take a young English wife. The Adan should be celibate. The elders had tried to banish my mother when she first came to our village, but he had fought for her. Water brought them together.

Mother and Father had gone out to wash in the river the morning after they met saving the life of a mother and her newborn twins. My mother was a practicing midwife back then, a woman with fiery red hair and freckles and strong opinions. She and the Adan had spent a long night of struggle and prayer over the laboring woman. Turning the babies gently; working carefully with the mother hour by hour. They were exhilarated when the twins were born alive and healthy. Delirious with joy, wonder, and weary beyond words, they walked down to the river. That summer morning, they joined together in the water and conceived me.

Babak lifted Jackrun from the sea, not on his back, but with his claws. He flew up, ten feet, fifteen, then dropped Jackrun with a splash. I smiled, hearing Jackrun's distant laughter when he surfaced. Tomorrow my work would begin again. Just for now, I would steal my hour of freedom as they were stealing theirs.

THE NEXT DAY, Lady Tess led five of us on horses through the forest toward Lake Eetha, with her youngest child, Kip, strapped securely to her front. In our party were Juliana, the girl with the mermaid costume who had danced with Jackrun at the ball, Queen Adela and Lady Olivia, one of Lady Tess's friends, a fey woman named Kaprecha, who had decided to join us at the last moment, and myself.

The queen looked jubilant. Lady Olivia told me the king had gone to her bedchamber last night.

"Race you, Lady O.," Queen Adela said with glowing cheeks. They galloped for the next tree-topped hill.

I wasn't about to let Her Majesty take a fall. I raced after them, my healer's basket full of ointments, bandages, and suture supplies thumping against my spine. The others cantered behind us. I could not quite catch up with the queen, who laughed when she reached the top, winning the race with ease. She sat sure and commanding in the saddle when I pulled up next to her, my horse shaking her brown mane. No one had told me what a fine horsewoman she was.

Lady Tess took the lead again, guiding us through the

whispering beeches. The woods were not as lush or as thickly overgrown as my forests back home. I missed the rich soil so riotous with life. We'd tamed small portions of the wild land to grow food, but the untouched places always thrilled me. Mother was the same; she'd explored the woods with Father when she could. The day she showed the Adan an herb she'd used in midwifery, he'd gathered it. Later he drew the contours of the leaves and wrote about it in his Herbal as she looked on. I felt a tug in my chest.

I could not let Her Majesty see me cry. I slowed my chestnut to be alone. The fey woman, Kaprecha, fell back with her charger and joined me.

"What's the matter?"

"Nothing." I swiped my eyes.

"You were the water lily last night, weren't you?"

"Yes."

Kaprecha swished her long black hair, sparkles flying out in all directions. Mine was a similar shade, but I could swish for the rest of my life and never send a single sparkle flying.

"The costume suited you."

I'd liked it too, but it belonged to the fey. I had to give it back. It wasn't meant for a life of daily work such as mine. It was made for dancing.

"Water lilies span two worlds," she said mysteriously. "They need the earth and a watery pool to grow."

What did she mean by that?

"You spent time with the fox," she added playfully. "I saw you dancing."

I'd stepped on Jackrun's feet more than once. "I do not know how to dance very well, my lady."

"Call me Kaprecha, Uma. I will teach you," she offered.

"I doubt I'll have the time to learn, but thank you."

"The queen keeps you busy," she said in a hushed voice. "Your people and mine have a long history, sharing the islands peacefully together well before the English came." Again she kept her voice low so the riders up ahead would not hear her.

I dropped back further still and said nothing to Kaprecha, who was looking to gossip behind the queen's back. She fell back again alongside me.

The alliance she spoke of was long ago. The fey had come to terms with the English in their own way. Dragonswood refuge was protected. We weren't as lucky.

"You had a name for us in your tongue. *Ateeyadain*?"

"*Ateeyudune*—the magical ones."

"Yes, that's it. We stood together when the prince kicked one of our children. A despicable act. I heard you gasp. You also took offense."

I gave a careful nod. So this was Butterfly Woman. The one who'd hissed.

"He was cruel, unthinking," Kaprecha whispered, running her long fingers through her horse's mane. Three will-o'-the-wisps flitted down from the trees like bits of sparkling sunlight, and landed on Kaprecha's shoulders. "We were proud of how Jackrun handled the situation," she went on. "The Son of the Prophecy was born to rule." Kaprecha eyed me sideways, waiting to see my reaction. Even the wisps turned their tiny heads.

What was I supposed to say? That he would make a better, more just king than Desmond? Of course he would, but Kaprecha must know it was treasonous to say such a thing aloud. The fey might have plotted years ago for Lady Tess to marry Arden, but she'd made her choice and it was done. The Son of the Prophecy was born a duke's son, not the king's. Jackrun was powerful in his own right and had his own life to live without the fairies' interference.

I did not even dare to nod at her remark this time. I kept my chin in the air, my eyes fixed ahead of us. Juliana laughed at something Queen Adela said. I'd thought her dangerous last night in her sea woman's costume. I heard something else now; the liquid laugh of innocence, of a woman yet untried.

"Lady Tess will see that girl weds Jackrun if she has her way," Kaprecha said.

The watery girl would drench his fire. "She is completely wrong for him," I blurted in a half whisper.

Kaprecha's brows shot up. "Do you think so?" she asked coyly.

I watched the horses on the trail ahead, hoping Kaprecha would leave me in peace if I ignored her.

"Look," she said, pointing up through the branches. At first I didn't see what she was pointing at. Then graceful winged movements caught my eye. Our party entered a small meadow. The will-o'-the-wisps vanished, flying back into the wood. By the time we reined our horses in, Jackrun and Babak had winged much farther south. Babak sped over the distant forest, his tail undulating in the air.

"Jacken! Jacken!" Kip cried, waving his small hands and bouncing up and down. Lady Tess held him in the saddle in case he wriggled out of his straps. Jackrun was much too far away to hear his little brother's cry.

"Where is Jackrun going?" Queen Adela asked.

"To settle a land dispute down south," Lady Tess said. "My husband cannot be everywhere at once. More and more he relies on Jackrun's negotiation skills in these matters."

Queen Adela turned in her saddle. "You should make people come to you with their troubles, as my husband does."

Lady Tess said, "Not everyone has the freedom or the means to travel, Your Majesty. Jackrun can reach them quickly on Babak. Besides, he likes settling disputes. He's quite good at it," she added proudly.

"Really? He used to have a terrible temper when he was a boy."

"He was nine years old on your last visit, Your Majesty," the duchess said tersely.

Queen Adela leaned out and tickled Kip. "You don't have a bad temper, do you, Kip? You are my little sweetmeat."

Kip giggled and squirmed. I dropped my eyes and rubbed my mare's neck. An infertile woman can attach herself to another woman's child, dreaming it is her own. Her Majesty was growing fond of Tess's little boy, perhaps too fond. It was good we were leaving in a few days.

We trotted across the meadow, the horse hooves crushing all too many wildflowers. Queen Adela rode on the duchess's left, in the mood for a merry argument. "Jackrun should not be flying off just now," she said. "I expect him to spend time with my son the prince while we are here."

Lady Tess took a moment to answer. "You are right, Your Majesty. The cousins should spend time together. They are the next generation of Pendragons to rule these islands when we are gone."

"King Arden reigns over both islands," corrected Queen Adela. "Your husband does not rule Dragon's Keep, he merely oversees the property for my husband."

"Of course, Your Majesty." Lady Tess looked like she would relish knocking Adela from her horse, fighting it out. Part of me wished she had the freedom to do it. But she reined her temper in, shot arrows with her eyes, and controlled her tongue.

"You should arrange an outing of some sort for the cousins while we are here," Queen Adela said, egging Lady Tess on.

"An outing," Lady Tess echoed noncommittally.

Lady Olivia and Juliana bent their heads toward the others. Kaprecha urged her stallion forward to join the conversation. I held back, catching the hint of honeysuckle in the soft breeze. The glassy air had turned the deep summer blue of Her Majesty's eyes.

No dragons flew above. Babak and his rider had long since vanished. No doubt Jackrun had grabbed the chance to put distance between himself and his cousin. The longer he stayed away, the better for them both. If these women had seen the two of them battling in my tower room, they would have known better than to force them on some cousinly outing.

I felt uneasy for the rest of the ride. My chestnut tossed her mane and pricked her ears, sensing my mood. I spoke softly to reassure her and calm myself at the same time. It didn't work.

LATE IN THE day I walked with Her Majesty in the walled garden. She bent to sniff a pink rose. "The king will visit me again tonight," she said with confidence. "Bring my potion up promptly after dinner."

"Yes, Your Highness."

"That's Your Majesty," she corrected. After all the months under Lady Olivia's tutelage, I was still getting things wrong. Her cheeks were flushed from our long day's ride, but she didn't seem at all tired. Pippin raced ahead of us barking, starlings flitted up from the bushes. Queen Adela laughed. "Such a mighty hunter, Pippin!" He wagged his tail and raced back to us, tongue lolling out the side of his little mouth. "That's my little boy."

I drank in the colorful plants, the bushes' fragrant summer breeze, grateful for Her Majesty's calm. I'd feared journeying to Dragon's Keep would worsen her health. I had to admit now, I'd been wrong. The trip had done her nothing but good.

A couple headed toward us from across the garden. Griffin and Tabitha walking very close together, though not arm in arm. Griffin bowed. Tabitha curtsied. "Your Majesty," they said in unison. Queen Adela nodded and passed them by, heading for the fountain. "Do you have a lover back home?" she asked.

"A . . . lover? No, Your Majesty."

She raised a brow. "Pity. You are young. It's good to find love in your youth." My cheeks grew hot, thinking of Jackrun. "I met King Arden when I was just fifteen. It was high summer, the most beautiful season. The days lasted forever. He taught me how to ride."

"You are a fine horsewoman, Your Majesty."

"Yes," she said. "I am." We stopped to admire the fountain. A butterfly landed on the queen's sleeve, its patterned monarch wings a tiny version of Kaprecha's costume at the fairy ball. We both stood very still, watching the tiny bit of life resting on her arm.

## CHAPTER FOURTEEN

# Pendragon Summer Castle, Dragon's Keep

### EGRET MOON
*August 1210*

THE QUEEN WAS in good spirits again the next day when I brought in her morning tonic. She drank it to the dregs, gazing out the window at the bright summer morning alongside Lady Olivia. I saw how Her Majesty's storms had settled, how her mood matched the weather. The bapeeta was working, but that wasn't all. King Arden had visited her bed two nights in a row. The soft glow coming off her skin made her seem years younger.

"That will be all, Uma," she said, indicating the door.

Lady Olivia eyed me critically as I curtsied in the fashion she'd taught me and backed out of the room.

Late in the day I heard Jackrun was back from his journey south. I searched the halls, hoping to run into him, and spied him at last in the weapons yard. He fought a bow-legged soldier twice his age, though not as muscled. Both men swung maces, fending off spiked blows with battered shields. Soldiers shouted, hurling cheers and insults in the sweaty, dusty side yard.

The man nearest to me said, "What is it you want, miss?" I was the only woman there. I left.

THAT EVENING I opened the trapdoor that led to the tower roof above my room. The wide round space with crenellated walls gave me the privacy I needed. I should perform the Moon Dance on Egret Moon's death night, but I would be too busy helping the queen pack tomorrow. I would have to do it now.

Turning slowly in my bare feet, arms raised, I greeted the four directions beginning with the sea in the east, the rolling hills along the coastline north and south, and ending with the forested mountain where the dying Egret Moon had fallen in the west. We danced to honor the moon and, some believed, to appease it. There were more deaths at the end of a moon's cycle than at any other time. Father had never told me why that was, but I had seen it myself in my village. Urette, the youth who worked with Father for a short time, died on the last night of Egret Moon when necks are the most vulnerable; a viper sank its fangs in his neck. And even here among the English it held true. Someone killed the lute player on Murderous Moon, the night Snake Moon died.

When I turned again, facing the sea, the duke's sentries had come out to light the torches along the distant curtain wall surrounding the castle grounds. I was jealous of their fire. Up here I couldn't build the customary bonfire for my dance. Even lighting a torch would draw the watchmen's eyes, so I had to make do with a candle for the element of fire. I unpacked the pouch of earth from Devil's Boot, the water bowl I used now that my mother's bowl was broken. Last, I raised the feather Jackrun brought me for the element of wind, and moved my feet to dance the death of Egret Moon, singing softly in the tongue I missed so much.

I longed to hear the men and women of my Euit family singing with me. Most of all I wanted to hear Father's deep voice and Mother's lilting one. But only the wind sang with me as I moved. The distant sea roared. Later the wolves joined in, howling hungrily for their Moon Month to begin.

I was still chanting softly, pressing the egret feather against my neck as Father used to do while I orbited the candle, when I heard a door shut and voices after that. I ducked behind a crenellation in the tower wall. Jackrun and Tabitha had come out of the eastern tower, taking the high walkway that linked the towers ten feet below me. I blew out my candle and was about to gather the rest of my sacred objects before Jackrun and Tabitha wandered up and caught me doing things I would rather not explain to any English, when I checked again and saw they were leaning against the wall looking beyond the torchlit curtain wall and out to sea. I stayed where I was, breathing hard, pressing myself against the cold stone and peering down through the open space between the crenellations.

Torch light pooled around Tabitha and Jackrun, she in her cloak, and he in a mud-streaked leather jerkin, his rolled-up sleeves exposing the dragon scales on his right arm. He had freed his hair from its usual leather strap. The side breeze blew it across his face as he looked out.

Tabitha said, "Juliana left earlier than planned. What happened?"

"Not sure," Jackrun said.

"You don't know why?"

"I can't pretend to understand women, Tabby."

"I think she didn't like the attention you were giving Uma at the ball."

"I can dance with whomever I please."

I gripped my elbows, liking the sound of that.

"Is that what you said to Juliana?"

Jackrun drummed the top of the wall. "I'm not a complete clod, little sister."

Tabitha laughed aloud. Her laughter carried far enough to alert one of the sentries on the outer curtain wall, who turned and waved at her. She waved back and was quiet for a while, then said, "I thought Juliana would be with us on tomorrow's picnic. Now I'll be the only female there."

"Does that bother you?"

"It wouldn't if *he* weren't coming."

"He's the point. It's all diplomacy. Mother and Father want the family to get along."

Tabitha reached up and covered her scales, rubbing them a little as if her neck were sore.

"Don't let what Desmond said shame you, Tabby. You're stronger than that. He has two scale patches himself; one on his arm, the other on his ass."

She laughed again, a sadder sound this time, and slowly lowered her hand.

"Point to his buttocks if he mentions your scales tomorrow," Jackrun said. "That will shut him up." I smiled from my hiding place.

"How do you know about Desmond's scale patch there?" Tabitha asked. I wondered that myself.

"Saw it when we dropped our breeches for a pissing contest."

She glanced up, surprised. "When was that?"

"On his last visit when he was eight and I was nine."

"Oh." She sounded relieved. "I was too young to remember much of that visit."

"He hasn't changed."

"He's been here less than a week, but it's long enough to see what he's like," Tabitha said, turning her back to the wall. I saw her profile and Jackrun's as she faced him. "He's a monster, Jack. He'll be a tyrant when he's king. It should be you on the Pendragon throne, like the prophecy said. You're the one the fairies wanted. You're the one with fairy blood."

Jackrun put his hand out, covering her mouth. "Stop it, Tabby. The prophecy never said I would be king, only the firstborn of three bloodlines. Besides, this is treasonous talk.

Things are the way they are. He may be no worse than I would be if I were king."

She pulled his hand away and spoke so softly I could barely hear her. "He *will* be worse, a hundred times worse, and you know it."

"How can you say that, knowing what I've done," he snapped. My ears pricked. What? What had he done?

Tabitha gazed up at her brother. "Tell me you hate him as much as I do, Jack. No one's listening. Tell me."

"Why?"

"Because I don't want to be so alone with how I feel," she said, her voice breaking.

"You are not alone," he admitted.

I saw her shoulders fall as she let out a sigh. "The fey think he's horrid too, spoiled and dangerous. I overheard some of them talking at the ball. They're worried about what will happen to Wilde Island when he's king. I agree with them. That's why you should be the—"

"Tabby, enough."

"I saw you talking to Uma after Desmond kicked one of their little boys. What did she think about it?"

I strained my ears, wondering what he would say, but Jackrun didn't talk about the ball.

"Uma has more reason than most to hate Desmond."

"Why? What did he do to her?"

Jackrun's shadow lengthened along the wall in the torch-light as if his dark thoughts bled into it, made it grow, as if it could swallow him if he let it. But it was just Tabitha he faced, his younger sister looking up at him, wanting to know what their cousin did to me, would have done to me if Jackrun hadn't stopped him.

"Did he hurt her, Jack?" Tabitha persisted.

Jackrun gripped his scabbard. "I've done my best to keep clear of him so I wouldn't . . ." He paused. "We'll have him to ourselves tomorrow."

"What will you do?"

"Give him a farewell he will remember," he said, smoke slipping from his mouth, coiling up around his angry face, crowning his head before it drifted away. Jackrun swung around and started back across the walkway. He made another sharp remark when he reached the door, but he was too far off for me to hear it. A moment later they were gone.

When I looked down, I saw I'd bent the beautiful feather in two and broken it. It was essential to release the ceremonial feather from a high place when the Egret Moon Dance was over so the wind could carry it far away. That was why I'd come to the roof to begin with, to dance, to let it go. Releasing it from on high ensured a safe transition from death moon to birth moon. I shivered, staring at the broken thing in my hand, wondering what I'd done, if any of my dancing and sacred songs mattered now that the feather was broken.

I was not sure what I feared as I cupped the wounded feather; I only knew I should not stay behind wondering what might happen tomorrow. I should follow.

## CHAPTER FIFTEEN

# Faul's Leap, Dragon's Keep

### DEATH OF EGRET MOON
*August 1210*

I WAS IN the kitchen right after breakfast when Cook finished preparing a picnic for the outing, so I offered to bring it out to Tabitha in the foreyard.

Tabitha took it from me. "Thank you, Uma."

Jackrun turned, startled. "Uma?"

"Uma brought us our basket," Tabitha explained. She looked about. "Where's Griffin?"

"He'll meet us on the way to Faul's Leap," Jackrun said.

Prince Desmond glared at me as he crossed the cobbles. "She's not coming with us, is she?"

"No, Your Royal Highness," I said with a curtsy, "I have work to do."

I left the three of them. Around the corner, I pressed myself up against the wall as the hostler led the horses from the stables. They rode past the gatehouse and through the portcullis gate.

The foreboding I'd felt last night hadn't left me. Following them wouldn't be easy on foot. The riders would reach the cliff they called Faul's Leap long before I got there at a run.

I breathed slowly in and out to put myself in balance, silently chanting *havuela*—become—then slipped past the gatehouse and took off, heading south toward the hills that ran parallel above the beach.

My slippers slid in the grass as I raced along. I pulled them off, wishing I could do the same with my heavy velvet skirts that blew sail-like and slowed my progress. Down on the beach, Griffin met the party on his white mare. They stayed a while talking, giving me more time to catch up as I ran in the hills above before they rode past the harbor toward the darker cliffs in the south.

Stopping at last, they tied their horses up and begin climbing the cliffside to Faul's Leap.

I couldn't scale the cliff in the same spot they were using without detection, but maybe I could find another place to climb. Thorny branches caught my skirts as I raced along the hillside.

I was out of breath by the time I reached the top and found a good hiding place where I could crouch and watch them all through the crosshatched brambles. The four of them stood catching their breaths and looking out to sea. No one spoke yet.

There was fresh yarrow growing beside me. A true find. I picked some while I watched and waited. Mixed with lavender oil and other herbs, yarrow made a superior ointment.

Four ancient standing stones dominated Faul's Leap. A short altar less than four feet high and carved with runes crowned the apex of the stone circle.

The power of this place coursed through my body; ancient rhythms here were as deep as the Earth's heartbeat. I am fox and of the earth; my body and bones knew I was on holy ground.

"I'm starving," Prince Desmond said. He grabbed the picnic basket, placed it on the altar, and dug inside for food.

Jackrun took the basket down.

"What did you do that for?"

"Can't you see what it is? It's not a table, Desmond."

The prince shrugged. "We have ruins like this on Wilde Island too. They're not sacred. Just stones people erected a long time ago. They serve no purpose now."

*Just stones people erected a long time ago.* Likely the Euit people. My people.

The picnickers sat twelve paces from the altar. Tabitha sliced the bread, passed around the cheese and meat. They talked little as they ate, avoiding one another's eyes.

The cool breeze that sang around the standing stones set my skin tingling. I felt a presence up here, as if invisible ancient beings were gathering all around us on the high cliff now that we had come to their place.

Desmond downed some ale and peered up at the sky. "We should have some dragons come pick us up and take us home."

"We don't fly dragons just to travel from one place to another like you do on horseback," said Tabitha. "You would know that if you ever rode one."

"I've flown many times, cousin. We have plenty of dragons in Dragonswood. And I've ridden one of the rare red breed who followed the Euits north."

*Liar! He's never ridden Vazan.*

"I thought reds were feral," Tabitha said. "I was told no one rides the reds, not even the fey folk." *She's never seen my father.*

"Well, you heard wrong." He pulled plums from the basket, throwing one at Jackrun, who swiftly caught it with his left hand.

Prince Desmond sucked plum after plum, spitting the pits on the ground. "Be back soon," he said, leaping up and bounding past the altar. I think he meant to piss behind the bushes. Before I could run, his boot was on the corner of my long velvet skirt, catching me in place.

The prince grabbed my hair. "What are you doing here, you little spy?" He yanked me up and dragged me toward the others.

Jackrun jumped up. "Let go of her."

"I won't. She was spying."

"I was not spying, Your Royal Highness. I came outside to gather herbs." My back was bent, my head held down in the prince's tight grip.

"I said let go, Desmond."

"She will run off like a rat if I do. You weren't picking herbs, little liar."

"I can prove it," I said. "Only let me go."

Prince Desmond jerked his hand, giving my hair a final painful tug before letting go. The stinging along my scalp made my eyes prick. I stood and pulled the yarrow from the basket on my back.

"There, you see," said Tabitha.

"You should apologize to Uma, cousin," Jackrun said.

"For what?"

Griffin stood with Jackrun. "He means about the other day."

Desmond's lip curled. "You're joking."

Jackrun stepped behind Prince Desmond and clamped his hands on his shoulders. "Get down on your knees to the queen's physician, cousin."

"Wait," I said, afraid. But already Griffin had stepped in to help. They both pushed down on Prince Desmond's shoulders until his knees buckled and hit the ground amid plum pits and crumbs.

"What do you think you're doing?" Prince Desmond snarled.

"Please," I said. "He doesn't have to—"

"Apologize for the way you attacked Uma Quarteney the other day," Jackrun ordered.

"I won't."

"That's enough," I said, trembling. I wanted Prince Desmond punished for everything he'd done to me and to my father. I had hungered for it, but this was wrong. We weren't alone here. Ancient presences surrounded us, the wind carrying their whispers in soft swirls. I could sense that, even if Jackrun, Griffin, and Tabitha could not.

"Look." Tabitha pointed up. Three dragons flew toward us. I saw Babak's colorful scales; the dragons flying on either side of him gleamed in the morning sun like polished brass.

Prince Desmond glared up at me with burning hatred. "Let go of me now, Jackrun!"

His shout seemed to bring the dragons down. They landed in a perfect triangle, holding their wings out as wide as sails. The animal scent was heavy with the smell of scorched meat. I stood rigid, all of us walled in by their wings.

Griffin released the prince and took a step back, but Jackrun persisted. Standing behind Desmond, he leaned his weight into his hands, pushing firmly down. "Say you are sorry, Desmond." He said each word slowly.

Grunting, Prince Desmond bent low as if he was ready to submit. Then, using the quick maneuver to trick Jackrun, he slid from Jackrun's grasp, rolled free, then leaped up, red and fuming, balling his fists, ready to fight. Desmond might have landed a punch if the dragons hadn't fixed their bright, menacing eyes on him. He met their eyes a moment, breathing hard, his fisted hands shaking at his sides.

No one moved, returning glare for glare. Then the dragons folded their wings, a sound like sails rippling in wind. Whether they agreed with Jackrun or not, Desmond was still the royal family's only son and future Wilde Island king. Their tall forms mirrored the standing stones behind them:

sentries of flesh, sentries of stone. Now the wings were down; a cool breeze began to dry my sweaty face.

"Uma," Jackrun said, "you have already met Babak and also his sister Nahal, who made the golden chain the night you arrived. This," he said, gesturing to the other copper-scaled dragon on his right, "is their sister Sitara."

"We are in this place together, warriors," I said, giving all three a formal Euit greeting, though I spoke in English. I bent down to them in turn, touching the top of each one's claw as one reveres an elder. They were young dragons, but still deserving of respect. Behind me I heard Jackrun catch his breath.

"We are together in this place," said Nahal, Babak, and Sitara in turn before I stepped away again. Tabitha had started repacking the picnic basket. I crouched down to help her, and wrapped up the remains of the barley bread. For a brief moment Prince Desmond had been on his knees before me in front of his cousins, their fey friend, Griff, and three powerful dragons. There was some consolation in that. I only wished Father had lived to see it.

I slipped the plum pits, future trees, into the herb basket still slung over my back. Nahal came closer, flicking her tail against the rocky ground.

"You do not need thissss," Nahal hissed, pinching Tabitha's lace scarf with her talons and pulling it off to unveil the blue-green scale patch on Tabitha's neck.

The dragons made an approving clicking sound with their tongues as Nahal held it up like a flag, the long lace fluttering in her hot breath. She blew it overhead, where it caught the breeze and twirled skyward. Tabitha put her arms around Nahal's lowered neck and rested her head against her.

"Sorry," Tabitha whispered. "I shouldn't have covered them." Nahal licked Tabby's neck scales with the tip of her forked tongue.

I looked away, feeling the private moment between them, and stood with Jackrun watching the white lace swirl over the choppy water, catching wind after wind until it vanished from sight.

"Jackrun," Babak said in a gruff voice behind us. "Will you leap now?"

Jackrun nodded, and Babak took off, flying south. I watched him make a swift, even turn, heading back toward Faul's Leap as Jackrun stepped to the edge of the precipice jutting out over the water.

"What is he doing?" Desmond asked.

"Hush," Tabitha warned. But I wondered myself. Was Jackrun truly about to leap on Babak from so high up? Babak vanished under the overhang. Knees bent, Jackrun swung back his arms. My heart caught in my mouth as he jumped.

"Hurrah!" Tabitha shouted as Babak soared upward with Jackrun on his back. I didn't feel like cheering. I wanted to scream at him for taking such a foolish risk. But now the other two dragons took off, their flapping wings sending dust swirling in my face.

"I'm next on Nahal," Tabitha said.

"Tabitha!" I called, but she was already running for the edge. Nahal had turned about in the sky flying for the rocky overhang. Tabitha waited on the edge, then leaped, arms out. Griffin came right behind her, giving a shout as he threw himself outward, landing on Sitara.

I went to the place where they had all jumped and peered down at the white roaring waves some fifty feet below. If any of them had fallen, they would have hit the water, and while it looked deep enough, it also looked rough where the tide crashed against the cliff rock.

Jackrun's dragon turned for the cliff again. The air filled with the sound of Babak's pumping wings as he sped back. Babak made a noisy landing near a standing stone. The others crossed the water and alighted near him.

"My turn to fly," Desmond announced. "One of you get off."

"These are our dragons," said Griffin. "We were all bonded from birth."

"Bonded? You're not a Pendragon."

"Fey also bond. My father is one of the fey folk and my mother is half fey."

"And I am the prince of Wilde Island, your future king, you wretch. You will obey me."

Griffin leaned down, the sunlight catching in his thick red hair. "We fey have our own laws. We don't live under your authority."

Prince Desmond started. "The fairy folk would have died out years ago if it weren't for my family. Maybe we should have let your kind die, and given Dragonswood sanctuary on Wilde Island and the greenwood here on Dragon's Keep solely to the dragons." He adjusted his belt. "Now dismount. I'm ready to go and I'm not climbing back down this bloody cliff."

Griffin hesitated.

"I will take you," Babak said, head tipped, eyes gleaming.

"No, Babak," Jackrun said.

"You heard Babak. Get off," Desmond demanded.

Jackrun peered down at me. "Have you seen him ride, Uma?"

"Once." Just the old dragon that often slept in the castle stables, a lazy creature nothing like the dragons here.

"Leave my mother's servant out of this, Jackrun. I can ride any dragon here."

Jackrun said, "You don't mean to jump from the edge, do you? I don't think—"

"What? You don't think I can do it? How hard is it to miss a dragon's back when he's just three feet below you?" His jaw was set with sudden determination.

Babak lowered his head and shook it. Jackrun's feet hit the ground.

*He shouldn't do this*, I thought. I was about to try and talk Desmond out of it when I heard rustling sounds. The brambles behind the altar stone moved. A moment later I caught a flash of the king's red livery before Sir Geoffrey stepped out into the open. "Your Royal Highness," he said with a quick bow.

The prince spun around. "What are you doing here?"

Sir Geoffrey cleared his throat. "Your father the king wished me to follow you and your cousins on your outing today. It's my duty to watch out for your safety."

"I'm no child," snarled the prince. "And why Father would send you to spy on me is beyond me."

"You are the heir, Your Royal Highness. Please let me accompany you safely back down the cliff the way you came. You should not take such a risk. You do not have the skills or training to do it."

Prince Desmond flushed purple. "Piss off, Geoffrey! I'm as skilled as anyone here!"

There was a hushed moment. Then Babak's claws scratched the ground before he ascended into the air.

"Your Highness, step away from the edge," Sir Geoffrey warned. "You are not—"

"I said piss off!"

Heart pounding, I watched Jackrun's dragon make a knife-wing turn in the soft blue sky and fly toward us. A heavy wind hit my back and filled my nose with a potent leafy smell a second before Babak dipped below the overhang.

"Prince Desmond!" I called out, fearing the sudden forceful gust would knock him off balance. The prince tipped forward in the brisk wind. Arms swinging wildly, he toppled over the side.

## CHAPTER SIXTEEN

# Faul's Leap, Dragon's Keep

### DEATH OF EGRET MOON
*August 1210*

W E ALL RUSHED to the edge and flung ourselves down on the rocky overhang. By the Holy Ones, Babak had missed, or Desmond had missed Babak!

I threw my arms out as if to catch the falling prince, but he was tumbling, screaming. Babak dove straight down, his wings pinned to his sides. The other two dragons plummeted after him, but Desmond hit the water and was sucked under the whitecaps. Babak plunged into the waves, surfaced, looked about frantically, and dove under again. The other two dragons landed on the rocks a few yards away, snouts down, watching the water.

"God help us!" cried Jackrun. "Desmond can swim, can't he?"

Griffin said, "We didn't ask him."

"Hurry!" Sir Geoffrey shouted. We all leaped up, and scrambled down the cliff.

BY THE TIME we reached the beach, Babak had fished Prince Desmond from the churning water, and laid him on the wet sand. I had seen death before, but this gruesome corpse with the broken bleeding neck was beyond me.

"Do something, Uma!" Tabitha screamed. "Fix him! Help him!"

I crouched in the sand. Blood spilled from his gaping mouth. The beach spun. The world went white. I'd called to him up on the cliff because I'd thought the forceful wind might throw him off balance. *Holy Ones, what have I done?*

"It's too late, Tabitha," Jackrun said, kneeling beside me. "We cannot bring him back."

"I hated him!" Tabitha cried, burying her tear-stained face in Griffin's shoulder.

*We all hated him,* I thought. *But this . . .*

I rocked on my knees by the prince's water-soaked body.

"Holy God. Jesus help us." Jackrun put his face in his hands.

"What do we do?" Griffin asked in a hoarse voice, hugging Tabitha tighter. Another wave washed up, the foam turned pink with blood before drawing back.

I made a feeble attempt to straighten the body, pulling tangled seaweed out from under Desmond's shoulder. We had tried to talk him out of jumping, hadn't we?

*The queen's only son.* No. I couldn't let myself think of the nightmare that was coming, of what his death would mean, not yet.

"Help me, Jackrun, will you?" Together we pulled the prince's body back from the water to a place where the waves would not reach him.

Sir Geoffrey stood firm, unable or unwilling to give us a hand. The dragons huddled in a group. Flies landed on Prince Desmond's face. I shooed them away. Tabitha still wept. Griffin bowed his head, resting it on hers.

Jackrun was praying over the body. I got to my feet, unsteady; still, I took twelve paces to the sea, brought water in my cupped hands, touched the prince's forehead with a wet finger, touched his eyelids, his mouth, his throat, with drops of seawater. Wind swirled around us; I took up a gull feather and placed it by his feet, blessing his spirit as it left his body.

The dragons had been clustering around Babak, who was soaking, shivering. Jackrun stood slowly and went to him. "Babak?" he croaked. "Are you all right?"

The dragon opened his golden eyes. "Why did you call out his name, Uma?" he snapped. "You threw him off balance. I could have caught him if you hadn't!" The words cut like thrown knives.

"I meant to warn him, I—"

Nahal growled. "*We* dragons will be blamed for killing the prince. The king will want *our* blood."

"Enough," Sir Geoffrey said, putting up his hand. "No one made him fall. You felt the gust come across the cliff."

He looked at all of us. "A strong blast that pushed against my back, it must have pushed him too and thrown him off balance."

"I felt it," Tabitha said, wiping her eyes with a shaking hand.

"Desmond walked to the edge on his own," Griffin reminded us. "No one made him go. He saw what we could do and wanted to prove he could do the same. He chose to jump."

I left the argument and walked a few feet from the body to rinse the hem of my bloodstained skirt off in the sea. What story would we tell the king and queen? The prince was dead. If any of us were blamed for it, our lives would be at stake.

My chest felt leaden as I lowered myself and washed away the blood. *He died of a broken neck.* Egret Moon had taken him on her death day.

"Someone has to go back and tell the king and queen what happened," Sir Geoffrey said. "Who will go?"

# CHAPTER SEVENTEEN

# Pendragon Summer Castle, Dragon's Keep

## DEATH OF EGRET MOON
### *August 1210*

IN THE END it was decided that Griffin would stay with Tabitha, and Jackrun and Sir Geoffrey would go tell Lady Tess and Duke Bion. I would accompany them, because the queen would need a strong potion the moment she heard the news.

At the castle stables, Jackrun swung down from his mount. "We should speak to my parents privately first."

He helped me from my saddle. "I'll go to the queen," I said.

Sir Geoffrey shook his head. "You had better come with us before you go to her."

"Let me speak first," said Jackrun. "I will tell them." He set his jaw, looking through the open stable doors into the sunny courtyard, preparing himself for the worst.

"What happened was not your fault," I said. I wasn't sure he heard me before he marched outside.

The sentries stationed outside the duke's presence chamber lifted their brows at the three of us in our wet clothing, uncrossed their pikes, and let us through. I stared at the blanket hanging behind Duke Bion's desk as we walked in: an intricate Euit pattern in red-orange, green, and brown, an owl in each corner. Seeing a blanket that could have been woven by my own grandmother on Duke Bion's wall left me deeply confused.

Jackrun's father looked up from his desk, and came to a stand. "What is it? What has happened?"

"An accident, Father."

"A terrible accident, my lord," Sir Geoffrey added. "You had better fetch Lady Tess."

"Who is hurt?" He belted on his dagger. "Not Tabitha?" he asked, his face dark with fear.

"Tabby is fine," Jackrun said. "Please, Father, wait a moment."

Jackrun's mother came in through the side door from her private chamber. When she saw us gathered in the room, she drew back and uttered the same words as her husband. "What's happened?"

Jackrun drew in a breath. "The prince has had an accident." How small and hollow the word *accident* seemed. Was there any word horrible enough to express what had happened? "He . . . fell from a great height. He's . . . he's—"

"Dead," Sir Geoffrey said.

Lady Tess screamed into her hand and fell back against the wall.

"God in heaven!" The duke eased his wife into a chair by the hearth, then gripped the back of her chair to support himself. Both were ashen faced. "You are sure he is dead?"

Sir Geoffrey nodded. "Would God it was not so, but we are sure, my lord."

"Where is he now?" the duke snapped. "Tell us exactly what happened. We will bring the body back to the castle before we tell my brother and his wife. In God's name, this is beyond belief!"

In fits and starts we three told them.

"You taught Tabitha to jump from Faul's Leap?" Lady Tess asked Jackrun. "How long," she asked, shaking, "has this been going on?"

"I've been doing it since I was thirteen," he admitted.

"And Tabitha only ten?" She was standing now, her face hard, her hands bunching her skirts as if to strangle them.

"No, Mother," he murmured, "Tabby was not allowed to try it until she too was thirteen. I take the blame for it," he added. "It is all my fault."

"No it isn't!" I said. "You tried to warn him."

Duke Bion turned to Sir Geoffrey. "And where were you when this was happening, man?"

"With them, my lord. I tried to talk the prince out of the feat, but he had seen the others jump and would not be persuaded to turn about."

Lady Tess strode to Jackrun, took him by the shoulders, and shook him. "Do you know what you have done, Jackrun? Do you know the danger we're all in?" He was taller than she, yet she shook him wildly as one would shake an orchard tree that withholds its fruit.

The duke stepped over to her and put a hand on hers as Jackrun looked down at his soaked boots. "Tess, they would not behead a member of the family."

"Won't they? You know the violence Queen Adela is capable of!"

The duke's face changed, some dark memory flashing before his eyes. "God help us," he said, squeezing his wife's hand on Jackrun's shoulder. "My brother is out riding now. Where is she, Tess? Where is the queen?"

"She is upstairs supervising the packing of her trunks for the journey home tomorrow."

He dropped his hand and spoke to Jackrun. "Look at me." Jackrun raised his chin, his face gaunt and darkly traced as death, but his eyes still burned. "We must do this right and do it quickly, Jackrun. You and Sir Geoffrey will show me where the body is and help me bear him home before the king and queen hear anything of this!" He glared at me. "Uma, the king and queen will need you, so gather your supplies from your chamber. An accidental death," he reminded us, "we are all agreed on this."

"Yes, my lord."

"We will bring him to my chamber through that door."

He nodded to his right. "Uma, as soon as you have finished, hurry back here and help us clean the body up before the king and queen see him."

I curtsied and ran out.

I had the tonics ready by the time they brought the prince home wrapped in a blanket. Lady Tess and I went to work in the duke's chamber, removing the sand from his torn clothes and washing the body. I tied a scarf around his broken neck to hide the bulging bone before we draped him head to toe with a clean linen sheet.

Lady Tess straightened up. "God have mercy on him, and on us all, by Christ." She closed her eyes and crossed herself, then opened the door to the fireside room. "He is ready, husband."

The duke nodded and continued his instructions to Jackrun. "You will tell them exactly what you told me and no more. He saw you mount your dragons from the cliff. He admired the sport. He insisted on trying it himself. You warned him. Sir Geoffrey tried to talk him out of it. The prince would not be dissuaded. He misjudged the timing when he jumped, and he fell."

"That's right. Babak tried to catch him and plummeted down after him, diving into the sea to rescue him, but it was too late."

Duke Bion studied Jackrun's face. "Do the dragons think they will be blamed?"

Jackrun nodded. Duke Bion heaved a breath and ran his fingers through his hair.

No one had mentioned how Jackrun and Griffin had made Prince Desmond kneel and apologize to me. Was Sir Geoffrey already hiding on the cliff watching us when that happened, or had he come later?

I looked sidewise at the broad-shouldered man who was straightening his windblown hair, wondering what he'd seen. What he would tell the king.

"Sir Geoffrey, the king will have returned now. Go and fetch him to this room."

"Yes, my lord."

"I will go and get the queen," Lady Tess said. "I'll tell her there was an accident today to prepare her as she comes, but no more than that."

"Tess," Duke Bion said heavily. "I know you'll do it rightly."

Tears brimmed in her eyes as she went to her husband and kissed him, not on the cheek, but on the mouth, and it was like a farewell kiss. She gave Jackrun a brief, strong hug and stepped back, looking at both of them with such love that I turned my eyes away. Nothing would be the same for them or for their family after this moment. Nothing would be the same for any of us.

Not long after, I heard Queen Adela's voice crying, "Let me see him!" The wailing could be heard down the hall-way, the clip-clip of her shoes as she ran toward the room. I braced myself as she burst in flying toward the door to the duke's private chamber. Lady Tess rushed up behind trying to stop her.

Duke Bion stepped in her path, putting himself between her and the door. "Don't enter yet, Your Majesty, wait for your husband." She pushed him aside, and hurried in. We all followed. None of us could stop Queen Adela from rushing to the bed where her dead son lay. She threw back the sheet and let out a pitiful knife-sharp scream that cut deep into my chest.

Sir Geoffrey rushed in with the king, who was still disheveled from his ride. He saw his son's body, his wife collapsed on her knees, sobs wrenching up her throat. One word came out between each sob: "No. No."

King Arden shook head to foot, like a quaking mountain. Growling with rage, he whipped out his sword. "Where is the murderer who killed my son? I'll slit the bastard's throat!"

Duke Bion stepped toward him. "There is no murderer, brother. It was a terrible accident. Prince Desmond fell off the cliff."

"Fell? Where? What cliff?" The king's face was scarlet, spittle formed at the edges of his mouth as he shouted at Jackrun. "*You* took him there. I saw you and your sister leaving with him this morning."

"Murderer," Queen Adela wailed.

"No!" Jackrun said. "A terrible accident. Desmond wanted to jump onto a dragon's back and fly just as we did. He wanted to prove he could do it too, only he . . . only he—"

The king rounded on Sir Geoffrey. "I sent you to watch

over my son. You let him die!" He flew at him and thrust the sword in Sir Geoffrey's gut, attacking with such speed, even Sir Geoffrey looked surprised as he groaned in agony, crumpled over, and crashed sideways to the floor.

"My God!" Duke Bion leaped between them to prevent a second stab even as Jackrun and I fell to the floor at Sir Geoffrey's side.

"Uma," he whispered. I pressed his belly trying to staunch the bleeding with my hand. He had never called me by my first name before. It shook me deeply to hear it now, as if he might be taking his last breath.

Jackrun gripped Sir Geoffrey's hand and squeezed as the man groaned.

"You will be all right," I said, panting with rising terror. I couldn't stop the flow of blood seeping through my fingers onto the floor. Over the queen's sobs, I heard Lady Tess ordering, "Take this wounded man to the soldier's infirmary. Now!"

Duke Bion still wrestled with the king, trying to hold him back. "An accident," he was saying. "Please, brother, release your sword."

When the men lifted Sir Geoffrey up to carry him out, I drew in behind to follow them to the infirmary. The wound must be stitched before he bled to death. Lady Tess grabbed my arm as I was about to reach the door.

"Father Ezra will look to him, Uma," she said with quiet urgency. "The queen needs you."

I looked behind me. The king was at the bedside now, kneeling by his weeping wife. He had laid his bloody sword beside his son's body. Cold dread filled me seeing the two of them. I knew the medicines Sir Geoffrey needed, but the queen's grief was beyond my skills. How could I possibly help her?

# CHAPTER EIGHTEEN

# Pendragon Summer Castle, Dragon's Keep

## DEATH OF EGRET MOON
*August 1210*

THE PASSAGE ECHOED with Queen Adela's sobs. Her body felt heavy and boneless as I guided her down the hall toward her rooms with Lady Tess. We found Lady Olivia turning down Her Majesty's bed. I hadn't seen her that morning when I'd brought the queen her potion. She'd retired to her room with a headache. No headache, no matter how painful, would keep her from her duty now.

The three of us eased Queen Adela onto her canopy bed. Lady Olivia and Lady Tess sat on either side of her, propping her up, coaxing her to drink my sleeping potion. Lady Olivia sang to her until she finally drifted off to sleep. Lady Tess drew the curtains. We exchanged haunted looks in the semidarkness. No one said "she will be all right" or "she will be better soon." A pitiful raw silence filled the room.

"May I leave her a while?" I asked Lady Tess.

"Do you need to mix more medicines?"

"Yes, my lady." *For the queen, and for Sir Geoffrey if I am not too late.*

"First tell me how it happened," Lady Olivia said.

"I don't want to speak of it, I—"

"I was told that you were there. You saw the accident. As the queen's companion, I must know the truth."

"She is right," said Lady Tess. "I wasn't there when the accident happened. Whatever I tell Lady Olivia would only be what I heard from you and Geoffrey and Jackrun. Take a breath, Uma. You will only have to do this once."

I gripped the bedpost, and I told the story as quickly as I could in a shivering voice, my words choppy. Lady Olivia's eyes were closed when I finished. She moaned softly, rubbing her temples.

"Do you want Uma to mix you a potion for your headache?" Lady Tess asked.

"No, my lady," said Lady Olivia, easing herself onto a chair by the bed, preparing for a long day and even longer night. "I will send word to you when she begins to stir, Uma. Be sure to have something ready."


THE SOLDIER'S INFIRMARY was housed near the weapons yard. Most of the cots were empty, but near the back,

I saw an elderly priest leaning over a cot. I had brought my wound supplies in my basket. Father Ezra carefully undid the bandage to let me check the wound. The reddened skin was finely stitched.

"A deep wound," Father Ezra said. "He has lost a lot of blood."

A thin sheen of sweat coated Sir Geoffrey's face. His breathing was too shallow, more like that of a small animal than of a man his size. Father Ezra replaced the bandage. "We will know by tomorrow if he is going to live. I have done what I can. The rest is up to God."

I pulled the small jar of the Adan's soldier's woundwort from my basket. It was the last of my store. I hadn't had the time to mix a new batch from the yarrow I'd picked that morning. "I hope this will help."

Father Ezra took it, removed the cork, and sniffed the jar. "Yarrow," he said, "and something else?"

"Herbs that grow in the mountains where I come from," I said. "They are powerful."

"Thank you, Uma. You are kind to bring it." He paused, then said, "You are young to have risen high enough to serve as queen's healer."

"I serve her because my father, the Adan, died," I said past the lump in my throat. "He was the one she wanted."

"But you took what God gave you."

"Did *God* give me this?" I snapped with sudden fury, thinking of Father's death, my own if I failed the queen.

The priest's face was calm. "You wanted another profession, perhaps? You have another calling?" His eyes were bright in the candle glow under his thick gray-black brows.

"No, Father. I have always wanted to be a healer."

He nodded. "I saw that when you inspected the wound, in the touch of your hands, and in your eyes when you gave me the salve."

"What would your God say about tradition, Father?" I asked, suddenly wanting more from this quiet man. "As a woman, I am not allowed to cure anyone back home in my tribe. It goes against our laws. Only the men are graced with the power to heal."

"Yet you are doing it now, Uma, because you must, am I right?"

"Yes," I whispered, "because I must."

"Already you answer your question," he said.

I left Sir Geoffrey in Father Ezra's hands, and made my way to my herbarium.

There is more to healing than mixing cures and stitching wounds. In our teachings, body and spirit are bound together. I had been studious. I'd read every page in Father's Herbal over and over many times. I'd watched him and learned much about the properties and uses of healing plants, but what Father hadn't taught me, what his Herbal could not show me, were the secrets passed from one Adan to another, ancient knowledge linking body and soul, flesh and dream.

*I am the healer who will cure her,* Father said. But he wasn't here. It was up to me.

I unlocked my father's Herbal. The pages made a whispering sound as I turned them, looking . . . looking. Grief. Despair. How do you treat a mother's pain at the loss of her only son? How do you treat her grief? Does grief reside in the heart or in the mind? In the body or the spirit? How was I to begin?

In the end I could only think to help Queen Adela sleep; give her dreams that would allow her to experience her pain from a safer place. The remedy I'd given the queen would wear off soon. Now I settled on the strongest sleep potion I knew. Lighting the fire to warm mulled wine, I sharpened my herb knife and slit the precious gyocana pods to get to the small purple seeds inside.

I also ground sleeping powder for the king, separating the doses out in packets to add to his wine, small amounts to calm him, larger doses to help him sleep. It would be easier to give the packets to another to treat His Majesty, but that broke tradition. Only the Adan or his apprentice touched these medicines. The king was still with his brother, Duke Bion, when I entered with his elixir. His Majesty's back was to me. He gripped the mantel hard, holding on as if the floor was moving under him and he could not stand without it. He refused my medicine until Duke Bion urged him on.

Down in the queen's bedchamber, Lady Olivia slumped over in her chair napping, the head veil covering her face fluttered gently in her breath. The queen moaned, stirring as she began to wake. Her bright blue eyes sprang open when I set the chalice on the bedside table. She blanched white at the sudden memory of her son's death, drew in a shuddering breath, and sat bolt upright.

"Your Majesty," I whispered, reaching for the curative.

The queen didn't seem to hear me. With a cracked scream, she gripped my arm, felt the knife under my sleeve. Before I knew what she was doing, she'd torn my herbing knife from my arm.

"No! Stop!" I lunged for her and gripped her wrists with both hands as she strained, trying to drive the point into her heart.

Lady Olivia awoke and leaped up, shouting, "Help! Someone help us!"

The sentries posted at Her Majesty's door burst in, followed by Lady Tess, who must have been on her way to check on the queen. They dove for Queen Adela. The guards pinned her down. At last I pried the knife from her clenched hands and raced across the room to store it on the bureau out of the queen's reach.

Queen Adela screamed, kicked, and clawed everyone who had come to throw his weight in and hold her down. Two guards forced her to sit up between them and managed to pin her flailing arms against her sides, but not without a few scratches.

The queen moaned and cried out, still squirming between her captors.

"Stop it, now, Your Grace." Lady Tess leaned over her, still breathing hard from the tussle. "You have had terrible news today. Your physician will give you something for the pain." Eyes to me, she jerked her head toward the potion.

"I don't want it! I want the knife!"

"No, you don't want the knife," said Lady Tess. "You are overcome with grief right now. You need rest. You need to heal from the horrible shock."

The tonic in the silver chalice had cooled. "Drink this, Your Majesty. It will help you rest."

"No," she sobbed, squirming.

Lady Olivia coaxed, "Sip some, Your Majesty, please."

Stepping closer, I pressed it to the queen's lips and got some in her mouth before she spat it out, spraying my face and Lady Tess's. Tess glared at me through strands of her disheveled hair dripping with potion. "Can you help her or not, Uma? How will we get her calmed down if she won't drink it?"

"Calmed down?" The queen laughed at us all, a horrid, leering laugh that ended in more sobs, another determined struggle to get free.

"Wait." I grabbed my knife and rushed down to the castle kitchen. Cook was pulling bread from the mouth of a fiery oven.

"The queen needs sweetmeats."

"Sweetmeats?" he asked, astonished.

"Now!" I shouted.

He went to the pantry and came back with a tin. There were just six inside. "Is that all?" I barked. It felt good to shout and spew a little of the dread that was building up in my chest. Cook did not deserve it. At the moment I didn't care.

"You will have to make more sticky nut balls for the queen. You understand she's stricken. You must do your part to help her. Lady Tess expects it," I added, unsure Cook would take orders from me.

I took the six with me up to the herbarium, where I slit more gyocana pods and pounded more seeds to powder. A small dose made the patient drowsy, a little more put him to sleep, too much killed him. I had to be careful. Slicing the sticky round nut ball in half, I scooped out the gooey filling, sprinkled in the purple powder, refilled the nut ball, and pressed it together.

The rumpled sentry outside the queen's door had long, angry-looking scratches down his left cheek. Inside, Queen Adela was sitting on her bed between Lady Tess and the second guard. Lady Olivia had wedged herself behind Her Majesty to keep her upright. Like the man's outside, all their faces were scratched. Somehow the three of them had managed to wrap a blanket about the queen's hunched shoulders while I was gone. One of Her Majesty's packed trunks had been opened and hastily gone through. We would certainly not be leaving Dragon's Keep tomorrow.

Queen Adela was breathing in great loud gulps. The blanket kept out the cold, but her racking shivers came from her core. I did not realize I'd halted to stand completely still, until Lady Tess gave an exasperated huff and motioned me forward.

I held out the sweetmeat. "Please eat this, Your Majesty. It will help you."

Queen Adela snarled. Lady Tess gave me a nod. Pulling the queen's mouth open, I popped the sweetmeat inside and made her chew it by cupping her jaw and moving it up and down. Queen Adela screamed into her closed mouth as I made her eat. I didn't like forcing her.

"It's all right," Lady Tess said. "You are not hurting her, Uma. She won't be as distraught the next time she comes to."

I wasn't sure that was true. I had treated the queen through many a strange mood. This was beyond me. Beyond all of us. She had never turned a knife on herself until today.

# CHAPTER NINETEEN

# Pendragon Summer Castle, Dragon's Keep

## DEATH OF EGRET MOON
### *August 1210*

W E KEPT CLOSE watch on her that night. The queen was too undone to attend chapel the next morn. Father Albus gave a short service by her bedside, and served Holy Communion.

The hours passed with painful slowness as I kept watch with Lady Olivia and Lady Tess. I slipped out when I had to mix more medicine for the king and queen. Always I hurried back.

By dusk a wild craving grew in me. I feared I would claw someone's face if I could not go outside and breathe some fresh air. There was no time to check on Sir Geoffrey's progress in the infirmary, no chance to find and speak with Jackrun.

The following day Queen Adela agreed to take luncheon with the king in his chamber. Afterward she strolled gingerly out in the walled garden with Lady Olivia on one side and me on the other. Guards followed so close behind I could almost feel them breathing down my neck, but I was grateful to be outside.

Queen Adela's face lit up for a brief moment when we'd passed the fountain. Kip was squealing happily on the sunny lawn, playing tug-of-war with Pippin. Her Majesty knelt down, patted the grass, and called, "Here, Pippin. Come here, boy."

Her lapdog was having too much fun to release his end of the rope. She stood again. "Bring him to me, Kip," she said sharply. Kip looked up and froze at the sight of her ghostly face. Dropping his end of the rope, he raced across the garden and through the gate on his short little legs.

"Come!" the queen demanded of her dog. Pippin whined as he inched closer, then rolled on his back and piddled all over his pink belly. Queen Adela grunted and pushed him away with her slipper. She nearly lost her balance doing it. Lady Olivia and I had to catch her by the elbows to keep her uptight. *I have overmedicated her,* I thought as we led her to a bench by the roses and sat her down.

I was feeling a velvety rose petal, wondering whether we should bring Her Majesty back inside, revolted at the thought of being shut up in her room again, when a servant rushed out, bowed briefly to the queen, and spoke to me. "You are wanted in the infirmary, queen's physician."

"Sir Geoffrey?" I said, pulling the petal so hard it came off in my hand. I regretted the name as soon as I'd said it.

"Geoffrey!" the queen said. "He was sent out to . . . to—" She looked confused.

"May I leave you for a moment?" I asked Lady Olivia, trying not to sound as urgent as I felt.

"Your duty is here and you know it."

"I won't be long." I left without her blessing, fearful of what I'd find when the guard led me through the weapons yard to the soldier's infirmary. Jackrun was already there with Father Ezra and a younger priest. He turned with a haunted look as I came in, his eyes ringed with circles over rough, unshaven cheeks. *Sir Geoffrey's dead,* I thought with a pang. Steeling myself, I stepped past Jackrun and saw the empty cot, the bloodstained sheets. "When did he die, Father Ezra?" I whispered.

Father Ezra shook his head, took up a candle, and motioned for us to follow him. When we reached a small still-room lined with medicine shelves adjoining the soldier's infirmary, the old priest bolted the door. "He did not die, Uma. He vanished sometime in the night. Brother Juniper has looked all around the castle and the grounds for him. Sir Geoffrey was near death. I did not think he could get far in his condition."

Father Ezra turned and held his candle closer to my face. "We have told no one else of this just yet. I wondered if you knew anything about this, Uma."

"Why would I know about it?"

"You seemed to care about him, coming here so soon after he was stabbed."

"To bring the woundwort, Father."

"Then it is safe to guess he left telling no one where he was going," he said with a sigh.

Brother Juniper blinked at Jackrun, at me. "I think he ran away out of fear for his life."

"His Majesty came down here last night demanding to see Sir Geoffrey," said Father Ezra.

"What did you do, Father?" I asked.

"What God would have me do. I protected the sick and did not let King Arden come near him, but I think Sir Geoffrey was awake enough to hear the king shouting in the outer hall. He must have crept away in the fourth watch of the night when I was at my prayers. He's not likely to live running off with such a deep wound."

Jackrun fingered a liniment jar on the shelf. "The king might see his running away as a confession of guilt."

"Was he guilty?" Father Ezra looked from Jackrun to me.

"It was an accident, Father," I said.

"You are sure, Uma?"

I breathed in the thick air laced with the scent of countless familiar and unfamiliar herbs and ointments.

"Sir Geoffrey tried to talk Prince Desmond out of jumping from the overhang onto dragonback," I said. "The prince refused to listen."

Father Ezra's penetrating eyes assessed me a moment. "I will go to Duke Bion with the news that Sir Geoffrey is missing, but not right away. I will wait a few hours more, you understand."

"Yes, Father." Guilty or innocent, Sir Geoffrey would be killed if King Arden caught him.

Father Ezra stopped Jackrun at the door. "And you agree with this plan, Jackrun?"

Jackrun gave a curt nod. "Meanwhile I'll search for him myself if you don't mind."

"Of course," said Father Ezra.

Jackrun slid the bolt aside, and left the stillroom. He didn't turn and wait for me as I'd hoped, but walked in a fluid motion across the weapons yard, disappearing into the stables.

Late that afternoon I mixed Her Majesty's fertility tonic. I doubted that she and her husband would bed together while they were both so grieved, but I couldn't risk letting her miss a single dose. At the very least the increased bapeeta I added to her potion would help to steady her. I was decanting the tonic when I heard someone coming up the stone stairs. A moment later I caught the scent of horses, of dragons, and knew Jackrun was at the doorway. I'd left the door ajar. It hadn't seemed as important to lock it now that Desmond was gone. I waited for him to speak as I poured the liquid through the strainer. He breathed heavily behind me as if he'd taken the stairs three at a time, which he likely had, knowing him.

The silence grew, then there were more footfalls, slower now as Jackrun started back down. I ran out onto the landing. "Jackrun?"

He turned with such a stricken look, I grabbed the iron railing. "What? What is it?"

He put a finger to his lips in warning, then sat down. I settled on a stair above his, the spiral staircase too narrow to wedge beside him without our bodies touching. It was chilly in this hollow place. The torches in the hallway below spread a dim, dun-colored light along the wall. I waited for him to speak, already wishing I had squeezed in next to him as I'd wanted to.

"Did you find Sir Geoffrey?"

He shook his head. "How is the queen?"

"She's in a bad way. I have to hurry back to her."

"You know what this does to me and my family?" Jackrun said. "Desmond was the only heir." I'd been so bound up with my work, so worried about the queen's health and what it meant for me, I hadn't taken time to think of what the death meant for Jackrun's future.

"I will help the queen have another child," I said.

"You have medicine for that?"

"It is what I've been treating her for all along. That and the condition of her mind."

He looked surprised. "She's not young anymore, Uma. Does she really think she can have more children?"

"She is about the same age as your mother, who bore Kip a little more than two years ago. She has to have a child now."

He rested his elbows on his knees, dangling his hands over the stairs. "I'll be future king if she doesn't have another child."

"Is that what you want?"

He said nothing for a moment. "The fey folk will be thrilled if I inherit. I used to think about it. What little boy doesn't dream of being a king?"

"Your wanting that when you were a child didn't make Prince Desmond die."

He curled his fingers inward, two fists hung in the air. "Babak blames you for what happened."

"Because I called out," I said with an ache.

Jackrun swallowed. "He's wrong. The wind blew my cousin off balance. I went to tell Babak so yesterday, but he wouldn't see me." So he'd gone to the dragons while I was penned up with the queen. Riding through the woods for the past day and night would explain his rumpled clothes, the new beard growth I'd seen earlier in Father Ezra's infirmary, and bramble scratches. He must have only just gotten back when he learned Sir Geoffrey was missing, and went riding off again to look for him. He scraped some dry mud off his boot.

The chill air felt as heavy as pond water between us. "There is something you're not telling me."

The mud he scraped off turned to powder. It filtered down to the stair below him. "My uncle looks for someone to blame for Desmond's death," he said. "People will begin taking sides now. The fey will stand behind the dragons."

"Will it come to that?" I asked, frightened.

"It already has."

I ran my fingers along the rough wall. "What should we do? What can we do?"

Silence.

Then Jackrun leaned his head close to mine. "It's not over yet," he whispered, his lips brushing my ear. I sat very still in the wake of his whisper, my ear tingling where his mouth touched it. "Uma?"

"Jackrun," I responded, not knowing what the question was.

He drew back and stood, gripping his dagger's jeweled hilt.

"Tell me you will keep your door locked from now on."

I swallowed, and managed a nod before I watched him descend toward the torchlit hall below, his shadow following after him.

## CHAPTER TWENTY

# Pendragon Summer Castle, Dragon's Keep

THE FAIRIES CAME that afternoon in a regal progression, bearing a thick glass coffin wreathed in wildflowers. I'd heard their pipes and drums and run to the window looking out.

Dragons flew over their solemn cavalcade in a V formation, Lord Kahlil in the lead with the copper-scaled sisters, Nahal and Sitara, behind him, a large green female and copper male flying in the rear. I didn't see Babak.

Hands still wet from scrubbing down my herber's table, I raced down the tower steps and out into the foreyard.

Through the gathering throng of soldiers and servants, I saw Jackrun by the portcullis gate, hands on his hips. Duke Bion, Lady Tess, and Tabitha came out the front door followed by Lady Olivia. I was surprised she'd leave the queen, but Her Majesty was asleep when I'd left her a short while ago and likely still was. More than a hundred people filled the foreyard, I guessed, many of them armed men. The dragons winged down and landed, clipping their talons on the crenellated walls, two on one side of the gatehouse, three on the other. *People will begin taking sides now. The fey will stand behind the dragons.* Babak blamed me for Prince Desmond's fall. Had the dragons and the fey sided with him? Would they draw me out? Accuse me? My skin felt strung tight as the fairies rode past the gatehouse playing their dirge. I pressed myself in among the curious servants as King Arden stepped outside.

The crowd parted. The piping and drumming ceased. King Arden's face was hard as packed earth as he took in the ornate cut-glass coffin meant for his son. Vines of inlaid gold and silver decorated the top and sides; gems sprouted from the vines like flowers.

The solemn fairy king dismounted and went to King Arden. His red-and-white silken robes fluttered like banners. He towered over the Pendragon king.

"Your Majesty," he said with a bow. "We have heard the news of the terrible accident. There are no words in our ancient language for such a terrible loss. Let our tears speak for us, our pipes and drums, our glass coffin inlaid with precious metals and gems, though there is nothing fine enough for the prince who left his life too soon."

Two fey guards placed the coffin on a rug they'd spread

on the ground near King Arden. It was too fine a thing to set upon the cobbles.

King Arden scowled down at it a moment.

"We dragons join you in mourning your loss, King Arden," said Lord Kahlil, in his gravelly dragon voice. "This fine coffin is also a gift from us. We breathed fire for the molding of the glass." He paused before going on. "We dragons wish that all be rightly done by the prince of Wilde Island now that he has passed from us." Smoke trickled from the dragonlord's nose. He whipped his tail against the wall with a slow slap, slap. The others did the same and it was louder and more unnerving than the fairy drums had been. I shrunk in amongst the crowd, glad Babak hadn't come, praying they wouldn't single me out.

Duke Bion said, "We thank you for your kind words, Lord Kahlil, and for your fire. We thank you too, King Morselid. We know you are doing all you can to help our family with this loss. This is a time of mourning for us all. This death was a terrible accident and no one is to blame. Prince Desmond would not want anyone punished for his accidental fall."

"How do you know what my son would want?" barked King Arden. "Where is the guard I sent to watch over my son on his outing? I have only just learned from one of my men that he has vanished from the infirmary. Run off like the guilty wretch he always was. Did he come running to you?" he demanded, turning to King Morselid. "Are you protecting him?"

The fey king looked offended. "We have seen no guard of yours, King Arden."

"Nor have we," said the dragonlord from the wall.

"And where is the dragon who was supposed to catch my son?" demanded King Arden, looking up. "Is he here to pay his respects, or is he hiding somewhere like a coward?"

Three things happened at the word *coward*. The dragons opened their jaws and roared a roof of fire over our heads, Lady Olivia ran inside screaming along with many others, and Jackrun raced across the courtyard, shouting, "How dare you call Babak a coward!"

I pressed my way forward through the guards, less afraid now for myself than I was for Jackrun, who might draw his blade on the king. But Duke Bion reached him first, pulled him back, and shouted, "Leave it alone, Jackrun!"

"Let the boy shout!" screamed King Arden, raising his fists under the fiery roof. "Let the dragons roar. My son is dead!"

One by one the fey horses bolted, racing madly through the portcullis gate. King Morselid mounted his black charger and rode after his people. The carthorses galloped out behind the king, the cart swinging to and fro behind them.

"Order here!" shouted the duke. "I will have peace and order on my castle grounds!"

The dragons took off all at once and flew toward the north woods.

My throat was dry, my body sweat-drenched in the nearly deserted yard. No one had pointed a finger at me. No one had mentioned that I'd cried out to Desmond in that last moment before he fell; still, I was shaking.

Jackrun stood red-faced and puffing hard like a man on the edge of battle.

I wondered if he would have fought for me if I had been named.

The dragon smoke cleared, revealing the pale green sky of early twilight. King Arden was slumped over by his son's coffin, his heavy breaths fogging up the glass. Lady Tess spoke. "We will bring Desmond's casket inside." She looked about. "Who among us will carry it inside for the king?"

Jackrun and his father stepped forward along with two of the king's men.

# CHAPTER TWENTY-ONE

## Cave,
## Dragon's Keep

WOLF MOON
*September 1210*

NEXT MORN THE rain swept in. I ran full tilt down the stormy beach. I'd dreamed of Sir Geoffrey, and I'd awakened knowing where to find him. When I arrived breathless, he was there in the cave the dream had shown me, sitting with his back against the wall.

I'd opened my herb pouch, then paused seeing the sharp blade in his hand.

He pointed it at me. "How did you know where to find me?" Angry lines traced his narrowed eyes and the edges of his mouth. I'd seen that furious glare aimed at Prince Desmond more than once; now he was giving me the same malicious look. I backed away.

"You think I would turn you in?" I said, "I told no one

where I was going. No one else knows where you are."
I regretted the words as soon as I'd said them. Now Sir
Geoffrey knew there was no one at my back if I needed help.

I drew my own knife out from under my sleeve, facing
him. "The priest, Father Ezra, kept your escape a secret as
long as he could," I said. "None of us want to see you killed.
But if you don't trust me at all, I will leave now and take my
food and medicine with me."

"I am trained to survive."

"So am I."

Kneeling at a distance from him, I unpacked the food,
water pouch, the herbs and salve I'd brought. "I will not
treat your wound at knifepoint."

He put the blade by his side, still within easy reach, I noticed. I slid mine back in its arm sheath and approached him.
The sweat on his skin glistened, giving his rigid face a strange
otherworldly glow. I removed his bandage and salved the
reddened skin around the sutures with the new woundwort
ointment.

It felt strange to use the yarrow I'd gathered the day
Prince Desmond fell to heal the knight King Arden blamed
for his death.

"You must do this twice a day. I do not think I will be
able to come back to attend to you."

"I wouldn't be here if you did." His face was hard, half
shadowed.

I took a few more steps back. "Where will you go?"

He looked at the cave wall seeing what I could not see.

I thought I had known this man. I realized I did not know him at all.

"It won't be long now before we set sail for Wilde Island." I paused, listening to the distant thunder as more rain swept in from the sea. The heavy downpour would soak me on my way up the beach as I headed back to the summer castle. "I have to go. The queen will need me again before long."

"Did Father Ezra say anything else?" he asked suspiciously.

I thought a moment. "He asked about Desmond's fall. If we were sure it was an accident."

Sir Geoffrey pushed himself up with his hands to lean against the cave wall. He gripped his knife again. "And you? What did you say?" His eyes were dark as sinkholes. The steady look made me back toward the cave entrance.

"I told him it was an accident." Father Ezra had not seemed completely satisfied with my answer. I didn't feel safe enough to tell that to Sir Geoffrey before I ran outside.

I was drenched when I reached the castle and was told to join the queen in the duke's presence room. With no time to run upstairs and change, I entered dripping wet and headed toward the hearth under Lady Olivia's critical eye. She considered herself responsible for me and disapproved of me coming in both late and wet.

The king and queen sat near the fire across from Duke Bion and Lady Tess. Jackrun and Tabitha were behind their parents. Jackrun's approving glance when I walked in was very different from Lady Olivia's. He too preferred outdoors to walled-in places and seemed to enjoy my damp wayfarer's look. But his pleasure was short-lived. A gloom lay over everyone. Only Kip seemed happy sitting with his mother, toying with the queen's red ball.

Pippin, opposite him on the queen's lap, looked jealously at Kip's toy, which by rights belonged to him. *I know the feeling,* I thought, staring at the Euit blanket on the wall. Hanging there for all to see; it felt like another part of my life was on display. My past, my people, my heritage nailed to the wall, held captive in this English castle.

I'd been staring over Jackrun's shoulder too long. He moved aside a little and was looking back at the blanket himself when his little brother slid down from Lady Tess's chair and crossed the great silent gulf on his short, stout legs, holding out the ball.

"Play doggie?" Kip asked. Queen Adela passed Pippin to Lady Olivia, swept Kip up, kissed him on the cheek, and sat him on her lap.

"You are looking rested, Your Majesty." Lady Tess spoke gently, as if she were addressing a frail old woman. Queen Adela didn't lift her gaze. She hummed to herself, wrapping one of Kip's brown curls about her forefinger.

The king said, "Kip eases my wife in our time of sorrow."

"I'm glad for it," the duke said cautiously. He and Lady Tess seemed to choose each word with care, as if knives were at their throats.

King Arden said, "My wife and I will leave tomorrow."

A wave washed through me. The sooner I could bring the queen safely home where she could rest and heal and have the child she wanted, the sooner the soldiers would leave my people. But a hollow spot ached below my breastbone when I thought of leaving Jackrun. No one had ever spoken to me the way that he had.

"Brother," said the duke. "I will order my men to provision your ship with whatever you need for a safe journey home. Jackrun will oversee the workmen."

"I expected you would do that for us, Bion. Now there is something else you will do for me and for my wife." I folded my hands behind my back, waiting for what else he might say.

"As you just said, Bion, you're glad your younger son gives my wife comfort. She sorely needs it now. You have three healthy children. As of this week, we have none." His eyes were dark flints. "We have decided to take Kip home with us. He'll be like a son to us, raised on Wilde Island with the best of care."

"No!" Lady Tess jumped out of her chair with such force she nearly knocked me into the fire. We steadied each other at the hearth before she gripped the mantel, sucking in a loud breath. "You cannot take my son away. He's two and a half years old."

Duke Bion came to a slow stand. "I know you're both in mourning, brother," he said. "But this would be wrong. He is our child. You cannot expect us to agree to this."

"You don't have to agree, Bion. I am king. I decree it. It will be done."

"Kip," Lady Tess said with a soft cry. "Come to Mommy, dear." She held out her arms.

Kip scrambled down from the queen's lap and went to Lady Tess. She swung him up. Thumb in his mouth, he rested his curly head against her shoulder.

Jackrun crossed the room and went down on one knee to the king. "Sire, let me go in my brother's stead. He's too young to . . . to travel," he stammered.

"Jackrun, don't," cried Lady Tess.

He kept talking, his dark head bowed. "I have always wanted to see our family home on Wilde Island. You won't have to sail home alone. Let me come and keep you both company, Your Majesty."

"Jackrun," his father cautioned, "you shouldn't have to . . . neither one of my sons should have to—" For once the eloquent duke could say nothing. Lady Tess clung to her little boy. The queen leaned over and whispered in her husband's ear.

"We'll leave you now," the king said.

"But what's your answer?" Jackrun asked, looking up.

The king scowled. "Not now, Jackrun. The queen is weary."

He helped his wife to a stand. Lady Olivia headed for the door. "Uma, bring Pippin with you, and follow us straightaway," she ordered. I went to fetch the lapdog from under the king's abandoned chair.

Lady Tess put her hand out toward Jackrun. "Come here, son." He went to her. So did her husband and daughter. The family gathered together by the fire as travelers huddle close in a storm.

# CHAPTER TWENTY-TWO

# Pendragon Summer Castle, Dragon's Keep

## WOLF MOON
*September 1210*

LADY TESS SENT a servant to fetch me later that evening and bring me to her solar. At the window the duchess looked out to the night sea. Her artist's studio was simply furnished. Brushes of all sizes bloomed from jars by the easel. It was comforting to see an English woman spending time on something she loved. Lady Tess had made her own choices defying convention as my mother had. If they ever met, I thought they could be friends.

One of the paintings along the wall showed Jackrun at age four or five building a sand castle on the beach with a smiling girl with startling features—green dragon scales across her forehead, golden eyes with dark slit pupils. I'd heard about King Arden and Duke Bion's younger sister,

Princess Augusta. She looked no more than five years older than her nephew Jackrun in the painting. The playful look on Jackrun's face reminded me more of Kip than of the Jackrun I knew now. I felt sad thinking that.

"They were very close," Lady Tess said.

"What happened to the princess?"

"She left us years ago." Her voice caught; her look told me to ask no more about the princess. These Pendragons had so many secrets.

"The king has made his decision," she said. "My older son leaves with your party on the ship tomorrow."

I felt a flutter of gratitude. I wouldn't have to say goodbye after all. But I masked my joy in front of her ladyship. Her son was leaving home. "Jackrun is strong to do this for his little brother, my lady."

We stood across from each other by the fire. "I know he's strong. That's not what worries me." She paused. "The first night you came here, Uma, I saw you on the beach. I know you saw Jackrun breathing fire."

She'd said nothing before this. Why bring it up now?

"You have told no one?" she asked.

"I promised Jackrun I wouldn't."

"Good." Her shoulders relaxed. "My husband and I don't think the king should know what our son can do. Not yet."

"Why? It is an admirable gift; a power only dragons have had until now. Your son has a great fire in him."

Lady Tess drew in a quick breath.

It was a strange thing to say. I didn't care. She'd asked me to her tower room knowing I would sail off with her older son tomorrow. If she wanted to know the way I viewed Jackrun's dragon power, I would tell her the truth. "Why should he have to hide it from the king and the queen?"

"The king views his dragon heritage differently than my husband does, Uma. He would not accept Jackrun's power."

*Do you?* I wanted to ask. "Jackrun seems to think he is dangerous. He wouldn't tell me why."

She sighed and took a chair, a deep sadness on her face.

"What did he do that was so terrible, my lady?"

"Fire is dangerous," was all she said. "It can kill."

"It also gives us warmth and light," I said.

Her hands were folded in her lap. I noticed her misshapen thumbnails again. Had they been crushed at some point? "Your thumbs, my lady—what happened? Forgive my asking."

"It happened when I was about your age. I didn't have a gifted healer like yourself to help me back then." She looked up. "The witch hunter used thumbscrews on me. Queen Adela wasn't always a queen, I'm afraid."

I leaned forward, heart pounding. "You were accused of witchcraft?"

Lady Tess gave the slightest of nods. "You must take care around the queen, Uma," she said at last, tucking her thumbs inside her folded hands.

"Do they still give you pain?"

"No. My injuries are light compared to some. Once, I met a half-fey girl who'd nearly burned to death in a witch pyre. Tanya was her name. A dragon flew in and rescued her before the fire killed her, but her flesh was so badly burned it's a wonder she survived."

"Tanya?" I thought of the dreadful night Queen Adela ranted about Tanya and the dragon who stole her. *Tanya has to burn!* she'd shouted. *Riders, bring the witch back to me!* "You said Tanya was half fey. Wasn't she also a witch?"

"Tanya was no witch, Uma, she was half fey like myself," Lady Tess said. "Adela had heard the fey song predicting that Prince Arden would wed a fairy's child, and she . . . well, she loved Arden and wanted to marry him herself, so she went about the countryside seeking half-fey girls out and . . ." Lady Tess glanced up and held me in her green eyes. She did not have to say *You know the violence of which Queen Adela is capable.*

The queen wouldn't hesitate to burn me if I failed her.

"There's a reason I asked you to come to me," Lady Tess said. "You cannot imagine my relief when Queen Adela agreed to leave my younger son with us here, but I've seen how fond she is of Kip, and I know her too well. I'm not sure she means to keep her word. If she should change her mind and send her husband's guards after Kip, we could not refuse her command. We would have no choice but to . . ." She took an uneasy breath. "I've watched you while you've been here, Uma. And we've worked side by side with the grieving queen. We are friends, I hope, even if we came together in the saddest of circumstances."

"Yes," I said, meaning it. *Never trust the English,* Father said. But I'd made some friends here on Dragon's Keep. I felt a flush of pride that this fine, independent lady considered me one.

"I need your help. I think you are the only one who can aid me tonight, but it is dangerous. I know you have the ability to creep through the castle unseen."

"My lady?"

"Don't worry. Your secret is safe with me. I understand the need to go out and breathe fresh air, the need to be alone. I broke the law and crept away to Dragonswood many a night when I was a girl. I met Prince Bion in Dragonswood while I was on the run from the witch hunter," she said. "There is something I need for you to do for me and my family." At that she leaned closer and told me what I had to do.


KIP WAS HEAVY with sleep when I took him from his cot, but he woke and whimpered as I headed down the passageway. "Hush now," I whispered, slipping into a dark alcove. "I bring you to your mother."

Kip's plump, sleepy weight made me awkward on my feet. My bulging shape with the blanket wrapped around us both made me appear round as a pregnant woman. I turned a corner and peered down the hall. Outside the queen's door, a sentry cleared his throat. The sudden noise made me jump. I wasn't sure now I could blend in carrying the heavy child past the queen's guards unseen. I turned back to find another way and was soon lost in an unfamiliar passage.

"Mommy?"

"Hush, Kip." I wrapped my arms tighter about him. "We're nearly there," I whispered, knowing it was a lie. Lady Tess trusted me with her little boy. Turning another corner, I stumbled on the base of a stairwell and gave quick thanks before climbing up. Lady Tess was tearing a sheet in long strips when I came in.

"Thank God," she said. "I was beginning to wonder." She took her child from me.

"Play game?" he said, bursting into a smile.

"Yes, we are going to play," she assured him, tousling his curly hair. Half asleep, he settled in again, sucking his thumb and laying his head on her shoulder. "You've done well, Uma. We haven't much time. Bind us together. I will only have one hand to hold him with."

I wrapped the long strip around them, tucked it between Kip's legs, and brought it around her back, crisscrossing the thick strips again and again, reminded of the years I'd bound my breasts.

Lady Tess tested my work, throwing out her hands and jumping up and down. Kip woke and laughed. "Again, Mommy." She jumped more until she satisfied herself that her son was securely tied.

"For you," she said, taking a package from her painting table. It looked too thick to be a painting.

"What is it, my lady?"

"Open it, Uma."

I undid the parchment and stared at the gift. She'd taken

the Euit blanket down from the wall, folded it neatly, wrapped it.

"I saw you looking at it and knew it belonged to you."

I was near tears. "My lady, I don't know what to say."

She turned, her eyes soft. "I see the trouble you're in, though you don't speak of it. You are leaving with my older son tomorrow, facing dangers I cannot imagine, but you are strong, Uma. I see that much."

She pulled the iron grille inward, secured it to the wall, and opened the tower window.

Wolf Moon hung thin as a brush mark over the sea. We waited for the sound of heavy wings. When they came, a great black shadow came with them and a warm wind that smelled of spice. Lord Kahlil flew at us like a piece of the night sky, deep and starless and heavy with life. He clipped his talons to the high ledge with a click-click, and folded his wings around the tower. We had saved two strips of sheeting tied together for this part.

I placed my Euit blanket on the table. "Do not be afraid, my lady," I said, tying the sheeting around her and securing the other end to the metal grill hook on the wall.

"This is one adventure of many." Lady Tess climbed up on the sill and paused. "Uma, thank you. Tell Jackrun—" She bit her lip. "Tell him good-bye for me. I could not risk going to the pier tomorrow. I hope he will understand what I had to do and why."

She climbed out onto the ledge and grabbed Lord Kahlil's leg. I held the sheet, letting it out slowly as she mounted the dragon, moving awkwardly with the weight of her son, then untied it and tossed the end to her once she was safely up. Lady Tess sat firm at the base of Lord Kahlil's long neck, one hand on his upturned scale, the other arm around her small son, whom she must steal to keep.

## CHAPTER TWENTY-THREE

# Ocean Voyage to Wilde Island

## WOLF MOON
### September 1210

J ACKRUN THREW OUT his hand and helped me over the wooden railing. "What are you doing up here, Uma?"

I climbed into the crow's nest high atop the ship's mast. "I could ask the same of you."

"I needed the exercise and the view," he said. "Did anyone spot you climbing up?"

"No." I steadied my feet and held the rail as we rocked to and fro high above the ship's deck.

I said nothing as he watched the vanishing island. I knew what it felt like to leave the home you loved. I had been dragged from mine. "Your mother sent her apologies for not coming to see you off."

"When did you talk to her?" he asked, surprised.

"Last night."

He turned and faced his disappearing isle again. "Do you know where she went with Kip?"

"No. But I saw her go."

A slow smile spread across his face as I told him how Lady Tess escaped with his little brother on Lord Kahlil.

"Of course the dragonlord would be in on it," Jackrun said. "The two of them have hatched more than one plan together. I used to slide down the old dragon's tail when I was Kip's age. He'd flip me in the air and catch me. It used to terrify my mother, but he always caught me. I never fell." He was smiling when he said it; we both looked over the edge, thinking of the one the dragon did not catch, the one who lay in the well-guarded coffin below deck. The silence drew out long between us. At last Jackrun said, "I knew why my mother stayed away. She was right to protect my little brother. I think my aunt would have tried to take Kip home with her."

"Queen Adela has wanted another child for years, Jackrun. She's tried many remedies and none of them have worked." My cloak felt too thin up here, where we clung and swayed like birds in a windy roost. I was glad we stood close enough for me to feel his warmth even if his scabbard pressed uncomfortably against my side.

"So you weren't the first to treat her with fertility potions?"

I shook my head.

"I hope no one offered her the cure Queen Gweneth used generations ago to have a child," Jackrun said.

"What cure is that?"

"The one that changed our family history." He looked at me. "You have heard of Queen Rosalind Pendragon?"

"The queen with a dragon's claw on her left hand."

"Her mother was barren for years. She tried everything to have offspring. Nothing worked. Finally she resorted to witchcraft." He leaned out a little farther. "A witch stole a fertile dragon's egg, put a spell upon it, made the queen drink the whole thing raw. After that she conceived her child, and later Rosalind was born."

"I don't believe it," I said with revulsion.

"It's true. It's how the dragon's bloodline entered our family."

For a moment I could not swallow. Of course a dragon had not taken a human for a mate. Of course it must have happened the way he said, but the one time I had sucked a raw egg, the slimy texture disgusted me. And a dragon's egg must be enormous compared to a hen's egg.

"I've heard many tales about your Pendragon family, but never that one."

"So the Euit tribe talks about us?"

"My mother did. She's English."

"You never told me that."

"You never asked." How sick the queen must have felt after drinking an entire dragon's egg. How desperate she must have been to do such a thing. Queen Adela was desperate too, but . . . "No one would risk stealing a fertile dragon's egg now. No one would dare to use spells on a former witch hunter who would burn them if she even suspected witchcraft."

"And so she takes your potions," Jackrun said.

"My father's potions," I corrected.

I caught the faint peppery scent of dragons, a smell I liked and was used to in him. I had always thought the hot tangy odor came from riding Babak so often. But they'd parted company after Desmond died.

The setting sun colored the sky and water, the billowing sails, Jackrun's face and chest. Crimson light filled my open hands as I leaned my elbows on the rail. Jackrun traced the long white scar on my left hand ending halfway up my middle finger.

"Cuts your lifeline in half," he said, frowning with concentration. "When did this happen?"

"When I was small. I tried to shuck an oyster and missed . . ."

When I did not cry, the chieftain had said I was strong, called me mi tupelli—my lad. Everyone loved what the chieftain loved, admired what he admired. For the first time in my life I felt accepted by the tribe, acknowledged for my courage. I hadn't wanted to lose their admiration, so I adopted the name. I became mi tupelli, a lad, a boy, my father's apprentice.

Jackrun's face was still washed in scarlet light, the hue of Vazan's scales. The color fed his fiery eyes. I said, "The knife was too sharp. The cut was deep. People marveled at my courage when I did not cry. It was . . . an accident. It changed everything."

We both peered down as if we could see the coffin below deck.

"Accidents can . . . change everything," Jackrun said. "But I wonder." He stopped and bit his lip, his teeth covering the tiny scar Prince Desmond made as he bit the words he'd nearly unleashed.

"Wonder what?" I asked. He released his lip, swallowed. The chill air between us felt thick the way it had when we'd talked in the stairwell. There was something he wasn't telling me, something he was holding back.

"Jackrun?" a knight called up from the deck far below.

Jackrun tugged my arm, making me duck down. "Yes?" he called. I crouched low with my cheek nearly touching his knee. The crow's nest smelled of men's boots and pitch down here.

"The king wants you," the knight bellowed.

Jackrun pulled my hood back over my head. "Will you stay low until well after I am gone?" he whispered. "We shouldn't be seen alone together."

I craned my neck at his silhouette framed in red-streaked sky. "Why not?"

He pressed his lips together, shaking his head.

"Come down," the knight shouted. "The king will not be kept waiting."

Jackrun swung his leg over the side and disappeared.

I hugged my knees in the rocking crow's nest as the sky dimmed from red to bruised purple to inky blue. There was no sign of Dragon's Keep by the time I stood again;

only dark sea and darker sky. The waxing Wolf Moon hung sharp as a sliver of broken eggshell over the sea. I thought of queens desperate for children, of fertile dragon eggs, of the dead prince in his glass coffin, the fragmented Pendragon family, the last look Jackrun gave me before he'd climbed down the ropes taking his secrets with him, and the moon did not seem the only thing that was broken. Everything seemed broken. All of it.

# PART TWO

## Broken

# CHAPTER TWENTY-FOUR

## Graveyard, Wilde Island

I RARELY HAD the chance to speak more than a few hasty moments with Jackrun in those first two weeks back at Pendragon Castle. He was caught up in Desmond's funeral preparations, while I raced from the queen's rooms to the herbarium and back again. Summer was over. September rains drenched the land, pounded on the windows, great puddles filled the foreyard. And the wolves were in their time of power. Rain didn't stop them.

At the full Wolf Moon a feral pack attacked a shepherd's son and killed him as he tried to defend his sheep. They found his torn body amid the sheep's carcasses. Packs were flooding the byways, decimating livestock up and down the countryside. Fear spread through Pendragon Castle like disease. King Arden ordered me to sprinkle wolfsbane across the drawbridge. Father Nicodemus held special prayer services. "Are you all right?" Jackrun whispered on his knees beside me in the chapel.

I nodded. "When can we talk?"

"Where can we talk?" He looked about.

That was two days ago. I hadn't seen him since.

Our brief encounters only made me want more. It was hard to mix the queen's medicines with thoughts of Jackrun crowding in. Wait until the prince is buried, I thought. I began chewing my nails again. In the brief hours when the deluge stopped, I peered out windows hoping to glimpse Vazan. She never appeared.

She was my father's dragon. Why should I expect her to stay here in the north with me? Then one afternoon two and a half weeks after we'd returned, I spied her from an upstairs window. The sight of her winging down to Father's grave made me want to shout, *She's here! She stayed!* I didn't have much time. I crammed Father's Herbal in my basket, threw on my cloak, raced down the tower stairs and out a servant's side door.

It was drizzling outside. Clouds obscured the sun one moment, split open like rotting fruit spilling light through the next. I passed the Pendragon tomb and climbed the hill.

Vazan crouched by Father's grave. Tail curled around her clawed feet, she eyed me as I came along and shook the raindrops from her head, her scales making the soft crackling sounds of newborn fire. I bowed to her. "We are being in this place together," I said in formal Euit greeting. I fought the urge to touch her claw as one reverenced an elder. She had never let me touch her.

"So you are come back, Uma."

"I have, rivule." I looked up and saw a flicker of approval at the word *rivule*—warrior. Wet wind blew back my cloak. I shivered.

Vazan narrowed her eyes. "Why are you wearing this frivolous English gown? It does not suit your station as a healer." I was still in scribe's clothing the last time we'd met here at Father's grave.

"I cannot help it, Vazan. The queen makes me wear it. And I agree. It doesn't suit, it—"

"Humph!" she said smokily. She didn't like excuses. Neither did I.

I raised my hand; the bell-shaped sleeve slid down, revealing the knife strapped to my upper arm. "Think of it as my battle garb, rivule. I wear it to do my job."

She gave a sharp appreciative nod.

I ran my palm across the tops of the thigh-high weeds on Father's grave, feeling a tugging in my heart. Hundreds upon hundreds of islanders had streamed past Prince Desmond's ornate glass coffin in St. John's Cathedral. Nobles, merchants, and peasants wept over him. Crowds marched behind the drummers, following the costly funeral procession through Dentsmore and up Kingsway Road to the Pendragon tomb. Meanwhile, the weeds had flourished on the Adan's grave as if he did not matter. As if he had been no one.

"Did the Pendragons across the water show their dragon scales?" Vazan asked testily.

I thought of Jackrun's arm scales, flashing in the sunlight when he sparred in the practice yard. Of the moment the dragon Nahal tugged the lace scarf from Tabitha's neck, *You do not need thissss*, and freed the lovely blue-green scale patch underneath. "Yes, they did, rivule."

Her look of pleasure was so fleeting, I barely caught the roundness of her silver eyes, the easing of her jaw before it vanished again. I wanted to remember the look. It was so rare.

"And the prince is in a box," she noted.

I cringed at her rough description. Dragons burn their dead and do not understand human burial. "A glass coffin the fey folk and the dragonlord made for him. Now he is laid to rest in a stone sarcophagus in the Pendragon family tomb." I jerked my head toward the stone tomb down the hill, large as a church with its round stained-glass window over the thick double doors.

"Very English," she hissed. "I do not understand the dragonlord's help in this," she added.

"He . . ." I paused, wanting to describe Lord Kahlil, the elder dragon who had greeted me in Euit my first night on Dragon's Keep, who'd whisked Lady Tess and Kip from the tower. I knew he had helped make the glass coffin to appease King Arden's wrath so he wouldn't turn on Babak and blame him for his son's death. "He did it to protect his own."

"And what have you done to protect your own?" Vazan asked.

"What?"

Vazan's narrowed eyes were thin as a line of light seeping

under a door. "How is your work with the queen? Is her belly rounding yet? Will she keep her promise to us and re-move the soldiers from our lands if she has her child?"

"I believe she means to keep her promise, but—"

"Yessss?"

"I don't know what she remembers anymore, Vazan. Her mind is worse now she's lost her son."

Vazan licked her extended talons until they shone black as polished boots, then she looked up again. "Concentrate on the king and get close to him."

"What do you mean by . . . close?" I asked, offended.

"I do not mean for you to spoil your virtue, Uma." She flicked out her forked tongue. "You are the Adan's daughter."

"Then what do you mean, Vazan?"

She clicked a talon on my handmade driftwood head-stone. "You tell me the mad queen is worse. It is the king's army who keeps your people captive. If King Arden suffers any pain, use your skills to heal him. Earn his respect, re-membering he is the one who holds the power."

Vazan's wits were as sharp as her teeth. "It is good coun-sel you give me, rivule."

She had grown too thin these last few months. The scales stretched tightly over her chest made her breastbone stand out like a ship's keel. "How long since you have eaten, Vazan?"

She held up five talons. Her last kill must have been small. A larger beast would hold her for a week, even two, but she didn't like the taste of the game she caught on Morgesh Mountain. "You could try hunting in Dragonswood."

"I am a free red," she huffed. "I will not fly over that prison."

"It is not a prison. It is a sanctuary."

"I will never land inside those wallssss!"

I cleared my throat and adjusted the heavy herb basket under my cloak. "I need your help, Vazan."

"Who do you need killed?" she asked, lowering her head with renewed interest.

"No one killed, rivule. I wouldn't ask you to break the dragon treaty."

"No red has killed or eaten men since the treaty was signed and Dragonswood walled in, but there are wayssss to do things secretly if you need them done, Uma. Bodies can be hidden."

"No one killed," I said again. "Something found. The plant called bapeeta. The one you brought back with the Adan to cure the queen's wind mind." I was completely out.

Vazan fixed her eyes on a flock of geese, easy treats for her to catch midair, if small. She was bored with the way the conversation was going and did not like being out in the drizzle. I would have to hurry before I lost her to the sky.

"The Adan drew the plant in his Herbal."

"I am no herbalist. That is man's business."

"And woman's," I corrected, pulling Father's book from my basket. I did not open it yet, fearing the ink would run in the soft rain. Vazan unfurled a wing, sheltering me so I could show her the page.

She huffed smoke as she peered down at Father's drawing; her gray breath ghosted over me as I held up the book.

"Do you remember where you took the Adan for this herb? Can you fly me there, Vazan?" I tried to sound calm as I asked her. Just saying the word *fly* sent tingling sensations across my tongue and sharpened my desire.

"You wish to pluck thissss?" she said, pointing to the ink drawing with her smallest talon.

"Yes, as much as we can as soon as we can. Everything depends upon my curing the queen."

"Giving her an offspring, not curing her wind mind."

"Both, Vazan. The king cannot go to his wife's bedchamber when she is raving."

"Humans," she said. "You fear emotions as if they had claws and teeth."

"Nevertheless."

She tipped her head and made a clicking sound with her tongue. "It is the king's duty more than ever to get an heir on her now his son is dead." She shut Father's Herbal, pinching it between two talons. Then she withdrew her wing and gave a low growl. Ears flattened against her scaly head, she lifted her snout, sniffed the air, and took off, letting out a screech like a thousand angry cats.

# CHAPTER TWENTY-FIVE

# Graveyard, Wilde Island

## WOLF MOON
*September 1210*

JACKRUN STEPPED OUT of the copse down the hill. Vazan must have scented him. So that was why she'd taken off, screeching. He climbed toward me in his fighting gear, a short sword strapped to his side.

I tucked Father's book deep in my herbing basket and shouldered it again.

Jackrun looked around, making sure we were alone before he glanced skyward. It had stopped drizzling. "A beautiful red," he said. "Desmond mentioned your father's red dragon. I've never seen that breed before. I wish she'd stayed." He hooked his thumb in his belt still looking up. "Desmond claimed he rode her once," he added.

"No one but my father has ever flown with her," I said. "Vazan is a free red."

"Vazan." He tasted the name and toed the grass with his

boot. "I was pretty sure Desmond lied about it. And the other dragon, the one he mentioned?"

"We just buried your cousin. Why does any of that matter now, Jackrun?"

"It matters, Uma. He told us he'd ridden dragons often before he tried to jump. If that's not true, I want to know."

"Desmond didn't lie about riding the other dragon, the one called Sorgyn that used to live near the king's stables." He'd seemed to care for the beast, bringing him prized meat slices from the kitchen.

"Where did Sorgyn go? No sign of any dragons near the stables now."

I pointed toward the dragon-sized mound by the yew.

"They . . . buried him?" He shuddered. "That's not right. Dragons burn their dead."

"Sorgyn didn't live as other dragons do. He lazed about and ate kitchen scraps. Vazan would have nothing to do with him when he died. She called him a winged pig. She refused to waste her fire on him to give him proper dragon rites."

"I don't blame her." Jackrun hurled a stone at the bushes. Starlings burst upward in a black shawl and flew toward the distant orchard on the grounds above Pendragon Castle.

Jackrun turned and read the name I'd carved on the driftwood headstone. "Estruva Quarteney. Adan—Healer. So *Adan* means 'healer'?"

I nodded, my head feeling too heavy for my neck.

"What happened to your father? How did he . . ." Jackrun cleared his throat. "Did Desmond do something, I mean did he . . . ?"

"Kill him?" I said. "No." I looked down, remembering the moment I found Father's body. A distant raven's caw broke the silence that had stretched out between us.

"I know my cousin's death has made your task that much harder," Jackrun said. "Her Majesty wanted a child, now she relies on you to help her have an heir. You had good reason to keep Desmond alive."

"I also had reason to want him dead. I was his dog to kick around at court. In private he liked to watch me being whipped. And . . . other things."

Jackrun clenched his fist. "The bastard. He never . . . overpowered you? He didn't—"

I shook my head. "I managed to fight him off. The one time he nearly . . . you crashed through the window and knocked him flat."

"I was glad to do it. The best cut arm and split lip I've ever had." He licked his lip, dropped his brows. "If you had told me *why* you needed the key—"

"How could I? A girl does not speak of such things." *Neither in my village nor in the English court.* "And we had only just met. I hardly knew you."

"You know me better now," he said.

I looked at him, wondering how much I really knew.

He was studying the name again. "Your father must have been proud of you," he said. "Are there many female healers where you come from?"

His question was too close to the wound of truth. "My father wanted a son to train up as was our custom."

"But he didn't follow custom himself."

"What?"

"Well, is it customary for an Euit healer to marry an English woman?"

I shook my head, gripped the folds of my blue velvet skirts. The gown was far more costly than my mother could have ever afforded growing up as an ironmonger's daughter. Jackrun was staring.

"I'm guessing your mother's a redhead."

"How do you know?"

"Sometimes the torches or the sun catches red highlights in your black hair."

I knelt, hoping my dark skin would guise my blush as I pulled weeds from the edge of the grave.

There was so much Jackrun didn't know about me. From the beginning he'd assumed I had chosen to serve as the queen's personal physician. That it was an honor I had wanted, perhaps even fought for. I'd let him think that, liking the respect it lent me. But I shouldn't let him believe any of those lies here at my father's grave. Here, if anywhere, I should tell the truth. "Father and I were abducted and brought here against our will, Jackrun."

"What?"

I pulled more weeds. He fell on his knees across the grave from me, yanking up weeds there and tossing them to my growing pile. "Tell me," he said.

"The queen heard about my father's fertility cure and wanted it, wanted him to treat her. She did not invite him to come north. She sent her husband's army down to capture him. She left an army there to hold the tribe captive until he succeeded. After he died—" My hand froze in a stranglehold around the weed stems. "After that, she kept me in her service. My father's tonics work better than those of her other physicians. They calm her moods, ease her stomach—the powder takes away her pain. She knows the Adan's medicines are powerful. She's willing to wait a little longer for his miracle cure to work. She won't let me go home until she is with child."

"Why didn't you tell me this before?"

I wanted to put my face against the earth. "I wasn't ready yet."

Jackrun started digging too, not just pulling. "She sent an army down," he said, fishing for more.

I told him about the day the king's army rode into our village. I dug deeper, more savagely, avoiding his eyes as I detailed the terrors, Prince Desmond slashing an elder's throat, the soldier killing my uncle in front of my father and me, our miserable trip north in the jail cart.

Jackrun's breath grew louder as he listened. Smoke trickled from his nose. Before I was done, he turned aside, a retching sound lengthening to a roar. The fire that poured from his mouth was silver orange as molten metal. Damp as the weed pile was from the morning drizzle, the weeds hissed and caught fire.

We did not speak for a long while. The crackling sounds of his fire filled my ears, the heat warming me. I could not burn away the ugly memories I'd just revealed to him, but his angry fire helped heal the ache.

"Sorry," he said, nodding at the fire.

"Don't be sorry. I wanted it. I needed it. It . . . helps."

He shook his head half in disbelief. "Do you mean that?"

"I do."

We watched the blaze blowing sideways now in the breeze. "You sound like my aunt Augusta. She didn't mind my fire either."

I thought of Lady Tess's painting of the girl and boy on the beach. "Where did she go?"

He shook his head. "She never told us where. Just somewhere far from us." He threw a hard glance toward the castle. "When you have so much dragon in you, it's almost impossible to live walled in with other people."

*He's speaking about himself*, I thought, wiping my hands on the damp grass.

Jackrun stomped out the flames and dumped the remains of the burned weeds behind the nearby bushes. Returned and took my arm to help me up. His hand clasped the blue velvet a moment longer, feeling the blade strapped under my sleeve. "Good," he said before letting go.

"Do you mean the gown or the knife?"

"Both."

I smoothed my soft skirts. I'd told Vazan the gown was fighting gear. But just now I was glad I wasn't dressed as mi tupelli, or in scribe's clothing. Some part of me liked how the dress pleased him.

"So raw," Jackrun said, looking at my red fingertips where I'd chewed the nails down to the quick. "You are worried," he added.

I was always worried, but less so when he was near me. I couldn't tell him that.

Jackrun said, "Uma, I have to go. They're expecting me in the weapons yard. I've stayed too long already. Don't head back right away," he added. "It's better if we are not seen together."

"Why?" I asked, hurt. "You said that once before when we were on the ship and didn't tell me why."

"Uma, just . . . Will you meet me this time tomorrow?" He pointed downhill to the grove he'd emerged from earlier. "In the trees. We can talk then. Maybe then I can, we can . . ." He did not seem able to finish. He left me with dirt on my hands, questions in my mouth, a dull aching behind my eyes. He was gone before I could argue more.

## CHAPTER TWENTY-SIX

# Elm Grove, Wilde Island

### WOLF MOON
*September 1210*

THE NEXT DAY, I found Jackrun in the elm grove. The sentries on the outer curtain wall could not see us through the foliage. *This is why he wanted to meet here,* I thought as he saw me approach. The air was heavy with the threat of storm, but for once it wasn't raining.

"Uma?" he said. A greeting and a question both.

"Jackrun." I drew back my hood, the chill September air nipping my cheeks. I was late to meet him, too busy with the queen to get away until the last moment. I feared I'd miss him, but he waited. He was dressed in fighting gear, sword and all.

"What do you remember about the day Desmond fell?" he asked.

"I don't like thinking about that day."

"Do you think it was an accident?"

"Yes, of course. What else could it have been?"

"Murder."

"Murder? It's not possible. We saw it happen in front of us. No one pushed him off or—"

"A very clever murder," he said again.

"No." I stepped back and leaned against an elm trunk for support, pressing my hands against the coarse, ridged bark.

"Tell me you didn't feel something wrong about that day," Jackrun said, his eyes boring into me. "Tell me what made you come to Faul's Leap in the first place."

"I . . . It was the last day of Egret Moon. A treacherous time some elders call the Murderous Moon. I knew you were all going to Faul's Leap. I sensed something might happen there."

He nodded. "Something like murder."

"Not murder, not especially murder, just . . . something bad. Some mishap. What happened was an accident," I said again more firmly. "Prince Desmond stood at the edge, Jackrun. He insisted on trying the leap. You tried to warn him. Even Sir Geoffrey stepped out to try and stop him."

"But do you remember what he said?" Jackrun asked.

I closed my eyes a moment. "I think so."

"I remember all of it," Jackrun said, "because it concerned me at the time and I've thought about it ever since. He said, *You should not take such a risk. You do not have the skills or training to do it.*"

Jackrun leaned against a tree across from me, bent his knee, and rested the sole of his boot on the trunk. "If anyone said that to me, I would have jumped to prove him wrong. I think he said it so Desmond would defy him, and jump."

"Why?"

"I think Sir Geoffrey wanted him dead." Jackrun crossed his arms. "I have an idea why." He frowned. "But I'm hoping it has more to do with the way Prince Desmond threatened Sir Geoffrey the day he broke up our fight. When he turned on him and said, *Breathe a word of this, and I'll let what I know about you slip, and you'll be hanged for your own filthy sins.* You remember how he said that and how Sir Geoffrey blushed crimson?"

"Would that be reason enough to kill Desmond?"

"If what he knew was vile enough to get Sir Geoffrey hanged, I'd say so."

I thought of the spit boy they'd hanged for murder before we left for Dragon's Keep. "There was a murder here at Pendragon Castle before we left."

"What? Who was killed?"

"A lute player. His throat was slit. An innocent boy hanged for the crime."

"How do you know the boy was innocent?"

"I saw him after the palace guards tortured him. He'd confessed on the rack just to make the pain stop, but he didn't do it, I'm sure."

"If Prince Desmond knew Sir Geoffrey killed the lute player, that would be a compelling motive for Sir Geoffrey to—"

"Wait. Now you're accusing Sir Geoffrey of not just one murder, but two."

"I'm looking for a strong motive, Uma, otherwise . . ." He paused, glancing at some twisted roots.

"Otherwise what?"

A silence had fallen on him. I thought of Sir Geoffrey, weighing the broad-shouldered knight who'd rescued Father and me from starvation against the one who'd informed on me later, telling Lady Olivia he'd caught the prince embracing me in the ship's galley. Then there was the man I saw in the cave, the man who'd threatened me with his knife; he'd kept his blade close even after he knew who I was, as if . . . as if, what? As if he was more than ready to kill me if he thought I'd give him away?

My eyes fell on Jackrun's dagger. I shivered, remembering Sir Geoffrey's feral look. The man was trained to survive. Prince Desmond knew something vile enough to get the man hanged. Had he killed to keep him silent?

"There is something you should know. I saw Sir Geoffrey once after he ran off."

Jackrun stepped in front of me. "You found him? Where? How?"

"I don't know how to explain. I had a dream. I packed food and medicines, and when I went to the cave the dream had shown me, he was hiding there."

"You are not only a healer; you are a seer, Uma Quarteney." I heard the awe in his voice.

"I am not a seer. It felt like"—I rubbed my damp hand on my skirts—"like Sir Geoffrey drew me there himself."

"You mean by some power?" Jackrun asked, his expression changing. "Yes . . ." He reached up and plucked a leaf. "That's what I've been afraid of. There's another reason Sir Geoffrey may have killed my cousin, a more radical one—something to do with me." He took a long breath and heaved it out. "I'd rather not believe that, but if the man had the power to draw you to him . . ." He stared at the elm leaf veined with autumn's gold and green.

"What?"

His head was still bent. Dark hair covered his forehead and eyes. "He would have needed some kind of magical power to bring you to him when he needed your medicine, Uma, powers like the fairy folk have." He looked up, his face wary now as a hunted creature caught outside its lair. "I think Sir Geoffrey was fey. He could have killed my cousin acting under orders."

"Fey? Why would the fey want to kill Desmond? Who would give him such orders anyway?"

"My grandfather Onadon, for one. I think he wanted Desmond out of the way so I would inherit the crown. If the fairies devised a way to remove Prince Desmond, it would put me in line for the throne."

He tore the elm leaf in his hand down the middle, renting the heart-shaped leaf in two.

We'd talked before about the fairies' hopes for Jackrun,

Son of the Prophecy. I tried to imagine Sir Geoffrey involved in such a plot. "But Sir Geoffrey did not even look fey."

"He could have used glamour magic to guise himself. Even the broken nose could have been a guise."

"The king trusted him enough to give him the responsibility of keeping an eye on Prince Desmond," I argued.

"Or the clever Sir Geoffrey convinced the king to entrust him with that job, waiting for his moment to set up a murder and make it look like an accident."

I took off, walking right then left in the pathless glade, the trees crowding in on me.

"Uma?" Jackrun called. I ran.

Jackrun caught up with me at the edge of the knoll where tree roots met the grass in the graveyard. He stopped and waited, breathing hard behind me.

A watery sun came out above. "I don't want to talk about murder anymore."

"We have to," Jackrun said. "I need to."

I turned and saw him framed by woven branches. Copper leaves fluttered in the breeze behind his back. "How long have you been thinking this way without telling me?"

"We've both been busy since we arrived here. Tell me you weren't."

"I was, but—"

Jackrun stepped closer. "I'm not here to convince you. Only we must talk together and share what we know."

I swallowed; his closeness drove argument from my mind. I blinked at his strong, resolute face in the half-light of the autumn sun and tried to regain my footing. "I don't think Sir Geoffrey could have killed the lute player. Whatever sins Prince Desmond knew about, whatever offenses the knight committed, I don't think it was that."

"So there could be more than one murderer about," Jackrun said.

"Or the same murderer?"

"How? There wasn't anyone else up there with us that day."

"I know, but . . ." I was trying to remember something. What was it?

"I still don't want to believe it was murder," I said.

"I knew you would argue with me about it. I wanted you to. Part of me still hopes it isn't true, because if the fey committed the murder, then it was done for me, because of me."

A gust blew up the hill; he fingered his sword hilt, looking left and right as if preparing for action, but there was just the two of us using sharp words that hurt in bloodless ways. "I've wondered about Lady Olivia."

"What?" I asked, startled. "Why ask about her?"

"I noticed her speaking with Sir Geoffrey a lot. She and Sir Geoffrey both seemed very interested in my cousin. She kept a close eye on him."

"Lady Olivia had every reason to keep the prince safe," I said. "She was hoping her daughter, Bianca, would marry the prince and become the next Pendragon queen."

"Oh," Jackrun said, raising a brow. His face changed. "Bianca. I've noticed her."

"You could hardly have missed her."

"That's true," he agreed.

I clamped my jaw a moment. Bianca and the prince had seemed happy together. She was giddy the day he'd generously given her one of the loveliest chestnut mares in the king's stable. She wept when she learned he was dead and had come to me often, begging for evicta to ease her headaches.

"So we are back to where we began," Jackrun said.

I thought of Sir Geoffrey's words on the cliff. "I can see how Sir Geoffrey could have insulted Desmond's pride so he would want to jump to prove himself. Still, we all agreed it was the wind that pushed him off the cliff in the end."

Jackrun was silent a moment. "That wind was the thing that got me thinking of murder to begin with," he said. "Do you remember how it felt? The sudden power of it? The smell of it?"

"Yes," I whispered. "The wind smelled different—not a sweet summery scent of August, but a thick smell, like pungent rotting leaves. And it blew in so powerfully, I called out a warning."

"My cousin was on the edge. A blast of wind was all that was needed to push him off, and the fey have power to stir the wind."

"But," I said, beginning to believe. "Sir Geoffrey was standing there with us. We would have noticed him doing it, wouldn't we?"

"He stood *behind* us," Jackrun reminded.

I fingered my embroidered waist pouch. "Can you . . . stir the wind?"

He tipped his head to the side and closed his eyes. Fingers spread, he moved his raised hand to and fro. Nothing happened at first. I felt a small dip of disappointment, then the leaves began to speak in whispers, a soft, cool breath crossed my skin. It was not human breath. No ordinary wind either, a green scent of living magic on it.

Elm leaves trembled, some flew off the branches and twirled down to my feet. As more spun down, Jackrun plucked a coppery leaf from the air, put it in my hand, and curled my fingers around it. He kept the other hand moving, wind swirled around me, finding its way under the eaves of my clothes, the walls of my skin until it hushed and the last of the green and golden leaves shuddered at my feet.

"I cannot make more than a small breeze like that," Jackrun said. "Tabby can stir up a gale," he added.

"And she hated him."

"What do you mean by that? Tabby would never—"

"I didn't mean to imply she'd stirred up the fey wind that day. Only you said she had the power to stir the wind. I'm sure she would rather see you, her brother, on the throne than her cousin who insulted her."

"Of course he insulted her! He insulted everyone. Tabitha might have girlish dreams, wrong ones, but she would never commit murder and neither would Griff. No matter how much fey power they have, no matter how much they care for me."

"Yes, of course, but this whole idea of murder . . ." I took a breath and looked out at the graveyard. "You told me you knew I would argue with you about it. I have questions now and you have to let me ask them."

"This was my free hour before I fight in the weapons yard. I'm expected back now. I can't stay much longer."

"Wait. You said your grandfather might have ordered Prince Desmond killed so you would inherit the throne, but that won't happen if Queen Adela has another child."

He studied my face a moment. "Yes, that would end their plans."

My mouth went dry. "Do you think the queen might be in danger?"

"They wouldn't risk killing her, Uma. Then my uncle could remarry a younger woman and sire an heir through her. I think she is safe for now. But you should watch out for yourself. Trust no one in the castle."

The elm leaves stirred again. We drew back, looking up, then he whipped his head around, hand on his hilt before saying in a hushed whisper, "I'll come to you again when it's safe to talk."

"I will want to argue more."

"I'm counting on that." Jackrun turned to go.

"Wait, take this." I pulled the small hand-sewn pouch I'd made the night before from the purse at my waist and held it out to him by its long leather straps.

"What is it?"

"I sewed wolfsbane inside. Wear it around your neck."

Jackrun slipped it on. "I used to carry wolfsbane back home." He pressed the calfskin pouch to his nose, breathing in the pungent scent.

"This bane is fresh," I said. "But it's not much against the feral packs in Wolf Moon. I have seen you ride out alone sometimes, you—"

"You watched me?" he asked, lowering the pouch, revealing a crooked smile. "From what window?"

"I . . . The stables are—"

"Don't worry." He reached up and brushed his thumb slowly across my lower lip in one smooth movement like a golden pour of honey. I held very still, hoping that if I did not move, said nothing, he would trace his thumb along my lip again. He gave me an intense look that said *Take care,* and other things I hoped to read but could not because it was not English or Euit or any language I yet knew.

He stepped through the leaf pile he'd made with his fey wind, and passed the moss-winged angel as he headed down the hill.

# CHAPTER TWENTY-SEVEN

# Pendragon Castle, Wilde Island

## WOLF MOON
### *September 1210*

I DIDN'T SLEEP well that night, picturing Desmond's fall again and again. The word *murder* whispered across my flesh, making the hairs along my arms stand up.

Part of me wanted to argue with Jackrun further. Another part had remembered something else in the dark, wakeful night.

I dressed quickly, mixed the queen's medicines so her brew was already cooling before she returned from morning mass. But my hurry made no difference at all. Jackrun had ridden out at dawn to visit a friend of his father's on his lands down south, and would not be back until the morrow.

Annoyed at his disappearance, I left the queen in Lady Olivia's care once my morning duties were done, and went again to Father's grave. A crisp clear day. Perhaps Vazan would come? She hadn't promised to meet me on the hill with the bapeeta leaves. She'd not even agreed to look for them before she'd winged off in a huff the other day; still, I paced the frosty ground below Father's grave, grumbling to myself, raw with lack of sleep.

After a few hours, I left the graveyard, hands empty, stomach empty.

The smell of fresh-baked bread drew me to the kitchen. Cook was pulling loaves from the brick oven on long paddles and setting them on the table. I'd not tasted bread before I'd come north, but I knew how much my mother loved it. She'd lived alone in town with her father the ironmonger. As a girl she'd cradled fresh loaves in her arms, racing home from the baker's shop to present them to her father warm. I thought of her as I sat on the long bench to take a meal with the kitchen staff, and buttered a steaming slice. My mother had had nowhere to go when her father died until the midwife took her in and trained her.

I ate here in the kitchen when I wasn't too rushed and had to take the meal to my room. The hardworking staff was friendly in a rough way that I admired. Today I longed to warm myself with soup, fill my emptiness with Cook's good bread, lose my worries a moment listening to stories. The raucous tales exchanged in Cook's kitchen were nothing like the ones I'd heard back home when the people encircled the fire. Still, they brought to mind the happy hours when Mother, Father, and I joined the tribe, listening to stories of Father Sun or Sister Sea, or the lighter animal tales.

Cook cleared his throat.

" 'Nother wolf attack last night," he said. "I heard it was a beggar woman this time. Tore out her throat."

"You sure it wasn't cutthroats with knives?" asked the server.

Cook eyed his row of knives hanging on the far wall. "Knives do a clean-cut job. I heard she was teeth-torn. Besides, she was poor with no coins for thieves ta steal."

"Not safe to go anywhere," said a scullery maid.

Cook said, "I wouldna step beyond the wolfsbane seal Uma Quarteney here spread to protect us." For a moment all eyes were on me. I wanted to say the wolf attacks would lessen after the death of Wolf Moon, but these folk wouldn't know what I was talking about.

"They won't cross the drawbridge," I said.

BACK UPSTAIRS, I buried my head in Father's Herbal, studying the pages.

Vazan hadn't promised to gather the bapeeta, so I might have to seek a vision, like Father did, ask the Holy Ones to show me where it grew and journey there myself. It couldn't be too far away. Father had gone after it with Vazan and returned the very next morning with a basketful of bright green hand-shaped leaves.

I felt a small flutter of hope as I set the four elements on the floor, a feather for wind in the north, a candle for fire in the south, a bowl for water in the east, a pouch for earth in the west. I wrapped the beautiful Euit blanket Lady Tess had given me around my shoulders. The Holy Ones visited Adans. I would sit very still as Father used to do, pray, and wait for a vision.

I lit the candle and closed my eyes. *Please, Holy Ones, show me where bapeeta grows*, I prayed. *If I am an Adan, bless me with a vision today. You know my need. You know my people are in trouble and why I have to please this queen so she will let them go.* An hour passed. My back ached. I did not move. Two hours passed. My legs cramped. I did not move. Three hours passed. Silence. Darkness. Emptiness.

Someone pounded on my door. "Mistress physician," a young voice called.

"Yes," I answered hoarsely. My feet had gone to sleep.

I hobbled to the door, slid back the iron bolt, opened it a crack.

"The king summons you." It was a page. "You're to come right away."

"Is he ill? Should I bring my medicines?"

The boy shrugged. "He didn't say, mistress physician. Come on." I pulled the blanket from my shoulders and folded it, deeply disappointed in myself. I'd had no vision. No proof I was an Adan. I might never be more than a well-trained girl who followed her father's teachings, who used his medicines until his trunk was empty and I had no more to give.

My feet were no longer putty; they were two pincushions pricked with needles from all sides. I gripped the iron banister, barely able to make my way downstairs behind the pageboy. It didn't help that he was bolting down two at a time. *As sprightly as a fey child*, I thought, which made me look at him again and wonder where he was truly taking me. *Trust no one*, Jackrun had said.

I sighed, relieved when the boy swept off his hat, bowed, and vanished at the king's door. *Jackrun has me suspecting everyone.* The sentries uncrossed their pikes to let me inside King Arden's privy chamber. He was alone. I curtsied. "Your Majesty, you wanted to see me?" How English I sounded now. How much of my Euit past, of me, had slowly leeched out of my bones in these past months?

King Arden poked a log in the fire. Flames sent his wavering shadow along the high-backed chairs behind him as if there were two kings in the room, one who faced the flames, and one who backed away from them. "My wife wants me to come to her chamber tonight." He jabbed the log again, sending up a spray of sparks. "You must know how . . . difficult it is with her."

I chose my words carefully. "Sire, she has been greatly troubled since we returned from Dragon's Keep, she—"

The king held up his hand to silence me. "How is she doing with your fertility cure?"

My heart thumped. "She has been taking it each day, Your Majesty. She continues to hope." They'd come together more than once on Dragon's Keep before their son died. She was a few days late, but women her age could be irregular. I didn't dare mention the lateness to His Majesty until I was more certain of what it meant.

"You have to help me." He kept his eyes on the fire. "My own physician is an imbecile in these matters. I am forced to turn to you."

"Sire, are you ill?"

"Not ill!" he barked, the veins swelling on his neck. "But you cannot expect me to . . ." He swung around with the poker. "No one could expect me to get a son on her the way she is now. Her condition makes it impossible to . . . I know my duty. I must have an heir. But the thought of going to her . . . You will have to mix me some kind of potion."

I understood him. They were both still in mourning for their son. Even if it weren't for that, how could he lay with a woman who was sweet one moment and snarling the next?

"Well?" he said. "Can you do it?"

I'd heard the Adan speaking of a virility cure. I had never seen him make it, but I thought I'd passed a page about it in his book. "I think I can prepare a remedy for you, sire."

"You think you can? Or you know you can!"

"I have to check my stores, but I am fairly sure I—"

"Do it. Make yourself useful." Still gripping the poker, he crossed to the barred window. "She wasn't always the way you see her now," he said with his back to me. "We had a good marriage. She was the brightest, most beautiful woman in all of Wilde Island once, a fine horsewoman, a brilliant strategist, a regal queen. You understand?"

"I do, Your Majesty." He was telling me he once loved her.

He turned. Dull autumn light fell across his features. "Is

there something in your store to help my wife . . . return?"
His face was a map of pain. I saw how hard it was for him to
speak of Queen Adela's madness.

"My father, the Adan, saw Her Majesty needed something to . . . balance her mind, sire. He began treating
her"—*don't say madness*—"*condition* soon after we arrived."
I swallowed. The bapeeta he'd picked was gone.

"Increase the dose, for God's sake," he said.

"Sire—"

"My wife still believes in you. If she did not, I wouldn't
waste more men and supplies on her cause."

"Waste more men, Your Majesty?"

"We got a report of an uprising down in Devil's Boot.
Nothing my soldiers couldn't handle, but I had to send
more men and weapons down. The enterprise will be worth
it if your father's miracle cure does what it's supposed to do,
a waste of good men and supplies if you fail. Go," he added,
waving me away with his poker.

My head reeled as I backed toward the door. *An uprising?*
I'd already lost Father. I couldn't bear it if my mother died
now. *Please Holy Ones, keep her safe!*

"One more thing, Uma, this potion you're going to give
me. Does it cause any ill effects? Is there any limit to how
often it can be used?"

"I believe it can make a man queasy at first."

He gave a dismissive laugh. "I am king, I can put up with
a little queasiness, young physician. Go now and come back
within the hour with your answer."

"Yes, Your Majesty."

I barely made it to my room before I broke down.

*A waste of good men!* By all that was sacred. I swiped tears from my eyes, gulping breath. What about the good men in my village, trying their best to protect their families or the elders who were too frail to fight? Had the reds joined in the uprising? I unlocked Father's Herbal. Tears blurred the pages. I cupped my wet eyes in my palms, pressing hard enough to feel the bony outline of my eye sockets. *No*, I thought, *not the reds*. The king would have said something if the dragons broke the treaty.

So my people fought alone. Who fell? Who died? How many more had to die before Queen Adela got what she wanted? It was all in my hands. It was too much.

I gulped against the pain, swiped my eyes again, and read the Herbal through a mist, my gut churning. I wanted to run back to the king's room, bash his face for his arrogance, feel his blood on my knuckles. I'd nearly smacked a guard the day we treated the spit boy's wounds. It was Father who stopped me, dragged me back up the stairs and pressed me into a dark alcove. *If you attacked one of the guards, they'd throw you in a cell,* he'd said in a harsh whisper. *Do you want that?*

He was right. If I did what I wanted to do now, they'd imprison me, hang me. There'd be no one left to free my people.

The candle had burned low. I thumbed through more pages until I found what I was looking for. I smiled a sad smile. Father knew I studied his Herbal. He'd worded it cleverly to protect me from understanding the effect of these herbs on men, but I was old enough to understand his code. I found the proper measurements needed for the curative's preparation, the list of herbs to crush to a fine powder before you mixed it with honey. And the indicated dose a man required. Each herb was not potent taken alone, but strong enough to increase a man's virility when combined.

I dried my eyes. The plants my father listed were in my trunk. The king had his army, but I had the remedy King Arden needed—plants that wielded the power of life. I could use this power as a bargaining tool to free my people if I was as wily as Vazan, as brave as my father.

## CHAPTER TWENTY-EIGHT

# Pendragon Castle, Wilde Island

WOLF MOON
*September 1210*

I T SEEMED THAT a night with her husband had eased
the queen. She looked calm, even contented when I
brought in her morning potion. If she wasn't already with
child, last night's visit gave her another chance. A flicker of
hope brushed light as a butterfly wing against my chest.

Bringing the king's cure hadn't been easy. "Mix a single
spoonful of this powder with an equal amount of honey
against the bitter taste, Your Majesty, and make sure to
take the dose just before you . . ." I'd paused then, sweat
trickling down the back of my neck. I was seventeen and
had never even kissed a man, yet here I was instructing the
sovereign king of Wilde Island, a man old enough to be my
father. I'd fixed my eyes firmly on the semi-precious gems
decorating his gaudy shoes as I spoke, and excused myself
as quickly as I could.

The queen was gazing out the window. "Look, there he is." Jackrun rode into the courtyard below. She tipped her head, looking down with her glass eye as he jumped from his mount. Horse and rider were both mud-spattered.

"He is looking very fit," she said. Her Majesty gave a little frown as Jackrun tossed the reins to a groomsman to lead his horse away. "Where has he been?" she said. "I've been missing him. And what is Desmond wearing?"

"Your . . . Majesty," I said. "Desmond—"

"Yes, Desmond." She turned. "What about him?"

By the Holy Ones, if she was mad enough to mistake Jackrun for her son, what would happen now? All my bapeeta was gone. There was none in her morning brew to treat this lunacy; still, I held it out to her.

"Your secret fertility herbs?" she asked.

"Yes, Your Majesty."

"Good. The king and I must have another child. Another—" She stopped before taking the chalice. Her left hand shook. She held it in her right like a caught bird whose wings she could not still. "My . . . my . . . son." Tears sprang to her eyes. Her mind had cleared enough to remember it was not her son in the foreyard below, that he was dead.

She snatched the goblet, drank it all, and shoved the empty cup in my hands. "Go now," she shouted. "Leave me alone!"

I stood partway down the stairwell, swearing under my breath at my father's stubborn dragon who would not stoop to herbing when I needed her so much, when I was out of the one thing that seemed to balance the queen.

Lute music drifted up from the queen's presence chamber below.

Lady Olivia came halfway up and stopped. We were alone; still, she greeted me in whispers. "How is the queen, Uma?"

"Not . . . well, my lady."

"I left her well and happy earlier this morning. What has happened since?"

I couldn't bear to repeat what the queen had just said about Jackrun. The delusion had passed. She had remembered her son was buried now in the family tomb. Maybe it would not come up again?

"She is thinking of Prince Desmond," I whispered.

"A mother never gets over the loss of a child," Lady Olivia said. She leaned closer. "Her courses are late," she whispered. "Do you think she carries another? Hope of that would cheer her." I tried to breathe. Her sweet perfume had overpowered the air in the stairwell.

"It is too early to tell, my lady."

"Maybe we will have good news to share with the king soon," she said.

"I hope so. Better not to mention it to Queen Adela or to His Majesty until we are sure," I added.

"She must suspect a possible pregnancy if she is late," said Lady Olivia in a hushed voice.

"She will when her mind is clear, but when she suffers with delusions—"

"Has the herb you use to treat her episodes become ineffectual?" she asked pointedly.

"No, my lady." *Do not tell her you've run out.* "It is not safe to give her too much too often."

"Yet she must be in her right mind to carry a child, Uma."

"I agree," I quipped. "My lady," I added.

"I know you are doing your best," she said as she lifted her velvet skirts and headed the rest of the way up the stairs.

I HAD TO pass through the queen's presence chamber below to access these private stairs to her bedroom. I heard the lute player as I entered through the well-guarded door. The ladies-in-waiting crowded in the window seats, veiled heads bent over their elaborate lace-making in the sunlight. The younger maids-in-waiting had left their sewing on the benches and were peering out the tower window. They drew back with guilty looks when I stepped in. Seeing it was only me, and not Lady Olivia, who presided over this room with strict rules of etiquette, they went back to their entertainment, chattering like treed squirrels as they watched the men in the weapons yard below.

The musician was playing "Fey Maiden," the fairy tune I thought of now as Jackrun's song. Still haunted by the queen's confusion of Jackrun for Desmond, I stood a moment, listening.

*In the enchanted woodland wild,*
*The Prince shall wed a Fairy child.*
*Dragon, Human, and Fairy,*
*Their union will be bound by three.*

*And when these lovers intertwine,*
*Three races in one child combine.*
*Dragon, Fey, and Humankind,*
*Bound in one bloodline.*

*O Bring this day unto us soon,*
*And forfeit weapons forged in strife.*
*Sheath sword, and talon, angry spell,*
*And brethren be for life.*

The last verse that spoke of sheathing swords did not sound like Jackrun, who relished sword fights, and sought matches in the weapons yard with the kind of intensity and passion he had for dragon riding. Bianca and Pricilla had squeezed up in front of the other pretty maids to get the best view of the men below.

"There's Jackrun," Bianca said breathlessly. I heard soft oohs and aahs. She was not the only one who'd noticed the athletic duke's son since he'd arrived.

"He's going to fight Sir Kenneth," Pricilla said. "Look, he's choosing broadswords from the rack."

I remembered Sir Kenneth from our trip to Dragon's Keep; a stout fighter years older than Jackrun. *She must be mistaken,* I thought, pushing my way through the little crowd to take a closer look. She was right. The two had broadswords, weapons so hefty you had to use both arms to swing them. I swallowed, wondering at Jackrun's pride going against a soldier whose muscled arms were as thick as Jackrun's legs. Did he enjoy getting injured? Knights gathered around the two below, some whistling, others shouting to cheer them on as the two men circled facing each other.

The minstrel played another song. I barely heard it as the girls made wagers on how many rounds Jackrun would last with Sir Kenneth. Pricilla pulled a ribbon from her hair; Bianca plucked a lovely tortoiseshell comb from hers. Her bright blond hair cascaded down her back as she held out her comb. "I say he lasts four rounds. Uma, do you want to wager with us?"

Her face powder did not hide the dark rings below her eyes. I knew her headaches kept her awake at night. They'd worsened since we'd come home with the dead prince, but she seemed well enough today.

I shook my head. What did I have to wager with that she might want anyway? My clothes had once belonged to Bianca. I didn't think she would want them back now I'd worn them. And I'd rather break out in boils than give away my dragon belt.

The sound of clanking metal made us all peer down again. The men were swinging their heavy weapons, the seasoned knight coming at Jackrun like a large bear, pushing him back as they both struck high and low, swords bashing. I caught my breath as Sir Kenneth landed a blow hitting Jackrun's upper arm, tearing his shirt as he drew it back. My hand went to my mouth as Jackrun stumbled, blood running down his arm. The same arm Prince Desmond slashed when Jackrun fought for me.

"Your Majesty," the ladies-in-waiting all said in unison with strained voices. They were rising to their feet to curtsy to the queen, who had just entered with Lady Olivia. *Don't let Her Majesty see Jackrun. She only just called him Desmond.*

I curtsied along with the maidens clustered by the window. The queen went to one of her ladies-in-waiting to inspect her embroidery work. The lute player sang as Her Majesty moved farther down the line, viewing each lady's workmanship. She would reach the maidens by the window soon. They'd thumped down on their bench squeezed together like a row of ducklings, some stitching vestments, others hemming plain-looking shirts. They appeared silent and demure now; only their blushed faces gave them away. My ears pricked to the sounds below; more clanking, a shout went up. For Jackrun or Sir Kenneth? I could not look.

I darted to the minstrel. "Come, sir," I whispered. "Stand here in the sunlight to entertain Her Majesty."

Lady Olivia shot me a questioning look as I tugged the man's sleeve, leading him in front of the window overlooking the weapons yard. He plucked a new tune. Lady Olivia drew me aside as the queen approached the maiden's window seats.

"Why move the minstrel there?" she asked in a hushed voice.

"We cannot let Her Majesty look out that window,"
I whispered back. "Jackrun is down there fighting in the
weapons yard. She saw him earlier through her tower window and called him Desmond."

Lady Olivia looked at me wide-eyed. "Are you sure?"

"Yes, my lady."

"Why didn't you tell me before when we spoke in the
stairwell?"

"I hoped it was a passing thing." We both turned. Her
Majesty was speaking with Bianca, who held out her sewing,
head bowed as if she expected a scolding.

"Chin up, daughter," Lady Olivia whispered under her
breath. "Show the queen your courage." She crossed the
room and enlivened the conversation between Her Majesty and Bianca. Bianca smiled as her mother pointed out
the finer qualities of her daughter's stitchery. I hurried out,
knowing the queen's clever companion would use her skills
to block Queen Adela's view of the yard below. Some battles are fought with broadswords, others with cunning and
words. I was only beginning to learn English ways. When
it came to courtly battle, Lady Olivia was a skilled fighter.

## CHAPTER TWENTY-NINE

# Pendragon Castle, Wilde Island

### WOLF MOON
*September 1210*

I DIDN'T KNOW the outcome of Jackrun's match until later that afternoon when Bianca came to my herbarium in the Crow's Nest. She did not speak of Jackrun right away, driven up the stairs by her usual need.

"My head pains me, Uma." She took a seat at my vanity, dusted the mirror with a strip of linen near the washbasin, and studied her reflection. Two knights had brought the vanity here after Father died. A gift from the queen, who'd said, "You will prepare yourself before you enter my rooms. I will not tolerate a physician with smudges on her face, rumpled clothes, or unkempt hair. Keep yourself properly combed and dressed the way Lady Olivia does."

"Look at these." Bianca pointed to the dark rings below her eyes. "Have you any face powder?" She tugged on the drawer.

I hurried over, pressing it shut. "You will not find any in my room." The powder she used was too pale for my dark skin. It would make me look like a lime-washed wall. "I'm sorry your head hurts," I said, "but I told you the last time it's not safe to take evicta very often. It can be dangerous." I caught her disappointed look in the glass. "You have to learn to use something other than Her Majesty's medicine," I said more gently as I went back to stir the queen's potion in its copper pot.

"I have tried," she moaned. "The king's physician bled me, which did no good at all, only made me faint. I prayed to Saint Agathius to help ease my pain. I was able to sleep that night, but he never helped me after that. I cannot think why he would answer my prayer once only to abandon me the next time. Perhaps I offended him by not being grateful enough?" She turned on the stool and looked across the room at me.

"I do not know what aggravates a saint," I said, measuring the honey.

"Your potions work the best of all, Uma. Even better than Master Ridolfi's."

I was determined not to give in to flattery. "Who?"

"The last queen's physician, who is in the dungeon. I wish Her Majesty would let him go. Master Ridolfi was nice to me."

Bianca wended through the room, touching my wardrobe, my worktable. Her pink fingers were everywhere. "Jackrun was wonderful today," she said in a half whisper. "You should have stayed to watch."

"Did the queen view the fight?" *Say she didn't.*

"Oh, no." I heaved a sigh as she went on. "She expects us to stitch reams of vestments or endless piles of shirts for the poor to earn our place in heaven. We had to keep our noses in our sewing and wait for her to leave before we could look out the window again. Jackrun withstood four rounds with Sir Kenneth before the match was called. I won Pricilla's ribbon from her."

"And he wasn't hurt beyond that first cut on his arm?"

"You are a healer. You could have gone to him if he was."

I thought a moment about that. "Her Majesty would not want me, a woman, to enter the soldier's infirmary."

"Oh, yes. Well, Jackrun seemed fit enough just now at the feast. Pricilla boasted that he was staring at her all through the meal, but I think his eyes were on me."

I pretended to ignore her as I capped the honey jar, though of course I spilled honey down the sides instead. No doubt Lady Olivia thought it wise for Bianca to catch Jackrun's eye, since he had a chance of becoming the next Pendragon king.

I was about to ask her to leave when she leaned against my worktable, the edge of a fine bracelet poking out from under her lace sleeve. Blue sapphires winked in the candlelight. A new bracelet. A gift?

"It's lovely," I said.

She drew back, covering the bracelet again.

"A beautiful piece. Who gave it to you?" *Someone as wealthy as the king.*

Bianca bit her lip and shook her head.

"A gift from some lord," I guessed. "Lord Godfrey?" *A widower.* "Lord Hastings? The king himself?"

She blushed bright red. "His Majesty gave it to me to cheer my heart when I was troubled," she said defensively.

I added the honey I'd measured to my brew to disguise the bitter herbs. "What were you upset about?"

"You know perfectly well. The wolves howl and I can't sleep. I lie awake and think of Prince Desmond lying cold and dead in his coffin. I remember when we used to ride together and it is just too horrible. I start crying and I can't stop. The king found me pacing the halls outside my room one night and he gave me the bracelet to comfort me."

King Arden knew he had to sire another heir. Was that the only reason he had wanted my virility powder? I hoped he wasn't thinking of inviting Bianca to his bed. She held the stones closer to the candlelight. Now that I had seen her prize, she could not resist displaying it. "He told me the sapphires match my eyes. Do you think so?"

"Have you shown it to anyone else, to your friend Pricilla?"

"Oh, it's a secret. I do not wear it in front of anyone, especially her. She is not as easy to talk to as you are."

"Why do you say that?"

"Well . . . because." She looked at me. "Pricilla is jealous of me. We both like to flirt. But you are not like that because you are . . . different."

*Because I am an Euit girl?* Did she think I did not notice

men? That my heart was a lifeless clump of bog? "I think you should leave now, Bianca."

"What? What did I say?" She grabbed my arm. "Don't cast me out, Uma," she pleaded. She had no idea how she'd just hurt me. "Please, don't be angry. It makes my head hurt all the more."

I glanced down at her hands. She let go of my arm, and pleaded again, this time with her luminous blue eyes. It was a look I had given in to before. "Does your mother know about the king's bracelet?"

"No." Bianca took a step back. "And you must not tell her. Promise me you won't." She seemed afraid now.

"I will mix you a small amount of evicta for tonight if you will you do something for me."

She brightened. "Yes, whatever you ask."

She paced as I wiped the drips from the sides of the honey jar. "All I ask is that you let me know the next time His Majesty gives you any more of his gifts, or treats you with other favors."

She frowned.

I stopped grinding the small black evicta seeds.

"All right, I will do it," she said anxiously. "Thank you," she added.

A moment later, Bianca licked the honeyed spoon laced with evicta, sighed, and rubbed her temples.

"The evicta will dull your pain soon," I said.

"I know it will. Thank you, Uma." She took my hand and squeezed it before going out the door.

Alone again, I strained the queen's early evening dose through the muslin cloth and left for her private rooms. Downstairs, Jackrun rounded a corner, nearly running into me. We stopped inches apart. He was in his courtly clothes. A hunk of hair had come free from its leather tie; his face was flushed.

"The queen's dose?" he asked, glaring at the chalice.

"Yes."

"Whatever you're using to treat her mind isn't working!"

"What?"

"She . . ." Jackrun paused, hissed out a breath, and looked about. "I can't talk about it here," he added before rushing off. I stood a moment feeling the heat he'd left in the passageway. We hadn't spoken since we'd met in the elms and this is all he had to say to me?

## CHAPTER THIRTY

# Pendragon Castle Cliffs, Wilde Island

WOLF MOON
*September 1210*

UPSTAIRS, HER MAJESTY turned from the letter she was writing at her vanity table when I entered and beamed at me. "Uma, isn't it wonderful? I feel life in me this time. I am sure it is another son."

I tried to return her smile. Had the queen noticed her late courses herself or had Lady Olivia said something in an effort to cheer her? I thought we had agreed not to bring it up so soon. "You are just five days late, Your Majesty," I said softly. "It is early yet."

She placed her hand on her red velvet gown, stroking her stomach. "I tell you I can feel it!"

"Yes, Your Majesty." I wished Mother were here. She had a midwife's knowledge, though she hadn't been allowed to practice it in our village, where the Adan presided over births. Would Mother have known the signs of early pregnancy? Would she be able to see something I could not? I did some quick calculations. If the king lay with her one of our first few nights on Dragon's Keep, she might have conceived. I felt a small flutter of hope, like a moth breaking from its cocoon. If I kept her and her child healthy, she might free my village and send me home at last.

"Give me my brew," Queen Adela said. "You are quite the healer, Uma Quarteney. I knew you would do for me what the other physicians could not."

"Thank you, Your Majesty." I warmed with pride watching her drink the chalice in five long gulps. "I have brought the utzo oil."

She turned to her mirror. "Good, apply it now." She was becalmed, her mind and heart in balance and at rest for once. Believing a child grew in her had done that.

I chanted silently as I uncorked the oil. For the queen, I sang the verse in English.

> *Utzo*
> *Round seeds white as moon*
> *Sweet poison*
> *Plucked nightfall from sky*

I watched her reflection in the glass as I rubbed the oil into her scalp. The utzo that made her dark hair shine would kill the lice and keep them away a good many days. Lice troubled courtiers and servants alike here at the castle. But my small store of utzo was reserved for the queen. Her fine-boned face in the mirror showed strength, even a kind of radiance. Her eyes were the same sapphire blue as Bianca's. I swallowed. *Had the king meant the bracelet for his wife? How dare he. It would kill her if she knew.*

The queen hummed to herself as I tugged the comb through her hair, removing the dead lice and their tiny eggs.

"I love the sweet perfume of this oil," she said, picking up the jar and bringing it to her nose. "Where did you find it?"

"The Adan found utzo growing in a secluded place in our valley. He understood its uses. No one else did. It should not go near your lips, Your Majesty," I added. "Sweet as it smells, it is a poison."

She was silent a long while and I watched her expression changing in the glass, already her happiness dulled, and I read a change of mood, sweet to sour. "There was another," she said, turning to me.

"Another what, Your Majesty?"

"Infant," she whispered, looking up with a solemn face. "A miscarriage when Prince Desmond was two. I don't talk about it because. . ." She shook her head with her eyes closed. "Do you think I'm cursed?"

"No, Your Majesty," I answered, my throat constricting.

"She came early. I was only in my fourth month, and she . . ." The queen dropped her voice. "Her foot was de-formed, shaped like a dragon's claw. My husband said it was better that she did not live."

I felt a flash of anger that he would say such a cruel thing to his wife after such a loss, that he would be glad, actually glad of his own child's death.

She held her hands up to me and I took them in mine. "You have known a lot of sorrow, Your Majesty," I said, looking down at her. "But it does not mean you are cursed." *Please Holy Ones let that be true.* "It does not mean you won't know happiness now. I am sure you and the king can have a healthy child."

"You know this? You have the Sight?" she asked, her eyes shining.

Jackrun had asked the same, thinking me a seer. I shook my head. And she drew her hands away, making me wish, this once, I could lie to her and give her the hope she was so desperate for.

She turned on the stool facing her mirror again. "Braid my hair with a velvet ribbon, Uma. I will look my best in case the king visits me tonight."

"Yes, Your Majesty."


WHEN I RETURNED to the herbarium I was too restless to stay inside. Unpacking the vayonaze leaves that red dragons love, and putting a small handful in my waist pouch, I left. The queen must have more bapeeta, especially if she was with child. There were caves in the cliffs by the sea. Father told me Vazan had chosen one of them to shelter in. I had never been there, never seen her den, but I would find her.

CLOUDS SCUDDED ACROSS the twilight sky as I passed the amphitheater walking south along the sea cliffs. The damp autumn wind blew my hood back before I reached the zigzag stairs leading down to the beach. When I stopped to tug it over my head, I heard a roar below, a sound not made by waves.

I peered down. Jackrun ran naked into the shallows, screaming fire; light flashed over the surface of the sea before he dove and vanished in the tumbling surf. I held my breath until he appeared again a little farther out, swimming alongside the shore. How could he stand the frigid water? Even dragons, with the exception of Babak, couldn't bear to swim. Dragon, human, and fairy—did all three bloodlines work together somehow to give him such strength, or was it the workings of the dragon fire in him?

In the dusky early evening light, I could just make out his curving arm moving in long, easy strokes beyond the breakers. He swam far down the beach almost out of my view before turning and heading back again to ride a cresting wave into the shallows. *Leave now, Uma, before he looks up and sees you.* My blood roared in my ears. I did not move as he came ashore cloaked in deep blue twilight, dressed in seawater. He didn't bother to dry off before throwing on his clothing and strapping on his short sword. When he started for the cliff, I drew back, heart pounding, thinking to leave, choosing not to. I'd come out to find Vazan, but Jackrun was here and I needed to see him alone, far from courtly eyes and ears.

A hand appeared at the edge of the cliff and up came Jackrun's head. The wooden stairs were less than a hundred feet to the south, but this was Jackrun. He chose to climb.

"Uma?" he said, grunting as he pulled himself the rest of the way up and stood across from me, hands on hips, catching his breath.

"What were you doing? Swimming in the sea?" I asked.

"You . . . watched?"

"Of course not! Your hair is wet and you smell of seaweed. Anyone would guess what you'd been doing."

He gave a wry smile. "And you came out here—"

"Looking for someone."

"Not looking for me?"

"For Vazan. You said the queen's medicine wasn't working. What did you mean by that?"

"I was going to tell you. I had to come here and cool off first."

"Cool off over what?"

Jackrun adjusted his sword belt. "My aunt ordered me to sit beside her at the feast. She called me Desmond, Uma." His brows were suddenly sharp, his eyes intense. "She made me stand up and give a speech as if I were her son."

"I'm sorry. It must have been . . . Her delusions have gotten much worse since he died."

"Aren't you dosing her for that?" Jackrun barked.

"I am trying to help her, Jackrun. She sees you and thinks of him. Your presence makes it harder!"

An enormous scaly head popped up in answer to my

shout. Vazan clipped her claws around Jackrun, shaking him.

"No, Vazan," I warned in Euit. "Let him go. We were just arguing." She blinked and reluctantly drew in her claws. Jackrun was breathing hard, looking squarely into her fierce face as he brushed himself off.

"Thank you," Jackrun said.

Vazan scrambled noisily the rest of the way up, causing a small landslide as she came. Once on top, she towered over us, her head swaying, her eyes narrowing as she fixed her intimidating silver stare on Jackrun.

Jackrun stood perfectly still. "Does she understand me?" he asked me out of the corner of his mouth.

"I know English!" Vazan snapped.

Jackrun bowed. "Of course, warrior Vazan. Dragons speak many languages. I want to tell you we were merely arguing. I would never harm Uma Quarteney. She is safe with me."

Vazan flicked her tail, uncertain.

"I am all right, rivule," I said. "But it's good you've come. I would have tried to find you if you hadn't. Were you able to harvest the plant I showed you in Father's Herbal?"

She dug her talons in the grassy ground. "I'm no herber!"

I felt myself flush. "I need it for the queen, rivule. I have to have it." I opened my waist pouch, letting the fragrant vayonaze speak. Vazan's nostrils flared. "I have more vayonaze if you bring me the plant. Will you promise to try?"

The red leaves drifted slowly from my hand to the ground.

"Promise?" Vazan said, weighing the word in her enormous, sharp-toothed mouth before she lowered her head and sniffed the leaves excitedly.

"Come," I said to Jackrun. We turned, walking north toward the distant castle. A moment later there was a loud thump followed by a snorting sound, and a groan of pleasure.

"Don't look back," I whispered. "She would not like you to see. Reds love vayonaze. She is rolling in it."

Jackrun laughed.

"Shh," I warned. It was good to be outside with him, walking under clouds and the early stars, the waning Wolf Moon barely visible, hanging like a broken lantern over the sea. Now that we were free to talk, I wasn't sure how to begin, but we'd reach the castle soon. If I didn't speak now, it would be too late. I told him the new thing I'd remembered about that day on the cliff. "I felt a presence there. Someone was watching."

"Sir Geoffrey hiding in the underbrush. He must have been there watching us a while before he stepped out."

"I don't think it was him. It felt . . . different."

"The murderer who killed the lute player?"

"I thought you ruled him out earlier," I said.

"That was before you mentioned sensing someone else up on the cliff with us. Someone hidden."

"Whoever watched us, they felt magical."

"We already know whoever did it had the power to stir the wind," Jackrun said. I kept pace with his long loping stride as we approached the enormous stone amphitheater on the hill. "The presence watched with a kind of expectation," I said, "like something was about to happen. The feeling grew stronger when the dragons came."

I thought of what the fey woman Kaprecha said the day we'd ridden with Lady Tess and the queen; *The Son of the Prophecy was born to rule.* She'd flashed me a conspiratorial look, expecting me to agree. "What if some fairies from Dragon's Keep were hiding there, watching us that day?"

We reached the amphitheater and stopped with our backs to the high stone wall. "I grew up with the fey folk on Dragon's Keep, Uma. I know them almost as well as I know my family. I don't think it would have been one of them. If what you suspect is true, it was more likely someone from Wilde Island. Some fey sent by my grandfather Onadon. Or . . ." He leaned against the wall, looking up.

"Or what?"

"Or some rogue element that split apart from the rest in Dragonswood, a secretive group who wanted the Son of the Prophecy on the throne and was willing to commit murder to make it happen. They could have worked alongside Sir Geoffrey, or worked alone."

In my mind's eye, I saw Sir Geoffrey scowling at Prince Desmond after he kicked the fey child. A tall fey man leaned down to talk with him. What passed between them? Were they planning something? I suppose some of the Dragonswood fey could have slipped into the summer castle the night of the fey ball. Everyone there was in some sort of disguise. But . . . "I don't think any Wilde Island fey folk sailed with us. How would they have come to Dragon's Keep?"

"Easily enough on dragonback, Uma."

I opened my hands to the wind coming up off the sea. It stirred my skirts, the grasses at my feet, and whistled around the amphitheater walls behind us. "Can the will-o'-the-wisps go dark?" I asked.

"A strange question," Jackrun said.

"I just thought if they were able to hide their light, they would make perfect little messengers."

"Or spies," Jackrun said, trailing my thoughts. "I don't know the answer, though I've seen them all my life."

I watched Vazan flying out over the bay to hunt bats or birds, tiny snacks for one so large, but she enjoyed them. We set out again toward the castle.

Neither of us talked again until we reached the Pendragon tomb, when Jackrun stopped and drew me under a massive oak. "I will have to go away soon."

"You just got back."

"I was only gone overnight. This time will have to be longer."

"Where will you go?"

"Dragonswood."

"Why do you have to go there?"

"You know why, Uma," he whispered. "I have to talk to my grandfather Onadon—find out what he knows about Desmond's murder. If he's not the one behind this and there's a rogue element hiding in the wood . . ." He frowned, lost in thought.

I knew it was selfish of me, but I didn't want him to go.

He and Vazan made Pendragon Castle bearable. Even when we couldn't get away like we were now to talk alone, knowing he was close helped me live a little easier, breathe a little easier. I wanted . . . I closed my eyes to push away his image, and saw his somber face still etched behind my eyelids before I gave up and opened them again.

Horsemen trotted up the road toward us. We pressed ourselves against the tree trunk listening to the muffled voices, hooves clopping in the packed dirt, then fading as two men-at-arms passed the tomb heading for the castle.

"We have to get back before they raise the drawbridge," I said.

"And the wolves start to howl," Jackrun added, glancing up the hill. I could barely see the outlines of the evergreens up beyond the graveyard at the edge of Dragonswood.

It hurt a little to see Jackrun wasn't wearing the wolfsbane pouch I'd made especially for him. "You should wait for the time of Wolf Moon to be over before you enter Dragonswood." *Please wait a little longer.* "It won't be long before Dragon Moon. You might be safer then."

He didn't speak. I knew I hadn't convinced him. Already he was crossing over the Dragonswood boundary wall in his mind because he was Jackrun and danger was his bread.

"I should tell you something before we go back inside," Jackrun said, turning his gaze from the distant woods back to me. "I'm afraid you won't like it."

I faced Jackrun under the widespread oak. "Tell me."

"If the fey of Dragonswood set up Desmond's murder,

they might have meddled in other ways to ensure my aunt has no more heirs."

"Are you saying the queen has been infertile all these years because of them? That they put some kind of . . . curse on her?"

Jackrun's eyes flicked toward the castle. "It's possible. A hex or a spell maybe."

Sickened, I leaned against the trunk, arms folded, barricading my heart.

"Uma?" Jackrun gripped my arms gently. "I know. It's a terrible thought. It's just an idea I had after we talked the last time. I might be wrong. I hope I am."

"Do you really think they would kill her only son *and* hex her womb? Are they that wicked, Jackrun?"

He frowned. "Not the ones I knew on Dragon's Keep, but there are good and bad folk among them, Uma. I cannot say what they would do."

I put my face in my hands.

"What is it, Uma?"

I shook my head. If Jackrun was right, it meant no matter what I did to help her, she would not conceive. My father had died for nothing, and I would lose. I would die. The army would do what they liked to my tribe.

"You need to come with me," Jackrun said.

"Where are we going?"

"Something I need to show you."

"It's too late. We have to get back."

He led me to the tomb, opened one side of the double doors, then motioned with his hand for me to go in first.

My feet went leaden as I peered inside the dark tomb. I'd forced myself to tolerate the thick castle walls and dank hallways with torches that smelled of burning pitch, but the Pendragon tomb was far worse than the many-windowed castle. The round stained-glass rose window over the double doors was the only source of light. Dark passageways inside led to underground catacombs filled with the remains of the dead. "I don't want to see anything in there, Jackrun."

"Trust me, Uma. This won't take long." Jackrun stepped over the threshold, gently drew me inside, and plucked an unlit torch from the wall sconce. He closed the door and whispered, "We cannot light this just yet. Sexton might see the torchlight shining through the rose window and come out here to inspect. We'll have to feel our way along at first, but the stairwell isn't far."

"Are you taking me to see Prince Desmond?" I'd heard his glass coffin was placed in a stone sarcophagus with his likeness carved on the lid. "I don't need to see where they laid him to rest."

"Not his burial place. It's a way into the castle. Come."

I took a tentative step. Father's warning whispered through me, *Never trust the English.*

*You never met Jackrun, Father,* I argued in my head. But my trust for Jackrun didn't ease my nerves. Our feet whispered against the floor.

Jackrun stopped abruptly. The dark air around me changed. Heated up. "Jackrun?" I asked, afraid.

He shoved me aside. I fell back, knocking my head against something hard.

"Jackrun!"

The next moment, he roared fire. The passage echoed his roar.

I half ran, half stumbled back toward the entrance.

"Uma!" I heard Jackrun calling. "Wait!" I turned on him in the narrow corridor. He caught up to me, his torch now lit.

"What do you mean 'wait'? You're the one who just shoved me aside and nearly lit me on fire! What's wrong with you!"

"Nothing, Uma. I pushed you aside so you wouldn't get burned when I lit the torch. You weren't afraid when I breathed fire when I was fighting Desmond, when I burned the weeds at your father's grave. What's changed now?"

"I knew what you were angry about then. This . . . this rage came out of nowhere. You aimed it right at me. What did I do to deserve it? Tell me."

"Nothing. Believe me. And I didn't aim it at you, Uma. I aimed it at the torch. I thought you knew I have to summon anger to breathe fire. That's how it works."

I was still trembling. "You summoned anger just to light a torch?"

"Yes, Uma." He handed it to me. "Are we all right now?"

"All right," I whispered.

He led me back down the corridor.

I held the torch up, lighting our path. "What if there is more to your dragon power than anger and destruction?"

He turned and stopped. "There isn't."

Yellow light pooled around us. Beyond that, all was dark. The small white scar on Jackrun's lower lip and chin was not much bigger than an apple seed. I resisted the impulse to touch the place where Desmond had split his lip the day Jackrun fought for me. "Just now you only wanted to use your fire in a good and simple way, to give us light to see by. The reds back home train their young. There are many uses. Fire for warmth, for illumination, for—"

"You think all I need is training?" he snapped.

"Yes. Why not?"

Silence.

"Tell me what you did that frightened you and your family so much that you had to hide your gift from everyone."

Silence.

A loud groan of cranking wood and metal came from somewhere in the distance. At first I couldn't place the sound. Then I knew. "They are raising the drawbridge"

"This way," Jackrun said, leading me down the stairs.

Jackrun stepped into a smaller chamber and crept behind a stone sarcophagus with the likeness of a Pendragon king holding a cross carved on the lid.

"There's a passage known only to the Pendragons. Father told me where to look for it in case I needed a quick way in or out of the castle. I've used it once before," he added. He pushed against a square stone at the base of the wall and drew it aside for me to see. A spider scuttled out of the low opening as I stepped closer.

I am Euit, used to wide-open spaces. The sight of the dark passage sickened me. My shaking hand made the torchlight jump along the walls. Jackrun held my wrist to steady the torch. The flame above us made a soft, deep-throated roar.

"Beautiful Uma, don't be afraid."

# CHAPTER THIRTY-ONE

## Pendragon Tomb, Wilde Island

WOLF MOON
*September 1210*

*BEAUTIFUL UMA.* My knees went to water at those two words. He had strung them together so easily like two pearls on a single strand. I wanted to stay with him and to run away from that dark gaping hole in the wall he expected me to crawl into. I was not sure at the moment if I could even walk.

Jackrun took the torch. "There are more spiders inside, I'm afraid. They like abandoned passageways."

"I am not afraid of spiders." *It's the passage itself. Stop trembling.* It made no sense that I should fear the underground when I am mostly earth element, when fox is my Path Animal and foxes live in dens. Shouldn't deep burrows and passageways feel like home to me?

Jackrun said, "There is no other way back inside the castle now."

"And you made it that way keeping us out so long!"

"We might both need this escape route with a murderer on the loose. Father said to tell no one our family secret, but I'm telling you in case you need a quick way out."

If he was waiting for me to thank him, he would wait a long while.

"Are you ready to try the passage, Uma?"

Of course I was not ready. I would never be ready.

Jackrun took my hand. "I'll keep you safe."

I ducked through the low opening. He shut the hidden stone door behind us. I took a few cautious steps. Hard to breathe. I began to sweat. Partway in, a large spider dropped to my shoulder. Jackrun quickly brushed it off, his hand lingering at my collarbone, warming the fox mark beneath my gown. He stood close to me as breath. He searched my face before we walked on.

I felt the terrible weight of rock and water over our heads as we stepped under the moat. *Holy Ones help me. I cannot do this.* I froze, unable to move my feet.

"It's not much farther, Uma, I promise." His palm was warm against mine. It was rough and calloused from sword fights in the yard, from clutching horses' reins, but the grip was light enough for me to pull away if I wanted to. I didn't want to.

The tunnel ended in the wine cellar deep in the castle, the door opening behind one of the many large barrels. He closed it again, the wood slats melding with the others, hiding the door.

"We have to part now," he said. "You can go up first. The stairs lead to the buttery. No one will be there this time of the evening, but wait and listen first to be sure."

"And if we need to talk again? How do I let you know?"

"Send a message through my page. The boy's a trouble-maker, but I can rely on him. Say only the queen is improving. When I get that message from you, I'll know you want to meet."

"Where?"

"Behind the tomb in the graveyard. That way we have a sure escape if we need it."

"Jackrun, do you think there are any fey folk around us in the castle now?"

"I've been looking out for any sign of them. If there are any on the castle grounds, they've guised themselves well. Remember to watch the windows and the mirrors as you move about. A glamour spell doesn't fool a mirror or any other shiny surface. You will always see the person's true reflection there."

"And if I should see something unusual?"

"Send your message so we can meet. I'll want to know right away."

"When are you going to Dragonswood?" *Leaving me here alone.*

"Soon."

"What will you do?"

"I don't know. I wish everything didn't seem so impossible." Jackrun looped his forefinger under my dragon belt and pulled me closer to him. He ran his fingers through my hair.

I closed my eyes, feeling his fingers weave along my scalp until he lowered his arm and brushed his thumb slowly across my lower lip. Cupping the back of my head in his large hand, he leaned down and kissed me. A foreign world turned in my chest; a still, dark place sensed dawn in his warm kiss. I went up on tiptoe wanting to strengthen the pressure of his mouth against mine. He tasted of sea salt, pine, and smoke.

We kissed longer, until we drew apart, breathless. His arms encircled me. I wrapped mine around his waist, pressing closer.

There was no going back to Uma, the lone healer.

No going forward with Jackrun, a royal Pendragon.

He was right. It seemed impossible.

BACK UP IN my herbarium, I washed tunnel dust and spider webs from my skin and hair. I caught myself grimacing in the vanity mirror as my brush caught a tangle, and laughed, still shy of my reflection. Back home I had only seen myself in pools. I'd seen a guise back then, a woven tunic top, proud boyish scrapes on my chin or cheek. I had not seen a girl.

Tonight I found my mother and father in the glass, both English and Euit wed together in my face: Mother's shapely lips, curved brows, and large eyes; Father's prominent cheekbones and darker coloring. I found sadness in my eyes, missing Mother, missing home.

But I also noticed something else: a faint glow that did not come from the rushlight, but from my own skin. I moved my lips, silently naming the source of the glow, *Jackrun*.

I opened the shutters to the endless night sky, felt the sting of the September wind and grabbed my Euit blanket. The scratchy weave rubbed the back of my neck where Jackrun had rested his warm hand, before he tipped my head back and kissed me. For that one moment, entangled in his arms in the semidarkness behind the casks in the cellar, I'd felt free.

But Jackrun would go to Dragonswood. I'd soon be on my own again, mixing medicines for the queen.

I leaned on the windowsill, cupping my chin in my hands. All my careful preparations and doses would not matter if the fey had been hexing Queen Adela to prevent her from having more children.

I'd doubted my gifts many times since Father died, leaving me alone to heal the queen, but I'd always had his fertility cure to rely upon. At least I had had that. But if what Jackrun said was true, Father and I had battled against fairy magic from the start. All the tonics in the world would not have given her a child. If the fey worked against me, it meant failure. Death.

I pressed my palms hard against my eyes. Tiny shooting stars darted behind my eyelids. If I died, who would free my tribe?

*She is late,* I reminded myself. *Her courses haven't come yet. There is a chance she's with child now and Jackrun's wrong.* My heart did not lift. Where was my faith? Why couldn't I believe?

I swept the floor, set out the four sacred elements, and knelt in the middle of the circle. *Holy Ones, if this is true, help me. Your magic is far greater than fey magic, but I am just a beginner, following what my father taught me. I was never trained to undo a powerful fairy spell. I don't even know how to begin.*

I stayed on my knees a long while, surrounded by silence in the chilly tower room. Before I put the elements away, I leaned over the water dish and touched the surface. Trembling circles broke around my finger, widening until they reached the edges of the bowl. I peered at my dark eyes when the surface was still again. Jackrun said, *A glamour spell does not fool a mirror or any other shiny surface. You will always see the person's true reflection there.*

I would watch for the fey hidden among the English. The barred castle windows would not show me much, but there were silver chalices and shiny food platters. I'd make sure to check the mirror in Her Majesty's bedchamber when I was with her. At least it was a start.

# CHAPTER THIRTY-TWO

# Pendragon Castle, Wilde Island

## WOLF MOON
*September 1210*

T HE SOUNDS OF the queen's ragged weeping echoed
down the stairwell the next morning. Halfway up, I
paused to listen, steeling my nerves before continuing up the
spiral stairs with Her Majesty's potion. Lady Olivia was on
the landing above, wagging her finger and hissing orders at
a cowering laundress. Spotting me, she gave the laundress a
little shove. "Show her," she said.

The girl hurried down, half tripping with her linen load.
On the step above mine she stopped and parted the wadded sheets, nodding down at the bloodstains. Not the small
droplets that might only mean spotting in early pregnancy,
but enough red to show the queen's monthly courses had
come in force.

Her lateness was only that. There wasn't any child.

The laundress folded the linen again, hiding the stain before she hurried down. My body went heavier than clay. Lady Olivia gave me a terse look as she reached for the door handle. "The queen won't see you this morning, Uma."

"She has to, my lady." I held out the steaming brew, the familiar scent filling the air in the landing. It was once the smell of hope, but now . . .

"She won't drink that today. She told me she is sick of your potion. She might not agree to take it ever again."

I gripped her arm. "But I have another month to help her conceive. She promised me I would have until the end of Dragon . . . the end of October."

Lady Olivia looked down at my hand and I removed it. "Please," I added. "What can I do?"

We listened to the sobs. "I have to go back inside. But Her Majesty needs whatever it is you give her to calm her nerves." She paused. "Can you guise it? Put the herb into some sweetmeats?"

I was afraid to admit I was out of bapeeta. "I can try, my lady."

"Go then, do it. I will bring her downstairs to her aviary. Her birds usually lighten her mood." There was a crashing sound beyond the door. "It might take some time to get her cleaned up. I'll send a messenger when she's ready," she added before letting herself back inside.

*Damn you, Vazan,* I thought, heading downstairs and through the long hallways to the kitchen. *If only you'd harvested the bapeeta when I first asked you to!* Cook had some sweetmeats in the larder. Back upstairs, I unlocked Father's Herbal and flipped through the pages searching for something, anything I could mix with the gooey paste in the center of the sweetmeats. None of the herbs or tinctures had the calming power of bapeeta. I slammed the Herbal shut, cut a sweetmeat open, killed a curious fly that showed too much interest in what I was doing.

At last I resorted to crushing the purple gyocana seeds I had used before to help Her Majesty sleep. A small amount would make her drowsy. I wasn't sure it would calm her tempest, but it was all I had.

It was another hour before Lady Olivia sent a message for me to bring the sweetmeats. I took only two with me, leaving the rest for later. Lady Olivia met me at the end of the long hallway outside the open aviary door. She eyed the queen inside as she quickly placed the sweetmeats on the enamel tray. There was a scratch on her cheek. The queen had long nails.

"I am afraid it's bad news," she whispered. Her face was a reservoir of worry. "Prepare yourself," she added. "I'm sorry. I did what I could to—"

"Come here, Uma," Queen Adela called in a chilled voice. I noted Her Majesty's puffy eyes and clammy-looking skin as I hurried into the room filled with chattering, tweeting, and singing. The birds didn't seem to know they were trapped. Had they ever been free? I glanced at the goldfinch, Mother's favorite bird, and called out to her in my mind, wanting her strong arm around me. Holding me up.

The queen put out her hand. I fell on my knees, kissing her ring.

"Your Majesty, I am sorry." I meant it for both my failure and her sore disappointment.

"Sorry?" She wrenched her hand back so speedily, her ruby scraped the tip of my nose.

She plucked a sweetmeat from Lady Olivia's tray, ate half, then broke the rest in tiny bits and tossed them to the birds in the large floor-to-ceiling cage. I jumped to my feet and exchanged a nervous look with Lady Olivia. Neither of us could say a thing as the bluebirds, goldfinches, and larks all fluttered down, taking the crumbs in their tiny beaks. Their bodies were so small. Would the sleeping powder kill them? *Please no*, I thought, watching them dance about on their tiny clawed feet as they ate every crumb.

"You are no better than the other physicians who have forced their sickening potions on me, Uma," Queen Adela snapped. "How many gallons of the Kuyawhat have I drunk these past two months?"

*Kuyawan, not Kuyawhat.* "It's hard to say, Your Majesty."

"Enough to sink a ship!" She took a second sweetmeat and ate it all. "Should we throw her to the dogs, Lady Olivia? Drop her in a bear pit? Behead her?"

"Your Majesty," Lady Olivia said with alarm, "please—"

"No, wait, I remember now," the queen said, raising her hand. "I have already chosen burning. This physician stinks like spoiled meat. We should cook her and start with a fresh physician."

I fell on my knees again. "Your Majesty, you promised to try my father's cure three more months. It has been only two. Give me one more month. Remember—"

"Remember? I remember everything. It's you who have forgotten your promise to me, mistress physician. Guards!"

"Wait, Your Majesty, please. Let me keep trying."

Four men marched in. Two yanked me to my feet.

"Take the blade she hides under her sleeve," said Queen Adela.

"It's an herbing knife, Your Majesty, not a weapon. I need it for my work." Too late; one of the men already pulled it from its sheath. He held it up, admiring the blade in the latticed window light.

"Another month, Your Majesty, please!"

"Throw her in a cell."

# CHAPTER THIRTY-THREE

# Dungeon, Pendragon Castle

## WOLF MOON
### *Late September 1210*

THEY LOCKED ME in a cell not much bigger than a rowboat. The single barred window high above me on the wall disgorged a pale gray light. I kicked the stinking rushes and crouched against the wall, clutching my stomach, the smell of rat piss in my nose.

The next day a guard wrapped a chain around my middle and tied my hands behind my back with a rope. Two men led me from my cell, one holding the end of the chain as if I were a leashed dog. Outside, a great mob filled the castle green from one side to the other. Common folk shoved past the well-dressed courtiers to jeer and hurl dirt clumps at me as I was led along.

Clods smacked me from all sides, but that was nothing to the dreadful sight of the great wood stack up ahead prepared for a burning. On the viewing stage, Lady Olivia and Bianca stood next to the queen. And on the left, seated between the bishop and King Arden, was Jackrun.

What in the name of the Holy Ones was he doing up there?

My heart cinched. I had let myself trust him . . . There must be a reason he sat with the king, but why wouldn't he face me?

The king's men positioned me below the stage, an arm's length from a filthy, middle-aged man dressed in brown sacking.

The queen ordered, "Bring Master Ridolfi up." It was the queen's previous physician.

Two guards brought the poor man up the stage steps and put him front and center, where he knelt on one knee to Her Majesty, head bowed.

Queen Adela said, "Master Ridolfi, you pricked me, leeched me, and lied to me. You sickened me with potions. You knowingly harmed your sovereign queen. For these crimes you will burn."

The crowd raised a cheer. Queen Adela held up her hand to silence them. "Do you have any last words to say before this crowd of witnesses and before God?" she asked.

"Your Majesty, have mercy," he begged. "As God is my witness, I used my cures to help you and heal you. I swear I meant you no harm. Reduce me to ruin. Exile me if Your Majesty sees fit. I will leave Wilde Island shunned and bereft and never return. But please have pity. Don't burn me."

The crowd booed. They'd come here to see a burning.

"Bishop, give him his rightful service," Queen Adela said flatly. The bishop was in full regalia, the golden stitching adorning his creamy robes matching the glittering threads in his tall hat. He stepped to the kneeling, trembling man, said a prayer in Latin, and crossed the man's filthy forehead with holy oil.

"Bring Mistress Uma up," Queen Adela called. My legs lost their bones. The guards hoisted me up the stairs. My head buzzed with screaming whispers like an aroused beehive. *I have another month. A month. I have until October's end. She promised me. She promised!* My tongue felt thick as a slug. Jackrun still wouldn't lift his eyes. He studied the stage as if it were a book.

Queen Adela's fey eye glinted as she appraised me. "You have disappointed me, Uma Quarteney. For that you will watch this condemned physician burn. Remember, this is your future, and your burning day will come upon you fast if you fail me again.

"Bring my physician down as close as you dare to the pyre," she told the guards. "And stake her in place so she feels the heat. Lady Olivia, you have been in charge of her. You may go and stand with her and keep her company. Bianca, accompany your mother," she added with a sly smile.

The guards dragged me ten paces from the base of the pyre, drove a stake in the grassy ground, and chained me to it, smashing my bound wrists against the post so I could not move or run. Looking over my shoulder for Jackrun, neck straining to find him, to read his face again, to understand,

I was crushed to find I could only see the far corner of the viewing stage, the king's ornate shoes and colorful hose, the base of his carved chair. The crowd surged on my left as people jostled closer to the pyre. The sweet scent of hyacinth perfume filled the air as Lady Olivia joined me with Bianca. A guard shoved them closer, but did not tie them to my post.

Bianca clutched her mother's sleeve, driving her fingers into the folds. "I don't want to watch," she said in a small voice. The large droplets of sweat on the edge of her upper lip quavered as she spoke.

Lady Olivia patted her hand. "I know, my darling. Be strong."

I could not think why Queen Adela ordered Bianca to stand this close to the pyre unless she somehow learned about the sapphire bracelet King Arden gave her and was punishing her for it.

Master Ridolfi gripped the ladder with his bony hands and was creeping spiderlike rung to rung. The guard prodded his backside with a pike until he reached the platform. He tied the man firmly to the stake with a long chain before climbing down and removing the ladder.

"There must be something you can do," Bianca pleaded. "Ask Queen Adela to call us back to the stage, she—"

"Hush, Bianca. It will all be over soon."

But it wasn't over soon. The king's men surrounded the pyre, jamming torches under the base where the wood had been blackened with pitch to assure a hotter blaze. The acrid odor of burning pitch filled my nose as the wood caught.

Bright flames leaped up. The crowd roared their approval, hungry for the burning as if it were a fine bit of entertainment after a day's work.

Thick smoke tumbled toward me. I swallowed and coughed, praying in my own language, asking for mercy, for the man to die quickly, for his soul to go where Christian souls went, a heaven I'd heard the priest describe that was as peaceful as Nushtuen, the place my father journeyed to after he left his body. The flames at the base of the stacked wood were the color of new-mown hay. They turned the darker yellow of wild iris as they rose higher, licking the wood, the platform, swarming in to the man's bare feet.

"God have mercy!" he wailed. The crowd cheered.

Lady Olivia gripped my arm. "Oh God," she cried as the fire rose up the screaming man's legs. "No one should have to die this way!" She hunched over, groaning. Bianca clung to her, sputtered and cried.

A sob wrenched up my throat. The searing heat coming off the pyre tightened the skin on my face, dried the tears that ran down my cheeks. Flames swept up and caught the man's sacking. *Save him. Someone save him.* I thought of the dragon who'd flown in to save Tanya, but this was no half-fey girl. No dragon would rescue him.

Bianca fainted in the heat and misery. Her mother bent over her, too weak to help her up, and I could do nothing to help either one of them with my hands tied behind my back. Bianca lay a long while at our feet like a cut flower as the inferno heated my body. I baked in my clothes. The pattern of my stitched bodice pressed against my skin like the hot wires Father used to burn the fox mark on my chest.

Master Ridolfi let out his last pitiful shriek and died.

The crowd roared with triumph. Lady Olivia leaned her head against my shoulder. The smoky smell of cooking flesh brought bile up my throat. *His pain is over. It's over.* But there were more insults to come. Small bits of burned sacking sent by a hot wind floated down over us where we stood close to the blaze. Lady Olivia weakly tried to brush off the falling smuts. Every wipe left a trail of black smears on her face, her sleeves, the gown she always kept so impeccably clean. I could do nothing to brush away the smuts landing on me. The soot settled like black snow on Bianca's pale blue gown, her face and outspread hair.

The inferno still raged. I sucked in ashes, choked. "Please unchain me," I begged. "It's over now. The man is dead."

Three men came out to aid Lady Olivia and Bianca, carrying the girl away. But they left me in place by the blazing pyre, letting me bake in hellfire until the queen allowed them to release me, and drag me seared and broken back up to the Crow's Nest.

# CHAPTER THIRTY-FOUR

# Crow's Nest, Wilde Island

## WOLF MOON
*Late September 1210*

"I HATE HER. I hate her. I hate her." I'd been crouched against this wall in the Crow's Nest, choking out the words with my head bent, my hands over the back of my sweaty neck since they'd hauled me up the stairs and shut me in.

"I hate her. Hate her. Hate her." She hadn't changed since her witch-hunting days when she'd burned women up and down the countryside. She was a ruthless monarch who executed people when they did not give her what she wanted. I'd believed her when she'd threatened to burn me after three months, but believing it was one thing, witnessing it another. The cruelty of Ridolfi's burning, the sight and sound and smell of it shook me to my core. I knew now what it meant to burn.

Someone was knocking at the door. I raised my head,

blinking in the shadowy room lit only by the dusky light from the open window. I hadn't lit a candle, revolted at the look and feel of fire, wanting nothing to do with it ever again.

"Uma?" Jackrun called.

Stiff from crouching, I went, slid the bolt aside, and opened the door to him. He flew in with a flurry of sudden storm, set a tray of food on the table, swept me in his arms, held me tight. "Uma, I'm sorry. I'm so sorry."

His body was too warm after Ridolfi's burning. I wanted cold. I hated him and his fire. He'd sat on the stage with Her. I pushed him away. "How could you do it?" I choked.

"It was all I could do to convince her to let you live," he said, drawing me close and holding me again. I was stiff in his arms, still not sure if I could trust him.

"I found out what was happening when the men left the weapons yard to build the pyre." He rocked me in his arms. "I went straight to my aunt. She was determined to tie two physicians to the stake. I had to use all the negotiation skills I've learned over the years to talk her out of burning you. She was fixed, mad. I talked ceaselessly yesterday and again with her last night, Uma." He passed his hand down my hair, my back. "I moved you step by step from the fire. She finally agreed not to burn you today on two conditions: that you must be staked down perilously close to the fire, and that I sit on the royal viewing stage to show my support of the Pendragon family, say nothing, not even give you a look."

He put his hands to my head, lifting it, kissing the tears

from my cheeks, kissing my ears, my neck, all the places the smuts still blackened. Through the open window I heard the sea crashing against the distant cliffs as he kissed me. He was the night and the sea and I melted, kissing him back, pulling him closer, wanting him closer still. The fire had nearly ended me. Now I wanted life, wanted him, admitted to myself how much I had wanted him and for how long. I wanted his flesh pressed against mine, no clothes between us.

I tugged his leather surcoat. He removed it and peeled off his shirt. I ran my hands along his warm chest and back, feeling the muscles underneath.

"Come away with me," he said, tugging the lacings on my gown and kissing my neck, my shoulder. "You have to come away with me tonight."

I slid my hand down the scale patch on his forearm, my breath catching. The overlapping scales were softer and cooler than I expected. "I can't run."

"I won't let her hurt you. She'll burn you if you stay." He kissed the tip of my ear, my throat. "Why didn't you tell me before that she'd threatened to burn you by October's end?"

"Quiet now." I didn't want to talk about that. I didn't want to talk at all, only hold him and kiss him, but he drew back a little, putting his hands on my waist.

"You *will* come away with me, Uma. We'll use the escape passage. I left two horses tied up near my family tomb so we could ride out tonight. That's what I was doing just before I came up here." He held out his hand. I didn't take it.

"I'll hide you in Dragonswood where she can't find you.

Later we can board a ship and sail anywhere in the world, away from her, away from the fairies' plans for me. Away from all of this."

"I have to stay."

"Why?" he asked, frowning, shaking me a little as if to shake sense into me.

"She has my village surrounded, Jackrun. If I run away now, they will never be free. If I stay and she conceives a child, she has promised to bring the army home, so I can't run. I won't."

"What chance is there when the fey folk have her hexed?"

"You're only guessing that's so. My father's medicines are powerful. I still might give her a child, an heir. I have another month, Jackrun. I have until the end of Dragon Moon."

"For God's sake, Uma, she'll burn you! She would have done it today if I hadn't stopped her. She's mad. She doesn't care at all for you. She'll kill you and move on to the next physician who promises her what she wants. You have to get out now." He pushed his arm through his sleeve, fighting into his clothes.

"Would you go if you were me? If your people were counting on you? My mother's down there, surrounded by soldiers!"

Jackrun put his fist against his forehead and turned his back to me. "This is the only way. You have to come."

"I won't."

His whole body shook. Then he swung around, smoke pouring from his nose.

"Are you going to roar fire now?" I said. "After what I just went through outside?"

He slid a knife from his belt. I leaped back. He gripped the blade and slapped the handle into my hand. My skin stung. He walked out, slamming the door behind him. When I looked down I saw my own herbing knife, the one the guard had taken.

My body hurt all over. Every joint ached with anger and passion and horror and need. It felt like I'd been thrown down the stairs.

I HAD TO stop crying, but I couldn't for a long while. I curled up and wept until my throat was raw. At last I struck the flints, lit a candle, and stared down at the food Jackrun had brought me. I hadn't eaten since yestereve. I was too sickened to touch it, too starving not to. I drank the small ale, tore at the bread, stuffing handfuls in my mouth, chewing with bloated cheeks.

The cut of beef sat untouched on the pewter tray, the smell of the roasted meat too much like the pyre. I pinched the revolting thing and threw it out the window.

Knocking again. My heart did a little flip in my chest. Jackrun? I ran to the door.

"Message for you, mistress physician!" said a boyish voice from the other side. I sighed, opening the door to the page, who handed me a note. I was used to a verbal summons. This was my first note. He rocked back on his feet as I opened the wax seal, glad Mother had taught me how to read English from her small prayer book. It was from Lady Olivia. I saw at once why she'd chosen to write the private message.

> Uma, the queen's flow is strong. She bleeds and groans with pain. Bring her a medicine to ease her cramps and something to help her sleep. Come immediately.

> Signed,
> Lady Olivia, Companion to Queen Adela, ruler of Wilde Island and the sister isle of Dragon's Keep

"Tell Lady Olivia I will come."

I shut the door and leaned against it. Queen Adela was giving me another chance to serve as her royal physician. How could I treat her tonight after she'd so ruthlessly burned Master Ridolphi?

I did not wish her well.

I wanted her dead.

I opened Father's Herbal to the *Adan-duxma*—physician's creed—and read the warning halfway down. *If you mix a remedy with hate in your heart, it will act like poison.* Mix her remedies now and I would poison her.

I read the other lines farther down. *All people suffer. All people feel pain. Adans do not take sides in battle. Adans heal the wicked and the righteous alike.*

*All people suffer.* I saw how Queen Adela suffered, driven by child lust, by raw unanswered need. I saw the love she wanted from her husband and didn't have, the madness that ruled her mind and isolated her from everyone. I saw how her wind mind scattered her thoughts and drove her into darkness. I'd listened when she'd grieved and raged, calling her God cruel for taking her only son from her, for giving her a stillborn daughter with a clawed foot, for not giving her another healthy child after years and years of trying. I stood a moment, hoping to feel my heart soften toward her, if just a little.

Nothing.

I took up the herbing knife, my palm remembering the sting of Jackrun's anger when he'd slapped it into my hand.

Light hurried footsteps came up the stairs. "Uma?" Bianca cried, tapping on the door.

"Not now. I cannot see you now."

"You have to, please. You must!"

When I slid the bolt aside, she flew straight into my arms, sobbing. "How could she do that to him? Every time I close my eyes I see him burning. I will never be able to sleep again."

We held each other. I cried with her, surprised I had any tears left when I'd already wrung my heart dry these past few hours.

"My head hurts so much," she said. "Please give me some evicta, Uma. I know I shouldn't ask again. You told me not to."

Her wet tears cooled my neck. "I'm sorry Her Majesty made you stand so close. I'm sorry that you had to come at all." I wiped my eyes, an idea forming. "I'm about to crush some evicta for the queen," I said, "but I think I can spare some for you."

"Oh, thank you." She hugged me again before she let me go, came and leaned against the table as I got out my mortar and pestle.

I crushed the purple gyocana seeds in the mortar, the tiny black evicta, softly chanting the Euit names under my breath. I focused on curing Bianca's pain and not the queen's, hoping if I kept my mind on Bianca, whose presence warmed me, whose watchful eyes made me feel less alone, I could prepare the remedies without turning them to poison.

Bianca licked the evicta-speckled honey as a kitten washes its paw, curtsied in gratitude, and kissed my hand as if I were a queen. When she left, I finished my preparations, filling the gooey centers of the sweetmeats with the black and purple powders, one for pain, one for sleep.

On my way to the queen, I paused partway down the stairs, hearing voices on the second story, and peeked around the doorframe. Dim as it was, I could see King Arden holding Bianca in his arms. She moaned, resting her head on his chest.

"I'm sorry you were made to watch, my dear," King Arden said, stroking her hair. It shocked me to hear him repeating almost word for word the very thing I'd said to her upstairs.

She wept softly, her satin gown crushed up against him. By all that was holy, what was she getting herself into? What would her mother, who was grooming her so carefully to marry someone of a high position, say if she knew?

I breathed a little silent sigh when Bianca pulled away at last, thinking she had seen sense. *She will curtsy to His Majesty now and they will part.* It did not go that way. Instead King Arden offered her his arm. They walked together, heads bent close to each other, strolling not toward his bedchamber where his private guards would be waiting, but in the opposite direction.

I had to follow. Taking a slow breath and whispering *havuela*—become—I stepped into the hall following them on silent feet as they rounded the next corner, hoping they wouldn't stop at Bianca's private room. They did.

He whispered in her ear and kissed her softly on the mouth before he opened her door and drew her inside.

THE QUEEN WAS in her bed propped up against the pillows, a lambskin draped over her middle. The embroidered drapery surrounding her canopy bed showed a summer's day outing with king and queen, knights and courtiers riding through wildflowers, feasting by a lake while minstrels played. Some long-ago time of ease and joy, or a time that never existed except in cloth and thread.

Lady Olivia read, "That I might watch the splendid birds over the well watered sea—" She paused and lowered the poetry book as I stepped farther in.

The queen glared at me when I curtsied. "What took you so long?"

"Her Majesty is in great pain," Lady Olivia added. She appeared proper as always, as if the pyre had never been lit.

"Cramps," the queen whispered as I brought the sweetmeats closer. "Ghosts. Get out," she snarled suddenly, not at me but at Lady Olivia, who dropped the little book, curtsied as she retrieved it, and backed quickly from the room.

We were alone. I held out the tray.

"Where is my tonic?" asked Queen Adela.

"I have added medicine to these sweetmeats for your cramp pain, Your Majesty."

She ate them both, moaning as she chewed. "Why are we made to suffer every month this way? God's wrath is on all women." She wiped the crumbs from her mouth and crossed herself almost as a second thought having spoken ill of her god. "I cannot sleep, Uma. Too many ghosts."

*Ghosts of all the people you've killed.* Hate flooded me again, thinking of Master Ridolfi. "The medicine will also help you sleep, Your Grace."

"Medicine," she said, drawing the sound out slowly as if it were a foreign word. "You saw what will happen to you if you fail me."

*I hate her.* "I will not fail you, Your Majesty."

"You seem very sure of yourself."

I looked away. If the fey had hexed her, I had no chance at all. I would die. She moaned. I adjusted the lambskin across her middle. Women heated them near the fire and placed them skin side down to ease cramps: an old cure and a good one. It was one thing women in our tribe were allowed to do without an Adan. Such a small thing.

Queen Adela petted the tiny curls in the wool. I thought of King Arden running his fingers through Bianca's hair, of what they might be doing in her room even now, and swallowed.

"A boy," said Queen Adela. "You have to promise me a boy. An heir." She looked up, the pupil of her living eye round and dark as an owl's. I stared at her. She could not make me promise that.

"Uma?" she said. "A boy child."

"Your Majesty, a boy to become Pendragon king, or a girl to become Pendragon queen."

"A boy. A king!"

"A king," I repeated just as loudly, promising nothing, only matching the intensity of her shout.

She smiled at me. "Very good," she said.


LADY OLIVIA LOOKED up from her book a few hours later when I entered her room. "How is she, Uma?"

"The queen is asleep." I had paused to listen outside Bianca's door before heading down the hall to her mother's room. I'd heard no sounds from within, but the king might still be in there. "The queen wants you to slide the trundle bed out below hers so you can be near her tonight if she should wake in need of anything."

Lady Olivia sighed at the news. I didn't look up in case she detected the lie. The queen had made no such demand. I wanted Lady Olivia back upstairs and out of the way as soon as possible so she would not run into King Arden exiting her daughter's room. I kept my eyes on the crumpled dark green gown in the corner on the floor. Threads dangled like webs from the smudged fabric. She had torn off every decorative pearl that once adorned the bodice.

Lady Olivia quietly closed her book. Whatever rage she'd taken out on the gown was long gone. "I will never wear that again," she said.

"A laundress could wash the ash—"

"Never," she repeated, standing and kicking it toward me as if it were a dead thing. "Take it if you want it. If you don't, I'll have it burned."

I had grown more accustomed to Bianca's gowns. But I had only two. The gray one I wore now needed washing; still, I couldn't seem to reach down to rescue the silken green dress that smelled strongly of Lady Olivia's perfume and smoke. I felt like the very richness of her gown would bind me to her proper Englishness, the lacings tie me inside her stiff, emotionless prison. I would lose myself in it.

"Thank you, no, my lady."

Upstairs, I was too exhausted to clean my worktable or put the mortar and pestle back in Father's trunk. I dragged myself across the room, collapsed on my narrow bed, and wrapped myself in the Euit blanket Lady Tess gave me, missing Jackrun, wishing we hadn't fought, wishing the world were different, that I was different, that no one depended upon me for their freedom and I could go with him.

I thought the worst day I'd spent in Pendragon Castle since my father died was over. Nothing else could drag me any deeper down in despair than I already was.

I was wrong.

# PART THREE

# Healing

# CHAPTER THIRTY-FIVE

# Vazan's Den, Wilde Island

## WOLF MOON
### *Late September 1210*

SOMEONE HAD BROKEN into the Adan's trunk, stolen all the medicines meant for the queen. I didn't discover it until the morning. The thief took everything but the wound kit I'd left in my herb basket. I nearly tripped running down the stairs to find Jackrun.

"He rode out," his pageboy said.

I cornered the boy, nearly pushing him against the wall. "When did he leave?"

"Last night."

"Did he say when he'd be back?"

The boy shrugged. "He doesn't tell me nothing."

Herb basket on my back, I took the wound supplies, the Euit blanket, and father's dragon belt, carrying the few precious things I still had left in my possession from my room. *Trust no one*, Jackrun said. I didn't.

You do not visit a red dragon in her den, but I was desperate. Thick fog rolled in from the sea as I headed out alone, shivering in my cloak, walking the edge of the cliffs. If this was September's chill, what would winter be like here in the north? *You won't be here that long. One way or another, you won't be here.* The thought made me shiver even more. At the bottom of the long, crooked wooden stairs, I stopped to fill a leather sack with sand and grabbed a stick before continuing on. Tracing the bottom of the high cliffs, I paused now and again and sniffed the air below the caves up in the rocky wall. When I caught Vazan's scent, I peeled off my slippers and started climbing up, catching tiny outcroppings with my fingers, finding a handhold here, a toehold there.

The keys to Father's trunk and Herbal clinked against the stone as I worked my way up. Useless to wear them now the Herbal was gone, the trunk empty. The small clinking sound scolded my ears. The noise must have also alerted Vazan. Either that or she caught my scent. A red scaly head poked out above. Silver eyes watched me struggling along the steep cliff with cool disinterest. *If I slip, she will simply let me fall to teach me a lesson for daring to approach her private cave,* I thought. But when I reached the mouth she moved her foreleg back enough for me to crawl inside.

I blew on my freezing fingers, missing the warmer caves I'd known back home, then greeted her in Euit. "We are being in this place together." I scooted far enough inside to reverence her, bowing with my hands on the stony cave floor, not touching her. She'd never allowed me that, though I wondered if her skin might be warm.

"We are being in this place," Vazan answered in kind, creeping backward to let me farther in while also blocking the way to the deeper recesses of her cave. Her sharp peppery odor stung my nose, and comingled with the ranker odor of rotting meat, which nearly overpowered me. Still, it worked both ways. I knew she would wash the walls with fire to remove my human smell from her den after I had gone. To lessen my offense, I kept as close to the mouth of the cave as I could without falling out.

"I won't stay long, Vazan. You have been courageous to remain here with me in my trouble."

"I am here to make sure the queen keeps her promise. The Pendragon soldiers have to go. We do not want the English so close to our mountain. If they stay long enough to overtake our hunting lands, they will lose the protection of our long-held treaty. They will meet our teeth, our claws, and our fire." She roared a heated jet. I flattened myself against the wall as it flared out the mouth of her cave.

Satisfied, she shook her head, her scales making soft crinkling sounds. She yawned. "Leave, Uma. I am sleeping now."

"I would not disturb your sleep, rivule, if—"

"You came for thissss." She reached back, filled her claw, and placed two green piles near my feet. My heart swelled as I fingered the pink root tendrils still clumped with earth, the hand-shaped bapeeta leaves with the precious dots of pollen on the undersides. She had gone to find it after all. "*Tuma-doa*—Thank you. I'm grateful, rivule."

Vazan flicked out her long tongue, ready for me to go.

I steadied myself and cleared my throat. "I have bad news. I need more—"

"Of that?" she said, pointing to the herbs with one of her talons. "I will not go after any more of it!"

"No, this is enough bapeeta, *tuma-doa*. It's—" I took a breath, afraid to admit what had happened. "I've been robbed, rivule. Someone came in last night while I was attending the queen. I was gone two hours. They used that time to break into the Adan's trunk and take everything inside. The queen's remedies are gone." I'd gone to sleep not knowing the robbery had already taken place. If I had cleaned the table, put the mortar and pestle back in the trunk, I would have seen it was empty.

"The fertility herbs to get her with child?"

"Yes, even that."

"Then the army will stay in Devil's Boot. These English will have won." She flattened her ears against her head. "How could you leave the Adan's medicines unguarded?"

"There was no one but myself to guard them! The herbarium door bolts from the inside. I had no way to lock the door from the outside, and whoever stole the herbs broke the lock on Father's trunk."

"You searched for them, of course. Where did you look?"

I shifted on my feet. "Where would I search? I'm not allowed to scour private rooms. I cannot ask the king's guard to do it. Tell them my herbs are missing and the queen might turn on me, burn me straightaway."

"Who would do thissss?"

"Someone wants me to fail. Jackrun thought it might be the fey folk working against me, but we—"

"Why would they work against you?"

"To keep the queen infertile so Jackrun can inherit the throne."

"Prophecy," she said, clicking her black talons on the stone floor. "Yessss."

"I plan to go on fighting, rivule."

"The herbs you need to win have been snatched," she reminded. "You are declawed."

I tugged the herb basket from my back, pulled out the leather sack, and poured a pile of sand on the cave floor.

"What's this, Uma?"

"You were with us when Father's Path Animal led him to the herbs to make the fertility cure, when he found the kea and when he sent me up the tree to pick huzana leaves from the vines." I smoothed the sand out with my palm and used the stick to etch the thorny kea stems and shape the serrated leaves.

"Why draw this on my floor?"

"To remind you of what the plants look like."

"Why not show me in the Adan's Herbal?"

My hand froze mid-drawing. I hadn't wanted to tell her that part.

"Uma?"

"It's gone with everything else, rivule."

Vazan hissed. She enveloped me in so much smoke, I had to rush to the entrance, hang my head out and breathe. She could not feel this loss as acutely as I did. No one could. At the mouth of the cave I hugged my stomach, remembering the years I'd watched Father engrossed in his masterful book, sketching the outlines of each plant and listing their medicinal properties. His life's work was in that Herbal. I thought it would always be near to study at my leisure. I thought I would have it forever.

When the smoke cleared enough for me to come back inside, I faced her again. "We have to harvest the fertility herbs, Vazan. It must be done, but I cannot go myself. I cannot leave the queen." She said nothing, just blinked at me as if I were an annoying rodent that had stumbled into her den. "You want the soldiers out of Devil's Boot as much as I do, Vazan. We have to keep working toward that. Everyone is depending on us."

"Ussss? I wasn't asked to cure this queen."

"I hope you will go south for us and pick the herbs we need, Vazan, for your clan and for mine."

She clicked her talons again. Sparks flew out this time. "The bapeeta you asked for grew in a crevasse. I had to crawl down the narrow crack. It cost me."

What did she mean by *cost me*? "Were you hurt, rivule?"

She did not answer. Of course she would not. I'd noticed the unusually pungent scent as soon as I'd entered. I'd ignored it thinking it was because I was inside her den. But what if the putrid odor came from a wound? Afraid for her, I said, "Let me see."

"There is nothing you can do, Uma."

She snapped her teeth when I ignored her and crossed to her right side, where there was more space to move between her large body and the cave wall. There was a reason why she'd given that side more room. I only had to look to see the long jagged tear running down her partly folded wing. The overlapping scales should have protected the wing skin beneath like heavy plumage, but they hadn't been thick enough to shield her against the sharp rocks that must have torn her wing in the narrow crevasse. "How in the name of the Holy Ones did you fly home with this torn wing, rivule?"

"I mostly walked," she said, snapping her teeth again. I felt like snapping mine. It was a terrible injury for her. Dragons had to fly great distances to hunt. An inability to fly would be a death sentence. Large and powerful as she was, she wasn't fast enough to chase a buck or a boar on the ground. I could scream at the injustice of an injury grounding her just when I needed her to fly south. But she'd gotten this way to begin with because I'd sent her to gather the bapeeta.

I needed to examine her more closely. She had never let me touch her. Ever.

I stepped closer and gently traced the edge of the tear. She growled. I kept my hand where it was.

Her dragon skin felt thick and leathery. The layered wing scales were varied shades, from bloodred with yellow edges, to poppy orange to red brown, to a rich vermillion. More beautiful than feathers, they shone like soft, living jewels.

"Do you trust me to help you?"

Her growl grew deeper.

I ignored it. I'd known her all my life. She'd been loyal to my father and borne him on his back year after year. "I can stitch your wing so you can fly again."

"Flying made the tear worse," she hissed.

"So you intend to keep to your cave and starve?" Smoke rolled from her nostrils. "The tear won't worsen in flight if it's sutured." I hurried back to the entrance and pulled the wound kit from my basket. The sea fog illumined the den in soft gray tones. Not enough illumination for what I had to do. "I'll need more light."

She shot a breath of fire.

"Wait," I added, dragging everything to the wall near her right side so she wouldn't burn me or my basket. "Now, give me a steady flare, please."

"You are not the Adan."

"I'm all you have."

There was a long silence. The Adan had trained me to thread his needle. He'd let me watch him stitch many kinds of wounds, small and large, deep and shallow, straight and ragged. I would not tell Vazan I had never sutured wounds myself.

I squeezed the needle between my fingers, waiting for more light. Vazan finally gave in and hissed out a low, steady fire so I could work. Her decision ignited a small flame of courage. I threaded the needle. "Open your wing a little and spread it out. Now tilt it upward." The topmost part of the tear was too high up for me to reach even with her lying on her stomach. "I will have to stand on your back foot."

"You will not," she said, her fire going out again.

"I will if you want to be healed."

She grunted and moved her leg forward, her claws fully extended in silent warning. It was one thing to touch her, another to stand on her back leg using it like a stool, but it had to be done. I steeled myself and stepped up. Her scales were soft, almost silken on the soles of my feet. I poised my needle. "This might hurt."

Vazan huffed bright, indignant fire over the warning. Her right eye swiveled back to watch me as I poked her skin, drawing out the thread. I wished her eyes couldn't move independently so I could work without an audience. I knew better than to suggest she look away.

Father said, *Be present with what you are doing.* I tried to put away my fears and focus on Vazan's torn wing, my needle. Mother was a gifted weaver. I'd been hopeless at it, all ventures ended in tangled threads. I'd been no better at stitchery. I was in the past again, trapped in fear. *Be present.* I began working stitch by careful stitch. I grew calmer. After a while my hands and fingers began to tingle. The small flame of courage I'd felt earlier burned in my chest, warmth spread down my arms to my fingertips. My hand was steady. My sutures sure. Was this what the Adan meant by being present?

The warm energy thrummed through me as I continued, repairing her wound with neat, even stitches. I was not my father. I was only Uma, but I knew this healing work. I knew it well. Vazan's breaths were slow and steady by the time I salved her wing with fragrant woundwort.

"It will be sore for a while," I said when I finished at last and climbed down from her leg.

"But I will fly?"

"Yes."

"Yessss," she said, scrabbling her claws against the cave floor.

"Not yet," I warned. "It's too soon!" Vazan ignored me. Her tail slapped my thighs, stinging them as she rushed through the entrance and launched into the air.

I cursed her impetuousness, watching her soar out over the water, anxiously called her name when she disappeared in the thick morning fog. Babak might swim, but if her weak wing failed her and she fell, she could not. *By all that's sacred. Fly out there and drown. That's just what we need!* I heaved a sigh when I could see her again. She caught a few gulls in her jaws before coming back inside, went to her favored spot, and spat her small prizes on the floor. Five dead gulls lay at her feet.

"I told you to wait," I shouted. "It should be two days at least before you do that again!" It was dangerous to raise your voice to a fire breather. I didn't care. I was her physician and she had to listen to me. She reared back, her silver eyes wide. I pressed myself against the wall, waiting for retribution. And waited.

"*Tuma-doa*, Uma," she said. My head swam. She had never thanked me before. I was sure I had never even heard her thank the Adan. Her *tuma-doa* should be acknowledged. Words stuck in my throat. "I'm . . . glad I could help you," I said, peeling myself away from the wall, still overcome with surprise. "I know what it means for you to be able to fly."

"You do not know what it means or how much it means," she corrected. Below the sharpness I heard a hint of gratitude.

Vazan lay down and speared the dead fowl, one on each talon of her left claw. She used her right to pluck the feathers the way I'd once seen Bianca tugging petals from a flower, saying, *He loves me, he loves me not,* then roasted her meal with a fiery breath.

When they were browned, she tore off some meat and held it out to me. "Hungry?" she asked, tipping her head.

My jaw dropped. What was happening? Reds never shared their food with humans. I stared at the meat within my reach, caught the alluring smell. My empty stomach growled.

"Take it, Uma," she said in a soft tone. This was not the Vazan I knew. She held her offering closer. I had not eaten any food since Jackrun's bread. I thanked her, plucked the meat from her talons, and stared at it in awe.

On the floor near Vazan I ate slowly. All my worries had melted while my mind was focused, working on her wing. Now my fears raced back with the full force of a raiding army.

"You are shaking," Vazan said.

I hadn't noticed that I was. Her dragon's body radiated warmth, so it was not from cold. "I don't know what I will do, Vazan."

"You said you would go on fighting, Uma."

How? I'd planned to send her down to Devil's Boot for the fertility herbs. A healthy dragon could fly there and back with speed, giving me a chance to continue the queen's daily treatments. By the time Vazan's wing was strong enough to fly the long journey to Devil's Boot, we would be halfway through Dragon Moon.

The feathers on the cave floor were white as the egret feather Jackrun gave me for the Moon Dance. I touched one with my finger. I should have listened to him. What did it matter that I'd stayed behind to fight now that the medicines were stolen?

I pulled the keys out from under my gown and wrapped my fingers around them. They were icy cold. The Herbal was stolen. Father's trunk ransacked. I should throw away the useless keys. I knew I wouldn't. I tucked the cord back under my stitched bodice, the back side of my hand rubbing against the pearl-studded collar. Father's keys were more precious to me than pearls. "I should return to the castle now," I said, coming to a stand.

"Sit," Vazan said.

"I cannot stay any longer, rivule. The queen—"

"Do it, Uma." She pointed to the floor at the base of her ruby red chest. So close to her? Vazan was waiting. Red dragons lived long. Their patience was short. I stepped between her muscled forearms spread out like two large roots, and sat with crossed legs in the shadow of her jaw.

"Lean your back against my chest and close your eyes."

"Why?"

She clicked her talons on the stone floor dangerously close to my knee and let out a small exasperated hiss.

I did as I was told. Her dragon warmth spread up my spine. Her throat made a windy sound as she drew breath in and out. She'd told me to close my eyes. The moment I shut them, my fear came at me in a torrent. It was over. I would fail. I would die. The army would stay in Devil's Boot. My heart split open like dry, cracked clay, broke like one of the jars I'd hurled against the wall in Father's healing hut. It hurt too much to sit still. I opened my eyes and struggled to stand. Vazan pushed me back down firmly with her claw and pressed me against her chest.

"I said close your eyessss."

I closed them and sank deeper into my despair. Each thought was a stab.

*The queen will kill me. Holy Ones help me. I don't know what to do.*

Hot tears ran down my cheeks. No answer came. The darkness went on and on. I walked on a dim path to nowhere, my feet moving in the rhythm of Vazan's heart beating against my back. I carried my broken heart with me as if in offering to the Holy Ones; Father Sun, Mother Earth, Brother Wind, Sister Sea.

After a while the darkness behind my eyes went from

pitch-black to a deep shade of twilight blue. Tall figures loomed ahead. I thought at first I had come to a place of standing dragons, but as the blue softened to daylight, I found I was walking in a forest, passing under ancient oaks and towering pines. Droplets fell from the branches pitter-pattering on the forest floor. The plants around the trees were unfamiliar, not like the ones in Devil's Boot.

A flash of red-orange caught my eye. A bristling fox tail vanished between the trees. The fox mark below my collarbone began to burn as I followed the moving tail through the underbrush. In a clearing I saw the distant snowcapped ridges of a familiar mountain before the dense forest hid the view again. I climbed a steep path in the foothills, passing golden-leafed beech trees where the ground leveled off again, then row on row of dogwoods.

Another bright flash of fox tail. I followed as it darted behind mulberry bushes and brambles. Then fox came out in full view. She sat and looked straight at me with her golden brown eyes, her ears pricked, her mouth open, panting. The fox mark on my skin burned hotter as if a living coal were pressed below my collarbone. I stared at my Path Animal sitting before a cane patch of tall thorny plants with serrated leaves and dark shriveled berries.

Kea plants.

I fell to my knees.

When I opened my eyes again, I found myself in the cave, still leaning against Vazan. I'd been with Father in the healer's hut, and later at Pendragon castle, when he'd prayed surrounded by the four sacred elements. A few times when he'd gone very still, he'd awakened saying, "I've seen where the herbs grow."

The Holy Ones had never given me a vision. Until now.

I stood up, turned, and bowed to Vazan, touching her feet.

"Did you find something?" Vazan asked.

I looked into her molten silver eyes. "I saw a place where kea grows, Vazan. How did you do that?"

"I did nothing. I just made you sit and look inside. Visions do not come when you are fleeing from yourself."

I looked at my small feet, her powerful claws. You could not run from yourself. But I knew what she meant. Visions had not always come quickly to my father. Nine years he'd prayed for the right fertility cure. I should not expect visions to be painless or to come easily. All Vazan had done was made me sit with my fears, feel them, move into them, pray my way beyond them. But it meant everything.

"Is the herb close by?" she asked.

I told her what I'd seen.

She flicked out her forked tongue. "Dragonswood," she said.

# CHAPTER THIRTY-SIX

# Pendragon Castle to Dragonswood

## DEATH OF WOLF MOON
### *September 1210*

"I HAVE HAD a vision, Your Majesty," I told the queen in a firm voice. "I saw fresh herbs I must gather for you."

The queen held very still for the artist painting her portrait in the throne room. I could not approach her throne and stood by Lady Olivia while the artist worked.

"A vision?" Her Majesty said.

"It is the way we find our cures." *The way an Adan finds cures,* I thought, still reeling from what happened in Vazan's cave. "Morgesh Mountain," Vazan said when I described the shape of the snowy ridge I'd seen in my vision. That told me two things: First, since this was the mountain that crowned the northernmost section of Dragonswood, the kea was not far away. Second, unlike Jackrun, I would have to get permission to cross the boundary wall and enter the refuge.

Her Majesty adjusted her jeweled crown, lifted her chin,

and posed again. "Why do you need these particular herbs?"

I couldn't risk admitting my supplies had been stolen. "The Adan and I brought what we'd harvested back home. But now I need a fresh supply, Your Highness."

"You are not telling me this so you can run away?" She'd turned her head. The artist paused mid-brushstroke.

"If I wanted to run away I would not be asking your permission, Your Majesty."

"Please, Your Grace, turn your head again," the painter said. She returned to her position. "Thank you, Your Majesty."

"I will be gone herbing only a day or two at most, if it pleases you."

"If it pleases me?" She laughed. "You are sounding very English these days, Uma Quarteney."

"I am half English," I said. I was less ashamed of my English blood now. Meeting Lady Tess had done that. Meeting Jackrun had done that.

Queen Adela turned to look at me. The painter tapped his foot, waiting for her to regain her pose. "You would risk the wolves?"

I shifted on my feet. "For you, Your Majesty, I would."

"Brave of you," said the queen.

"Or very foolish," Lady Olivia whispered at my side.

"Jackrun interceded for you." She was speaking out of the side of her mouth, her body frozen in place for the portrait. "He begged me to let you live and continue to serve as my physician. My nephew is very persuasive. But I can always build a new pyre. Come here," she said to Lady Olivia.

The artist sighed, having to pause again as the queen conferred with Lady Olivia, their two heads bobbing close together as doves in a dovecote. Queen Adela frowned, spoke again in whispers, then nodded.

"I will send Sir Giles to assure you keep your promise and come home safely to us."

Everything in me revolted against this. I couldn't work with a soldier at my heels. *Easy,* I thought, taking a breath. *She can be persuaded.* Jackrun used diplomacy. I could do that too. "There is no need to send anyone, Your Majesty. I have gone herbing all my life. I will keep myself safe, and return to you as—"

"I insist, Uma," she said holding out her hand. I crossed the room, curtsied, and kissed her ruby ring.

Half an hour later, I paced in the stables as Sir Giles readied the horses and supplies for our journey. He was not a tall man, but strong, thick-necked, a loyal soldier whose jutting jaw lent him a defiant look. At least this man wasn't one of the soldiers who'd ridden down and taken Father and me from Devil's Boot.

At last we were on our way. I rode Lady Gray, who did not know me well enough to appreciate my kicking heels as I urged her south on Kingsway Road. Dragonswood's boundary wall on my right was only four feet high. The stacked stones, more property line than wall, could be easily crossed, but we had to ride south first to reach the place I'd seen in my vision. We needed to make time. I nudged Lady Gray to a canter. Sir Giles trailed me on his charger.

We'd covered a good twelve miles or so before I glimpsed a bright orange tail moving in the scrub beyond the wall. Heart pounding, I reined in Lady Gray. "We stop here," I said.

"Thirsty?" Sir Giles asked, reaching for his ale pouch.

"No. I need to climb over the wall here."

Sir Giles shook his head. "That place is meant for dragons and fey folk only, mistress physician. No one's allowed in there without the king's permission."

"I have the queen's permission. I am going in. You may stay here on the road or ride home if you like."

Sir Giles spat and wiped his mouth. "What about the wolves?"

I did not look him in the face. I was keenly aware we traveled on the last day of Wolf Moon. I'd stashed a small handful of wolfsbane in his provision bag and mine before we left. If I could have waited another day to travel, I would have. But there was too much at stake with the queen now and not enough time to turn things around.

"If you're worried about the wolves, then we had better get going while we have this much daylight." I dismounted and tossed him Lady Gray's reins.

His brows shot up as he caught them. "You don't plan to abandon your mount, do you?"

"I have to walk when I go herbing, sir."

Grumbling to himself, he led the horses to a yew tree across the road. I had my own reasons to grumble. I needed to be alone to follow the vision. The man was trouble.

Sir Giles tied the horses' reins to the bushes and rubbed each one's neck. "We won't be gone too long," he promised, taking his bow and quiver down along with the provisions bag he'd crammed with food and a plump ale skin for the journey.

He followed me over the wall, then stood back adjusting his quiver. "You're not planning to go too far in?" he asked nervously. I didn't answer.

"Dragons and fey patrol their sanctuary, mistress." He looked around warily. "The fey might turn us to Treegrims if we're caught in here."

"My mother told me that story too, Sir Giles. I'm sure it's a made-up tale to frighten people and keep them out of Dragonswood." I suspected the game was plentiful in the vast forest. Poachers would be tempted to come in after the meat if they weren't afraid to step inside.

"I'm not so sure," Sir Giles said, frowning at a stunted oak that hunched between two pines. "I'm not passing that poor sinner," he added, crossing himself.

Holy Ones! How could I shadow my Path Animal with this man along? Was it like this for Father when I'd followed him herbing? At least I'd trained myself to be silent, not complain or ask foolish questions. "You will have to walk a good way behind me," I said. "Move quietly and do not speak."

"Yes, Your Highness." He gave a mocking bow.

I checked the sun's position. I had three, maybe four hours of hard walking to find the herbs before the sun set. I abandoned the grassy spot near the wall and gave the gnarled oak a wide berth as I looked for the place I'd seen the flash of orange tail. Soon we moved into the tall whispering trees. The air felt moist and cool. Branches dripped on the earth as they had in my vision. It seemed a good sign that I was on my way at last.

The forest floor muffled the sounds of Sir Giles's boots. It did not soften the grumbling noises coming from his mouth. I needed to concentrate. "I asked you not to speak," I said, glaring back.

He shrugged. "I didn't say a word, mistress."

I was used to traveling miles on foot each day in the mountains, but I had always followed the Adan. I had never walked in such an unfamiliar place. The forest changed as we moved deeper in. Layered scents swirling in the breeze made a rich, giddy tonic. With each step, I felt I was moving deeper into Dragonswood's wildwood magic.

Sir Giles had stopped his grumbling, silenced by the towering evergreens in this part of the wood. But I saw he'd drawn his knife. There's an Euit saying: *Sharp weapons do not vanquish fear.* I did not say this to the man behind me.

We hiked mile after mile under the boughs. Clouds scudded over the treetops, sweeping eerie shadows along the forest floor. *Courage, mi tupelli.* Farther along, thick canopy darkened the way almost completely. I had to push through a creeping fear that was taking hold.

I chose a new path. The fleeting glimpse of a bushy tail led me on again. The wider path cutting through the trees left a blue river of sky above, more light, more air, less gloom.

"Well now," whispered Sir Giles with an audible sigh, though he still gripped his dagger.

I began to sense ancient presences all around me, as if the spirits in the trees saw me moving here among them, knew why I had come, what I was looking for.

Somewhere far off a whippoorwill sang, the bright sound startling me in the deep silence. Taking the low foothills toward Morgesh Mountain, I came to a place where the path split in two directions.

Sir Giles took a few noisy gulps from his ale pouch. "Where now?"

"Shhh." I hadn't seen fox for some time and didn't know which way to turn. The forest gave no clue. I did what I'd seen Father do a few times when he was following a vision. I closed my eyes, waiting to feel my way. *The map is within me,* Father once said.

If the Holy Ones had given me this vision, the map was in me now.

I felt a low heartbeat in my back as if I still leaned against Vazan's broad chest. A twinge of heat shot down my right arm. I turned that way, taking the trail bringing us closer to the mountain. A few moments later the sight of a fox tail far ahead confirmed the choice I'd made and my heart did a little joyful flip. We stepped over thick roots and large tumbled rocks.

In the place where the trail leveled out again, I saw elms and oaks growing between the pines, but it was the row of beeches like the ones I'd seen in my vision that made me run. A great gust of wind sent hundreds of leaves swirling down as I raced toward them. I caught the golden hope in my hands and threw the leaves up again. The knight stood back, making tutting sounds as I played. The kea was near. I knew it.

Fox darted out ahead. I followed her, leaving the beeches for the dogwood trees, and there they were, the kea plants, a great green patch of them ready to be cut. Fox glanced at me with a look of satisfaction, then she vanished in the underbrush. "*Tuma-doa,*" I called after her. Thank you.

I fell to my knees and pulled out my blade to cut the stalks.

"Need help?" Sir Giles asked.

I glanced up at him, surprised. He had a knife and the work would go faster with two. "Yes," I said. "Thank you."

"No trouble," he said with a shrug as he came closer. "Thorny buggers, aren't they." He bent down. "Too late for the berries. They're all shriveled up."

"It's the leaves and stalks I need to boil for their rich cure, Sir Giles, not the berries. Cut the stalks low to the ground, like this." I showed him. "We'll pile them up and tie the kea stalks in bundles when we're done."

"We can reach the road before dark if we start for it soon," he said, kneeling and cutting with his dagger. I didn't tell him I still had to find huzana vines. I needed both herbs for the fertility cure. Back home I'd climbed the oaks Father's Path Animal, owl, showed him growing near a kea patch, and pulled the heart-shaped leaves from the creeper. I looked up now. No oaks here, and I didn't see any vines in these trees. Kea first, I told myself. The rest will come.

I SCANNED THE branches for huzana vines as we walked. Three boulders marked the place where the trail leveled out. They tipped one to another like giants' heads in conference. A stream ran behind them. We stopped to drink and fill my water pouch before starting off again. The rope around the kea bundle had rubbed my fingers raw. Thorns caught at my cloak as I took it in my left hand. The scar along my palm and middle finger would complain soon. I would have to switch hands again before too long.

Sir Giles carried his bundle a few feet behind me. We had miles to go yet. Like Sir Giles, I wanted to reach the road before dark. I also knew I had to find the huzana. Torn between rushing back and holding out for the plant I needed, I set an uneven pace for the two of us. Walking fast at times, other times slowing to look up, checking the branches for vines. Where was fox? Why hadn't I seen her again? Didn't my Path Animal know how much I also needed the huzana? It didn't seem right that she'd deserted me.

The chilled air felt cold as lake water in the dense trees.

"Look," Sir Giles said, pointing at the low gray mist beyond the brambles. No, not mist. The hair rose on the back of my neck. Wolves. Creeping low on their haunches, heads down, ears back, stalking us on silent paws.

I drew out my knife. They burst through the underbrush

snarling and snapping their jaws. "Run!" screamed Sir Giles, jumping in front of me. He shot one through its eye before it reached us. But there were more careening through the trees.

A wolf bounded up, knocked him down, jaws snapping around his throat. I screamed, stabbed its back, kicked it, stabbed again as I tried to pull it off. Blood spurted from Sir Giles's neck, covering his attackers' fur, my skirts. The wolf bit my hand. I screamed, reared back, grabbing my hand, losing my knife. Three more wolves bounded toward me. I ran and threw myself against a tree, desperate to scramble up, but the branches were too high to reach. The trees on either side of me were the same. No way to climb.

A wolf leaped at my back. I clung to the tree, tried to shinny up. I'd trapped us both in my desire to get the medicine. We would die here.

A terrible burning heat washed up my back. I turned and saw a figure leaping from his horse. Roaring fire. Wolves yelped and scattered, some racing past me, yowling, fur ablaze. Bright yellow flames screamed around me in furious scorching rivers, as if the sun had fallen to earth, destroying all with its fire. More wolves fell in the burning. I panicked and ran.

The yelping sounds lessened and faded. The great golden fire died away. I stopped, clinging to my hand in the swirling smoke. The silence was deafening. A figure raced through the thick smoke. Jackrun threw his arms around me. "Are you hurt? Did they hurt you?"

"I'm . . . all right. Sir Giles?"

We went to him. The knight's throat was torn wide open, exposing the muscle and bone. Sir Giles had trained up to battle men, not ravaging wolves. His chain mail hadn't protected him in this attack.

"I tried to fight the wolf off," I said, my ears ringing. "It went right for his throat." My shaking voice sounded very far away.

Jackrun tugged off his cloak and draped it over mine. It did not stop my trembling.

"You're bleeding," he said, tugging my left hand toward him. He tore a strip from the hem of his shirt to bind the puncture wounds.

"I have bandages in my basket," I whispered.

"Too late to tell me that."

I clenched my teeth against the throbbing pain as he wrapped the linen strip around my hand.

"I'm hurting you."

"No. It's good to wrap it."

I swallowed, glancing down at Sir Giles's dull, unseeing eyes. His jaw was defiant even in death, but there was horror in his fixed gaze. I wanted to wipe the terror from his face. I didn't seem to have the power to kneel down and do it. I didn't even have the strength to drag the sob I felt crammed down in my chest all the way up my throat.

Jackrun said, "I could have saved his life if I'd come sooner."

"You saved mine."

He spotted my blade, fetched it, and wiped the blood from it. "You harmed one of the wolves at least."

"It wasn't enough to save him. If I'd come in here alone he'd—"

"Alone to Dragonswood?" Jackrun put his arm around me. "It's dangerous in here."

"You seem to be alone," I said, my cheek against his chest.

"That's different. I'm a trained warrior."

"So was Sir Giles."

"What are you doing in Dragonswood?" he asked.

"Herbs." I nodded at the bundles we'd dropped on the path. "For the queen."

"Still fighting the good fight, I see," he said.

I looked down at my bloodstained gown. "I had no choice but to come."

"Why, what happened?"

I shook my head, too tired to tell him about the stolen medicines right now.

Jackrun knelt over Sir Giles and closed the dead man's eyes. "A good man. I used to fight him in the weapons yard. We should cover him with rocks at least before we go." I shuddered, wanting to leave now, but the wolves might return to eat their kill if we didn't do something to cover him.

Jackrun was not afraid to stay a little longer. If the wolves tried to attack us on our way out of Dragonswood, he'd burn them again. We were safe enough. He gathered stones from the trail's edge, piling them in the crook of his left arm. I wondered at the powerful blaze I'd seen pouring out of him—too much fire for an ordinary man to house in his body, even if the man was Jackrun.

The task would take less time if I gathered stones too. I walked weak-kneed up the trail to seek out rocks the right size, using the time to think more before I spoke to Jackrun about the power I'd seen. We covered the knight's body, but for the base of his left leg and his booted feet. I went to gather a few more stones to finish what we'd started.

My back was turned when I heard a terrible guttural sound. I swung around. A wolf had pounced on Jackrun's back, knocking the wind out of him, flattening him on the trail. It had planted its paws on Jackrun's spine, pinning him down. A wild growl came up my throat. I flew. Hurling rocks at the wolf. I couldn't tell if Jackrun was moving or if the jolting motions were from the wolf shaking him in its powerful jaws.

I jumped on the wolf's back, threw my arm under its thick, furry neck and tugged with all my might until I forced its head back, drove my blade into its gullet, and slit its throat.

The wolf's eyes rolled back. It made a strange gurgling sound before collapsing atop Jackrun.

"Jackrun? Are you all right?" *Holy Ones help me!* I tried to push the wolf's dead body off. *So heavy.* I spread my hands on its furry side, heaving my full weight against it and straining. At last the wolf rolled onto the ground with a sickening thud.

Jackrun was motionless. His clothes and skin were torn. He was covered in blood.

# CHAPTER THIRTY-SEVEN

# Dragonswood, Wilde Island

DEATH OF WOLF MOON
*September 1210*

"JACKRUN!" I TURNED him over. So much blood. I couldn't tell how much was Jackrun's, how much the wolf's.

"Uma?" he said in a husky voice. I checked him more closely. Blood covered his ripped sleeve. There were teeth marks in his shoulder, perilously close to his neck. If I hadn't killed the wolf when I did . . .

"Where does it hurt?"

"Everywhere."

"Where does it hurt the most?"

"My arm."

"Can you walk?" I had to get him to a safer place where I could clean and stitch the wounds. We'd passed boulders not far from here. Jackrun clenched his teeth and moaned as

I helped him up. "If I'd tethered my horse," he muttered. "We could ride out now."

"There was no time to tether it, and anyway, you couldn't ride out now in your condition." At the boulders, I laid out the cloak Jackrun had given me, helped him to the ground, removed his short sword from his belt, and carefully peeled off what was left of his ravaged shirt and tunic.

"Press this against your skin to stop the bleeding," I said, handing him a bandage from my herb basket. "I'll be right back." I ran for the provisions bag and the rest of the things I'd left near Sir Giles's body, tossed them on the ground by our little campsite before soaking a bandage and potion sponge with a steady stream from my water pouch.

Jackrun winced as I washed the bite marks on his shoulder, the deeper wounds on his upper arm, and the bloody places below his elbow tearing down and through his dragon scale patch.

"Thank you," Jackrun said shakily, "for killing . . ." He gulped in a breath, unable to finish. Pressing the damp gauze to his deepest wound, he watched me with utter faith as I threaded the needle. The look chilled me to the core. My hands shook. He did not know I'd never stitched a person, only a dragon's wing, and that was just this morning. I braced myself to tell him how little experience I had, glanced at his face, fixed with pain, and lost my nerve.

Somehow I managed to thread the needle. Jackrun's skin was soft and vulnerable compared to Vazan's. I was afraid I'd hurt him. "This will dull the pain," I said, lifting the potion sponge.

He waved it away. "I don't want that."

"Breathe in just a little." I held it under his nose.

"Uma, you can't make me take this. I can handle . . ." He did not finish before his eyelids drooped over his eyes.

I bent over him in the last bit of daylight falling through the forest. I had to keep dabbing away the blood. My hands shook like windblown leaves. I couldn't work this way. *Help me!*

Father's voice whispered through me: *Be present with what you are doing.* I focused my mind on Jackrun, thought of nothing but the wounds I had to mend, the needle in my hand, the way Jackrun's arm would look when it was whole again if I served him now with all I had.

I chanted *Ona loneaih*—be you well. *Ona loneaih, Jackrun.* Chanting in my home tongue warmed my chest. I took a long, slow breath. My hands no longer shook. The warmth had somehow steadied them. I would have called this feeling a gift of magic from this forest if I hadn't felt the warmth earlier in Vazan's cave. *Tuma-doa*—Thank you, Holy Ones. I bent closer, my sutures clean and straight and true.

The wound in the forearm wasn't as deep or ragged as the one above. But the dragon scales made it more challenging. I gently lifted the torn scales, and stitched the blue-green skin beneath.

Dusk had dimmed the woods by the time I finished bandaging his wounds. I wrapped the cloak around him, covered him with the Euit blanket, and leaned back with a sigh, thankful Jackrun was still asleep and not awake yet to pain.

He breathed in and out. His expression was determined even in his dreams. I touched his cheek and ran my hand along the landscape of his fierce, beautiful face inch by inch. My fingers traced his cheekbone, his nose and strong chin.

*Ona loneaih*—be you well. Leaning closer, I brushed his mouth with my fingers, kissed him in his sleep. His lips were sweet and smoky. When they parted in a moan, I kissed him once more, lightly this time, and was drawing back when he awoke.

"Hurts worse now than before," he said with a half smile.

"That would be the sutures. Can you sit up?" He did so gingerly. "Drink now," I said, handing him my water pouch. He took three long gulps and wiped the droplets on his chin with a shaking hand.

"No ale?"

"Water first, ale later." We shared some food. Jackrun ate with his left hand, his right arm and shoulder too sore to lift.

"It pounced on me from behind. I didn't see it coming. How did you kill it?"

"Slit its throat." Jackrun's shaking hand made it hard for him to eat. He needed food. "Let me help you."

"No," he said, but he took the bit of bread, and smiled, caught my hand and kissed it when I brushed crumbs from his chin.

"No more," he said, leaning back and wincing.

"You will feel better in the morning," I said.

"Lucky for me you brought your wound kit along, Adan."

I let out a small gasp.

"I pronounced it right, didn't I?"

I put my hand to my throat as the word traveled through me. No one had ever called me Adan before. I had waited all my life to hear it. I wanted to claim the title, believe it, but . . .

"Only men can be Adans in my tribe," I admitted under my breath. "A woman can't be a healer, only a healer's helper."

"What?"

"That's the tradition."

"You're more than a healer's helper. You're a skilled physician," he said, raising his bandaged arm before he winced and lowered it again.

"The chieftain and the elders back home don't know that."

"You can tell them when you return."

"It's not that simple, Jackrun."

"Why not?"

"It breaks all tradition for a woman to be the Adan. It's never happened before in the history of our tribe." He gave me a wry look. "It wasn't long ago you English burned women who used healing herbs, calling them witches," I pointed out, feeling suddenly defensive for our ways.

"They aren't burned now. Female healers haven't been put to the stake for practicing medicine here on Wilde Island since my mother was young."

"Not too long ago," I repeated.

He was out of breath. I'd only just stitched his wounds, now I was arguing with him.

"I'm in your care," he said, leaning back and closing his eyes. "I won't call you Adan if you don't like it."

I liked it. I wanted it to be true, not just here between us, but when I went back home, *if* I went back home. Wind whistled around us. Jackrun scooted stiffly back in the triangular cave made by the leaning boulders, using his strong left arm to pull himself along. Something was wrong with his left leg.

"The wolf didn't bite you there, did it?"

"Struck my knee on a stone when I fell, I think."

I rolled up his breeches to check his sore knee. It was bruised and swollen, but the skin wasn't torn. I salved it and wrapped it using the last of my bandages. Some of the teeth marks in his shoulder were clean puncture wounds like the ones in my hand. They'd been too small to stitch. I gently rubbed them now.

Jackrun breathed softly, eyes closed, as I salved the bites, feeling the curve of his muscles below his skin. I wanted him strong again. I whispered the Euit plant names in the ointment. Four in all. Each joined the others to strengthen the healing effect.

Jackrun's eyes opened. "What about your bites? Have you stitched them?"

"No, better not suture the smaller wounds. They will close up on their own. I didn't stitch your puncture wounds either, only the tears."

He reached out, unbound my bandage, and frowned at the arc of bites dotting my skin like small red burning stars. "Why haven't you put anything on it?"

"I'm all right. I don't need any—" I swallowed. He'd already dipped his finger in the jar and was gently spreading woundwort over the punctures on the top of my hand. "Stop," I said. "We need to save the rest for you."

"Just hold still, Uma." He turned my hand over, dipped his fingers in the salve again to sooth the wolf's teeth marks in my palm, his fingers awkward as a man unused to careful work. "You should take better care of yourself."

My eyes welled up. I turned away, bound my hand again, and went to lean against the far end of the boulder trying to breathe past the lump in my throat.

"Did I do something wrong?"

"No, I just . . . need to take a breath." Night spread its stars across the sky. Earth, wind, fire, water. All was in balance here, but I was not in balance. I never used Father's medicine on myself.

I was losing mi tupelli, the hardened, studious boy I'd been for years—the uncomplaining boy who used to work alongside Father, who earned his trust, won the right to practice medicine with a stern, manly confidence. The change had been happening slowly ever since I met Jackrun. Mi tupelli slipped away with Jackrun's touch. He'd kissed it away, salved it away. I did not know how to be a healer and a woman at the same time. No wonder I'd felt strange when he called me Adan. As much as I yearned for it, the resistance the chieftain and the elders had against women healers was also in me. I didn't want to believe it, but it was true.

# CHAPTER THIRTY-EIGHT

# Dragonswood, Wilde Island

## DEATH OF WOLF MOON
### *September 1210*

MY BANDAGED HAND stung each time I struck the flints. Cold, needing fire's warmth, I ignored it, banging them again and again in frustration.

Jackrun awoke. "Let me, Uma."

"Sorry, I didn't mean to wake you." Teeth chattering, I moved back, cradling my hand, grateful for his help as he filled his lungs and breathed onto the small woodpile I'd been trying to light. But no fire came. Jackrun made a hoarse roar, trying to summon the anger he seemed to need to awaken his dragon power, then tried again—still no flame.

"Gone," he whispered, terror in his voice.

"No. The wounds have weakened you, that's all." Hoping I sounded more convinced than I felt, I turned and struck the flints fiercely, each sharp jerk sending fresh pain through my hand. Sparks flew. When the kindling lit at last, I bent down, blowing a thin stream of air at the base of the wood stack to nurse the tiny flame.

Jackrun leaned his head against the granite boulder. "The fire wasn't there when the wolf knocked me down. I had none left by then. You had to kill it with your knife."

"Jackrun, it knocked the wind out of you back there. You will be fine. You have lost nothing."

"You're right," he muttered. "It was a gift no one wanted me to have."

"That's *not* what I meant."

Somewhere in Dragonswood, wolves began to howl. The sound ripped through me. I grabbed Sir Giles's bow and arrows and scooted next to Jackrun, wedged between the protective boulders. It was the death of Wolf Moon. We were in the strangest of forests whose magic was darkening all around us. Jackrun had no fire left to defend us if the wolves came.

More baying filled the night. Jackrun's body tensed beside me, his hand rested near the bow.

"Where did you put my sword?"

"Over there." I pointed. "I removed it when I stitched your wounds." I brought it to him and sat again. "They sound like they are a long way off."

"I hope you're right." He took the short sword from me and laid it beside the blanket.

"They don't like fire, that will help," he said. He swallowed and glanced down at his sword.

"Your fire will return."

"I'm not so sure." He was trembling. I touched his hands. His fingers had always been so warm. They were icy now. I looked away to keep him from seeing my fearful expression. If he'd lost his fire, he'd done it to protect me.

He lifted the thick blanket. "Come." I scooted in close to him, sharing the colorful blanket by our small fire.

"I'm better off without it," Jackrun said.

"How can you say that when I would be dead now if you hadn't used your fire to scatter the wolves?"

He clenched his jaw.

"I saw a new power in your fire this time," I said. "It came out in a torrent that should have burned me and Sir Giles and the trees all around us, but you aimed it like a weapon and chased off the wolves. You burned only them. You told me once you'd never trained your fire. You cannot convince me of that now."

"I used to go to a secret place with Babak to roar fire. I've had to run off many times to scream it out when it burned too hot inside me. I don't think you could call that training."

I'd seen how he'd tried to exhaust himself fighting in the weapons yard, riding, swimming, doing whatever he could to keep active to channel his anger. "That time you left the king's court to visit a friend of your father's down south?"

"I made him up. I had to get away to breathe . . ."

"Fire," I whispered, finishing for him.

"I used to think it would be easier when I got older, that I could learn to control it, but it burns within me like a black-smith's forge; each year it grows hotter and hotter." He paused. "I don't think I could ever learn to . . . This power is meant for dragons, not for a man."

"Don't say that."

"It's true, Uma."

I sat a long while with his words. At last the howling died away. I hoped it was gone for good and that part of the night was over. The fire near our feet was small compared to the vast darkness of the wood. I felt deep sadness for Jackrun, for Sir Giles lying dead under piled stones on the trail. He'd followed me over the wall. I should have left him on the road.

Jackrun's breathing grew quiet. His head drooped. I scooted closer so he could rest it on my shoulder.

I watched the stars moving in the heavens, a slow sweep of broken glass across a black floor. An owl hooted hours later, waking Jackrun again.

"It's only an owl," I said. "Try and sleep."

"Not sure I can. You try, I'll keep watch."

"We'll keep watch together."

We ate some food. Jackrun leaned his head back, drinking from the ale skin. He sighed, wiped his mouth with the back of his hand, and passed the skin to me. I drank, then tugged the corner of the blanket up to my chin. "Are you warm enough?"

"I've never felt this cold before," he admitted.

I pressed myself up against his side, careful not to bump his sore knee. "Better?"

"Mmmmm."

I watched his profile. His hand stroked my hair, eyes

on the burning log closest to our feet. The red-orange bark glowed in scaly patterns like Vazan's scales.

"My family will be happy at least to see my fire gone."

"Why do you say that?"

"Do you really want to know?"

"I do."

"You'll hate me," he said.

"I won't."

He looked up, speaking to the night sky. "I did a terrible thing when I was three." He went silent a long while before going on. "Tabby was just a baby. I was jealous of her for taking all of Mother's attention away from me. One day Mother was holding Tabby and wouldn't take me up on her lap the way she used to. I screamed and roared fire at them both. Mother's gown and the baby's blanket burst into flame. Mother jumped up screaming. Father tore a tapestry from the wall, raced over and smothered the flames. The baby's screams filled my ears. Mother bore down and shouted at me. She shook me hard and locked me in my room.

"I could hear Mother crying outside my door. Father's angry voice. There were shouts. Someone was running. But the worst thing was, I couldn't hear Tabby anymore. I didn't know if I'd killed my little sister. They wouldn't let me out of my room. They wouldn't tell me anything. I cried and pounded the door for hours until my fists were red and raw. No one came to tell me what happened. Not that day or all that night. I curled up on the floor at the base of the door with my blankets.

"Father finally let me out of my room. He was stern. He didn't say much, but he told me my sister lived. I was given a new guardian, a strict man with a wrinkled face and soul. My mother wouldn't let me near Tabby again for three months. If Father hadn't been able to put the flames out when he did, Tabby could have died. Mother's knees were burned. Tabby had burn scars all down her arm and the lower part of her left side. She still has the scars I gave her. So does Mother. Thank God for long sleeves and long skirts, or I would see those scars every day." He looked aside. "I told you I was dangerous."

"What you did was terrible, Jackrun, but you're wrong."

"I burned them. I could have killed them both."

"You were a little boy when you threw that tantrum. You haven't burned anyone since."

"Not people, but I've come close too many times. Animals," he admitted. "I've burned them in a rage, and I don't just mean the wolves that were attacking you today." He pulled in a breath. "Tell me something awful you've done. Do it quickly. It's only fair."

I thought about the day I broke Father's medicine jars after I'd learned I had to marry Ayo, then dismissed it for another, more personal story. "I once crept into Father's healing hut and stole some of his precious evicta medicine to ease my pain. My father, the Adan, came in and caught me swallowing his powder."

I shut my eyes remembering my father's face when he saw me licking the black seed powder in my hand.

"What is this, Uma?" His voice was cold earth.

"Adan?" I drew back, frightened.

"You are having pain?"

*Yes, terrible cramps.* "I'm sorry, Adan."

"You have broken trust, Uma. Do not step where a woman should not walk! Now go and wash yourself."

I did not tell Jackrun I'd taken the evicta for my menstrual cramps. Some things were too personal.

"Is that all?" he asked, unimpressed.

He wanted more? "You don't understand. I'd broken a sacred tradition. Only the Adan is allowed to administer his medicines. I should have gone to him with my pain, but I didn't. I kept it to myself and stole a cure instead."

I stared at the flames a moment. I was not ashamed about breaking the law the day I healed Melo. But that first time was different. I'd been selfish. I'd stolen the evicta in secret because I feared he would take another apprentice if he knew how much I suffered from my courses. The Adan never complained of any illness or pain. I couldn't admit my weakness to him, especially a womanly weakness. I lost my position anyway once he caught me.

The wolves began to howl again, a cry of fury on the death of Wolf Moon. I could not scoot any closer to Jackrun than I already was. He took the short sword from the ground and laid it by the bow across both our laps.

"What happened then?" he asked.

"After that my father let me go. He took on a male apprentice named Urette."

I'd gone back to working at Mother's side, feeling ashamed of myself, ashamed of my womanhood that had betrayed me. Mother welcomed me, offered me my own loom. I thought I'd lost everything.

"When the Adan and his new apprentice came home from their week of harvesting herbs in the valley, I stole plants from Urette's basket and hid them so he'd get in trouble and Father would send him away."

"Did he get in trouble?" Jackrun seemed more interested now.

"Yes. But Father didn't dismiss him. And when Father asked me if I knew what had happened to the medicines, I lied and said his apprentice must have lost them. 'He's not good enough to work for you, Adan,' I said. Still Father didn't let him go. 'He will learn,' Father said. That enraged me!"

Jackrun smiled. "What happened then?"

"Some would say fate intervened, but I don't think so. Urette would have taken my place for good if he hadn't died a month later from snakebite."

"Ah," said Jackrun. "I see."

"See what?"

"How fate intervened."

"I wanted him gone," I admitted. "I wanted my old position with my father . . ." I stopped.

"Uma, you can tell me. I've told you the worst thing I did."

I leaned back, listening to the wolves. "Part of me was . . . glad he was dead," I whispered. "Father had no time to train someone else. Urette was gone forever. My father had to take me back." Shame flooded through me at hearing my own words. For a moment I hated Jackrun for making me admit such a despicable thing. I didn't move, couldn't look at him. After a while, he took my hand in his, rubbing my knuckles with his thumb.

The distant sounds of baying filled the darkness all around us.

"It's a strange world, Uma. If Urette hadn't died, then you wouldn't have become a healer. You wouldn't be here, right now, with me."

JACKRUN FINISHED HIS meal and sipped the warm tea from the copper pot. "Pine?" he guessed.

"Pine needle tea. It will warm you." Across the fire, I removed bits of caked-on mud from my slippers with a twig. I could do nothing to remove the dried blood from my cloak or gown; at least I could clean the shoes. We'd fallen asleep sometime near dawn and slept away the morning hours, awaking hungry sometime after midday. I watched him sip the tea.

Tiny patches of blue appeared between the scudding clouds above. I longed for sunlight. Jackrun offered me the copper pot. I waved it away.

"It's a chilly day. You need some warmth yourself, Uma."

"I'm all right."

"Have some or I won't drink any more." He passed it to me and I took a few sips, tasting the rich forest flavor before giving it back. Jackrun downed the rest and said, "Better get going."

"What?"

"You have the herbs you came for?"

"Not all of them. There's one more I have to find, but I can't see us walking out. You're not well enough to travel so far. Your wounds need time to heal."

"I have to enter the fairy realm, Uma. Confront my grandfather in DunGarrow; find out if he or any of the fairies in Dragonswood are behind Desmond's murder."

"When you're stronger," I argued.

"Now. I also need to find out if the fey hexed the queen to keep her from having more children. You'll need them out of the way to succeed with her."

"You were going in to speak to the fey on my behalf?"

"What else could I do to help you when you refused to run away and save yourself from her?"

Suddenly shy, I held my palms out to the fire, studying my torn nails and raw fingertips. He had not rejected me after our fight; he'd entered Dragonswood to confront the fey and help me. "Thank you," I managed.

"You are the most stubborn person I have ever met," he added.

"So are you."

"We should get you back to the road. This part of Dragonswood isn't a safe place for you."

"And it is for you?"

"I grew up hunting on Dragon's Keep. I know how to stay alive in the forest."

"And I lived outdoors with the Adan weeks at a time," I argued, drying the pan.

"Not in woods as wild as these."

I slammed the pot down on the ground. "You don't need to escort me."

"Think of it as selfish, then. I need to retrieve a new horse from Pendragon Castle to ride to DunGarrow. It's much too long a journey on foot."

I slid the copper pot into my basket. "It's miles to the boundary wall. We're not going until you're better."

Without another word, he shoved the arrows into the quiver and strapped it on. Then he took up one of the kea bundles and started off, walking with a limp. I shouldered my basket and provision bag, and grabbed the second bundle, too angry to speak.

Jackrun kept his wounded right arm pinned against his side as he walked. His swollen knee made our progress slow. Early on, he found a branch and stripped the twigs and leaves away to make a staff for himself. Leaning on it seemed to help. He still couldn't move with much speed, but whenever he cringed and paused to catch his breath, he shot me a fierce look, warning me not to say a thing. I eyed both sides of the trail for a flash of red as we passed through a glade of gnarled oaks, still hoping fox would lead me to some trees where the huzana vines grew.

"Water?" I passed Jackrun the pouch. Watching him lift his chin and close his eyes to drink, I thought of the warriors back home passing the jar hand to hand, drinking sega as part of the Dragon Moon dance.

"Jackrun?"

"Hmm?" He handed me the pouch.

"Promise me if I don't succeed with the queen, if I die—"

"You won't die," he said fiercely. "I won't let that—"

I put my fingers on his wet mouth. "That if I die, you will convince the king and queen to free my people. You're skilled in persuasion. I know it. You already saved my life, talking Queen Adela out of burning me. She won't have a reason to hold my people captive anymore if I'm gone, but I'm afraid she'd keep the troops there anyway. The English and the Euit have a long, bloody history. We've been surrounded and driven off our lands before."

I watched his face change as I lifted my fingers.

"You don't need to ask. I won't let the queen hurt you. I—"

"Please, Jackrun."

Oak leaves whispered all around above us in the long silence. He took my hand, kissed my damp fingertips. "I promise."


WE WALKED ON together until the light faded from blue to deep purple under the towering evergreens. I'd still seen no sign of fox. It looked less and less like we would make it to the boundary wall before dark. I pulled up my hood against the early evening chill, letting go of my search for huzana for the more urgent one of a safe place to sleep. The trail widened. I was hoping to find boulders tall and broad enough to protect us from the wind and the wolves.

Jackrun pulled an arrow from his quiver. "Run," he whispered. "Climb a tree."

Soft cracking sounds came from the underbrush up ahead to the right of our path. Gray wolves paced between the pines, heads down, ears pressed back, two, then four. I looked wildly around for branches low enough to reach. They were all too high. Even if we could both run fast, which Jackrun couldn't do, where would we climb?

"Go," Jackrun ordered in a whisper.

"No, I won't leave you here." I swept small sticks into a pile and quickly tried to light them with my tinderbox. I could barely hold the flints in my shaking hands. The sparks caught and started a tiny flame. So small. Too small. I added more sticks and in my haste nearly doused the fire. The largest male sniffed the air, then he crept closer.

I lit Jackrun's walking stick and held it out like a warning torch. Jackrun's arrow struck the male's neck. It yelped, staggered a few paces, and fell over. Blood pooled around it. The others drew back snarling. But another charged and there were more behind it.

Jackrun shot again. I shouted and waved the torch. Still one leaped and knocked me down, planting its paws on my chest and bearing its teeth. Thick drool splashed on my face. Throwing my arms up, I screamed, pressing hard against its furry chest. A halo of yellow fire exploded over us. All was blinding light around the wolf's snarling jaws. *Jackrun's breathing fire!* I thought.

But the flames were not from Jackrun.

# CHAPTER THIRTY-NINE

# Dragonswood, Wilde Island

## DRAGON MOON
### *October 1210*

A GREEN DRAGON with a golden chest swooped down and landed on the wide path. The male wolf jumped off me and fled. The others yelped, racing from the flames.

"Uma? Are you all right?" Jackrun helped me sit up. Angry barking filled the wood. "We'd better get out of here now." He swung my herb basket over his shoulder by his bow and helped me onto the dragon. I straddled the base of her lowered neck like a great tree trunk.

"My herb bundles." I looked frantically around. One was burning. Jackrun threw the other up to me.

I grabbed it, heart pounding, amazed to be alive, to be seated on a dragon. A lifelong dream and it was happening so fast, too fast to take it all in.

Jackrun grunted in pain as he climbed up and scooted in behind me.

"Jackrun, if you tear open any of the wounds I so carefully sutured—"

"Worried about your stitchery?" he asked from behind,
as if I were a maid-in-waiting fussing over some pretty lace-
work. He wrapped his strong left arm around me. "Grab her
upturned neck scale, Uma," he called.

I threw myself forward over the kea bundle and grabbed
the jutting scale with both hands. The dragon leaped from
the forest floor, rising and dipping in frightening jerks under
our weight. My stomach went down to my feet, then up
again until she managed to crest the treetops and soar over
the canopy. Wolves ran below, fanning out between the
pines like scattering gray leaves.

"Thank you, warrior," I called to her. I held on, stunned,
chest aching where the wolf's paws had held me down, heart
pounding with the sheer excitement of the unexpected ride.
I'd wanted this since I was a small jealous child watching Father ride Vazan.

As the dragon winged us over the forest canopy, I thanked
the Holy Ones. We were alive, the wolves were far below us,
and I was flying for the first time in my life. High above the
moving forest, I felt I was a part of the evening sky, a part of
the wind that blew past in chilly gusts, stinging my cheeks
and eyes.

My hands were cold, gripping the scale, but the dragon's
neck warmed my legs, and Jackrun warmed me from behind. He pressed his chest against my back, peering over my
shoulder.

"She's not flying toward the boundary wall," Jackrun said, waking me from my reverie. To her he called, "Where are you taking us, warrior?"

When she did not answer, he raised his voice again. "What is your name?" he shouted. Still no answer as she flew west. "We are not trespassers in Dragonswood. I'm Jackrun Pendragon."

Stars overhead brightened to polished jewels as she flew west, skirting Morgesh Mountain. A warmer, sweeter wind washed silken across my skin. It was redolent with flowery scents as if the dragon had somehow flown us from autumn to summer. I wanted to say something to Jackrun, but I didn't have to. His arm tightened around my waist. His breath warmed my neck. We were entering the fairy realm. He felt it too.

The dragon soared down, following a dark river that cut a sinuous path through the forest. Stars winked out one by one in the thickening clouds above. The lower she flew, the colder it got. "Where are you taking us?" I called. Still, she didn't answer.

A barge came into view and I saw the large outline of another dragon seated at the prow. Our dragon landed on the edge of the barge, gripping the timber rail with the talons on her back legs as a bird on a branch, beating her wings to keep her balance. At last she steadied herself and lowered her neck for us to dismount.

"Tell us where we are, warrior," Jackrun said.

Silence.

We got off, and the dragon abandoned us, shifting the barge, rocking it violently up and down. We stumbled forward, gripped the rail until the motion eased, then turned to face the dark outline of the other dragon at the prow.

Jackrun did not draw his bow or his sword. Bowing to the dragon, he said, "I am honored to meet you, warrior. I am Jackrun Pendragon." The beast opened its jaws and breathed golden fire, lighting the torches bracketed to the rails on our left and right. It was then I saw the woman in a crimson gown on a carved throne before the seated dragon. Her golden eyes and blue-green scales along the left side of her forehead matched the dragon's at her back, her eyes were sparkling jewels in the torchlight. I knew her from Lady Tess's painting in her solar.

Jackrun gasped and rushed forward, knocking over a bench on his way to Princess Augusta. She came to a stand as he rushed to her, a strong, slender woman not much older than Jackrun. I was surprised to see the dragon curl her long green tail around their feet. The tail had three sharp-tipped curved spikes on the end, like Vazan's.

"You're a man now," Augusta said. "You were nine when I left, just a boy."

I saw the top half of Augusta's face over Jackrun's broad shoulder. Our eyes met for a moment. Hers were astonishing, as if they had caught fire.

Jackrun was fighting to catch his breath. "I . . . wasn't sure I'd ever see you again, Augi."

The dragon huffed smoke at the nickname. Princess Augusta gestured to her companion. "This is Filalda."

I bowed to the fierce-looking she-dragon along with Jackrun.

"Please introduce me to your friend," said the princess.

"This is the queen's physician, Uma Quarteney."

"You serve Queen Adela?" Her eyes flashed with anger. I met her look and didn't quaver under it. Between us, Jackrun leaned over. Augusta's expression softened. "You are hurt, Jackrun. Please sit."

I stepped forward and helped the princess right the bench Jackrun had knocked over. He groaned as he sat, clutching his right arm.

I said, "He is recovering from a wolf attack, Princess."

"Uma saved my life," Jackrun said, stretching out his sore leg. A section of the bandage I'd wrapped around his knee peeked through his torn pants.

Augusta's face was all concern. "When I learned you were in Dragonswood, I sent my dragon out to find you. I see I acted too late."

"How did you know I was here?"

"We have our border patrols. I'm only sorry it took us so long to locate you, Jackrun. How bad are your wounds?"

"I am on the mend," he said.

I slid onto the bench beside him, wanting desperately to check his arm to see if the stitches had torn out. "Bleeding?" I asked him.

"No, just sore."

Princess Augusta returned to her throne and sat, fingering the carved rosebuds on the armrest.

Jackrun's breathing was still unsteady.

"The attack was only just last night, Princess," I said. "The wounds are new. Food and rest would help."

"Yes, of course." Princess Augusta waved her hand. Tiny lights flitted across the water. Soon scores of will-o'-the-wisps flew toward the barge bearing a small table, long-necked ewers, and food on silver trays. The last time I'd seen these smallest of fairies was the day the fey king of Dragon's Keep brought us the glass coffin.

A soft humming filled my ears as they flew down, set their table before us, and placed the trays on it. The fresh bread brought a heady scent to my nose. I folded my hands to keep from reaching for it or for the sliced cheeses layered and arranged like blossoms, the relishes and fresh berries covered in cream.

The will-o'-the-wisps startled me, tugging my hands apart, washing my unbandaged one with warm water from their ewers and drying it with tickling cloths before cleaning Jackrun's hands. They could do nothing for his torn clothes, my bloodstained cloak and gown. I drew back as I felt one trying to clean under my fingernails. This was all a little too close for me.

"Uma cannot eat fey food," Jackrun said, glancing at the meal. My stomach lurched. I was hungry.

"I cannot eat their food either," said the princess. "I have my own cook who's human. Uma may eat whatever she likes." I heaved a grateful sigh as the wisps filled our goblets with wine. I began to feel less light-headed as I ate the luscious berries and the sharp cheese that stung the back of my tongue. I was chewing the warm bread when the will-o'-the-wisps darted back over the water.

At last Jackrun spoke again. "You have to tell me why you left us for good. Why you never came home even for a visit."

Small wrinkles formed on the half of her brow not covered in scales. She gazed at the trees lining the shore, then at the sky. Dark clouds had mounded up in the heavens. "I don't belong in the human world. I won't be going back."

"The family misses you, Augusta. Mother and Father and Tabby and . . ." He paused. "You haven't even met my little brother, Kip, but I know he would love to meet you. Dragon's Keep is still your home."

"It was never my home, Jackrun. I was banished from Wilde Island at birth because of my face scales and my eyes. My father rejected me and sent me there to live my life as an outcast."

"You weren't any more of an outcast than the rest of us were on Dragon's Keep."

"Don't lie, Jackrun. It only makes things worse." The heavy clouds opened overhead, letting down a sudden rain. Filalda spread her wing over the three of us. *The princess must be well esteemed,* I thought. Babak was the only dragon I knew who could tolerate water, so I understood what it meant for Filalda to stay out in a sudden heavy downpour just to keep the princess dry.

Filalda's chest heaved in and out as she pumped her lungs like bellows to stoke her inner fire and stay warm. Vazan had used that trick whenever she was caught out in a shower. Flares shot from her mouth high above each time she puffed, illuminating her wing and sending short, bright flashes of light over us sheltering below.

Jackrun seemed oblivious to the rain. "If you stay away, it will mean King Arden, Queen Adela, and Desmond won, Augusta. It will be as if you agree with the ones in the family who always thought you—"

"Were a monster," she finished.

"Thought you didn't belong," he corrected, tensely.

The expression on Augusta's face changed from anger to sadness to resignation to pride. Whatever Duke Bion and Lady Tess did to help the princess feel loved, to heal the wounds the other family members caused, wasn't enough. Something made Princess Augusta run here for sanctuary.

I saw more likeness to Jackrun in those looks. These two had more dragon in them than the rest of the family, but their gifts had come with a price.

"Things can be different for you," Jackrun said, "now Desmond is dead."

Augusta said, "We heard of his death." I caught her vindictive look. What I saw sent a cold chill to the back of my neck.

She was glad her nephew had fallen. I ate more sharp

cheese, rain pattering the outstretched wing above as I chewed. I wondered just how much she knew about the death.

The cheese clumped in my mouth. I couldn't seem to swallow it.

Jackrun had mentioned the possibility of a rogue element in Dragonswood. What if . . .

"Augi," Jackrun said, interrupting my thoughts, "we think Desmond was murdered."

"Murdered?" She sucked in a quick breath. All went dark a moment. When Filalda breathed fire above us again, the princess was standing over us. "No more talk about this here," she warned. "Wait until we arrive."

# CHAPTER FORTY

## Princess Augusta's Castle, Dragonswood, Wilde Island

### DRAGON MOON
*October 1210*

**P**RINCESS AUGUSTA SAT again. I felt the barge
moving mysteriously, following her gaze as if her eyes
directed it. We drew north against the river's current, then
toward the trees until the barge bumped against a short dock
in the riverbank.

A small steep-roofed castle made of river stones waited in
the woods. The two dragon sentries, curled up tail to snout
on either side of the entryway, leaped up as we approached.
They bowed to the princess, one using his talons to pinch
the door handle and let us in.

I hung my filthy cloak on the hook next to Jackrun's, keeping my herb basket and kea bundle with me. Lifting the hem
of my bloodstained skirt, I followed the princess to the large

central room. A fire bloomed in the hearth as we came in. I'd seen no one light it, but this was Dragonswood after all, a magical place. As soon as we took the chairs by the hearth, will-o'-the-wisps flew in and flitted about Augusta's head like little jewels, straightening her wind-tangled hair.

*The wisps and dragons serve her as if she were queen of Dragonswood. A queen is used to giving orders, getting what she wants.* I thought again of the triumph I'd seen on her face earlier at the mention of Desmond's death, and glanced away, my temples pounding.

Jackrun watched her, his face tense in profile, his hands gripping the armrest. I wanted to reach out and run my finger along the small smooth hills of his knuckles. My chair was close enough to his. I kept my hands in my lap.

Golden firelight danced around the large high-roofed room, and illuminated the glass sculptures on the shelves and the mirrors hanging on the walls. Light swirled about the room like stirred honey. A fey child of five or six entered and set down a tray of steaming mugs. Her curls bounced as she skipped off and shut the door.

Now that it was fully dark outside, the wolves began to howl, a chilling sound even in such a sturdy dwelling. My eyes caught Jackrun's before he turned his to the fire. I took a sip from my mug, saw my hand shaking, and set it down again.

The wisps finished grooming the princess and flew back down the hall in a flurry of small shooting stars. If the will-o'-the-wisps could go dark, they would be perfect little messengers—or spies. How much had they overheard? Were any silent wisps hiding in the shadows now?

Princess Augusta rose and shut the hall door firmly. She leaned forward when she sat again, her eyes shining bright as polished copper coins with black slits down the center. "Now we are alone," she said quietly. I hoped she was right. "Tell me what you meant by murder."

"I don't know where to begin, Augi."

"Begin with the day it happened unless you can think of a better place." Her look was all too intense. What did she know already? What was she expecting to hear?

Jackrun described the picnic on Faul's Leap. When he reached the place in the story where he forced Prince Desmond to his knees in front of me, his aunt interrupted him.

"Did Desmond do something grievous to Uma?"

Jackrun glanced at me.

Princess Augusta turned. Her sudden look of sisterly understanding surprised me.

"Do you want to tell her?" Jackrun asked me. I did.

"And Desmond called *me* a monster," the princess said in a ringing tone when I was done. "After he attacked you, you still served as physician to his mother, the queen?"

"I had to, Princess."

"No one has to do anything, Uma Quarteney."

"You're wrong," I said. "Some of us are not given any choice."

"What illness does she suffer from?" Her searing eyes were on me. I nudged the kea bundle with my ankle facing her.

"The queen is not right in her mind," Jackrun interjected.

"She never was," Augusta said shrilly.

"Well, she is even worse than you remember her to be, Augusta."

"That is hard to imagine!" She lifted her brow and turned her face from me. I'd gone silent under her interrogation. "Go on and finish your story, nephew. I'm anxious to hear why you think your cousin's death was not an accident."

I watched her closely while she listened, narrowing her bright eyes one moment, pressing out her chin the next. Night slipped away as he spoke. When he was done, she sat in silence with her elbows on her armrests, her fingers forming a steeple under her chin.

"Sir Geoffrey telling the prince not to jump so he would do the opposite, and jump. A rogue wind, possibly stirred by fey power." She tapped her fingertips a few times. "From what you have told me, I would still say it was most likely an accident. Desmond leaped a moment too late."

Jackrun would not let go that easily. "Sir Geoffrey might not have done this all on his own," he said. "He may have had help." He fixed his eyes on her. "Have you lived here the whole time since you went away?"

"Yes. What does that have to do with anything?"

"You've come to know my grandfather Onadon?"

"As much as anyone can come to know someone with such power. He is king once more, Jackrun. He earned the crown again when he challenged the former king to magical battle, and won."

"What?" I asked.

"The fey monarchy isn't like our own, Uma," Jackrun said. "Kings are not born, they earn kingship through battle. The one with the strongest magic rules."

It was like that in the animal kingdom. I thought of elk locking horns, fighting for dominance in rutting season, of the alpha wolf who ruled the pack. The princess came to a stand and jabbed the logs with her poker. "You don't think Onadon is behind Desmond's death? Your own grandfather?"

I saw she was shivering.

"I don't know, Augusta, but he'd had his eye on me from the beginning. Mother said he wanted his grandson on the throne. She told me how angry he was when she married the wrong prince."

She stiffened. "The wrong prince?"

"Not wrong by me, Augi, I love my father; wrong by fey standards, since he was the youngest and not the one who would be king."

"The fairy prophecy never said the one with three bloodlines would be a king."

"Maybe not, but that's what they were hoping for. Tell me I'm wrong."

She was silent, poking the fire.

I watched Jackrun's alert expression. It struck me that he'd taken the chair closer to the fire than mine. He had never done that before. It used to be he didn't need the warmth, but now with his fire gone . . .

Jackrun said, "The fey here in Dragonswood must have

noticed how Prince Desmond was turning out. They must have thought if I were king, I would protect this sanctuary, I would stand up for the fairy kingdom in the future, and Desmond would not."

She turned. "Even when you were a little boy we played the game where you were king. Now you have a chance, Jackrun." Her voice was soft, expectant. A striped cat padded up and clawed the hem of her crimson gown. She ignored it.

"It was a game, Augi. We were children. And you played the part of queen, remember? I knew I'd never actually become king. And even if I dreamed of it as small boys do, I learned I wasn't suited to it. There are reasons why I could never perform the daily duties of a king."

"Reasons?"

"Reasons," he repeated, snapping his mouth shut.

She nudged the cat away. "Whatever you want, you will do your duty, Jackrun. You will become a king if you must."

"I can't let that happen. It would be the end of Uma and her people."

"What do you mean?"

I stared at the kea bundle near my feet. All I had to treat the queen with, and it was not enough. I still needed huzana for her fertility cure. I didn't know how I'd find it now. Or what would happen to me upon my return, having been gone so long with no one to care for the queen.

"Queen Adela holds Uma's people captive until she helps her get the child she wants."

"You would help this queen have another heir?" Princess Augusta asked, pointing her poker at me, the tip glowing.

"I have to, Princess."

She was rigid a moment, the poker aimed at me. I rose from my chair. I was exhausted, needed sleep, but . . . "If you want me to leave—"

"No." Jackrun jumped up and stood between the two of us, shoulders back, hands at his sides. Protecting me from her or her from me, I did not know which.

At last Princess Augusta hung the poker on the hearth. "It's getting late," she said, scooping up her cat. "We all need some sleep."

Jackrun didn't move. "I have to see Onadon, Augusta."

"Tomorrow," she said. "You are recovering from your injuries. Rest tonight. I'll take you to him myself in the morning."

I wasn't sure I liked her plan. But I saw no way to change things just now.

The princess showed us down the hall, cat in her arms. She opened the door to my room, then took Jackrun farther down the corridor to his.

I was storing the kea under the bed when I heard a tapping sound and opened my door. Jackrun leaned against the doorframe. I wanted to tell him I didn't trust his aunt. Ask him what he thought of her, if she might be setting a trap. His face was pale. He moved his arm and winced.

"How are your injuries?"

"Don't ask," he said, stepping quietly inside.

"I'm a healer. I have to ask."

"They're no worse than the ones I've gotten in the weapons yard, Adan."

"Liar."

He smiled, drew me close, and kissed me, running his hand down my back and tugging the ends of my hair. Once, his lips tasted moist and salty from his night swim in the sea; once they tasted of smoke, but not now. Tonight his kiss was sweet.

We broke apart when we heard footsteps coming toward us.

"Good night, Uma Quarteney," he whispered, his lips tickling my ear.

I watched him limp past a fey girl in the hall. The candelabra in her hand lit her heart-shaped face, her red hair, so like my mother's, and her green eyes. She carried herself like a young woman, but looked no more than twelve.

"I'm Tanith," she said with a curtsy. "The princess said you might wish to bathe."

"I do," I said immediately. A door closed somewhere down the passage. Jackrun's kiss had sent my rational mind flying in all directions like startled birds. I'd meant to talk with him about his aunt. He was too trusting. Princess Augusta might be connected to the murder. I was sure he hadn't seen that, or hadn't let himself see it. I'd have to catch him in the morning if I could.

Tanith led me around the corridor at the back side of the castle to a room of smooth gray stone with an enormous copper tub in the middle set on clawed feet. As soon as I stepped in, the large window near the ceiling flew open. I reared back and clung to the doorframe as Filalda poked her head through. She breathed a long stream of fire engulfing the large copper tub, heating the water that filled it to the rim. *So this is how the princess bathes,* I thought with wonder. I waited with Tanith, feeling the heat of Filalda's steady blaze until steam rose from the water and she withdrew her head again.

"Thank you, Filalda," I called out the open window. Black talons gripped the casing and it shut again.

I placed my knife and dragon belt on the side bench and carefully removed the bandage from my left hand. The cloth strip was filthy; still, I felt a little sad discarding it. Jackrun had torn his shirt to make me the bandage.

"Come," Tanith said, easing me out of my soiled gown and small clothes before she helped me into the deep copper tub. The steaming bath felt as soothing as the volcanic pools back home. The wolf bites stung, but I held my hand under the surface until it grew less stiff and gave in to the cleansing water. I hadn't felt this warm in days.

Tanith washed my back, scrubbed and rinsed the dirt from my dark hair, pouring pitcher after pitcher of water over my head and letting it stream down my back. "Thank you, Tanith," I said reveling in the unexpected luxury. "Please thank the princess for me, and Filalda too. I don't think she heard me."

She lit a second candelabra on the bench, using a candle

from her own, then pointed to a soft tan robe hanging from the wall. "You may wear this when you're done. I will lay out a fresh gown for you to wear tomorrow, a gift from the princess. And this?" she asked, pinching my gown between her fingers. It was the gown I'd worn the day Prince Desmond attacked me, the day he died, and the day Master Ridolfi burned. The bloodstains on the bodice and long skirt were mine and Sir Giles's, Jackrun's, and the wolf's whose throat I'd slit.

"I never want to see it again."

Tanith looked relieved. "I'll destroy it then, shall I?"

She left me alone to soak awhile. Steam rose and coiled around the high crossbeams on the ceiling. I eased back in the tub and relaxed for the first time in a long while. My parents joined and conceived me in water. I had heard my mother tell the story so many times. She always began with, *Your father never meant to marry,* saying it with a wry smile that told me it was not a mistake, that it was meant to be.

I pictured Mother now, the way she tipped her head so even her eyes seemed to smile. She had been so certain of her place, even in the early days when she wasn't fully accepted by the tribe.

She'd found me weeping the day Father caught me taking the evicta for my cramp pain. Resting her hand on my back, she said, *You are not a mistake.* I didn't know what she meant. I thought my femaleness was a terrible burden, the thing that prevented me from my life's desire of becoming an Adan.

My skin tingled in Filalda's fiery water. I traced my lips where Jackrun kissed me, slid my finger down my chin and neck and along the fox mark under my collarbone; my breasts were twin hills on the landscape of my body. The cloth I'd used to wrap them and press them flat was gone, discarded like the bandage I'd just taken off.

Was it possible I was never meant to be born male? That I was supposed to be born a female? Was it possible I was not a mistake?

I closed my eyes. My tears fell soundlessly. The salty drops became one with the steaming pool warmed by dragon fire.

## CHAPTER FORTY-ONE

# Princess Augusta's to DunGarrow, Dragonswood, Wilde Island

## DRAGON MOON
*October 1210*

T HE GREEN GOWN Tanith left out for me to wear
the next morning was silken like the costume I'd worn
to the fey ball, but slightly heavier and more substantial. It
had no ornamentation other than the subtle scrolling vine
patterns that caught the light, revealing the shades of green
from palest new leaf to a deep mossy color. The gown whispered as I slid it on. In the wardrobe mirror I ran my hands
down my sides, reveling in the soft, sleek cut that traced my
curves, yet somehow wasn't binding.

I walked about, swinging my arms. The skirts were so
much lighter than the heavy velvet ones I'd grown used to. I
tested the sleeves, pulling gently, then gave them a few hard

tugs, and smiled, relieved. The material was light and strong. I could run in this gown, work in it, dance in it. I brushed my clean, dark hair and tied it with the ribbon Tanith left. Knife strapped under my green sleeve, dragon belt around my waist, I slipped on the gown's matching cloak and went outside to meet Jackrun and Augusta.

Jackrun stood near the riverbank between Princess Augusta and two dragons. I heard his breath catch when he spotted me. The wind coming off the river rustled my green skirts. His eyes drank me in as I approached.

"Uma," he said, his brows raised.

"Good morning," I said. He was newly dressed in huntsman's garb, one sleeve slit to allow for his bandaged arm. His green cloak was a shade darker than my gown. We were leaving earlier than I had expected. I'd missed my chance to speak with him alone.

"You know Filalda," Princess Augusta said. "This is her sister, Eaudan."

I recognized the dragon who'd rescued us. "Thank you for saving us from the wolves last night, Eaudan," Jackrun said, bowing. I curtsied to her.

"All right, queen's physician," Jackrun said, putting out his hand.

I should go back to Pendragon Castle. The queen was sure to need me. But if this was a trap, I could not let him go alone, not with his injuries. I touched his fingers, sad to feel the coldness of his skin. I mounted Eaudan. Jackrun stifled a grunt of pain as he swung up and sat behind me.

I clung to the green's upturned scale and prepared myself. Still, my stomach somersaulted as she launched skyward.

We traveled mile on mile as the dragons followed the river, their dark shadows skimming along the water below. When we rounded the last bend, we saw a roaring waterfall that tumbled down the mountainside and straight through the middle of the castle set against the mountain. I'd seen the Pendragon castles, and Princess Augusta's smaller one, but they were nothing to DunGarrow, home of the fey king. Look one way and it seemed a natural setting, a place of towering gray-black pinnacles and mossy ledges cut into the mountain rock. Look again and you saw the recessed windows shining behind the flowered terraces.

Eaudan soared over the castle spires to a grassy plateau above the falls where fourteen dragons waited. A large marble fountain, and the mound of earth in the golden pot to its right, indicated a kind of a ceremonial place. The dragons were seated in a semicircle behind King Onadon and his colorful courtiers.

Eaudan landed near the fountain. As soon as Jackrun and I dismounted, Princess Augusta and our dragons joined the sentinels behind the fairies. She climbed a boulder, Filalda and Eaudan on either side.

King Onadon stood a few paces in front of the rest, gripping his golden staff. He wore his crown tipped on his head as if he had just clapped it on as an afterthought. He nodded to Filalda, who lengthened her neck and shot a red flame toward us.

I jumped.

"It's all right," Jackrun whispered, taking my hand. "He's gathering the elements."

King Onadon drew circles in the air, turning the long red flames into a spinning golden orb over the fountain. Filalda no longer breathed fire. Still the orb remained, revolving bright as a small sun.

The king waved his hand again, summoning water from the river. A wave sped toward us, tumbling in midair before it fell, filling the marble fountain to the brim. The fountain came to life, the carved birds and dragons spraying water from the three-tiered layers down to the lowest bowl.

I felt Jackrun's cool hand surrounding mine as we waited for King Onadon to raise the final element.

The king made a small motion with his fingers. A gust blew across the meadow, spinning the fiery orb faster until it flung out chains of brilliant light. Wind whistled around us, lifting cloaks and hair and skirts, blowing the tops of the grass. A strong gale shoved against my back, chill as the windy blast I'd felt on Faul's Leap.

The gust softened to a breeze. Princess Augusta said, "Jackrun, meet your grandfather King Onadon."

Jackrun went down on his good knee.

"And this is Jackrun's friend the healer and queen's physician, Uma Quarteney."

I curtsied beside Jackrun.

"Come closer," said King Onadon, motioning with his finger. Suddenly Jackrun and I were both moved across the grass as if the king had tugged the earth, pulling us toward him on a green carpet. Onadon had moved us against our will, handled us like chess pieces when we could have just as easily walked! I hid my fists in the folds of my skirts, the bite marks stinging under the new bandage.

"I have waited long to meet you, King Onadon," Jackrun said in a clear tone.

"As I have you, Jackrun." He eyed Jackrun's bandaged arm. "We heard you battled wolves. How are your injuries?"

"Better, sire. Uma Quarteney treated me. She is a great physician."

I bit my lip at the exaggeration. Will-o'-the-wisps flew across the river, some landing in the trees to our right, a few circling over King Onadon's head as he appraised me.

"You are welcome here, Uma Quarteney. Your people and ours shared Wilde Island along with the dragons count-less generations before the English came."

"Yes, Your Majesty."

"But your customs must have changed recently," he added. "The Adans we have known were all male." I low-ered my eyes and studied the chained light patterns on the ground. When I looked up again, I had to blink at the flitting movements of the crowd. The fey folk had seemed constant at first; now I noticed fairies appearing and disappearing, as one winked out, another took his or her place. The rippling light from the fiery orb had confused my eyes. I hadn't noticed the constant change until now. At least King Onadon was con-stant, as were Princess Augusta and the dragons behind him.

"You took your time, coming to see me, grandson."

"I had duties to perform at my uncle's castle. We had to bury his son. I noticed none of your court came."

"We were not welcome. King Arden has hardened his heart against us and the dragons."

"He blamed a dragon for his son's death," Jackrun said, "but my cousin's murder wasn't the fault of any dragon."

I cringed at the blunt remark as King Onadon repeated the word. "Murder?"

The word echoed through the crowd behind him. The dragons' tongues slithered in and out, licking up the sound.

"We heard it was an accident," King Onadon said. "We were told you were there with him when he fell."

"I was there, and so was Uma."

"And what makes you think it was murder, grandson? This is news to me and my court."

"We felt the wind that pushed him over the edge."

"A wind can blow from anywhere," Onadon argued with the wave of a hand.

"Or it can be summoned by those who have the power to do it, as you've just shown us, Grandfather."

A frown was growing on the king's noble face.

"Are you so completely innocent?" King Onadon continued. "You knew the kind of man he was. Can you honestly say you wished *him* to be king?"

Jackrun clenched his jaw. No one thought Desmond would make a good king except his doting parents and Lady Olivia, who envisioned her daughter beside him on the throne. Tabitha's words whispered through me: *He's a mon-ster, Jack. He'll be a tyrant when he's king.*

"In a fair fight for the crown, the strongest wins," King Onadon said. "That is how we do it in Dragonswood."

"That is not how humans inherit, Grandfather."

"Are you sure? Many kings in your human history were toppled by those who challenged them. Brother has gone against brother, cousin against cousin. Or don't you study your own English history?"

Silence.

"Very well, Jackrun, if a man is born to become king, an-swer me this: Were you?"

The crowd hushed. Even the dragons looked expectant.

*The Son of the Prophecy was born to rule.* All the fairy folk believed that. I could see it in their faces.

"I never wanted a crown purchased by my cousin's blood," Jackrun said icily.

King Onadon narrowed his eyes.

A piercing raptor's cry tore through the sky above. All looked up.

"Vazan," I called, surprised. She had vowed never to enter *Dragonswood prison,* as she called it. Yet she had flown in with her newly stitched wing. I watched her wheeling down.

"Come, Uma." It was not a plea but an order.

"What's wrong, Vazan?"

"The queen is worse."

Onadon called, "You have entered our domain, red dragon."

"I will not set claw down in your domain," she answered with distaste. "I am here for Uma Quarteney." She darted closer in. "Come now, Uma, if you don't want to lose everything we are fighting for."

"What do you fight for, Vazan?" demanded Onadon.

"Freedom!"

"Then come down and speak with us. We are a free people here."

Vazan whisked down, I thought to land, but instead she hovered by the cliff and lowered her head. "Get on, Uma."

"Your stitched wing. Can you carry my weight so soon?"

"Yessss!"

I adjusted the herb basket on my shoulder and looked at Jackrun, torn.

King Onadon said, "Before you go, queen's physician, I say this. Her Majesty Queen Adela owes us for her glass eye. If we had left her marred, she would have never wed King Arden. Remind her of it."

"I will do my best to remind her, Your Majesty," I said, not knowing when or how I could possibly pass on such a message to the queen.

I turned to Jackrun. "She is injured. She won't be able to carry us both."

"I can't leave yet anyway." He put his lips close to my ear. "If they've placed an infertility hex on the queen, I'll make sure it's removed before I come back to you."

"Uma!" roared Vazan, hovering by the cliff's edge. The stubborn dragon wouldn't land to make mounting easy. I grabbed the kea bundle, ran to her, and barely managed to straddle her neck before she backwinged from the cliff. She raised her head and sent me sliding down her long neck. I came to a sudden painful stop against her shoulders, the kea bundle flying from my grip.

"We can't leave that behind," I screamed as it fell. Vazan dove for it, jolting me forward. I would have joined the falling bundle if I hadn't grabbed her protruding scale and driven my knees into her. She snatched the kea in her talons and winged back up again. In the air, I craned my neck to look once more at the high plateau above DunGarrow Castle. Jackrun stood at the cliff's edge, his dark hair blowing back, the crowd of fairies and dragons behind him. He lifted his hand and touched his ear, reminding me of the words he'd just whispered in mine as he watched us go.

## CHAPTER FORTY-TWO

# Dragonswood to Pendragon Castle, Wilde Island

### DRAGON MOON
*October 1210*

"WE CANNOT GO straight back. I still have to find huzana vines."

"Gone two nights and you still don't have all the herbs you need?"

I did not feel like explaining. Too much had happened since I'd entered Dragonswood. "Go as I guide you," I said, watching the treetops for the vines, the ground for a sign of fox. The cold wind chased us. I worried about Vazan's stitched wing as I hunched under my new green cloak, shivering and looking down. When I saw fox darting through the bracken, I called, "Follow her."

So far Vazan had managed not to land in Dragonswood prison.

"Those trees there." She swept lower, gripped a high branch with a claw, and pumped her wings slowly, waiting for me to climb to another branch. Her weight bent the tree-top down. It was a good thirty-foot drop to the earth below. One of my slippers tumbled to the forest floor as I clambered onto the safest-looking branch, holding on to another. The tree leaned at a dangerous angle. I hung on with one hand, pulled leaves off the huzana vine with the other, filling the top of my basket. When I heard a loud crack, I climbed up and threw a leg over Vazan's neck. The tree broke as she took off, and crashed to the forest floor.

The wind continued to harass us over Dragonswood. Almost as if Onadon were using his magic to sweep us out. Midday we landed near the Pendragon tomb. I would have used the secret way in, but the gatehouse men must have seen Vazan coming; already a soldier crossed the drawbridge expectantly.

Vazan handed me the kea bundle she'd carried in her claw.

I dipped my head. "*Tuma-doa*—thank you." She kept a claw out a little longer for me to touch. I teared up, running my hand over her scales, ending at her talons, black as marble, sharp as spears. "Go rest your wing now, rivule." For once she did not argue. I watched her mount the sky, then met the soldier at the drawbridge. He reached for the kea bundle, but I would not let him carry it for me.

"The stables first," I said to him. "I have a message for the head groom." We asked around and found the man currying a fine white charger.

"I had to leave the horses we took tied up by Kingsway Road."

The man stopped brushing and looked back at me. "How far away, mistress physician?"

"Twelve miles or more to the south."

"Those mounts belong to King Arden," he said gruffly. "Where is Sir Giles? I have a word or two to say to him."

"Dead, sir," I said with a thick throat. "We were attacked by wolves."

His eyes widened. He was crossing himself, brush still in his hand.

We left the stable. "He was a good knight," the soldier said, leading me inside the castle. "I'll have to tell the commander he's dead. But first I'm to take you to Her Majesty."

"I should mix her remedy before I see her."

He paused in the hall. "I was told—"

"It won't take long," I said.

The man paced outside the door to the Crow's Nest as I cut off portions of the new kea stems, adding them to the huzana leaves and bapeeta in the simmering pot.

"Ready?" he called through the door, pounding it at the same time with his fist. I shed my slipper, no good wearing it when the other was lost, went out barefoot to the cold stone alcove at the top of the stairs, and followed him through the winding halls toward the queen's tower.

I'd been away two full days and nights; still, I was not prepared for what I met when I opened the queen's door. The bedchamber was in shambles, every drawer was open, gowns and shoes were strewn across the floor as if a tempest had swept in.

Her Majesty wandered through the clothing piles talking to herself. I saw no sign of Lady Olivia.

"Your Majesty?" I said with a curtsy. When she ignored me, I approached her cautiously, holding out the brew, staying close in case she grabbed it and tried to hurl it across the room. I sighed when she drank it, and began picking up her things. I could have called down to the guard at the base of the bedroom stairs, demanded he send up a chambermaid at once, but I thought better of it. She was worse than I'd seen her since the early days after her son died. I wanted a little time to restore her before anyone else came in.

"Her eye will do," the queen said, still pacing. "Then we will dig out her heart."

"Here, Your Majesty," I said, helping her sit before her vanity.

"I'll execute him," she said to the mirror. "He murdered Pippin."

"Who murdered Pippin?" I asked, astonished.

"The guard, see the blood?" She pointed to a tangled red gown on the floor, then put her face in her hands and wept.

"Your Majesty, I will be right back."

I hurried downstairs to speak to the man below. "Where is the queen's lapdog, Pippin?"

"The page left with Lady Olivia to take Pippin on his morning walk."

"So the dog is all right?"

He cocked a brow. "Course he is, why?"

"The queen is unwell. Do not let anyone up to see her while I'm gone. I won't be a moment," I said before going out. I found Pippin in the walled garden pissing in the ferns while the freckle-faced page stood by. Lady Olivia was seated on a stone bench under a covered archway. Seeing me, she stood up glaring.

"So you've returned to us at last," she said, wrapping her cloak tightly around herself. Her nose was pink and her face looked paler than usual if that were possible.

"I need to take Pippin back to the queen, my lady."

"Have you any idea of the distress you caused Her Majesty by staying away so long?" Turning aside, she sneezed, and dabbed her nose with a lace handkerchief.

*Didn't I say I might be gone two days?* "There was trouble. A wolf attack. Sir Giles was killed." There wasn't time to go into all the rest of the story before I raced back up the stairs.

She saw my bandaged hand. "And you were injured," she said, her voice softer now. She sneezed again.

"It's nothing. How long have you been feeling ill, my lady?"

"I'm only a little bit tired, Uma. I have had to attend Queen Adela day and night since you left." The short speech seemed to exhaust her. Sighing, she sat again. "How is she?"

"Very bad, I'm afraid."

"I only just left her, but I'll go to her. I just came out for some air while the lad walks Pippin." She dabbed her nose. "What?" she added, seeing my expression.

"I don't think you should attend Her Majesty until you're feeling better, my lady."

She was about to protest, when she coughed into her handkerchief.

"You should be in bed," I added.

"You will watch over her?" She gazed up, uncertain.

"I will. I promise. Now go."

She raised her brows at the insistence in my voice, but gave in, knowing I was right, and headed for the garden gate. I turned and went for Pippin, who was already wriggling in the boy's arms and licking his face.

The boy grinned. "I'll take 'im up, mistress."

"No, give him to me. I have to do it." I hurried back inside and entered the queen's solar with my small prize.

"Here's Pippin alive and well," I said triumphantly. "No one has harmed him as you can see."

The queen glanced up, neither surprised nor pleased, and made a clicking sound with her tongue. "Filthy paws."

I looked about for something to wipe Pippin's paws with before I set him down. Knowing better than to use the queen's facecloth by her washbowl, and finding nothing else, I had to head back downstairs and snatch a cloth from the queen's presence room before returning with the dog.

The rest of the day was a whirl of activity. Later when I was in the herbarium, mixing her bedtime dose, Bianca came up the stairs and poked her head through the door.

"I'm sorry; I cannot give you any more evicta, Bianca."

"Mother said you were attacked by wolves." She pushed into the chilly room, put her candelabra on my worktable, and placed a pair of slippers on my floor.

"How badly are you hurt? Let me see." Her pink gown swished as she came closer, her face soft with concern, reaching for my bandaged hand.

I stepped back. "I'm all right, Bianca." I was used to her coming here to beg for evicta, not to ask after my health.

"Mother also said you were barefoot, so I thought you might need these." She looked down at the slippers she'd placed near the table leg. "They might be too small for you, but . . ."

The black slippers were covered with embroidered vines and delicate leaves.

"Try them. They will match your pretty moss-green gown," she said, touching my silken sleeve. "The gown suits you," she added. "No lace or pearls, still it's beautiful."

"A gift from someone in Dragonswood," I said.

Her eyes grew wide.

The slippers were a little too narrow for my feet "They are so fine. Are you sure?"

"Oh, it's nothing. I have so many shoes and gowns, a whole wardrobe full. Mother wants me to dress like a princess." She frowned at her hands, her skin pale as tallow, her lovely nails curved like crescent moons.

I fought for what to say as the silence drew out longer. "How is Lady Olivia feeling?"

"She coughs some. But she . . . is strong."

"She hasn't sent you to ask me for a curative for her?"

"She wouldn't. She says your medicines are strictly for the queen. She doesn't like having to stay apart from Her Majesty, but she knows she mustn't spread contagion." Bianca swished to my vanity but did not sit. "I shouldn't have come to you myself to take the queen's medicine those other times," she said, blushing. "I never told Mother I came to you."

"I won't tell her, Bianca."

"Thank you," she whispered. "You are so brave," she added, fingering the hairbrush on my vanity, "going herbing with the wolves still out there. I only wanted to say . . . we are friends, aren't we?"

The soft words stole into me as she looked up. I saw the rings below her eyes that she never could quite cover with her powder, and remembered the last time I'd seen her in tears in the castle hallway with the king holding her close, drawing her into her room. Her flirtations with His Majesty went against all I was trying to do to help Queen Adela conceive an heir. For that we should be enemies.

She was waiting.

"Thank you for coming to see how I am," I said, putting my hand on her arm. "And for the slippers. The castle floors are cold."

The little smile she gave in return made my eyes prick. "You should . . . go now. I have work to do."

"Don't you ever rest?" Bianca surveyed the Crow's Nest, the boiling pans lined up in a neat row, the mortar and pestle on the worktable. "I suppose you can't rest in your profession," she added, retrieving her candelabra. I closed the door behind her, leaned my head against it, and swiped away tears. It was always kindness that undid me.

I should mix the queen's night remedy. Instead, I crossed the room, pulled woundwort from my woven basket, and undid my bandage. The red teeth marks were slowly healing. I applied the salve along the back of my hand, then on my palm.

Jackrun had dipped his calloused finger in this same jar, rubbed it gently on my puncture wounds. I didn't know if I was weeping now from the cooling relief or from the place in my heart Jackrun had unknowingly opened when he'd salved my hand. I remembered the trusting look he'd given me before I'd stitched his wounds. As a healer, I had known just what to do. But as a woman, I was lost. He was leading me into a new country, a mysterious place where I did not walk alone, but beside him.

I'd left him on the cliff just this morning. Already it seemed too long ago.

OVER THE NEXT week I potioned Queen Adela and tried to keep her happy as she went from tearful to vindictive to forgetful. She was approaching the fertile time of her cycle again. I had to balance her as quickly as possible, or the king could not visit her bed.

Afraid to leave her overnight, I took to sleeping in the trundle bed Lady Olivia sometimes used. At first my remedies didn't seem to make a difference to her wild moods. But after seven long days of lacing her fertility tonic with ever increasing doses of bapeeta, I saw the angry lines around her mouth smooth out, the strange mad look went out of her face. I waited one more day to be sure she was in balance. Hopeful my cure was finally working; I sent a message to King Arden. The queen was well enough to join her husband at the feast table, and, with any luck, he'd come to her room for the night.

I watched the queen dine from a place in the shadows in the crowded Great Hall. I still preferred to take my meals privately away from the noisy feast tables, or in the kitchen with the staff, but when a server offered me wine, I took it and sipped it gratefully. Queen Adela's eyes were bright as she spoke with her husband at the high table. Her cheeks were rosy with health. King Arden caught my eye and shot me a positive glance halfway through the meal.

Stars winked through the high windows. The waxing Dragon Moon grew more powerful every night. Father taught me this animal moon had great healing powers, ruling earth, wind, and fire; it needed only the element of water for complete balance. I decided I would order Her Majesty a restorative bath tomorrow. No bath could match the one I'd had in Dragonswood warmed by Filalda's fire, but I would sprinkle the water with scented herbs and give the queen the best bath available here at the king's court.

An hour later the sentry put out his hand and stopped me at the base of the queen's stairs. "The king is with his wife, queen's physician."

"Oh." I backed up. "Yes. I see. I'll return in the morning, then." He winked at me before I left.

A smile leaped to my face as I hurried through the torch-lit halls, greedy for a night alone in my own chamber, a full night of uninterrupted sleep. The Crow's Nest smelled faintly of huzana leaves. I lit the fire in the hearth, a luxury I rarely allowed myself, and sat cross-legged on the floor. The king and queen could be creating a new life even now. A child. An heir. Thank the Holy Ones I'd prepared a jar full of virility powder before my medicines were stolen, and given it to King Arden. I'd mixed the remedy all at once partly to avoid the work of grinding more leaves, partly to skip the embarrassment to both of us each time he had to renew his request. I slipped off my shoes and warmed my toes before the fire. Tonight, at least, I would let myself hope. I was too tired to do much else.

I draped the woolly Euit blanket over my shoulders, pressing my cheek against the owl woven in the corner. The blanket was barely big enough for two. Jackrun and I had had to lie very close together to soak in its warmth the night he confessed what he'd done to his sister, the night I admitted how I'd sabotaged Urette, the night he called me Adan for the first time.

"Jackrun," I whispered into the woolly owl's ear. "When will you come home?"

My fingers found a hardened spot. I looked closer. Dried blood. I did not know it was a sign of things to come. I folded it over, hiding the red stain.

# CHAPTER FORTY-THREE

# Pendragon Castle

## DRAGON MOON
### October 1210

THE NEXT MORNING, I set the queen's elixir on the side table a moment, tossed a handful of breadcrumbs to her songbirds, and watched them flutter down in a riot of bright colors. "There is plenty for you all," I said through the cage, but they did not think so. I left them squabbling amongst themselves.

The sentry in the presence chamber on the second floor leaned on his pike at the base of Queen Adela's private stair.

"Is Her Majesty alone?"

He nodded. I climbed the stairs to the bedchamber, stepped inside, and shut the door. Her Majesty sat with her back to me in her rumpled sleeping gown. The room was in shambles. Gowns and small clothes hung half across the chairs or lay on the floor by the smoking fire. The queen's four-poster canopy bed was mounded with covers; tangled sheets lay in the corner on the floor.

Her Majesty mumbled something and I stepped a little closer.

"Witches," she hissed, holding her glass eyeball in her open hand. "I had to be a virgin, you see. Satan's sacrifice." She looked up at me. The empty eye socket on the left side of her face was wrinkled as a wasps' nest.

Her voice changed to a growl. "See the curse?" She aimed the glass eye at the corner, showing it the tangled sheets. "My husband abandons me."

The news struck me dumb. What happened last night? Did the king do his duty? Or did they only fight, ravage the room between them? I had to know, but how could I ask her when she was raving?

She moved her hand, aiming her glass eye at me. "Who is the witch?" she asked, tipping her head, her voice seesawing from harsh to musical as if she were speaking to a young child. "We know she joins her coven in secret places. We know she tortures innocents."

She'd never called me a witch before, but then, I wasn't sure she was even speaking to me. I blinked back disappointed tears. Only last night I thought the bapeeta was healing her madness at last.

Sick inside, I picked up the dirty sheets as she chattered on. "See the witch?" she asked the eyeball in her palm. "She's a woman with a devil's heart."

I called to the sentry down below. When the chambermaid ran up, I met her on the landing. "Take these sheets away. Bring me clean linen and get a breakfast tray up here for Her Majesty, now!"

Green-faced, she darted back downstairs. I bolted the door, took up the golden ewer, and filled the washbasin. The queen had placed her eyeball on her vanity and was pulling the gray strands from her brown hair. "An eye for an eye. A tooth for a tooth. Silver hair, where is your youth? Gone, gone," she sighed, pulling more gray.

"I will clean this for you, Your Majesty, shall I?" I dipped the eye in the basin. *Queen Adela owes us for her glass eye. If we had left her marred, she would have never wed King Arden. Remind her of it.*

King Onadon expected me to speak to someone in her right mind, not this queen. Not as she was now. She hummed her strange tune behind me.

When the fey eye was rinsed clean, I approached her vanity table. "Here, Your Majesty, if you tip back your head a little." Opening the upper and lower lid, I gently slipped the glass eyeball back inside the socket. She blinked a little. Stood unsteadily, then sat again. I grabbed a brush and ran it gently through her hair. A few gray strands still silvered the long, dark tresses. She peered at her reflection; her eyes in the glass were blue as hyacinths. Both seemed lost as desert oases within her vacant face.

There was a furtive tapping at the door. I took the clean sheets and breakfast tray from the chambermaid on the landing, bolted the door again, and encouraged the queen to eat while I made the bed. Once again I'd have to keep vigil. No one could be allowed in her room until my treatments dispelled her delusions.

She had eaten some of her pudding and drank her elixir. She'd need a stronger dose of bapeeta. I hated to leave her even for a moment when she was this way, but I'd have to run to the Crow's Nest for it. "I will be right back, Your Highness."

The sentry watched as I came down the stairs. "The queen is unwell today," I said. "She must have complete rest. I will attend to all her needs. Do not let anyone other than me inside."

In the tower, I shut the herbarium door and leaned against it. The Adan should be slow to prepare medicines, paying close attention to each detail. But in the past week I'd felt the queen's lunacy seeping into my work. My breath was unsteady, my hands damp with sweat as I scraped bapeeta powder from the undersides of the leaves. Father had used bapeeta on the old people back home so long ago, I could not remember the traditional Euit chant for the herb. Was that why its powers had failed? Or was it the poor decisions I'd made regarding how much I should use?

Father hadn't had time to teach me more about bapeeta before he died. What secrets had died with him? I leaned against the table and cursed the thief who'd stolen my remedies, and worst of all, the book Father had put his life's knowledge into.

I had nothing and no one to guide me here.

I was alone.

I found Queen Adela conversing with her reflection when I returned. "Why did he shout at me?" she said. "What have I done? Why won't he love me?" She wept into her hands.

"Your Majesty?" *Did he sleep with you before you argued? Did you come together as man and wife last night?* Questions fought to climb out of my mouth.

She raised her head as I approached with the silver platter. I'd made a decision to follow my own way, mixing the bapeeta powder in the sweetmeats as I'd done in the past, two for now, two for later—the last two hidden in my waist pouch. This way I could give her what she needed without running off to the herbarium to mix another dose. The queen ate one. By the time she consumed the second and licked her fingers, her mood began to soften. She called me Uma again, put out her hand for me to kiss her ring, and did not call me witch.

I ordered a bath set up next door in her changing room. When it was ready, I sent the woman out, and brought the queen in myself. Helping her out of her robes and into the copper tub, I sprinkled the water with the sweet herbs, and gently washed her body and her long, dark hair. She hummed as I poured the water through her tresses. I dried her off and took her in her robe back to the larger bedchamber, where I built up a blazing fire so I could brush out her damp hair by the hearth.

As the day passed I fed her when she was willing to eat. Her mind seemed far away, like a ship adrift in some dark sea. I cared for her body as her mind lost its mooring, hoping I could do something to bring her back. She looked at me and took my hand.

"I'm afraid," she whispered, part of her knowing how lost she was.

I put my arms around her. "I won't leave you. I'll stay with you."

I rocked her as she cried. Her tears melted me. What could I do for her? How could I help her? She needed so much more than Father's rules, so much more than herbs. But there was nothing in his treatment store for this.

Mother had been a midwife, a healer. Women bathe the sick, rub sore muscles, offer food, and sing pleasant songs. My father would never do such things. I had to walk far beyond what my father the Adan would have done to ease the queen's suffering. In the passing hours, I mined stores I'd buried deep inside myself, a woman's knowledge I did not even know I had. I sang to her, rubbed her back, fed her, moved her from place to place to make her more comfortable.

Slowly the raging winds within her calmed.

At dusk a storm battered the windows with hail, as if Adela sent her tempest through the window to the greater world outside. We were both exhausted from the long day. At last she lay down on her bed in her clean gown, her hair neatly plaited.

Putting the rushlight by Adela's bed, I sang her an English lullaby my mother used to sing, half remembering the words. *Poppies and roses in her hair. She is queen of the May. Oh sing to her gladly and never sing sadly, she is the light of our day....* I could not remember the rest, though I knew it named more flowers; there was lavender and mallow in one part. I sang the same verse over and over until I grew tired of it and made up a new verse with songbirds in it. Adela smiled with her eyes closed, her head on the silk pillow. She loved birds.

WHEN IT WAS very late and she fell asleep at last, I stayed by her bed, listening to her breath go in and out. My fingers smelled of potions and the scent of all my father's dreams and mine gone to ruin.

I would sleep in the trundle bed again tonight. I would keep treating her, keep trying to help her find her mind and have the child she needed, but would it be enough? Even now high above the storm clouds, Dragon Moon waxed toward fullness.

## CHAPTER FORTY-FOUR

# Pendragon Castle

### DRAGON MOON
*October 1210*

I HURRIED DOWN the halls to the aviary on the first floor of the queen's tower, her morning elixir sloshing in its chalice. The birds flew wildly about as I rushed in, disturbed as if I were hurling gravel at them.

"What's all the fuss? It's only me. You know me well." I would have turned for the stairs then if I hadn't seen movement through the ground-floor window. A man had just ridden into the muddy foreyard on a black charger. I pressed my face to the lattice, squinting through the glass. *Jackrun.* He turned his horse for the stables. My breath went out of me.

I had to grip the ironwork to keep my feet in place. I'd left the queen sleeping in her bed to make her brew and I'd already been gone too long. I didn't want her to wake up alone. *Soon,* I promised myself. *When Her Majesty's had her elixir and eaten a little breakfast.*

The moment I entered the second-floor presence chamber, I knew something was wrong. The sentry had deserted his post. I'd told him to guard her when I left, to let no one but me upstairs. Where was he? A deep moan drifted down the dark stairwell. Not the queen's voice, a man's. My heart dropped to my feet. Leaving the curative on the table, I crept upstairs and pressed myself against the landing, well out of sight.

I could not look directly into the room from my hiding place. But I saw the image of the small crowd reflected in the queen's vanity mirror. The king was kneeling at his wife's bed. Weeping. Two guards flanked His Majesty. The woman praying at his side tucked a dark strand of hair under her veil. One of the guards stepped to the right. What I saw in the glass sent a pike through me. Queen Adela's face was a ghastly shade of green. Her head was thrown back from the convulsions she'd had as she died, her swollen purple tongue protruded from her mouth. Vomit ran down the side of her cheek. I made no sound on the landing as the bile washed up my throat. Adela. I'd only just left her. I'd only just . . . The floor swayed underfoot. I leaned against the wall, trying not to faint.

"Looks like someone poisoned her sweetmeat," said one of the guards.

"Why weren't you with her?" King Arden demanded to the lady kneeling at his side.

"I have had a fever, Your Majesty. Uma warned me to stay away from the queen." Her back was to the mirror, but I knew Lady Olivia's voice.

"Who else was . . . up here?" the king asked with a shudder.

"Just the queen's physician," said the guard. "She said not to let anyone see her. I let no one else up the stairs but her, sire, I swear it. I only came up myself when I heard a strangled sound after Uma left, and I found the queen like . . . this."

"Queen's physician must have done it, then," said the second man.

*No!* I screamed in my head. I ran down the stairs. Before I reached the bottom, I heard the king shouting, "Find her. Arrest her!"

I was out the door, racing through the long passage, the guards' distant footfall sounding loud as a cavalcade behind me. I skidded around a corner, running straight into a courtier, who took me by the shoulders and peered at my face.

"Queen's physician, what's your hurry?" he demanded.

I pulled away from him, ran again. My head pounded. If I could slow down, calm myself a moment, use the *havuela* chant to blend in, but I was too terrified. I couldn't think, couldn't stop running. My feet took me outside.

The guards shouted "Stop her!" as I raced for the stable.

"Jackrun!"

He came out, blinking in the morning sunlight, saw the men chasing me and drew his weapon.

"Get behind me, Uma." He raised his sword at the king's men. "Stay back!"

The blacksmith came out of the forge with the weapons

master; others emerged from the kennels. The yard was filling up with those who were suddenly my enemies.

"Out of the way, Jackrun, the woman's wanted for murder!"

"Don't come near her or you'll feel the point of my sword." Jackrun backed us toward the stable. I drew my knife and moved in unison with him, guessing we were going for his horse.

"We don't want to fight the king's nephew," one man said. We were nearly to the stable door.

"Turn her over, Jackrun. We're to take her by King Arden's order."

"Who accuses the queen's physician of murder?" Jackrun said, waving his sword as one man got too close. "Who died?"

"The queen is dead."

I heard Jackrun's quick intake of breath. Men reeled with the news.

"God have mercy," cried the blacksmith.

"Heaven help us!"

"Grab her!" called the weapons master, marching toward us.

"I didn't kill her," I called to them from behind Jackrun. "I would never harm Her Majesty."

"I believe her," Jackrun said, inching us under the lintel. "This woman is the queen's physician. She was appointed by the queen herself. No man among you will touch her while I'm alive."

Someone grabbed me from behind. Jackrun rounded on the head groom the moment I screamed. Already the groom had thrown a harness over me and held a hammer to my head. I tried to wriggle free, used my knife to slice the leather. He knocked the knife from my hand and threw a muscled arm around my throat.

"Now then," he said, "let's do this rightly."

"Let her go, Horace," Jackrun said, putting his sword to the man's throat. "You're a good fellow, but bring that hammer down and I'll have to cut your throat. Uma's riding out with me. Boy!" he added, calling to a stable lad watching the action from one of the mounting blocks. "Saddle my horse. There's half a crown in it for you." The boy hopped down and grabbed a saddle.

"Ready that horse and you're out on your ear," Horace the master groom shouted.

Outside, I heard someone calling "Raise the drawbridge." Jackrun heard it too and urged the stable boy to hurry.

More men had flooded in, swords all drawn at Jackrun. One sliced Jackrun's left shoulder, drawing blood. Jackrun didn't move from his spot, his eyes moving between me and Horace and the stable boy. He kept his sword point at Horace's throat. "You'll let her go and she will mount my horse now."

I felt the master groom shifting on his feet, smelled his fearful sweat under Jackrun's blade. With a grunt he let me go and slowly backed away, his hammer still in the air. I threw the halter off my head and mounted the black charger. Jackrun tried to climb on after me, fighting the men off at the same time. He was halfway up. I was reaching for him when the king's men dragged him off. He slapped the charger's rear, sending him bolting out of the crowded stable, shouting "Ride Uma!" He'd made it out of the stable, clashing swords with the men as I looked back. I circled around for him, but the charger reared at the battling crowd. "Go, Uma!" Jackrun screamed as he fought. The charger understood even if I refused to leave him. He turned, galloping for the drawbridge and had to pull away again before smashing against the solid wood. The drawbridge was up.

WE WERE MARCHED back inside to the king's throne room. His Majesty's face was still white from shock. His hands shook on his armrests. A few favored councilmen stood near the throne along with the castle priest. None stepped near Queen Adela's empty throne. I swallowed another wash of sickness down as Jackrun and I were forced onto our knees on the square of red carpet at the base of the dais.

"The murderess, sire," the chief guard announced. "Your nephew fought us out in the yard and tried to help the Euit woman escape."

"Rise," the king said. "And face me."

King Arden did not look at me. "You dared cross my men, Jackrun? Didn't they tell you that this . . . this devil killed my wife?"

"They told me, sire. I didn't believe them. Someone else committed this terrible crime. Uma would never—"

"No one else went in or out of my wife's bedchamber this morning, Jackrun," roared the king. He wiped his brow with a shaking hand. The throne room was hushed.

I looked at the many faces turned on me with anger, terrified to speak, terrified not to. "Your Majesty," I said, curtsying, head bowed. "I did not poison her. Someone must have—"

"So you know she was poisoned! How would you know that? Did anyone in my guard say she died of poison?" he barked.

"We said the queen was dead, sire, that's all."

"I . . . saw!" I cried out. "I came up the stairs and saw you kneeling by her bed. I saw what had happened. Then I ran. I didn't—"

The king snapped his fingers and a guard clamped his hand over my mouth.

"Jackrun, if you continue to side with this murderess, you are no nephew of mine. Step away from her."

"You're wrong about her, sire. I won't step away."

A shiver of anger passed through the king's body. The councilmen and priest leaned forward, ready to help him as he stood slowly to his feet, pointing a finger at Jackrun. "Lock him in the tower." Three men dragged Jackrun from my side.

"And that . . . that," King Arden said to the guard whose hand was planted on my mouth. "Throw that devil in the dungeon."

I WAS LEFT alone in my small stinking cell for hours. At nightfall they hauled me to the torture chamber. The large cell smelled of sweat and blood and fear. Would they burn me with the pokers leaning by a lit brazier, hang me from one of the many ceiling hooks, stretch me on the rack, force me into the chair with hundreds of three-inch nails poking from the seat and from the back?

The jailer stepped in rubbing his hands together. "King said to rack her, men."

"Please, I didn't do it. I didn't kill her!" The innocent spit boy confessed when they stretched him on the rack. I was terrified I'd do the same.

I struggled, but of course they were too strong for me. The jailer gave me a brown-toothed smile as the men manacled my wrists and ankles. "We'll stretch a confession out of you soon enough, Euit devil." His eyes shone with excitement. I hadn't screamed or cried when he'd whipped me in front of Prince Desmond. The man seemed to be looking forward to some real entertainment now.

"Crank her," he said, stepping back and resting his hand atop the nailed chair. Men at the top turned the handles of the roller bars. The first few cranks didn't hurt too much, but the pain increased as the rope attached to the manacles pulled my arms and legs tighter and tighter.

Another crank tore a moan from my mouth. I broke into a sweat. "Holy Ones, help me!"

"Holy Ones," said the jailer. "Who are they?"

I focused on the ceiling, trying to see beyond the heavy hooks. I knew just outside Pendragon Castle, Dragon Moon looked down on us, surrounded by sparkling stars, but I could not feel the light as the intense ripping pain shot down my arms and up my legs. "Stop! Please!"

"Are you ready to confess?" asked the jailer.

*Yes. Anything to stop the pain.* "No! I didn't harm the queen!"

"Again," he said.

The cuffs bit into my ankles and wrists. Wrenching pain stabbed my shoulders, the sleeves ripped under my arms. Cracking sounds came from my spine. I clenched my mouth. Screamed into my teeth.

"Ah! That's it now," said the jailer, pleased.

Sobs came up my throat. They would wrench my arms from my sockets. "Have mercy!"

"Confess?"

I screamed, felt myself breaking till there was an explosion of light behind my eyes. Sunburst. Agony.

"Stop before you kill her. The king wants her kept in one piece so he can watch her burn."

White-hot fire. Searing pain. Darkness.


I AWOKE CURLED up on the floor in my cell, every joint in my body throbbing with excruciating pain. I buried my face in the rushes, moaning. The rushes smelled like my herbing basket. The memory of Mother singing as she wove it came to me. For a moment she was in the cell. *Poppies and roses in her hair.* I could almost see her, almost hear her song. I tried to breathe, sobbed. My wrists throbbed, my shoulders, my ankles, my hips. The stabbing pains were as deep as if someone were attacking me with icy knives.

*Move your arms.*

*I can't. Poppies and roses in her hair. She is queen of the May. Oh sing to her gladly and never sing sadly, she is the light of our day.* The song faded and I was lost in dark again.

# CHAPTER FORTY-FIVE

# Dungeon, Pendragon Castle, Wilde Island

## DRAGON MOON
*October 1210*

THE NEXT DAY the guards dragged me to His Majesty's chamber before the king's council. They gave me a swift trial that consisted of the queen's guard claiming that no one but I had entered the queen's bedchamber before the murder, and of me pleading my innocence. Shaking in my manacles, joints aching, chains clinking, I relayed what I'd seen from the landing, told them the scent I'd caught coming from the room. "Whoever stole my medicines used the utzo oil to poison Her Majesty."

"You did not report your medicines stolen."

He was right. I'd kept that hidden. "I was afraid to, Your Majesty. I feared the queen would turn me away. It was why I was forced to go after more herbs."

The council conferred with one another all too briefly. The sheriff said, "The fact remains, the physician was the only one seen going up and down the queen's stairs."

My heart hammered. "The fey," I barked, remembering what Jackrun said. "They can guise themselves to look like someone else. Please believe me. I didn't—"

"Now she blames the fairy folk," the sheriff said with a huff.

The king squeezed his eyes shut. "Take the Euit woman out of here. Now."

Rain drummed outside my underground cell. By nightfall a stream of muddy rainwater flowed down the wall from the courtyard outside, forming a black puddle near my cheek where I lay in the straw. I stayed awake for what might be my last night on earth, trying to understand my life, the sacrifices I had made to learn the healing craft, throwing away my girlhood, shedding the company of others to serve the Adan.

What had it brought me? Jackrun was in the tower because of me. My mother and my people were still surrounded by soldiers. I was afraid to walk into the afterworld carrying all my failures with me. I had washed my father's feet for his spirit walk to Nushtuen. No one would wash mine.

The puddle grew larger, slick and still as a black mirror. I slapped the surface, shattering the image there. The water drew together again, healing itself. The sight of the queen's dead face reflected in her mirror came back to me with sickening clarity. Jackrun had warned me that mirrors told the truth, but I never thought I would see such horror and misery in one.

I rubbed my sore wrists. I wanted to black out that last horrible image of Adela's contorted face, the agony she must have felt. Who poisoned her so cleverly? So heartlessly? How had they gotten away with it?

Someone passed by with a torch outside. Yellow light glanced across the dark puddle. I sat up blinking.

I'd seen something else in the queen's mirror.

The torchlight was gone. The puddle went dark again. But the memory of what I'd seen in the mirror remained. The questions swarming through my head settled.

I knew who had killed the queen. I just didn't know why.

I CALLED OUT and banged against the door, anxious to tell someone what I knew. No one came all that night.

"I'm innocent," I cried the next day when the cell door opened. "I know who murdered her. Bring me up to see the king."

"Shut up with your babbling." The muscled guard tied my hands behind my back.

"You'll see the king all right," the second man said with a chuckle.

I blinked in the harsh sunlight on the crowded castle green. They dragged me forward.

"No, wait. I demand a trial."

"You got yours already. It's the fire for ye." People threw dirt clods. The ones loaded with rocks stung my chest and thighs.

"Best pray to your Holy Ones, whoever they are. See if they'll hear ye."

King Arden waited on the viewing stage, the sheriff and the bishop to one side of him, Bianca and Lady Olivia to the other. My whole body shook as they led me up the stage steps. It did not help to see Bianca crying as if I were already dead. The king linked his arm through hers and glared at me with cold hatred.

People on the lawn below us crowded closer to the edge of the stage, hungry to hear my confession before I was taken to the pyre.

By the Holy Ones I didn't want to die this way, executed by the English. I didn't want to die so far from home.

Two guards ushered Jackrun outside and made him stand to the left of the stage. His hands were tied behind his back like mine. Men on either side held him by his upper arms. I looked down at the face of the one I wanted to remember most as I left this life. His cheek was bruised. He'd fought his captors and paid for it. His eyes burned, looking up at me. We'd kissed by the escape tunnel, in the Crow's Nest, in Dragonswood. Three times. I'd hoped for more.

Jackrun started pushing and shoving like a young bull. "Let me speak!" he shouted. "I have something to say that must be heard! Uma did not—"

At the king's signal, the guard to Jackrun's left clamped a hand over his mouth. The man didn't drag him away for his disturbance. King Arden wanted Jackrun to see. Watching me die was part of his punishment.

My stomach stormed as the sheriff read out my crime.

"Uma Quarteney, for the heinous murder of Queen Adela, you are sentenced to be burned at the stake by order of our sovereign, King Arden Pendragon, on this fourteenth day of October in the year of our Lord 1210."

Ravens circled overhead, landing noisily on the wall edging the castle green. Where was Vazan? A bitter taste came to my tongue. I should not blame her for keeping to her cave with her hurt wing when I'd been the one who told her to rest, but I did.

The bishop stepped up. "Kneel, Uma Quarteney."

Just before the guards pressed me down to my knees, I saw her. Fox had come out to the lawn to sit by the wall. My Path Animal was here to lead me from one life to another. My eyes teared up as the bishop sprinkled my head with holy water, praying over me.

"Do you have any last words to say before us and before God?" he asked as I was helped back up to my feet.

I turned to the king. "Your Majesty. I did not do this crime. The woman who used magic to guise herself to look like me is—"

"Sorcery and magic?" King Arden shouted over me. "Is that your confession?"

The crowd booed, yelling, "Burn the murderess!"

Jackrun broke free from his guards below and raced for the pyre, shouting, flames roaring from his mouth in radiant reds, oranges, yellows. The sound was almost deafening; the brilliance stung my eyes. People screamed, leaping back in terror.

I gave a secret shout of joy seeing his fire again when I'd feared it might be gone. The pyre burst into flames, devouring the stacked wood at the bottom, crackling and licking up the sides. Jackrun ran to the far side, he screamed fire: spoke with fire, a speech every human soul on the castle green feared but me. I was alive with it, alive because of it. No one could get near enough to tie me to the stake now. The ladder leaning up against the pyre blazed along with the platform, the stake they were about to bind me to.

King Arden shouted furious orders behind me. I couldn't make out the words over the inferno. A few men rushed toward Jackrun with their weapons drawn, but they all stopped short, afraid to go any nearer.

In the bedlam I did not notice the black shadows sweeping across the lawn, did not look up until I caught the familiar spicy scent.

Craning my neck I saw two dragons winging in with Vazan. My Vazan. She hadn't stayed in her cave at all, hadn't abandoned me. Filalda and Babak flew in behind her with riders on their backs.

Jackrun went silent now, looking up, surrounded in coils of smoke.

The crowd drew back even farther than they had for Jackrun as Babak and Filalda winged in, landed on the grass before the royal stage, and lowered their heads. King Onadon and Princess Augusta dismounted gracefully onto the stage a few feet from me. The dragons took off again, joining Vazan, who'd alighted on the high crenellated wall just behind the stage. Six dragon eyes peered down at us, four golden, two silver. I caught Vazan's silver ones. Loyal dragon. Did she see the gratitude in mine?

The king was staring openmouthed at his younger sister, whom he hadn't seen in years.

King Onadon bowed. "We came as quickly as we could, Your Majesty. We hoped we would not be too late."

"You are still in time to see the execution," King Arden said, recovering his dignity.

"Then we are not too late to see justice served, Brother King," said Princess Augusta.

Jackrun climbed the steps onto the stage, his wrists still tied behind his back.

"You are not welcome up here," King Arden cautioned, putting up his hand. "You're still under arrest."

King Onadon moved his smallest finger. The ropes slipped off Jackrun's wrists and coiled like a dead snake by his boots.

"More magic," King Arden growled. "You cannot stop justice through sorcery. Guards, grab Jackrun. See that you hold on to him."

"I didn't use sorcery, Your Majesty," Jackrun said as the men surrounded him, swords and daggers drawn. "I only used the fire I was born with as part of our Pendragon heritage."

"To save a murderess."

"To save an innocent woman. Uma Quarteney couldn't have committed the murder."

"Let him go, please, Your Majesty," I said. "And I will tell you who poisoned your wife. You didn't let me finish before."

"Don't move," King Arden warned the men around Jackrun. "Speak, woman," he said bluntly. "And give me no more prattle about fairies and magic, I warn you."

The courtiers closed in on the stage, faces upturned. The guards held me firm. I swallowed, looking down as if to find courage by my feet. The delicately embroidered toes of the slippers Bianca had given me poked out from under the hem of my gown. I hated accusing the woman who'd watched out for me since I'd come to Pendragon Castle, but everyone was waiting and the king was impatient. I sensed I did not have long to tell my story. When I raised my eyes, I took heart from Jackrun's encouraging look. The king's guards still pointed their daggers at him, yet his face was intent. He believed in me.

"The sentry at my trial told the truth, Your Highness," I began. "He saw no one else but me climb the stairs to go in and out of the queen's bedchamber that morning." I searched the armed men in the crowd until I found the one I was looking for, and nodded at him before going on. "I don't blame the man for saying what he said. A woman guised to look like me took the poisoned sweetmeat to the queen. A fey glamour can fool anyone. But it cannot fool a mirror. I went upstairs later that morning with the queen's potion. Four people were already there in her bedchamber. I could not see them straight on from the spot where I stood in the stairwell, but all four were reflected in the queen's mirror. There were two castle guards and two others at Her Majesty's bedside. I saw you kneeling, Your Highness, and the woman praying at your side who tucked a dark strand of hair under her veil."

"Yes," said the king. "And so?"

"And so, I heard the woman's voice and knew it was Lady Olivia. The voice told me one thing, the mirror another. Lady Olivia's hair is blond, not dark. The mirror showed her true hair color. If she'd turned her head just then, I would have seen her true face as well, but I heard the guard accuse me of the crime, and I ran."

Vazan suddenly flew down from her perch, catching Lady Olivia, who had just edged down off the back of the stage. Vazan lifted her up and set her back in her place. "You will not sssslip away." Vazan's silver eyes had the look of polished daggers.

"Let me go!" Lady Olivia screamed, still caged in the red's long talons.

"Help her," Bianca pleaded, tugging the king's arm.

"I demand you let her go, red dragon," King Arden said. "She was my wife's closest companion. Onadon, Augusta, you and your dragons were not invited to this execution. If you care anything for the refuge we have provided for the fey folk and the dragons for more than six decades, you will leave my —"

"Wait," King Onadon said. "There is a way to settle this."

"A mirror," I said. "Just bring a mirror out."

"Would you listen to a murderess?" Lady Olivia called from her clawed cage. "Your nephew has put on a show so the fairy king and his dragons can carry his lover off to safety."

"Have I?" Jackrun nodded to the knights at my side. "You still hold Uma Quarteney firmly, don't you?"

"Aye, we do, and her wrists are tied."

"More show!" said Lady Olivia. "King Onadon can make her vanish and whisk her away with the twitch of a finger."

Jackrun raised a brow, then smiled. "If that were the plan, he would have done so already, my lady. If you are innocent, you won't mind standing in front of a mirror, will you?"

"Now," said the king, "we'll clear this up. You and you," he said, pointing at two armed men alongside the stage, "bring me the large mirror from my own privy chamber."

The men made their way through the whispering crowd and returned shortly, hefting a large oval mirror up to the stage. Two more followed them with a long sturdy bench. Vazan moved her captive aside while the men climbed onto the bench set at the back of the stage, holding up the heavy glass between them by its wooden frame. They were up high enough to tilt the mirror slightly so all the onlookers could see whoever stood before it.

For a moment I was afraid. The sight of the queen's dead body the other morning had thrown me into shock. Had I imagined the dark strand of hair I'd seen in her mirror? What if the mirror told us nothing?

The rest of us on the stage moved to the outer edges to give all a clear view. The guards dragged me to the side opposite from Jackrun.

"Let her go, red dragon," said the king.

"I am called Vazan."

"Let her go, Vazan," he said impatiently. "My guards will take her for now."

Vazan released her and flew back to the wall, lowering her head with the other two dragons, guarding us all from behind.

Lady Olivia moaned when they tugged her hands away and pinned her arms to her sides in front of the mirror. One man pinched her chin between his fingers, lifting it up toward the glass. And I saw. We all saw.

"Oh," cried a courtier.

"Look," said another.

The reflection showed two men holding a woman of middle years who did not look a thing like the fair-skinned Lady Olivia. You could still see the dark-haired woman's regal beauty on one side of her face, but the other half was mottled with red-and-white burn scars that stretched in branching patterns up her neck and across her cheek to just below her ear.

I was shaken by the sight of this total stranger's face. I thought I'd known her. Lady Olivia had been stern, sometimes severe when she'd schooled me in courtly manners. But she'd come to my defense more than once and pointed out my successes early on when I was too reticent to own them myself. We'd clung to each other while Master Ridolphi burned.

Why did she turn her back on me, steal the medicines, use my utzo to poison the queen? I didn't understand. The king's face was carved with shock. Bianca held his arm, tears streaming down her cheeks.

"This is a trick mirror," Lady Olivia said. "It is a lie!"

"Mirrors do not lie." Princess Augusta stepped beside Lady Olivia and her guards and gazed up at the glass so all could see her face with its dragon scales and golden eyes.

"Guards," King Arden said, "turn Lady Olivia about." She faced the crowd again, every bit the beautiful pale-skinned Lady Olivia we had all known.

"This is all sorcery and trickery," she said with icy calm. "King Onadon and the Princess Augusta flew here to free Jackrun's lover. We all know Princess Augusta would do anything for her nephew, and the fey king would do anything for his grandson, the Son of the Prophecy. You've heard the song about him taken from an old fairy prophecy.

"King Onadon and his fey court have wanted Jackrun to inherit the Pendragon throne all along. They have manipulated this court, used magic and murder to get what they want. Of course they schemed to destroy Her Majesty the queen so she would not birth an heir and displace Jackrun. Don't you see what they are doing? Are you all blind?"

King Arden tilted his head, caught a moment in her lie, then shook himself as if waking from a dream. "Turn about!" her ordered. "Turn her!"

The men forced Lady Olivia to look in the glass again.

"Who are you?" demanded King Arden.

King Onadon, who had held his powers in since freeing Jackrun's wrists, spoke out. "I know this woman."

## CHAPTER FORTY-SIX

# Pendragon Castle Green, Wilde Island

### DRAGON MOON
*October 1210*

KING ONADON GESTURED with his hand. "Sire, may I introduce Lady Tanya, known to you as Lady Olivia."

I blinked at her. Tanya? The girl the dragon saved from Queen Adela's witch pyre? King Onadon went on, "What you did not know because she kept it from you is that she is half fey. Eighteen years ago, we brought half-fey maidens to Pendragon Castle, hoping you would marry one. You welcomed my daughter, Lady Tess, and another to your court. Do you remember?"

"Yes, of course," King Arden said.

"Two came courting that year, but not Lady Tanya. She'd been burned for witchcraft a month before, and only just saved by one of our dragons."

"She's a witch?" asked the king. The crowd murmured, moving about as if an invisible hand stirred them.

"All lies," shouted Tanya.

"Guards, cover her mouth," said the king.

"Not a witch," King Onadon corrected. "Some of the women accused of witchcraft in those days were simply half-fey girls with powers others feared or could not explain."

I thought of Lady Tess, who'd endured the agony of thumbscrews. "We managed to rescue Tanya and tried to help her, but she was badly damaged. Even using all our powers, we could not fully heal her burns." Lady Tanya was struggling, trying to shout into the guard's broad hand.

"She was adept at glamouring herself to hide her scars, as you can see," said King Onadon. "Still, we knew a mirror, any mirror, would reflect her as she was and show the truth. So we kept her away from Pendragon Castle court then. She was bitter, disappointed. I think Tanya wanted to be the next Wilde Island queen more than the other half-fey girls we escorted here that year, but she could never wear the crown after she'd been burned.

"She lived with us a year longer and left DunGarrow when she was with child." I sucked in a breath, turning to Bianca. She'd once told me her father was an English lord. The girl was shaking, biting her lip. What fairy powers did she have? How had she hidden her fairy blood so well? Suppressing power: Had that caused her severe headaches? She looked weak, powerless now, her pale skin seemed almost translucent; I could see the tiny blue veins in her neck.

King Onadon said, "We did not know how deep Tanya's scars were, or guess that she was capable of murder when she left our care."

"Stop," cried Bianca. "It's not like that. She didn't come here to hurt anyone. It wasn't like that!"

"Quiet, girl!" barked King Arden, stepping away from her.

"Your Majesty, this is difficult news for you," King Onadon said. "We did not come to put on a show before your entire court, only to see justice done. If you are willing to hear the rest of my testimony along with Jackrun's, I might suggest you dismiss the people who came out to see a burning this morning, and keep only those trusted courtiers you want to remain here while we speak further."

"Yes," King Arden hissed. Angry as he was, he saw the sense of King Onadon's suggestion. He called on his armed men, the sheriff, the bishop, and his privy council to remain and dismissed the rest of the villagers and courtiers from the castle green. Bianca did not leave. I think she did not have the strength to move.

His Majesty faced the prisoner. "How could you poison my wife? What evil—?"

"Evil?" Tanya dropped her glamour spell, raising herself up to her full height. "Your wife was the evil one. She tortured me and burned me. Not because I was a witch, but for my fey blood. She knew the first lines of the prophecy: *The Prince shall wed a Fairy child.* She didn't want you to marry any half-fey girl. She didn't care whom she maimed or killed to get what she wanted," she shouted, spittle flying from her mouth. "She got the death she deserved!"

"Mother," cried Bianca. "You didn't. You didn't—"

"I've heard enough." King Arden yanked the sword from the nearest soldier's belt. Jackrun broke free and leaped between Tanya and the king. We'd both seen him stab Sir Geoffrey. King Onadon put one hand on His Majesty's shoulder and raised the other toward Lady Tanya. "Don't move," he said to her.

If she thought to use magic to vanish and escape, he would hold her down; his power was far greater than hers.

Bianca knelt on the stage, weeping with her face in her hands. King Arden, who'd kept her constantly at his side in these past days, seemed to want nothing to do with her now. "Remove your hand," King Arden said to Onadon.

"Not until you sheath your sword. She will be punished soon. It's not time yet and you know it."

King Arden lowered his weapon, turned and stared at his enemy. "You came to us guised to take revenge? Who gave you the right to harm my wife?"

"I had every right after what your wife did to me!"

"And Prince Desmond?" Jackrun said behind the king's back. "What did he do to you?"

"Desmond?" said the king, taking a slow step closer to her as if approaching a wild animal. "M-my son?"

"Your son was in the way," she said.

"In the . . . way?" His face broke. His mouth opened, no words came.

Tanya smiled. "How does it feel to lose everything, Your Majesty? To see all your dreams go up in smoke?"

King Arden swayed on his feet. Two men ran out to hold him up between them.

King Onadon took charge. "Take Tanya to the dungeon." Armed men surrounded her and led her off.

King Arden glared at Bianca as if she were no more than a cowering dog, before walking unsteadily across the stage. Stepping down on the green, he paused and turned, looking back at us. "King Onadon and Augusta, stay with us a little longer while we get this sorted out. Stay as our guests," he added hoarsely.

The stage was less crowded now. Jackrun opened his mouth a little, pursed his lips to shape a word—*Uma*. He said it soundlessly, yet I felt as if his lips brushed mine, naming me.

A moment later I heard small celebratory voices as my wrists were freed. I thought the sounds came from my own heart until I saw the songbirds flying in from the orchard, calling *see-dear, see-dear* in liquid song. *See-dear, I am free.*

# PART FOUR

## Free

## CHAPTER FORTY-SEVEN

# Pendragon Castle Cliffs, Wilde Island

### DRAGON MOON
*October 1210*

THE KING HELD a royal funeral for his queen in St.
John's Cathedral. Through my veil, I watched in awe
as Jackrun supported his uncle, staying at his side through-
out the service and the long funeral procession to the Pendragon tomb.

Then King Arden retired to his rooms, leaving orders for
tents to be erected on the castle green for Tanya's trial the
next day.

"WHERE DOES IT hurt?" Jackrun asked. We'd met near
the amphitheater to steal a little time together and walk

south along the high cliffs before Tanya's trial, Babak and
Vazan winging over us.

"It doesn't hurt so much now."

Jackrun stopped. "Liar. You were stretched on the rack.
Tell me."

"My wrists are—" He was already pulling up my sleeves,
putting his large warm hands over the ringed bruises the
manacles had left behind.

We'd searched Tanya's room for any remains of Father's
medicines; she'd kept and used the utzo, but we'd found
nothing else. Worse, we'd found no trace of Father's Herbal.
A few men helped us look other places in Pendragon Castle. Nothing. It was clear she'd destroyed my father's life's
work. Alone in my room, I wept.

"Things keep haunting me," I said.

"What sort of things?"

"Memories of Lady Olivia before I knew who she was."

He cradled my wrists, listening.

"She always wore a veil that fell to her shoulders. I'd
thought it had to do with her strict sense of fashion, but its
real use was to hide her face and hair whenever she was near
a mirror."

"Clever," Jackrun said.

"Very. And she was careful, so proper most of the time,
but I saw her break down twice. The first time was the night
Queen Adela had a kind of waking dream, reliving Tanya's
burning. Her Majesty shouted at the dragon who rescued
Tanya from her witch pyre, screamed for him to bring her

back. Lady Olivia—Tanya," I corrected, "collapsed, hid her face in the covers and sobbed."

"Because it was her story," Jackrun said.

"Yes, but I didn't know it then."

"And the other time?"

"The day Queen Adela burned Master Ridolphi and made Tanya watch. We clung to each other. She was crying, saying, *No one should have to die this way.* The man's suffering must have been a torture to her, reminding her of her own."

"Yet she was willing to let you burn for her crime," Jackrun said.

"I know. I'm only trying to piece it all together so I can understand."

"Why she hated Queen Adela? That's clear enough."

"More than that—why she killed Desmond. Why she framed me."

"Uma, I think she killed Desmond after she discovered he'd attacked you on Dragon's Keep. She wouldn't want her daughter to marry a man like that. She saw another way for her daughter to be queen by marrying me."

I looked down at his large hands cupping my wrists.

"But I failed her too," he added. "I wasn't interested in Bianca."

He raised my chin and gave me a soft kiss that felt like a question. I answered his question with a silent yes. He was warm again. Full of fire.

Swirls of heat swept down from above. "Jackrun," Babak called.

Jackrun pulled away and looked up. "Not now, Babak. I'm busy." He tugged me closer again, both of us laughing as we kissed.

Babak flew in lower, his pumping wings blowing back our hair. "It's your father's ship!"

This time we broke apart in earnest. Down in the bay, a vessel had pulled into the harbor, a large green dragon flying above. Squinting from the cliff top, I could just make out Duke Bion's colorful flag whipping in the breeze.

We flew to the harbor on Babak and Vazan. Our dragons landed on the shore near Lord Kahlil. As soon as we dismounted, Tabitha raced up the beach ahead of her parents and threw her arms around her brother.

"Jackrun, you're safe! We thought something terrible must have happened to you when Babak left so suddenly. And, Babak, you should have said something before you flew off," she said, scolding the great beast as if he were no larger than a housecat.

Babak flattened his ears against his head. "There was no time. Jackrun was locked in the tower. He needed my help to rescue Uma Quarteney before she was burned."

"Burned?" Lady Tess stepped toward me, taking my arm.

Vazan nudged Babak's shoulder. "You did not work alone, Babak."

"I did not say I did, my lady."

She flicked her tail, sending up a spray of sand. "Call me rivule, not my lady!"

"Yes, rival."

"*Rivule,* which means 'warrior,' not *rival,*" she said with a snarl.

"Please, warriors," said Lord Kahlil, "let Jackrun speak."

The wind whipped the words from Jackrun's mouth as he told his family all that had happened to us in the past month and a half since leaving Dragon's Keep. When Jackrun spoke of Princess Augusta, Lady Tess stopped him. "You've seen her?"

"Yes, she's well, Mother. She's here. You'll see her at the trial."

Lady Tess drew in a breath. "Alive and well," she whispered, blinking back tears. Duke Bion squeezed her hand. "Go on, son."

Jackrun's voice dipped when he told them about the queen's murder, about Lady Olivia's true identity, how I nearly burned for her crime. I looked from one astonished face to another. We all stood a moment, listening to the distant waves when he was done.

Lord Kahlil dug his long claws in the sand and fixed his golden gaze on Lady Tess. "It is not our way to regret the past," he said, "but you know my part in this."

I wondered what he meant by his part. Lady Tess stepped closer and placed her hand on the jagged scar along the dragonlord's neck. "Did you see the future when you rescued Tanya from Adela's witch pyre, sir?"

He tipped his head as she stroked his neck. Lord Kahlil was Tanya's rescuer?

"I saw many possible futures, Tessss."

Duke Bion joined his wife. "Tanya chose her path, Kahlil. You had nothing to do with that."

Jackrun and Tabitha stood wide-eyed. I must have looked the same, taking in the revelation. If the dragonlord had not rescued her, she wouldn't have lived to take her revenge on the queen. But if I'd had the courage, I would have run my hand along Lord Kahlil's neck as Lady Tess was doing now. I agreed with her and Duke Bion, it was not the dragonlord's fault. Tanya had made her own choices. Not even the fey folk had guessed what she would become.

Lady Tess turned to Jackrun. "Is it safe to bring Kip to shore now?" she asked.

"It's safe, lady Mother."

She waved to the knight, who carried the little boy down the gangplank and along the beach. Lady Tess sent me a look of gratitude as she took the sleepy child from Sir Geoffrey's arms. It was good to see him again, especially now that I knew he was innocent.

Duke Bion glanced north along the cliffs. "We should go support my brother. I cannot imagine the agony he's experienced these last few months, first losing his son, then his wife."

Jackrun mussed his little brother's hair, wavy like his own, but a lighter shade of brown. "King Onadon asked King Arden to hold the inquiry on the castle green so there would be enough room for the dragons to participate in the trial."

"Jackun," Kip said, yawning and stretching in his mother's arms.

"It's a ways back," Jackrun said. "We should borrow some horses here in the harbor so we—"

"Ride dragonback," said Lord Kahlil. "A few can double up."

Sir Geoffrey made a swift bow. "The rest of you ride. You are all needed at the trial. I will come on my own and catch up with you." I wasn't sure if he declined out of courtesy or fear, having never flown before. But one less rider would be easier on the three dragons. I sidled over to Vazan. Her wing was still on the mend. She would hiss if I said she must only take one rider, but I didn't have to. Tabitha climbed on Babak with Jackrun. Lord Kahlil took Jackrun's parents and their younger son. Kip squealed with delight as we all took off, the great wings pounding like thunder.

IT DRIZZLED WHEN we began to gather later that afternoon on the green. There were seven dragons in all, including four from Dragonswood. King Arden invited King Onadon to join his privy council for the trial. A half-fey woman who had lived in DunGarrow, even if it was only for a year, was on trial. Both kings would sit in judgment of her.

Lady Tanya's crimes had brought all the factions of Wilde Island and Dragon's Keep together in one place. Dragon, human, and fairy encircled the fire pit in the pavilion tent as the sky outside let down its rain. Jackrun sat with the fairies closest to his grandfather King Onadon. Duke Bion and Lady Tess took their places by Princess Augusta. Somber as this day was, Lady Tess and her husband could not help exchanging grateful looks now and again knowing Augusta was alive and well after hearing nothing from her for so many years.

Vazan and I sat close to the dragons, but not with them. As much as Vazan had been willing to fly into the sanctuary to help me, she did not consider herself a creature of Dragonswood. We were, as always, set apart from the rest. But I stole glances of Jackrun, as he did of me.

Castle servants had propped up His Majesty's mirror between the kings' thrones so we could all see the face of anyone seated on the white oak chair. In Euit traditions, the oak is a wizened tree—a tree of truth. And here, the English were also using oak to seek truth. How strange to think that there were ancient beliefs that the Euit and English shared, beliefs that were bigger than our differences.

Bianca was summoned outside first.

I glanced around the circle. Many looked relieved to see the same girl with milky skin and hair of spun honey in the glass that they'd always seen. I was not surprised. She'd peered at my vanity in the Crow's Nest more than once.

Bianca struggled through tears to answer the questions put to her the first half hour. She shook visibly later when King Onadon asked, "Did you know your mother killed Prince Desmond?"

Bianca looked down at her clenched hands.

"Answer me, Bianca."

"I didn't, Your Majesty."

"You had no idea of her intentions when she sailed to Dragon's Keep?"

She shook her head vehemently. "No."

"Did you know she planned to poison the queen?"

"I didn't. How could I know . . . believe she would do such a terrible—" She broke down again. The council members looked uncertain, but I believed her. She had always obeyed her mother, first courting Prince Desmond, and later Jackrun.

No doubt her mother was angry with her when she didn't win Jackrun's affection. But there was a quicker way for Bianca to be crowned, if the queen were dead. When had her mother discovered the king's interest in her daughter? Had she found the sapphire bracelet, cornered her and asked questions? I couldn't guess what had gone on between mother and daughter, but I was sure Bianca was innocent of murder. She had no cruelty in her.

The girl slumped in the oak chair, weeping. For the first time since she'd entered the pavilion, King Arden allowed himself to glance in her direction. His expression swirled from grief to love to fury, and finally regret until his face broke, and he had to look away. He did not speak as the rest of the council conferred together, heads tipping this way and that.

When Bianca was dismissed, she stood unsteadily. Suddenly, she threw herself at her lover's feet. King Arden looked down miserably as she cried, "Please, Your Majesty, please spare my mother's life. She's done evil things, m-many evil things, but please don't . . ." She choked, unable to finish, kissed the ring on his hand, then wiped her golden hair across his boots.

The king blanched white, rigid as one of his onyx chess pieces. Duke Bion leaned forward and spoke gently. "Bianca, you must leave us now. Go with the guards."

I did not reach out to comfort her when she passed my bench. Her mother would have let me die in her place. Tanya had ended two people's lives, nearly three, nearly mine. That was not Bianca's fault, I knew. Still, I could not put out my hand.

THREE FEY MEN brought Tanya in, staying close to her lest she try and use magic to escape. She was still guised as Lady Olivia, walking with regal steps to the oak chair. Once seated, she scanned the council members, dragons and fey in the great circle. I shivered when her cold blue eyes landed on me before moving on to King Arden.

His Majesty glared back at Lady Olivia, then turned to see Tanya in the glass. His fingers tightened around the throne's clawed armrests.

King Onadon began the questioning, and Tanya shifted her focus to him. "You have already confessed to two murders," he said. "We are here to question you further and hear your side of things before we pass sentence."

"My side?" she scoffed. "Who was ever interested in my

side? Did you listen to me when I begged you to bring me here to Pendragon Castle when I was a girl? Did you give me the chance to become queen in my own right? No. You were too afraid King Arden would see my burns in the mirror. I proved you wrong, didn't I? I lived two years in Pendragon Castle guised as Lady Olivia and no one was the wiser. Only one man found me out, and I silenced him in his sleep."

The lute player.

I blinked back tears thinking of the poor spit boy who hanged for her crime.

"What were your intentions when you came two years ago to live in Pendragon Castle?" asked King Onadon.

"I intended to give my daughter the chance I never had."

"To marry a Pendragon king?"

"Why not? She was Prince Desmond's age. My daughter came here as a pure maiden. Her father was fey," she added with a glance to King Onadon. "She would have fulfilled the prophecy you've all longed for if she married a Pendragon."

"If you had that in mind, why kill Prince Desmond?" King Onadon asked.

"Would you let your daughter marry a cruel woman-izer? He tried to rape Uma," she said, nodding in my direc-tion. Heat stormed my cheeks. I looked down at my hands. "Tell them what you discovered back on Dragon's Keep, Sir Geoffrey," she commanded.

Sir Geoffrey stood up, uncertain.

"Sit!" King Arden ordered, and he dropped to the bench

again. "You are not in charge of this trial, Tanya!" A hush fell on us all. I heard small rustling noises of cloaks and clothing as people shifted on their seats.

King Onadon said, "Did you think I would condone your twisted methods to put fey blood on the throne? If any fairies plotted with you on this, they went outside my authority."

"I didn't need anyone's help. I have my own powers."

Jackrun said, "You are no doubt a woman of tremendous power. Not every half fey can command the kind of wind you used to push my cousin off the cliff."

Jackrun knew how to win her attention. A slow smile crept across her face.

He went on. "Did you also use your fairy magic to hex the queen? To keep her ill?"

I found myself holding my breath, grateful for the question as much as frightened by it.

"Hex her?" Tanya raised a brow. "No." I felt my insides folding up like a fan. "Adela was infertile and going mad all on her own," said Lady Tanya. "All I had to do was stand back and watch."

"Enough," said King Arden. "You sicken me to death. I don't want to hear any more."

Tanya leaped up. "I sicken *you*? Your wife was no innocent. Look what she did to me." She yanked up her sleeve, showing her ruined arm, then tugged her thick skirts up to her knees to show the ropy burn scars on her legs.

"I made sure to show Adela who I was while she was

dying. She saw the scars she gave me when she burned me. And I told her I killed her son."

IT WAS NIGHTFALL before the kings and council reached a decision. King Onadon proposed taking Tanya back to DunGarrow, and imprisoning her in a cell of mirrors with no escape from her reflection and no means to shatter them. It seemed an apt punishment for one who had hidden so much for so long. But King Arden had lost his son and his wife. "She must be beheaded," he said. No one crossed him.

## CHAPTER FORTY-EIGHT

# Castle Green, Wilde Island

### FULL DRAGON MOON
*October 1210*

AFTER THE SENTENCING, they dragged Tanya away. I stepped out of the tent and saw Dragon Moon rising full and bright in the darkening sky.

The flames of the long-poled torches roared in the wind, flying sideways like bright orange flags. We were in the twilight hour when there was no daylight to cast our shadows and we became shadows ourselves.

Across the green, Jackrun stepped out from under the awning with King Onadon. He was talking, gesturing. The crowd had broken into many small groups around the lawn. I could not hear him.

Vazan flew down and settled on the grass. "We will leave tomorrow," she said. I heard the longing in her voice, for home and for her first good meal in six months. I stroked her scaled neck. She let me touch her now. So much had changed between us since the day I'd stitched her wing. I had removed the stitches, but I could still feel rougher skin in the place where it had torn.

"It's strong," she said.

"I can see that. But strong enough to fly all the way to Devil's Boot with a rider on your back?"

"Yessss."

I should be overjoyed at the thought of going home at last. "The king's soldiers are still there," I said to her.

"We'll ssssweep them off our land," she said with confidence.

I would arrive in Devil's Boot with my own terrible news. No one back home knew Father was dead. I would have to tell Mother.

"Uma?"

Augusta had stepped beside Vazan. I'd been too distracted to sense her approach. It surprised me to see Vazan lowering her head to greet the princess. Vazan did not bow to anyone, not even my father when he was alive.

Augusta nodded. "Rivule Vazan." I felt a pang of guilt for suspecting her when I'd first met her in Dragonswood.

The princess had her eyes on Jackrun. "He used his dragon power well the other day," she said. "He told me you encouraged his gift."

I nodded, suddenly shy.

"If I'd remained on Dragon's Keep, I would have helped him. No one else in his family did. But I think that will change now. He deserves the freedom to grow into his dragon power." She did not say *as I've grown into mine.* She did not have to say it. I saw animal power and dragon beauty in her. I saw the way she balanced the different parts of herself. I felt a sudden kinship with her, as I was beginning to do the same.

"Princess, I'm wearing the gown you loaned me when I stayed with you." I fingered the mysterious soft green cloth that seemed almost a living thing; the gown had welcomed me, but it was hers. "I can return—"

"Please, keep it, Uma. You look beautiful in it, and I have plenty. The fairies make my gowns now."

"Thank you." Did she truly think I looked beautiful in it?

Jackrun stepped across the lawn to talk with King Arden.

"Princess, your brother the king seems to have accepted you back in the Pendragon family now. It means you can visit your family here and on Dragon's Keep if you like."

"Yes, but I am not planning to stay among men, Uma. I do not want to try to fit in, not anymore. I live in Dragonswood."

"The queen is dead," I said, "and her son. The ones who hurt you are gone. Are you sure you want to live apart?"

"Uma," Vazan said, "you do not understand."

The princess rested her hand on Vazan's chest. I felt a wave of envy when Vazan did not hiss and back away. There was something the dragons seemed to know about Princess Augusta; even Vazan knew it, and she did not count herself a creature of Dragonswood.

"Uma does not have to understand to be a friend, rivule,"

said the princess. She turned her copper eyes to me. "I'm happy in Dragonswood. Well loved. It is not where I was born, but it's become my home."

I heard contentment in her voice, and the challenge in it. "Vazan mentioned you're returning to Devil's Boot," she said.

"Yes," I whispered.

"I found my home in an unexpected place. It was not where I grew up, but a place where I could grow," she offered.

Across the lawn, Jackrun was laughing with his grandfather, his head thrown back. "How many hearts will you break if you go?" asked the princess.

"Princessss," hissed Vazan.

"Let Uma answer, rivule."

I could not answer. Too many tears filled my throat, blocking my words.

"Uma," she said, lifting my chin. "Think on it not only with your head but with your heart." She turned and walked away with Vazan. The dragons on the far side of the green bowed their heads as the princess approached. Even Lord Kahlil bowed. They did not hold their heads down long, dragons would not, but the gesture showed the love they had for her.

THE FIRST FEW stars appeared as Jackrun crossed the green, his stride long, his arms swinging. His hair had tugged free of its leather strap. I drew in a long breath as he moved closer, as if my breath were pulling him toward me.

"*Veritas vos liberabit,*" he said.

"What?"

"It's Latin for 'The truth shall set you free.'" Jackrun stepped closer. "I need . . . I have to swim," he said. "Will you come with me? Do you mind?"

We went out the gate, taking the road between castle and graveyard, leading to the cliffs beyond the amphitheater. Farther south, we climbed down the zigzag stairs to the deserted beach below.

"I won't be long," Jackrun said. "Sorry, Uma. I'm too full of everything that's happened. We can talk once I've . . ." He left the rest unsaid, hurriedly pulling off his cloak and shirt. His muscled skin shone in the full moonlight.

Someone in Dragonswood had removed the stitches from his arm. The small, even patterns in the scales matched perfectly. A scar line would remain, but there would be no distortion. I smiled to myself. I'd done well by him.

"You're healing quite quickly," I told him.

"I am, thanks to you," he said, pulling me close to him. "Now, no peeking." He jumped out of my arms and ran toward the water, where he pulled off his breeches. I was surprised to see a second, longer scale patch running down the back of his right leg. He had been too far away the other times I'd watched him swim for me to see this second patch. Jackrun raced for the water, strong limbed and swift footed on the uneven sand.

I slipped out of my shoes, lifted my skirts, and headed for the water's edge as he dove into a curling white wave.

The sea swirled around my ankles. I was used to steaming pools at the base of our mountain, not this freezing ocean. I couldn't go in after him. I didn't think he wanted me to.

Jackrun's arms rose and fell in rhythm on the surface until he was no more than a black dot in the water where Dragon Moon made a shining path of polished pearl. The path shone right up to me as if I could walk out on it, but it was all water, all moonlight, all wish.

I stood watching, trembling with cold as Jackrun swam back. Bending down to gather driftwood, I busied my hands and watched under my lashes as Jackrun dried his body off with his cloak before tugging on his shirt and trousers. His wet hair stuck out at odd angles.

Cold as it was here by the shore, he did not bother putting on his cloak. When he saw me shivering, he took a slow deep breath and sent a soft yellow flame down by our feet, lighting the driftwood logs. Then he shot me a smile, waiting.

For a moment I didn't understand what he expected me to say, then I knew. "You didn't have to summon anger to make fire this time."

His smile widened. "My power returned as I got stronger, just like you said it would. When it did, I decided to experiment with it, see what I could do."

I thought of the explosive flames he'd roared to destroy the pyre, the soft breath he'd used just now to kindle our beach fire. Destructive fire, warming fire: The two couldn't have been more different. Princess Augusta was right. He deserved the freedom to grow into his dragon power. He'd have the freedom he needed in Dragonswood. Suddenly Dragonswood and Devil's Boot seemed as far apart as the earth and moon.

Jackrun broke a stick across his knee with a loud crack. "Vazan told me you were leaving."

"Yes, tomorrow."

He tossed the broken pieces in the flames, looked down, and slid his fingers through his wet hair. My scalp tingled. "Come closer," he said. "Look into my fire and tell me what you see."

Some fey had the fire-sight. I would not pass his test. "I don't have fey powers, Jackrun."

"No, but you are a seer."

"What do you mean?"

"You thought Sir Geoffrey used fey magic to draw you to his hiding place, but the man was not fey after all, was he?"

I knelt to brush the thin layer of sand from my ankles, using the moment to turn Jackrun's words over in my mind. Only men could be seers in my village, yet the Holy Ones had gifted me with sight more than once. The vision in Vazan's cave led me to fox in Dragonswood and to the kea.

"Adan?"

I looked up. "I told you not to call me that," I said.

Smile lines formed in the corners of his eyes. "Adan?" he asked again. The word fell like rain on a parched place deep inside me. This time I let it soak in. He had seen me for who I was, spoken truth.

I stood again, planting my feet. *Look into my fire and tell me what you see.*

The flames flew upward in long leafy shapes of growing light. They pitched and swayed. How could anyone see visions in such constant motion? If I could see something, it would be the face and form of the one who'd made this fire with his breath so I could have him twice, across from me, still damp from his swim, and in the ever-moving blaze.

"I see only fire," I whispered.

Jackrun swept the blowing hair away from my face. He'd worn his finest castle garb to sit with the council today, and still, loose threads hung from the cuffs of his damp linen shirt. He could never quite fit into the courtly fashion. I'd been trying to hold my emotions in my heart, already preparing to leave him tomorrow, but the little threads undid me.

My eyes burned. Jackrun brushed the tears from my cheek with his finger, kissed the place where they had fallen, and put his arms around me.

"Don't," I whispered as he leaned down. "I'm leaving tomorrow. This will only make it worse." But I didn't pull away when he kissed me. His body was still cool from his swim, his lips were warm. It was a kiss that grew deeper, sadder. He held me close in the circle of his arms as if he would refuse to let me go. I wove my fingers through his dark hair at the nape of his neck.

I don't know how long we would have kissed like this

if we hadn't heard the telltale swooping sound and felt the warm wind swirling over our heads. Babak gusted in. I moaned his name before we drew apart. *Jackrun.*

Babak landed on the beach directly in front of us. "Come," he said. "Both of you."

Jackrun retrieved his cloak. "Is it the king?"

"Yes, the king."

Babak flew us back up along the cliffs.

"What about the king?" I asked.

Babak swiveled one eye back. "He wants to see you, Uma."

The answer startled me. Jackrun tightened his grip around my waist. "Don't be afraid," he said into my ear.

I glanced back. "Do you know something about this, Jackrun?"

"I might."

"Tell me," I said. Jackrun held his tongue as Babak circled down. Many had left the green, but the fey king and the English king remained by a newly built bonfire along with Jackrun's family, Princess Augusta, and the dragons.

Jackrun leaped down and helped me dismount. Vazan narrowed her silver eyes at Babak. "We have been waiting. What took you so long to find them?"

"I did my besssst!" he hissed. Would these two ever stop fighting?

Lady Tess motioned me over to King Arden.

I curtsied, awkwardly, then stood with my feet spread apart on the ground, a warrior's stance, though I did not feel much like a warrior at the moment. I wanted to feel the earth's power wicking through me as I faced the king. "Vazan, will you come here?" She lumbered over, wrapping the tip of her red tail around my skirts. "*Tuma-doa*—thank you, rivule." I felt a little better with her on my left and Jackrun to my right, but not much.

Jackrun bowed. "Tell Uma what this is about, will you, sire?"

King Arden's shoulders were hunched as if he carried some great invisible weight. I had no herbs to heal his grief, no mixture for the pain in his soul. I could only pray.

His Majesty appraised me. "You are a fine physician, Uma Quarteney." I saw admiration in his look. "You attended my poor wife, God rest her soul, and saved my nephew Jackrun's life after the wolf's attack." I'd helped him too, though that would remain a secret between us.

Jackrun reached out and gave my hand a squeeze. I blushed twice, first at the compliment, and then at Jackrun's boldness, touching me here in front of everyone. Jackrun did not let go of my hand until he gave it another squeeze and even then he linked his smallest finger with mine.

The king was still addressing me. "Tanya tricked us into thinking you were a murderer. I am glad for your sake the truth came out in time."

"Thank you, Your Highness." This was as close to an apology as you could expect from a monarch.

"I am sure you are pleased with the outcome of today's proceedings," he added.

I did not think beheading Tanya would ease his suffering. And I'd preferred King Onadon's suggestion of a mirror prison for Tanya, but he would not want to hear my thoughts on execution. "I am, Your Majesty."

"Jackrun spoke to me of your concerns for your people. My soldiers have been stationed there long enough. I've already sent a messenger to Devil's Boot with an order for my army to break camp and come home."

Song broke out in my body. There would be no army threatening my people when I returned, no one surrounding the village, keeping them hostage. King Arden was smiling. Jackrun beamed. I felt warmth glowing in my chest as if I'd been given a new heart.

"Thank you, Your Majesty." I trembled so much I could only half curtsy if I hoped to keep my balance.

"Don't thank me, Uma, thank Jackrun. He convinced me it was the right thing to do."

Jackrun's eyes were bright. On my left, Vazan shivered snout to tail. The quaking rumbled through my body. She craned her neck and blew a riotous fire skyward. I raised my hands high in the air, palms up to her victory blaze, cupping fire and stars and Dragon Moon. Jackrun lifted his chin and roared brilliant red-orange flames. Then everyone seemed to be moving. Lady Tess dashed over with Duke Bion and Augusta. All three joined me, raising their hands palms up to the light in sudden celebration. And the dragons joined Vazan, breathing their flags of fire until the night bloomed bright with it.

# Free

King Onadon made circles with his hand, turning branching flames to shining orbs spinning overhead. This was not their moment of victory, but everyone joined in and hailed it just the same. My people were free. The reds were free.

The sky blazed brighter than the bonfire until the flames subsided. Jackrun's father laughed and slapped him on the back.

My arms still felt warmed by dragon fire, silken with caught moonlight when I lowered them at last to link fingers with Jackrun again.

"It has been a long day," King Arden said. "There is one last thing I promised Jackrun I would say before I retired to my rooms."

I blinked up at Jackrun's face. What now?

His Majesty said, "Your talent has not gone unnoticed. You have earned the right to become our royal castle physician, Uma. I offer you the position along with ample payment for your services."

"Your Majesty, I . . ." Words fell away. I could not move.

"You would take Uma from ussss?" Vazan hissed at the king.

"Vazan, let me speak."

"Are you English now?" she snapped.

"No, rivule. I am half English, half Euit."

Her eyes flashed. "And you don't know where your home issss?"

I couldn't bear to look in her quicksilver eyes, or at Jackrun as they both waited for my decision. He wanted me to stay. She wanted me to go. But what did I want? The king's offer was tempting. I would be honored as the royal castle physician. And what he said was true. I had earned the right to practice medicine here.

But Jackrun's presence made this place home for me, nothing else. I looked from one face to another in the small, prestigious crowd.

*How many hearts will you break if you go?* How many hearts would break if I stayed?

The king breathed a sigh of impatience. "Answer me, Uma."

"Thank you, King Arden. It is a very generous offer, but I cannot accept."

Jackrun withdrew his hand. I shivered as his warm energy drained out of me.

King Arden frowned. "You refuse my offer?" He was not used to anyone turning him down.

"My tribe is dying out, Your Majesty." I straightened my shoulders. "We intend to live. Some of the women wait for my father's cure. They cannot have children without it. I am the only healer who knows how to find the herbs, prepare them, and administer them. I have to go home."

"Uma, please," Jackrun said under his breath.

Did he think this was easy for me? "Don't you understand anything? I was brought here against my will. My home is in Devil's Boot. My medicines are needed there."

"Even though you told me a woman cannot be a true healer in your tribe?"

"I have to try."

Jackrun drew back. "You could work here as an honored physician, Uma. I would have made a home for you."

*You are my home,* I thought. I pressed my lips together. I'd cry out, take it all back if I didn't.

His face fell. I wanted him to tell me he understood. He wasn't about to say that.

One by one people left the bonfire. Jackrun crossed the green with his father and His Majesties. The dragons spread out on the wide lawn. Lady Tess and Princess Augusta stayed outside under the stars.

"Uma," said Lady Tess. "Come here." The two women welcomed me between them by the burning wood stack. I could not feel its warmth.

The fire I wanted was gone.

My companions rested their hands on my shoulders as we faced the fire.

# CHAPTER FORTY-NINE

## Castle Green

DRAGON MOON
*October 1210*

AT DAWN I set the Adan's trunk on the castle green and looked around again for Jackrun. He'd promised to meet me here before I left. Checking the gates and terrace stairs once again, I heaved a breath and adjusted my cloak. Damp grass soaked into Bianca's slippers. My toes were numb with cold. I wiggled them and stomped my feet to try and keep them warm. *Hurry!* I thought, as if I could summon Jackrun with my need the way my father used to call Vazan. She'd return from her hunt soon and would expect me to be ready to go the moment she landed, knowing her.

Once again I looked back at the deserted stairs and gates. King Arden's flags tugged and slapped on the battlements. A windy day to sail. Tess and her family planned to ship out today. She didn't want to linger and see Tanya's execution any more than I did. Last night I'd told her about

Bianca's many small kindnesses to me while I was captive here. I asked Tess if she might take Bianca home to Dragon's Keep before King Arden turned his anger toward her. Bianca might feel more at home in the summer castle where half-fey people like her, like Tess, were welcome. "I'll talk with Bion," she said. I hoped he would agree.

In the distance, two small dots soared down from Morgesh Mountain's snowy ridge. As they flew closer I saw Vazan's red wings pumping in unison with Babak's mottled golden green. Vazan was a solitary hunter. I was surprised she'd let Babak join her this morning. Wispy clouds blushed pink in their wake. They landed side by side on the grass. Vazan licked fresh blood from her claws with her long forked tongue. Babak snapped his jaws and picked his teeth with the tip of his talon.

I bowed. "Was it a good hunt, rivule?"

"Not the choicest kill," she said with a growl.

At last Jackrun crossed the lawn bearing two cloth sacks. *You're too late.* A sharp pain entered my heart. I'd wanted to be alone with him, to say good-bye before Vazan returned from her hunt.

He dropped the sacks and took me aside, leading me partway across the lawn, but not out of earshot—Vazan's and Babak's sharp ears could hear a mouse squeak from a mile away. We stopped in a darkened spot under a passing cloud. "Can't you wait a little longer before you go?"

Vazan was already flicking her tail. "I can't. I have to go home now."

Jackrun touched the ribbon in my hair. It was the same color as the one that blew free the night we'd faced each other on the beach at Dragon's Keep, Jackrun offering to carry Father's trunk, me refusing his help. I had learned to stop refusing him. Now I had to again. "Why did you come out here so late?" I said, my voice pinched with anger.

He gripped my upper arms. "Tell me what you want."

I turned my head; a sharp pain tore my heart like teeth. "Don't ask. It hurts too much."

"Look at me, Uma. Tell me."

"Let me go."

"Uma," Vazan growled. "It'ssss time."

I freed my arms and crossed the lawn. Vazan eyed the Adan's trunk suspiciously. She took in the netting I'd brought out to strap it to her back. "You expect me to carry that?"

"Yes please, rivule."

"I am not a mule."

I put my hands on my hips. "It was the Adan's. It's full of medicine." Father's Herbal was gone, but at least I could bring this vital part of his life home with me. The women needed the precious kea and huzana I'd carefully packed inside.

She dug her claws in the ground. "I will do it for you this once, you understand."

"Thank you, rivule."

Vazan lowered herself. Jackrun set the trunk on her back and threw the net overtop to secure it in place for the flight. My clammy hands felt useless as I helped tug the net down. Jackrun took it from me. I wanted to touch the dark curls that had pulled free from the leather strap at the nape of his neck as he tied the knots below Vazan's underbelly.

He straightened up before I had the courage to do it and held out one of the sacks he'd brought. "Food for your journey."

I pretended not to notice his strained expression as I took it. No doubt I looked just as gray-faced. "We'll be all right, Jackrun."

"Remember," he said, but he could not finish. I drank him in, standing on the lawn in his fighting garb. He'd make his way to the weapons yard as soon as I left. Jackrun handed me the second sack. "Don't look, just put your hand inside."

I pulled the drawstrings and reached in, feeling the shape of what must be a book, the back side of smooth leather, the front embossed. I bit my lip when I drew it out. The two trees burned onto the dark leather cover had strong trunks and branches. The oak and the willow did not touch aboveground, but their roots intermingled underneath. A disk that might be sun or moon hung in the sky above them.

I ran my hand along the sturdy-looking trunks and slid my fingers down to feel the interwoven roots.

"I couldn't sleep last night," Jackrun said. "I breathed fire to heat the stylus nib and burned the tree patterns into the cover."

"A new way to use your fire," I whispered, my throat thick. "You are an artist like your mother."

"No, not like her," he said, shaking his head and looking down.

I wondered what book he'd chosen from the castle shelves. Wilde Island history or a book of verse or . . . I opened the cover. It was blank.

"An Adan needs an Herbal," Jackrun said.

Tears sprang to my eyes. The loss of Father's Herbal was a hollow space nothing could ever fill; there was so much knowledge in its pages. But this blank book was the seed of something new.

Jackrun tugged my belt, drawing me closer. The impatient smoke tumbling from Vazan's nose coiled over Jackrun's dark head as his lips touched mine.

I leaned in. His arms were tight around me, his kiss deep and sorrowful until Vazan's hiss drew us both back heaving for breath.

Vazan was kneeling, waiting for me to climb on. I wavered, unsteady on my feet. The tearing pain in my heart was almost unbearable now.

"Uma," Jackrun said fiercely. "Tell me what you want." He took my arms again, gripping them harder than he had before as if to squeeze an answer out of me.

"I want to be the first female Adan of my tribe. And I want you." I couldn't have both. Saying it aloud only drove the pain deeper.

"Why did you make me say it?" My tears blurred his face; I saw a smile in the watery sheen. He still held my arms, but gently.

"What," I said with a sniff.

"You only had to say it, Uma."

"But you can't."

"Don't tell me what I can or cannot do, Uma Quarteney." He kissed me, softly, quickly, and turned back to Vazan. "I've already said my good-byes inside in case Uma asked me to come south. Our castle physician shouldn't have to return to Devil's Boot alone. I'll escort her home."

Vazan lowered her head and gave a low hiss. "Do not expect to be welcomed in Devil's Boot, king'ssss nephew."

"It is an honorable thing for Jackrun to escort Uma home," Babak said.

Vazan flattened her ears. "She needs no escort!"

"She is a lady, is she not?"

"She is a healer. A woman of power."

"Babak, could you and Vazan stop arguing for once?" Jackrun said. "It's going to be a long journey as it is."

Vazan narrowed one silver eye on Jackrun, the other still firmly on Babak. "If you come, you will not only enter Euit tribal territory, you will also enter mine."

"As your guest, I hope, rivule," Jackrun said.

"As a guest?" She shook her head, her neck scales crackling. "I cannot speak for the other reds back home. They have their own teeth and fire. I will be flying very fast," she added, both eyes swerving to Babak.

I wanted to hold on to the joy that was bubbling up inside of me, but I was worried. "Vazan is right. You won't be welcome in Devil's Boot."

"I don't expect to be. Not after my aunt and uncle abducted you and your father and left a garrison down there. If you could withstand living with the English, I can withstand whatever awaits me."

He was leaving so much behind. A chance to train his fire with the dragons in Dragonswood, and there was another thing. "Jackrun, you are the heir."

"I am, that is unless the king weds again and has another child. But King Arden has years of rule left in him. And if I'm to rule Wilde Island, I intend to see the whole of it first. A future king should know his people."

"But—"

He put his fingers on my lips. "Uma, I've made up my mind." He kissed my forehead, one cheek, then the other, the tip of my nose, as if his lips were searching out the right place until I thought I would go mad, until at last he found my mouth.

My earlier sorrow fell away as an old flower falls from the stem giving room for a new bud, opening to the sunlight that is warm and rich and full of life. His life, my life. Beginning now.

# EPILOGUE
*Two and a Half Years Later*

# Devil's Boot

FOX MOON
*May 1213*

I KINDLE FIRE to cook breakfast in our cave. Jackrun could easily light it, but I do not want to wake him yet. We flew to the south side of the volcano with Babak and Vazan yesterday to gather herbs. Jackrun sat up late with his documents, studying a civil dispute King Arden has asked him to settle. He can sleep a little longer.

I flip the spicy griddle cake and watch the batter bubble. I used to pick herbs here with my father in the spring. I grew up in his shadow, reading his Herbal, learning his secrets, revering the strong healing ways of men. In those years I buried my womanhood, my Englishness among the willow roots. Back then I didn't believe I could belong to my tribe just as I was. I buried much, hid much, just as Jackrun smothered a vital part of who he was when he hid his fire.

Things have changed, but they did not change quickly. The chieftain didn't want a female healer when we flew home more than two years ago. Nothing I said or Jackrun said changed his mind. He and the elders followed tribal law. They wanted things done as they had always been done. Even Vazan, who stood proud and vehement beside me, hissing words of praise over how I'd healed her wing, did not sway him.

But there are other ways: the slow-growing ways of plants, the ways of song, the ways of touch. The women who wanted children were hungry for my medicine. As the months passed, the men began to come to the healer's hut with their complaints. And I cured them. In winter, in the time of Cardinal Moon, the chieftain limped in with an inflamed foot. The *Adan-duxma*—physician's creed—says: *All people suffer. All people feel pain.* I suppose even the chieftain does. I treated him. When his foot healed and he walked easily upon it, he nodded sternly and called me Adan.

He was not the first one to call me that. Jackrun saw me both as a woman and a healer before I could join the two together. He saw it as far back as our time in Dragonswood. At first I did not understand how to use the softer part of my being that Jackrun opened up—the part that loved as a woman loves, and healed as a woman heals. But in those last hours with the queen, I was forced to look to my womanly powers.

Queen Adela was so lost in the end. Father would not have fed her, bathed her, rubbed her sore back. He wouldn't have sung to her the night before she died. I'm glad I was there to sing her to sleep, to give her those last hours of care and peace before she was poisoned. Wicked as she was, she was human and she was suffering.

Joy and sorrow are songs women have long known. For women are healers.

I kneel down by Jackrun and say his name like a chant. He awakens, stretches, and gives me a loud kiss that makes me laugh before he goes outside to wash in the stream.

A year after Queen Adela died, King Arden sailed to Dragon's Keep and met Bianca again. His love for her rekindled. They married on Dragon's Keep. Jackrun attended the wedding and saw them happy. I hope King Arden will not turn on her someday and blame her for his losses. I hope he will always remember her innocence. Bianca has given him a son—a child with dragon, human, and fairy blood—so the fey have their wish fulfilled in another. And Jackrun is free.

Free to explore what it means to be the Son of the Prophecy, the firstborn of his kind. Free to live the life he chooses. He trains up his fire with the red dragons here, gaining mastery of his power. He hunts with our warriors, preferring the wilderness to walled castles. He answers King Arden's requests and travels north to south, east to west, settling island disputes as he once did for his father. I hum the last two verses of the fairy song as I wait for him to come back inside.

*And when these lovers intertwine,*
*Three races in one child combine.*

*Dragon, Fey, and Humankind,*
*Bound in one bloodline.*

*O Bring this day unto us soon,*
*And forfeit weapons forged in strife.*
*Sheath sword, and talon, angry spell,*
*And brethren be for life*

These words speak of a man with power. Not a king so much as someone who is free to travel place to place, communicate for all, settle conflicts so that sword and talon and angry spells are set aside. Jackrun has just begun this challenging ambassador's work, the work of a lifetime that might take him to other islands, even other countries if it's necessary or if it pleases him. He loves to travel. He's not a man who can stand still for long.

Jackrun steps back inside and looks down at me, tucking his thumbs under the red dragon belt Mother gave him as a wedding gift. Mother and I both cried when he looped the Adan's belt around his waist.

"Maybe I shouldn't take it," he'd said, awkward at our tears.

"No," Mother said. "It's perfect for you." And it was. It is.

Jackrun squats by the fire. "How is my queen of the May?"

I smile. He'd heard Mother's song. "Do you call me that because it's May or because I am your queen?"

"Both," he says, leaning down and kissing the back of my hand. He eats a spicy griddle cake, drinks the brew I seethed, and frowns.

"You'll get used to the bitter taste," I say. "It's good for the stomach."

He laughs. "I don't have to like it, do I?"

"No. You just have to drink it." The scar on his lip gleams under a drop when he pulls the cup away. He wipes it off with his little finger, and stares at me across the fire. His smallest finger is the length of my fox mark. I know because he likes to rest it there.

"Where do you want to hunt for herbs today?"

"In the valley six or seven miles from here." We'll bring home more kea and huzana this month. Three women gave birth the first year we were home. Five more our second year, including Ashune. Melo has a little sister. Mother helps me in the birth hut, beaming as she passes on her midwife's knowledge. A widow now, she finds joy in midwifery. I hold the wriggling newborns in my arms, males and females, tiny but strong. They are our future.

This year I'll treat more women, and though we will be away up north for a while on Jackrun's business with the king, I plan to fly home in time to cradle the precious little ones a moment before I give them to their mothers. This is a small price I demand.

Jackrun finishes his last griddle cake. He likes the spicy food I prepare. It would be difficult if he did not. I don't know how to cook anything else.

"Shall we walk or fly today?" he asks.

"Fly if Babak and Vazan don't mind taking us."

Jackrun gives me a wicked smile. We watched their mat-ing dance in Dragon Moon. I never would have thought Vazan would choose such a colorful male, but they love to fight and she is fierce in her love for him.

"We'd better wait a little longer before we ask them," Jackrun says. He knows if he disturbs them in their den before they are ready, he's likely to be scorched by Vazan's ferocious fire. Jackrun leans closer. "Uma."

The way he says my name stirs the secrets of my origin, the dreams the earth feeds me down in the dark underneath. Some people say my name and do not hear the sound; they do not know who they are calling, what they might awaken. He awakens the heart, the memory of my beginning in the stream, deep waters, sun, wind; he awakens my powers.

He kisses me, and we stay in our cave longer to shed our clothes, touching skin to skin, entangling like roots, searching for the darker places where we are fed with joy.

# AUTHOR'S NOTE
## The Moon, Medicine, and More

THIS BOOK'S DEVELOPMENT began with cliff jumping, magic, dragons, and murder, before it focused back on the primary character of Uma and her Euit culture. The moon entered somewhere along the way, setting a strict lunar timeframe, enhancing the drama as it orbited the story.

As the animal moons rooted themselves into the story with greater force, I was inevitably drawn to research. I found ancient peoples that named various calendar moons after plants, weather, or animals. I discovered moon stories in the Hawaiian, Native American, African, Asian, and European cultures. The most commonly known moon names still used today are: September's Hunter's Moon, October's Harvest Moon, and the occasional Blue Moon. Both Native Americans and medieval Europeans called January the Wolf Moon.

The Euit Moon Months entered this story not only as tribal tradition but as an integral part of the healing approach of the Adan who seeks to balance the elements of earth, air, fire, and water within the human being. He also pays close attention to the dangerous and enhancing animal power released each Moon Month.

Tribal and medieval medicine also played another vital role. I created the Adan's medicinal approach from many sources starting with books about medieval medicine, and expanding to books and articles on tribal medicine, preferably written by indigenous healers themselves. I was also privileged to listen to firsthand accounts of traditional healing practices. All these influences quickened my imagination and helped me create the Adan's close relationship with plants, and his healing philosophy. The Adan's cures mirror some of the herbal remedies I studied, but I changed them and guised them with Euit names. Thus all the remedies are from my imagination and have an implied "don't do this at home" disclaimer. There were a few exceptions to this. Yarrow, for example, was made into a highly valued wound ointment in ancient times, and went under such names as soldier's wound wort or knight's milfoil.

I was with two wise women healers, Lei'ohu Ryder and Maydeen Iao, on the Maui Immersion when I first heard about Peruvian healer Eda Zavala Lopez. I'd already written the first draft of this book and was taking a breather (note: Writers never really stop working. When not writing we "sit around plotting and scheming," so says my husband). I felt that familiar tingling sensation as I learned Eda's story. Eda is a descendent of the Wari people of the Peruvian Amazon rainforest who comes from a lineage of native women healers. She travels the world as a healer and educator with an ongoing mission to save the indigenous healing plants and healer's knowledge that are quickly passing away in her homeland. From her website:

*The beautiful and pristine sacred forests, the head waters of the river basin where pure, crystalline waters feed the waterways and woods, the incredible biodiversity of plant and animal life where scientific observations have identified medicinal plant species yet to be documented and studied ... will be forever and irrevocably changed if the plundering of the Peruvian rainforest continues.*

In the course of writing this book, I learned more about the ways so many plants vital to curing human diseases are being destroyed. Research often leads to action.

Readers who would like to join me to help save the plants in the Amazon Basin can visit the "giving back" page on my website: http://www.janetleecarey.com. Or go directly to Nature Conservancy and join in their effort to preserve the Amazon rainforest: http://www.nature.org/ourinitiatives /regions/southamerica/brazil/placesweprotect/amazon.xml.

Thank you, and as Uma says: *Ona loneaih*—be you well.

# Euit Moon Months Chart

*Euit Moon Month calendar beginning spring 1210*

### ⤜ SPRING ⤛

SEAL MOON (WATER)—MARCH: *affects skin*

FALCON MOON (WIND)—APRIL: *affects arms and feet*

FOX MOON (EARTH)—MAY: *affects ears and legs*

### ⤜ SUMMER ⤛

SNAKE MOON (FIRE)—JUNE: *affects spine and tongue*

WHALE MOON (WATER)—JULY: *affects chest and lungs*

EGRET MOON (WIND)—AUGUST: *affects throat and neck*

### ⤜ FALL ⤛

WOLF MOON (EARTH)—SEPTEMBER: *affects nose and teeth*

DRAGON MOON (FIRE)—OCTOBER: *affects head, heart, and hands*

SALMON MOON (WATER)—NOVEMBER: *affects mouth*

### ⤜ WINTER ⤛

OWL MOON (WIND)—DECEMBER: *affects eyes*

BEAR MOON (EARTH)—JANUARY: *affects stomach and bowels*

CARDINAL MOON (FIRE)—FEBRUARY: *affects blood*

# ACKNOWLEDGMENTS

MAYA ANGELOU SAID, *"We delight in the beauty of the butterfly, but rarely admit the changes it has gone through to achieve that beauty."* The same can be said for any book that passes through countless stages from gawky to glorious. And though the author works alone in her darkened chrysalis, no book achieves flight all on its own. I have many people to thank.

I'm indebted to the people at NAMI (National Alliance on Mental Illness) http://www.nami.org/ for support in understanding brain disorders and mental illness. Their education classes helped our family, and provided needed information for Queen Adela's condition.

Warmest thanks to Lei'ohu Ryder, and Maydeen Iao http://www.leiohuryder.com/; Hawaiian spiritual leaders, visionaries, and advocates for the indigenous soul in all people, who gave their love and knowledge so generously on the Maui Immersion retreats. Lei'ohu and Maydeen introduced me to Patrick O'Rourke, who told me the inspiring story of his encounter with the indigenous healer Eda Zavala Lopez. Thanks, Patrick, for putting up with the scratchy older-than-Moses tape machine we used to interview you. The story you told about Eda Zavala Lopez's journey from her home in the Peruvian rainforests, and the remarkable healing practices she generously shared at Blue Deer Center and across the U.S., strengthened Uma's story.

This book would not be in readers' hands without my critique group the Diviners: Peggy King Anderson, Judy Bodmer, Katherine Grace Bond, Dawn Knight, Roberta Kehle, Molly Blaisdell, and Nancy White Carlstrom. Thank you all for bearing with me during the far from cuddly caterpillar stage. Heartfelt thanks to Justina Chen and Sofia Headley for hauling a four-hundred-page manuscript along on their mother-daughter trip to Alaska and returning it with priceless insights; and to my former agent, the Lioness, Irene W. Kraas, and current agent, the Incandescent Ammi-Joan Paquette.

Deepest thanks to my richly talented editor, Kathy Dawson, whose vision and tireless work gave this book wings. And to all the people at Kathy Dawson Books and Penguin who release finished books like butterflies to brighten our world: assistant editor, Claire Evans; copy editor, Regina Castillo; jacket designer, Tony Sahara; and interior designer, Jenny Kelly, to name only a few.

Last but not least, thanks to my husband, Thomas, for his generosity, patience, and travel savvy as we adventured to different destinations researching this book.

## ABOUT THE AUTHOR

JANET LEE CAREY was born in New York and grew up in California. She is the award-winning author of several young adult novels, most notably her epic fantasy novels set on Wilde Island—*Dragon's Keep, Dragonswood,* and *In the Time of Dragon Moon. Dragon's Keep* was an ALA Best Book for Young Adults and a *School Library Journal* Best Book of the Year, while *Dragonswood* made the YALSA Best Fiction for Young Adults list. Janet lives near Seattle with her family, where she writes and teaches writing workshops.

Find Janet online at:
WWW.JANETLEECAREY.COM
@JANETLEECAREY
/JANET.L.CAREY.3